I0576975

George Alfred Henty

Through the Fray

A Tale of the Luddite Riots

George Alfred Henty

Through the Fray
A Tale of the Luddite Riots

ISBN/EAN: 9783744758901

Printed in Europe, USA, Canada, Australia, Japan

Cover: Foto ©Andreas Hilbeck / pixelio.de

More available books at **www.hansebooks.com**

NED DEFENDS HIS MOTHER'S MILL AGAINST THE LUDDITES.

THROUGH THE FRAY:

A TALE
OF THE LUDDITE RIOTS.

BY

G. A. HENTY,

Author of "True to the Old Flag," "St. George for England," "In Freedom's Cause,"
"With Clive in India," "By Sheer Pluck," "Facing Death," &c. &c.

*WITH TWELVE FULL-PAGE ILLUSTRATIONS
BY H. M. PAGET.*

LONDON
BLACKIE & SON, Limited, 50 OLD BAILEY, E.C.
GLASGOW AND DUBLIN

PREFACE.

My dear Lads,

The beginning of the present century, glorious as it was for British arms abroad, was a dark time to those who lived by their daily labour at home. The heavy taxation entailed by the war, the injury to trade, and the enormous prices of food, all pressed heavily upon the working-classes. The invention of improved machinery, vast as has been the increase of trade which it has brought about, at first pressed heavily upon the hand workers, who assigned all their distress to the new inventions. Hence a movement arose, which did much damage and for a time threatened to be extremely formidable. It had its ramifications through all the manufacturing districts of England, the object being the destruction of the machinery, and a return to the old methods of work. The troubles which occurred in various parts of the country were known as the Luddite Riots, and the secret body which organized them was called King or General Lud. In the present story I have endeavoured to give you an idea of the state of things which prevailed in Yorkshire, where, among the croppers and others employed in the woollen manufactures, was one of the most formidable branches of the secret association. The incidents of the murder of Mr. Horsfall and the attack upon Mr. Cartwright's mill are strictly accurate in all their details.

In this story I have left the historical battle-fields, across so many of which I have taken you, and have endeavoured to show that there are peaceful battles to be fought and victories to be won every jot as arduous and as difficult as those contested under arms. In *Facing Death* my hero won such a battle. He had to fight against external circumstances, and step by step, by perseverance, pluck, and determination, made his way in life. In the present tale my hero's enemy was within, and although his victory was at last achieved the victor was well-nigh worsted in the fray. We have all such battles to fight, dear lads; may we all come unscathed and victorious through the fray!

Yours sincerely,

G. A. HENTY.

CONTENTS.

ILLUSTRATIONS.

THROUGH THE FRAY.

CHAPTER I.

A FISHING EXPEDITION.

T has just struck one, and the boys are stream-
ing out from the school-room of Mr. Ha-
thorn's academy in the little town of Marsden
in Yorkshire. Their appearance would create
some astonishment in the minds of lads of the present
generation, for it was the year 1807, and their attire differed somewhat materially from that now worn. They
were for the most part dressed in breeches tight at the
knee, and buttoning up outside the close-fitting jacket
nearly under the arms, so that they seemed almost devoid
of waist. At the present moment they were bare-headed;
but when they went beyond the precincts of the school
they wore stiff caps, flat and very large at the top, and
with far-projecting peaks.

They were not altogether a happy looking set of boys,
and many of their cheeks were stained with tears and

begrimed with dirt from the knuckles which had been used to wipe them away; for there was in the year 1807 but one known method of instilling instruction into the youthful mind, namely, the cane, and one of the chief qualifications of a schoolmaster was to be able to hit hard and sharp.

Mr. Hathorn, judged by this standard, stood very high in his profession; his cane seemed to whiz through the air, so rapidly and strongly did it descend, and he had the knack of finding out tender places, and of hitting them unerringly. Anyone passing in front of the schoolhouse during the hours when the boys were at their lessons would be almost sure to hear the sharp cracks of the cane, followed sometimes by dead silence, when the recipient of the blows was of a sturdy and Spartan disposition, but more frequently by shrieks and cries.

That Hathorn's boys hated their master was almost a matter of course. At the same time they were far from regarding him as an exceptional monster of cruelty, for they knew from their friends that flogging prevailed almost everywhere, and accepted it as a necessary portion of the woes of boyhood. Indeed, in some respects, when not smarting under the infliction, they were inclined to believe that their lot was, in comparison with that of others, a fortunate one; for whereas in many schools the diet was so poor and bad that the boys were half-starved, at Hathorn's if their food was simple and coarse it was at least wholesome and abundant.

Mr. Hathorn, in fact, intended, and as he quite believed

with success, to do his duty by his boys. They were sent to him to be taught, and he taught them through the medium then recognized as most fitting for the purpose —the cane; while, as far as an abundance of porridge for breakfast, and of heavy pudding at dinner, with twice a week an allowance of meat, the boys were unstinted. He would indeed point with pride to his pupils when their parents assembled at the annual presentation of prizes.

"Look at them!" he would say proudly. "None of your half-starved skeletons here—well-filled out and in good condition every boy of them—no stint of porridge here. It keeps them in good health and improves their learning; for, mark you, a plump boy feels the cane twice as much as a skinny one; it stings, my dear sir, it stings, and leaves its mark; whereas there is no getting at a boy whose clothes hang like bags about him."

This was no doubt true, and the boys themselves were conscious of it, and many had been the stern resolutions made while smarting in agony that henceforward food should be eschewed, or taken only in sufficient quantities to keep life together. But boys' appetites are stronger than boys' resolutions, and in the end there was never any marked falling off in the consumption of viands at Hathorn's.

Like other things punishment fails when administered in excess. There was no disgrace whatever in what was common to all; for although some boys of superior ability and perseverance would escape with a smaller amount of punishment than their fellows, none could hope to escape

altogether. Thus it was only the pain that they had to
bear, and even this became to some extent deadened by
repetition, and was forgotten as soon as inflicted, save
when a sudden movement caused a sharp pain in back
or leg. Once in the playground their spirits revived,
and except a few whose recent punishment incapacitated
them for a time from active exercise, the whole were soon
intent upon their games.

One only of the party wore his cap, and he after a few
minutes left the others and went towards a door which
led from the playground into the road.

"Don't be long, Sankey; come back as soon as you can,
you know we agreed to go fishing this afternoon."

"All right, Tompkins; I will come back directly I
have done my dinner. I expect I shall have finished
quite as soon as you will."

Edward Sankey, who was regarded with envy by his
school-fellows, was the only home boarder at Hathorn's;
for, as a general thing, the master set his face against
the introduction of home boarders. They were, he considered, an element of disturbance; they carry tales to
and from the school; they cause discontent among the
other boys, and their parents are in the habit of protesting
and interfering.

Not, indeed, that parents in those days considered it in
any way a hardship for their boys to suffer corporal punishment; they had been flogged at school, and they believed that they had learned their lessons all the better for
it. Naturally the same thing would happen to their sons.

Still mothers are apt to be weak and soft-hearted, and therefore Mr. Hathorn objected to home boarders. He had made an exception in Sankey's case; his father was of a different type to those of the majority of his boys; he had lost his leg at the battle of Assaye, and had been obliged to leave the army, and having but small means beyond his pension, had settled near the quiet little Yorkshire town as a place where he could live more cheaply than in more bustling localities.

He had, when he first came, no acquaintances whatever in the place, and therefore would not be given to discuss with the parents of other boys the doings in the school. Not that Mr. Hathorn was afraid of discussion, for he regarded his school as almost perfect of its kind. Still, it was his fixed opinion that discussion was, as a general rule, unadvisable. Therefore, when Captain Sankey, a few weeks after taking up his residence in the locality, made a proposal to him that his son should attend his school as a home boarder, Mr. Hathorn acceded to the proposition, stating frankly his objections, as a rule, to boys of that class.

" I shall not interfere," Captain Sankey said. " Of course boys must be thrashed, and provided that the punishment is not excessive, and that it is justly administered, I have nothing to say against it. Boys must be punished, and if you don't flog you have to confine them, and in my opinion that is far worse for a boy's temper, spirit, and health."

So Ned Sankey went to Hathorn's, and was soon a

great favourite there. Just at first he was regarded as a
disobliging fellow because he adhered strictly to a stipu-
lation which Mr. Hathorn had made, that he should not
bring things in from the town for his school-fellows.
Only once a week, on the Saturday half-holiday, were the
boys allowed outside the bounds of the wall round the
playground, and although on Wednesdays an old woman
was allowed to come into those precincts to sell fruit,
cakes, and sweets, many articles were wanted in the
course of the week, and the boys took it much amiss
for a time that Ned refused to act as their messenger;
but he was firm in his refusals. His father had told him
not to do so, and his father's word was law to him; but
when the boys saw that in all other respects he was a
thoroughly good fellow, they soon forgave him what they
considered his undue punctiliousness, and he became a
prime favourite in the school.

It is due to Mr. Hathorn to say that no fear of interference induced him to mitigate his rule to thrash when
he considered that punishment was necessary, and that
Ned received his full share of the general discipline. He
was never known to utter a cry under punishment, for
he was, as his school-fellows said admiringly, as hard as
nails; and he was, moreover, of a dogged disposition,
which would have enabled him, when he had once determined upon a thing, to carry it through even if it killed
him.

Mr. Hathorn regarded this quality as obstinacy, the
boys as iron resolution; and while the former did his

best to conquer what he regarded as a fault, the boys encouraged by their admiration what they viewed as a virtue.

At home Ned never spoke of his punishments; and if his father observed a sudden movement which told of a hidden pain, and would say cheerfully, "What! have you been getting it again, Ned?" the boy would smile grimly and nod, but no complaint ever passed his lips. There was no disgrace in being flogged—it was the natural lot of school-boys; why should he make a fuss about it? So he held his tongue. But Mr. Hathorn was not altogether wrong. Ned Sankey was obstinate, but though obstinate he was by no means sulky. When he made up his mind to do a thing he did it, whether it was to be at the top of his class in order to please his father, or to set his teeth like iron and let no sound issue from them as Mr. Hathorn's cane descended on his back.

Ned Sankey was about fourteen years of age. He had a brother and a sister, but between them and himself was a gap of four years, as some sisters who had been born after him had died in infancy.

Ned adored his father, who was a most kind and genial man, and would have suffered anything in silence rather than have caused him any troubles or annoyance by complaining to him. For his mother his feelings were altogether different. She was a kindly and well-intentioned woman, but weak and silly.

On leaving school she had gone out to join her father in India. Captain Sankey had sailed in the same ship and, taken by her pretty face and helpless, dependent manner, he had fallen in love with her, knowing nothing of her real disposition, and they had been married upon their arrival at the termination of the voyage. So loyal was his nature that it is probable Captain Sankey never admitted even to himself that his marriage had been a mistake; but none of his comrades ever doubted it. His wife turned out one of the most helpless of women.

Under the plea of ill health she had at a very early period of their marriage given up all attempt to manage the affairs of the household, and her nerves were wholly unequal to the strain of looking after her children. It was noticeable that though her health was unequal to the discharge of her duties, she was always well enough to take part in any pleasure or gaiety which might be going on; and as none of the many doctors who attended her were able to discover any specific ailment, the general opinion was that Mrs. Sankey's ill health was the creation of her own imagination.

This, however, was not wholly the case. She was not strong; and although, had she made an effort, she would have been able to look after her children like other women, she had neither the disposition nor the training to make that effort. Her son regarded her with the sort of pity not unmingled with contempt, with which young people full of life and energy are apt to regard those who are weak and ailing without having any specific disease or malady which would account for their condition.

"All the bothers fall upon father," he would say to

himself; "and if mother did but make up her mind she could take her share in them well enough. There was he walking about for two hours this evening with little Lucy in his arms, because she had fallen down and hurt herself; and there was mother lying on the sofa reading that book of poetry, as if nothing that happened in the house was any affair of hers. She is very nice and very kind, but I do wish she wouldn't leave everything for father to do. It might have been all very well before he lost his leg, but I do think she ought to make an effort now."

However, Mrs. Sankey made no effort, nor did her husband ever hint that it would be better for herself as well as her family if she did so. He accepted the situation as inevitable, and patiently, and indeed willingly, bore her burden as well as his own. Fortunately she had in the children's nurse an active and trustworthy woman.

Abijah Wolf was a Yorkshire woman. She had in her youth been engaged to a lad in her native village. In a moment of drunken folly, a short time before the day fixed for their wedding, he had been persuaded to enlist. Abijah had waited patiently for him twelve years. Then he had returned a sergeant, and she had married him and followed him with his regiment, which was that in which Captain Sankey—at that time a young ensign—served. When the latter's first child was born at Madras there was a difficulty in obtaining a white nurse, and Mrs. Sankey declared that she would not trust the child to a

B

native. Inquiries were therefore made in the regiment, and Sergeant Wolf's wife, who had a great love for children although childless herself, volunteered to fill the post for a time.

A few months afterwards Sergeant Wolf was killed in a fight with a marauding hill tribe. His widow, instead of returning home and living on the little pension to which she was entitled at his death, remained in the service of the Sankeys, who soon came to regard her as invaluable.

She was somewhat rough in her ways and sharp with her tongue; but even Mrs. Sankey, who was often ruffled by her brusk independence, was conscious of her value, and knew that she should never obtain another servant who would take the trouble of the children so entirely off her hands. She retained, indeed, her privilege of grumbling, and sometimes complained to her husband that Abijah's ways were really unbearable. Still she never pressed the point, and Abijah appeared established as a permanent fixture in the Sankeys' household.

She it was who, when, after leaving the service, Captain Sankey was looking round for a cheap and quiet residence, had recommended Marsden.

"There is a grand air from the hills," she said, "which will be just the thing for the children. There's good fishing in the stream for yourself, captain, and you can't get a quieter and cheaper place in all England. I ought to know, for I was born upon the moorland but six

miles away from it, and should have been there now if I
hadn't followed my man to the wars."

"Where are you going, Master Ned?" she asked as the
boy, having finished his dinner, ran to the high cupboard
at the end of the passage near the kitchen to get his
fishing-rod.

"I am going out fishing, Abijah."

"Not by yourself, I hope?"

"No; another fellow is going with me. We are going
up into the hills."

"Don't ye go too far, Master Ned. They say the
croppers are drilling on the moors, and it were bad for
ye if you fell in with them."

"They wouldn't hurt me if I did."

"I don't suppose they would," the nurse said, "but
there is never no saying. Poor fellows! they're druv
well-nigh out of their senses with the bad times. What
with the machines, and the low price of labour, and the
high price of bread, they are having a terrible time of it.
And no wonder that we hear of frame-breaking in Nottingham, and Lancashire, and other places. How men
can be wicked enough to make machines, to take the
bread out of poor men's mouths, beats me altogether."

"Father says the machinery will do good in the long
run, Abijah—that it will largely increase trade, and so
give employment to a great many more people than at
present. But it certainly is hard on those who have
learned to work in one way to see their living taken away
from them."

"Hard!" the nurse said. "I should say it were hard. I know the croppers, for there were a score of them in my village, and a rough wild lot they were. They worked hard and they drank hard, and the girl as chose a cropper for a husband was reckoned to have made a bad match of it; but they are determined fellows, and you will see they won't have the bread taken out of their mouths without making a fight for it."

"That may be," Ned said, "for everyone gives them the name of a rough lot; but I must talk to you about it another time, Abijah, I have got to be off;" and having now found his fishing-rod, his box of bait, his paper of hooks, and a basket to bring home the fish he intended to get, Ned ran off at full speed towards the school.

As Abijah Wolf had said, the croppers of the West Riding were a rough set. Their occupation consisted in shearing or cropping the wool on the face of cloths. They used a large pair of shears, which were so set that one blade went under the cloth while the other worked on its upper face, mowing the fibres and ends of the wool to a smooth even surface. The work was hard and required considerable skill, and the men earned about twenty-four shillings a week, a sum which, with bread and all other necessities of life at famine prices, barely sufficed for the support of their families. The introduction of power-looms threatened to abolish their calling. It was true that although these machines wove the cloth more evenly and smoothly than the hand-looms, croppers were still required to give the necessary smoothness of face; still the tendency had been to lower wages.

The weavers were affected even more than the croppers, for strength and skill were not so needed to tend the power-looms as to work the hand-looms. Women and boys could do the work previously performed by men, and the tendency of wages was everywhere to fall. For years a deep spirit of discontent had been seething among the operatives in the cotton and woollen manufactures, and there had been riots more or less serious in Derbyshire, Nottingham, Lancashire, and Yorkshire, which in those days were the headquarters of these trades. Factories had been burned, employers threatened and attacked, and the obnoxious machines smashed. It was the vain struggle of the ignorant and badly paid people to keep down production and to keep up wages, to maintain manual labour against the power of the steam-engine. Hitherto factories had been rare, men working the frames in their own homes, and utilizing the labour of their wives and families, and the necessity of going miles away to work in the mills, where the looms were driven by steam, added much to the discontent.

Having found his fishing appliances Ned hurried off to the school, where his chum Tompkins was already waiting him, and the two set out at once on their expedition. They had four miles to walk to reach the spot where they intended to fish.

It was a quiet little stream with deep pools and many shadows, and had its source in the heart of the moorlands.

Neither of them had ever tried it before, but they had heard it spoken of as one of the best streams for fish in that part. On reaching its banks the rods were put together, the hooks were baited with worms, and a deep pool being chosen they set to work.

After fishing for some time without success they tried a pool higher up, and so mounted higher and higher up the stream, but ever with the same want of success.

" How could they have said that this was a good place for fish?" Tompkins said angrily at last. " Why, by this time it would have been hard luck if we had not caught a dozen between us where we usually fish close to the town, and after our long walk we have not had even a bite."

" I fancy, Tompkins," Ned said, " that we are a couple of fools. I know it is trout that they catch in this stream, and of course, now I think of it, trout are caught in clear water with a fly, not with a worm. Father said the other day he would take me out some Saturday and give me a lesson in fly-fishing. How he will laugh when I tell him we have wasted all our afternoon in trying to catch trout with worms!"

" I don't see anything to laugh at," Tompkins grumbled. " Here we waste a whole half-holiday, and nothing to show for it, and have got six or seven miles at least to tramp back to school."

"Well, we have had a nice walk," Ned said, " even if we are caught in the rain. However, we may as well put up our rods and start. I vote we try to make a straight cut home; it must be ever so much shorter to go in a straight line than to follow all the windings of this stream."

They had long since left the low lands, where trees and bushes bordered the stream, and were in a lonely valley where the hills came down close to the little stream, which sparkled among the boulders at their feet. The slopes were covered with a crop of short wiry grass through which the gray stone projected here and there. Tiny rills of water made their way down the hillside to swell the stream, and the tinge of brown which showed up wherever these found a level sufficient to form a pool told that they had their source in the bogs on the moorland above. Tompkins looked round him rather disconcertedly.

"I don't know," he said. "It's a beastly long way to walk round; but suppose we got lost in trying to make our way across the hills."

"Well, just as you like," Ned said, "I am game to walk back the way we came or to try and make a straight cut, only mind don't you turn round and blame me afterwards. You take your choice; whichever you vote for I am ready to do."

"My shoes are beginning to rub my heel," Tompkins said, "so I will take the shortest way and risk it. I don't see we can go far out of our way."

"I don't see that we can," Ned replied. "Marsden lies to the east, so we have only to keep our backs to the sun; it won't be down for another two hours yet, and before that we ought to be in."

By this time they had taken their rods to pieces, wound up their lines, and were ready to start. A few minutes' sharp climbing took them to the top of the slope. They were now upon the moor, which stretched away with slight undulations as far as they could see.

"Now," Ned said, "we will make for that clump of rocks. They seem to be just in the line we ought to take, and by fixing our eyes upon them we shall go straight."

This, however, was not as easy to do as Ned had fancied; the ground was in many places so soft and boggy that they were forced to make considerable detours. Nevertheless the rocks served as a beacon, and enabled them to keep the right direction; but although they made their way at the best of their speed it was an hour after starting before they approached the rock. When they were within fifty yards of it a figure suddenly rose. It was that of a boy some fifteen years of age.

"Goa back," he shouted; "dang yer, what be'est a cooming here vor?"

The two boys stopped astonished.

"We are going to Marsden," Ned replied; "but what's that to you?"

"Doan't ee moind wot it be to oi," the boy said; "oi tell ee ee cant goa no further; yoi've got ter go back."

"We sha'n't go back," Ned said; "we have got as much right to go this way as you have. This is not your land; and if it is, we ain't hurting it." By this time they were at the foot of the pile of rocks, and the lad was standing some ten feet above them.

" Oi tell ee," he repeated doggedly, " yoi've got vor to go back." The boy was so much bigger and stronger than either Ned or his companion that the former, although indignant at this interference, did not deem it prudent to attempt to climb the craig, so he said to Tompkins:

" Of course we ain't going back, but we had better take a turn so as to get out of the way of this fellow."

So saying they turned to the right and prepared to scout round the rock and continue their way; but this did not suit their obstructor.

" If ee doan't go back at oncet oi'll knock the heads off thee shoulders."

" We can't go back," Tompkins said desperately, " we are both as tired as we can be, and my heel is so sore that I can hardly walk. We shouldn't get to Marsden to-night if we were to turn back."

" That's nowt to oi," the boy said. " Oi bain't agoing to let ee pass here."

" What are we to do, Ned?" Tompkins groaned.

"Do!" Ned replied indignantly. " Why, go on, of course. Marsden cannot be more than three miles off, and I ain't going to walk twelve miles round to please this obstinate brute."

" But he is ever so much bigger than we are," Tompkins said doubtfully.

" Well, there are two of us," Ned said, " and two to one is fair enough when he is as big as the two of us together."

"We are going on," he said to the boy, "and if you interfere with us it will be the worse for you."

The boy descended leisurely from his position on the rocks.

"Oi don't want to hurt ee, but oi've got to do as oi were bid, and if ee doan't go back oi've got to make ee. There be summat a going on thar," and he jerked his head behind him, "as it wouldn't be good vor ee to see; and ye bain't agoing vor to see it."

But Ned and Tompkins were desperate now, and dropping their rods made a rush together against him.

CHAPTER II.

THE FIGHT ON THE MOOR.

HE lad threw himself into a position of defence as the two boys rushed at him.

"Oi doan't want vor to hurt ee," he said again, "but if ee will have it, why, it won't be moi vault;" and swinging his arm round, he brought it down with such force upon the nose of Tompkins that the latter was knocked down like a nine-pin, and, once down, evinced no intention of continuing the conflict.

In Ned, however, the lad found an opponent of a different stamp. The latter saw at once that his opponent's far greater weight and strength rendered it hopeless for him to trust to close fighting, and he worked round and round him, every now and then rushing at him and delivering a telling blow, and getting off again before his heavy and comparatively unwieldy companion could reply. Once or twice, indeed, the lad managed to strike him as he came in, each time knocking him fairly off his feet; but in the fair spirit which at that time animated English men and boys of all classes he allowed Ned each time to regain his feet without interference.

"Thou bee'st a plucky one," he said, as Ned after his third fall again faced him, "but thou bain't strong enough for oi."

Ned made no reply, but nerved himself for a fresh effort. The blows he had received had been heavy, and the blood was streaming from his face; but he had no idea of giving in, although Tompkins, in spite of his calls and reproaches, refused to raise himself beyond a sitting position.

"It's no good, Ned," he replied, "the brute is too big for us, and I'd rather try to walk home all the way round than get another like the last. My nose feels as big as my head."

Ned hardly heard what his companion said. He would have been killed rather than yield now, and gathering all his strength he sprang at his opponent like a tiger. Avoiding the blow which the boy aimed at him, he leapt upon him, and flung his arms round his neck. The sudden shock overthrew him, and with a crash both boys came to the ground together. Ned at once loosened his hold, and springing to his feet again, awaited the rising of his opponent. The latter made a movement to get up, and then fell back with a cry:

"Thou hast beaten me," he said. "Oi think moi leg be broke."

Ned saw now that as the lad had fallen his leg had been twisted under him, and that he was unable to extri-

cate it. In a moment he was kneeling before the prostrate
lad.

"Oh! I am sorry," he exclaimed; "but you know I
didn't mean to do it. Here, Tompkins, don't sit there like
a fool, but come and help me move him and get his leg
straight."

Although the boys did this as gently as they could, a
groan showed how great was the agony.

"Where is it?" Ned asked.

"Aboove the knee somewhere," the lad said, and Ned
put his hand gently to the spot, and to his horror could
feel something like the end of a bone.

"Oh! dear, what is to be done? Here, Tompkins, either
you or I must go on to the town for help."

"It's getting dark already," Tompkins said; "the sun
has set some time. How on earth is one to find the way?"

"Well, if you like I will go," Ned said, "and you stop
here with him."

The lad, who had been lying with closed eyes and a face
of ghastly palor, now looked up.

"There be soom men not a quarter of a mile away; they
be a-drilling, they be, and oi was sot here to stop anyone
from cooming upon em; but if so bee as thou wilt go and
tell em oi has got hurt, oi don't suppose as they will
meddle with ye."

Ned saw now why the lad had opposed his going any
further. Some of the croppers were drilling on the moor,
and the boy had been placed as sentry. It wasn't a pleasant business to go up to men so engaged, especially with

the news that he had seriously injured the boy they had placed on watch. But Ned did not hesitate a moment. "You stop here, Tompkins, with him," he said quietly, "I will go and fetch help. It is a risk, of course, but we can't let him lie here."

So saying, Ned mounted the rock to get a view over the moor. No sooner had he gained the position than he saw some thirty or forty men walking in groups across the moor at a distance of about half a mile. They had evidently finished their drill, and were making their way to their homes.

This at least was satisfactory. He would no longer risk their anger by disturbing them at their illegal practices, and had now only to fear the wrath which would be excited when they heard what had happened to the boy. He started at a brisk run after them, and speedily came up to the last of the party. They were for the most part men between twenty and thirty, rough and strongly built, and armed with bill-hooks and heavy bludgeons, two or three of them carrying guns. One of them looked round on hearing footsteps approaching, and gave a sudden exclamation. The rest turned, and on seeing Ned, halted with a look of savage and menacing anger on their faces.

"Who be'est, boy? dang ee, what brings ye here?"

Ned gulped down the emotion of fear excited by their threatening appearance, and replied as calmly as he could:

"I am sorry to say that I have had a struggle with a boy over by that rock yonder. We fell together, and he has broken his leg. He told me if I came over in this direction I should find someone to help him."

"Broaken Bill's leg, did'st say, ye young varmint?" one of the men exclaimed. "Oi've a good moinde to wring yer neck."

"I am very sorry," Ned said; "but I did not mean it I and another boy were walking back from Marsden from fishing, and he wouldn't let us pass; it was too far to go back again, so of course we had to try, and then there was a fight, but it was quite an accident his breaking his leg."

"Did'st see nowt afore ye had the voight?" one of the other men inquired.

"No," Ned replied; "we saw no one from the time we left the stream till we met the boy who would not let us pass, and I only caught sight of you walking this way from the top of the rock."

"If 'twere a vair voight, John, the boy bain't to be blamed, though oi be main grieved about thy brother Bill; but we'd best go back for him, voor on us. And moind, youngster, thee'd best keep a quiet tongue in thy head as to whaat thou'st seen here."

"I haven't seen anything," Ned said; "but of course if you wish it I will say nothing about it."

"It were best for ee, for if thou go'st aboot saying thou'st seen men with guns and clubs up here on the moor, it ull be the worsest day's work ee've ever done."

"I will say nothing about it," Ned replied, "but please come on at once, for I am afraid the boy is in terrible pain."

Four of the men accompanied Ned back to the rock.

"Hullo, Bill! what's happened ee?" his brother asked.

"Oi've had a fight and hurted myself, and broke my leg; but it wa'n't that chap's fault; it were a vair voight, and a right good 'un he be. Doan't do nowt to him."

"Well, that's roight enough then," the man said, "and you two young 'uns can go whoam. Marsden lies over that way; thou wilt see it below ye when ye gets to yon rock over there; and moind what I told ee."

"I will," Ned said earnestly; "but do let me come up to see how he is getting on, I shall be so anxious to know."

The man hesitated, but the lad said, "Let um coom, John, he bee a roight good un."

"Well, if thou would'st like it, Bill, he shall coom."

"If thou coom oop to Varley and ask vor Bill Swinton, anyone will show ee the place."

"Good-bye," Ned said to the boy, "I am so sorry you have got hurt. I will come and see you as soon as I can." Then he and Tompkins set off towards the rock the man had pointed out, which by this time, in the fast growing darkness, could scarce be made out. They would indeed probably have missed it, for the distance was fully a mile and a half; but before they had gone many yards one of the four men passed by them on a run on his way down to Marsden to summon the parish doctor, for a moment's examination had sufficed to show them that the boy's injury was far too serious to treat by themselves. Tired as the boys were, they set off in his footsteps, and managed to keep him in sight until they reached the spot whence Marsden could be seen, and they could no longer mistake the way.

"Now, look here, Tompkins," Ned said as they made their way down the hill; "don't you say a word about this affair. You haven't got much to boast about in it, sitting there on the grass and doing nothing to help me. I sha'n't say anything more about that if you hold your tongue; but if you blab I will let all the fellows know how you behaved."

"But they will all notice my nose directly I get in," Tompkins said. "What am I to say?"

"Yes, there's no fear about their not noticing your nose," Ned replied. "I don't want you to tell a lie. You can say the exact truth. We were coming home across the moors; a boy interfered with us, and would not let us pass; we both pitched into him, and at last he got the worst of it, and we came home."

"But what's the harm of saying that you and he fell, and he broke his leg?"

"A great deal of harm," Ned replied. "If it was known that a boy's leg got broke in a fight with us it would be sure to come to Hathorn's ears; then there would be an inquiry and a row. Like enough he would go up to see the boy and inquire all about it. Then the men would suppose that we had broken our words, and the next time you and I go out on a fishing expedition there's no saying what mightn't happen to us. They are a rough lot those moor men, and don't stick at trifles."

"I will say nothing about it," Tompkins replied hastily;

"you may rely on that. What a lucky fellow you are to be going home! Nothing will be said to you for being an hour late. I shall get a licking to a certainty. How I do hate that Hathorn, to be sure!"

They now came to the point where the road separated, and each hurried on at his best speed.

"You are late to-night, Ned," the boy's father said when he entered. "I don't like your being out after dark. I don't mind how far you go so that you are in by sunset; but, hallo!" he broke off, as he caught sight of the boy's face as he approached the table at which the rest of the party were sitting at tea; "what have you been doing to your face?"

Captain Sankey might well be surprised. One of the boy's eyes was completely closed by a swelling which covered the whole side of his face. His lip was badly cut, and the effect of that and the swelling was to give his mouth the appearance of being twisted completely on one side.

"Oh! there's nothing the matter," Ned replied cheerfully; "but I had a fight with a boy on the moor."

"It is dreadful!—quite dreadful!" Mrs. Sankey said; "your going on like this. It makes me feel quite faint and ill to look at you. I wonder you don't get killed with your violent ways."

Ned made no reply, but took his seat at the table, and fell to work upon the hunches of thick brown bread and butter.

"I will tell you about it afterwards, father," he said; "it really wasn't my fault."

"I am sure I don't wish to hear the story of your quarrels and fighting, Edward," Mrs. Sankey said; "the sight of you is quite enough to upset my nerves and make me wretched. Of course if your father chooses to support you in such goings on I can say nothing. Neither he nor you seem to remember how trying such things as these are to anyone with a broken constitution like mine."

Captain Sankey, knowing from experience how useless it was to attempt to argue with his wife when she was in this mood, continued to eat his meal placidly. Ned seized his mug of milk and water, and took an impatient drink of it.

"Is there anything I had better do for my face?" he asked his father presently.

"I don't think anything you can do, Ned, will make you presentable for the next few days. I believe that a raw beef-steak is the best thing to put on your face; but there is not such a thing in the house, and if there was, I don't think that I should be justified in wasting it for such a purpose. I should say the next best thing would be to keep a cloth soaked in cold water on your face; that will probably take down the swelling to some extent."

After tea Ned repaired to the kitchen, where Abijah, with much scolding and some commiseration, applied a wet cloth to his face, and fastened a handkerchief over it to keep it in its place. Then the boy went into the little room which his father called his study, where he used to read the papers, to follow the doings of the British armies in the field, and above all to smoke his pipe in quiet. He laughed as Ned entered.

"You look like a wounded hero, indeed, Ned. Now sit down, my boy, and tell me about this business; not, you know, that I have any objection to your fighting when it's necessary. My experience is that it is the nature of boys to fight, and it is no use trying to alter boys' nature. As I have always told you, don't get into a fight if you can help it; but, if you once begin, fight it out like a man."

"Well, I couldn't help it this time, father, and I will tell you all about it. I promised not to tell; but what was meant by that was that I should not tell anyone who would do anything about it; and as I know you won't, why, of course I can tell you."

"I don't know what you mean in the least, Ned; a promise, whatever it is about, is a promise."

"I know, father; but all that was meant in my case was that I would say nothing which would cause injury to those to whom I promised; and it will do them no injury whatever by telling you in confidence. Besides, it is probable you may learn about it in another way; because, unfortunately, I broke the other fellow's leg very badly, and there is no saying what may come of it, so I think you ought to know all the circumstances."

"Very well, Ned," his father said quietly; "this seems to be a serious business. Go on, my boy."

Ned related the whole circumstances, his father saying no word until he had finished.

"You have been in no way to blame in the matter, nor could you have acted otherwise. The breaking of the boy's leg is unfortunate, but it was a pure accident, and even the boy's friends did not blame you in the matter. As to the illegal drilling, that is no new thing; it has been known to be going on for many months, and, indeed, in some places for years. The authorities take but little notice of it. An outbreak of these poor fellows would, indeed, constitute a considerable local danger. Mills might be burned down, and possibly some obnoxious masters killed, but a few troops of dragoons, or half a regiment of light infantry, would scatter them like chaff.

"The Irish rebellion thirteen years ago was a vastly more formidable affair. There it may be said that the whole country was in arms, and the element of religious fanaticism came into play; but in spite of that the resistance which they opposed to the troops was absolutely contemptible; however, it is just as well that you did not see them drill, because now, if by any chance this lad should die, and an inquiry were made about it, there would be no occasion for you to allude to the subject at all. You would be able to say truthfully that finding that he was hurt, you went off, and happened to come upon four men on the moor and brought them to his assistance."

"I promised to go up to see the boy, father. I suppose that there is no harm?"

"None at all, Ned, it is only natural that you should entertain the wish; in fact you have injured him seri-

ously, and we must do all in our power to alleviate his
pain. I will go in the morning and see Dr. Green. I
shall of course tell him that the boy was hurt in a tussle
with you, and that you are very sorry about it. The
fact that he is some two years older, as you say, and
ever so much stronger and bigger, is in itself a proof that
you were not likely to have wantonly provoked a fight
with him. I shall ask the doctor if there is anything in
the way of food and comforts I can send up for him."

Accordingly, the next morning the first thing after
breakfast Captain Sankey went out and called upon the
doctor. Ned awaited his return anxiously. "The doctor
says it's a bad fracture, Ned, a very bad fracture, and
the boy must have had his leg curiously twisted under
him for the bone to have snapped in such a way. He
questions whether it will be possible to save the leg;
indeed, he would have taken it off last night, but the
boy said he would rather die, and the men were all against
it. By the help of half-a-dozen men he got the bones
into their place again, and has bandaged the leg up with
splints; but he is very doubtful what will come of it."

Ned was crying now. "I would give anything if it
hadn't happened, father, and he really seemed a nice
fellow. He said over and over again he didn't want to
hurt us, and I am sure he didn't, only he thought he
oughtn't to let us pass, and as we would go on he had to
stop us."

"Well, it can't be helped, Ned," his father said kindly.
"It is very natural that you should be grieved about it;

but you see it really was an accident; there was nothing wilful or intentional about it, and you must not take it to heart more than you can help."

But Ned did take it to heart, and for the next fortnight was very miserable. The doctor's reports during that time were not hopeful. Fever had set in, and for some days the boy was delirious, and there was no saying how it would turn out. At the end of that time the bulletins became somewhat more hopeful. The lad was quiet now from the complete exhaustion of his strength. He might rally or he might not; his leg was going on favourably. No bad symptom had set in, and it was now purely a question of strength and constitution whether he would pull through it.

Mrs. Sankey had been kept in entire ignorance of the whole matter. She had once or twice expressed a languid surprise at Ned's altered manner and extreme quietness; but her interest was not sufficient for her to inquire whether there were any reasons for this change. Abijah had been taken into Captain Sankey's counsels, and as soon as the fever had abated, and the doctor pronounced that the most nourishing food was now requisite, she set to work to prepare the strongest broths and jellies she could make, and these, with bottles of port-wine, were taken by her every evening to the doctor, who carried them up in his gig on his visits to his patient in the morning. On the third Saturday the doctor told Ned that he considered that the boy had fairly turned the corner and was on the road to recovery, and that he might now go up and see him. His friends had expressed their warm gratitude for the supplies which had been sent up, and clearly cherished no animosity against Ned. The boy had been informed of the extreme anxiety of his young antagonist as to his condition, and had nodded feebly when asked if he would see Ned should he call upon him. It was therefore without any feeling of trepidation as to his reception that Ned on the Saturday afternoon entered Varley.

Varley was a scattered village lying at the very edge of the moor. The houses were built just where the valley began to dip down from the uplands, the depression being deep enough to shelter them from the winds which swept across the moor. Some of those which stood lowest were surrounded by a few stumpy fruit-trees in the gardens, but the majority stood bleak and bare. From most of the houses the sound of the shuttle told that hand-weaving was carried on within, and when the weather was warm women sat at the doors with their spinning-wheels. The younger men for the most part worked as croppers in the factories in Marsden.

In good times Varley had been a flourishing village, that is to say its inhabitants had earned good wages; but no one passing through the bare and dreary village would have imagined that it had ever seen good days, for the greater proportion of the earnings had gone in drink, and the Varley men had a bad name even in a country and at a time when heavy drinking was the rule rather than the exception. But whatever good times it

THE VISIT TO SEE BILL SWINTON.

may have had they were gone now. Wages had fallen greatly and the prices of food risen enormously, and the wolf was at the door of every cottage. No wonder the men became desperate, and believing that all their sufferings arose from the introduction of the new machinery had bound themselves to destroy it whatever happened.

A woman of whom he inquired for John Swinton's cottage told him that it was the last on the left. Although he told himself that he had nothing to be afraid of, it needed all Ned's determination to nerve himself to tap at the door of the low thatched cottage. A young woman opened it.

"If you please," Ned said, "I have come to see Bill; the doctor said he would see me. It was I who hurt him, but indeed I didn't mean to do it."

"A noice bizness yoi've made of it atween ee," the woman said, but in a not unkind voice. "Who'd ha' thought as Bill would ha' got hurted by such a little un as thou be'st; but coom in, he will be main glad to see ee, and thy feyther ha' been very good in sending up all sorts o' things for him. He's been very nigh agooing whoam, but I believe them things kept un from it."

The cottage contained but two rooms. In a corner of the living-room, into which Ned followed the woman, Bill Swinton lay upon a bed which Captain Sankey had sent up. Ned would not have known him again, and could scarce believe that the thin feeble figure was the sturdy strong-built boy with whom he had struggled on the moor. His eyes filled with tears as he went up to the bedside.

"I am so sorry!" he said; "I have grieved so all the time you have been ill."

"It's all roight, young un," the boy said in a low voice, "thar's no call vor to fret. It warn't thy fault; thou couldn't not tell why oi would not let ee pass, and ye were roight enough to foight rather than to toorn back. I doan't blame ee nohow, and thou stoodst up well agin me. Oi doon't bear no malice vor a fair foight, not loikely. Thy feyther has been roight good to oi, and the things he sends oi up ha' done oi a power o' good. Oi hoap as how they will let oi eat afore long; oi feels as if oi could hearty, but the doctor he woin't let oi."

"I hope in a few days he will let you," Ned said, "and then I am sure father will send you up some nice things. I have brought you up some of my books for you to look at the pictures."

The boy looked pleased.

"Oi shall loike that," Bill said; "but oi sha'n't know what they be about."

"But I will come up every Saturday if you will let me, and tell you the stories all about them."

"Willee now? That will be main koinde o' ye."

"I don't think you are strong enough to listen to-day," Ned said, seeing how feebly the boy spoke; "but I hope by next Saturday you will be much stronger. And now I will say good-bye, for the doctor said that I must not talk too long."

So saying Ned left the cottage and made his way back to Marsden in better spirits than he had been for the last three weeks.

From that time Ned went up regularly for some weeks every Saturday to see Bill Swinton, to the great disgust of his schoolfellows, who could not imagine why he refused to join in their walks or games on those days; but he was well repaid by the pleasure which his visits afforded. The days passed very drearily to the sick boy, accustomed as he was to a life spent entirely in the open air, and he looked forward with eager longing to Ned's visits.

On the occasion of the second visit he was strong enough to sit up in bed, and Ned was pleased to hear that his voice was heartier and stronger. He listened with delight as Ned read through the books he had brought him from end to end, often stopping him to ask questions as to the many matters beyond his understanding, and the conversations on these points were often so long that the continuance of the reading had to be postponed until the next visit.

To Bill everything he heard was wonderful. Hitherto his world had ended at Marsden, and the accounts of voyages and travels in strange lands were full of surprise and interest to him. Especially he loved to talk to Ned of India, where the boy had lived up to the time when his father had received his wound, and Ned's account of the appearance and manners of the people there were even more interesting to him than books.

At the end of two months after Ned's first visit Bill was able to walk about with a stick, and Ned now discontinued his regular visits; but whenever he had a Saturday on which there was no particular engagement he would go for a chat with Bill, for a strong friendship had now sprung up between the lads.

On Ned's side the feeling consisted partly of regret for the pain and injury he had inflicted upon his companion, partly in real liking for the honesty and fearlessness which marked the boy's character. On Bill's side the feeling was one of intense gratitude for the kindness and attention which Ned had paid him, for his giving up his play-hours to his amusement, and the pains which he had taken to lighten the dreary time of his confinement. Added to this there was a deep admiration for the superior knowledge of his friend. " There was nothing," he often said to himself, "as oi wouldn't do for that young un."

CHAPTER III

A CROPPER VILLAGE.

BAD as were times in Varley the two public-houses, one of which stood at either end of the village, were for the most part well filled of an evening; but this, as the landlords knew to their cost, was the result rather of habit than of thirst. The orders given were few and far between, and the mugs stood empty on the table for a long time before being refilled. In point of numbers the patrons of the "Brown Cow" and the "Spotted Dog" were not unequal; but the "Dog" did a larger trade than its rival, for it was the resort of the younger men, while the "Cow" was the meeting-place of the elders. A man who had neither wife nor child to support could manage even in these hard times to pay for his quart or two of liquor of an evening; but a pint mug was the utmost that those who had other mouths than their own to fill could afford.

Fortunately tobacco, although dear enough if purchased in the towns, cost comparatively little upon the moors, for scarce a week passed but some lugger ran in at

night to some little bay among the cliffs on the eastern
shore, and for the most part landed her bales and kegs in
spite of the vigilance of the coastguard.   So there were
plenty of places scattered all over the moorland where
tobacco could be bought cheap, and where when the right
signal was given a noggin of spirits could be had from
the keg which was lying concealed in the wood-stack or
rubbish heap.   What drunkenness there was on the moors
profited his majesty's excise but little.

The evenings at the "Cow" were not lively.   The men
smoked their long pipes and sipped their beer slowly, and
sometimes for half an hour no one spoke; but it was as
good as conversation, for every one knew what the rest
were thinking of—the bad times, but no one had anything new to say about them.   They were not brilliant,
these sturdy Yorkshiremen.   They suffered patiently and
uncomplainingly, because they did not see that any effort
of theirs could alter the state of things.   They accepted
the fact that the high prices were due to the war; but
why the war was always going on was more than any
of them knew.   It gave them a vague satisfaction when
they heard that a British victory had been won; and
when money had been more plentiful, the occasion had
been a good excuse for an extra bout of drinking, for
most of them were croppers, and had in their time been
as rough and as wild as the younger men were now; but
they had learned a certain amount of wisdom, and shook
their heads over the talk and doings of the younger men
who met at the "Dog."

Here there was neither quiet nor resignation, but fiery talk and stern determination; it was a settled thing here that the machines were responsible for the bad times. The fact that such times prevailed over the whole country in no way affected their opinion. It was not for them to deny that there was a war, that food was dear, and taxation heavy. These things might be; but the effect of the machinery came straight home to them, and they were convinced that if they did but hold together and wreck the machines prosperity would return to Varley.

The organization for resistance was extensive. There were branches in every village in West Yorkshire, Lancashire, Nottingham, and Derby—all acting with a common purpose. The members were bound by terrible oaths upon joining the society to be true to its objects, to abstain on pain of death from any word which might betray its secrets, and to carry into execution its orders, even if these should involve the slaying of a near relation proved to have turned traitor to the society.

Hitherto no very marked success had attended its doings. There had been isolated riots in many places; mills had been burned, and machinery broken. But the members looked forward to better things. So far their only successes had been obtained by threats rather than deeds, for many manufacturers had been deterred from adopting the new machinery by the receipt of threatening letters signed "King Lud," saying that their factories would be burned and themselves shot should they venture upon altering their machinery.

The organ of communication between the members of
the society at Varley and those in other villages was the
blacksmith, or as he preferred to be called, the minister,
John Stukeley, who on week-days worked at the forge
next door to the "Spotted Dog," and on Sundays held
services in "Little Bethel"—a tiny meeting-house standing back from the road.

Had John Stukeley been busier during the week he
would have had less time to devote to the cause of "King
Lud;" but for many hours a day his fire was banked up,
for except to make repairs in any of the frames which
had got out of order, or to put on a shoe which a horse
had cast on his way up the hill from Marsden, there
was but little employment for him.

The man was not a Yorkshireman by birth, but came
from Liverpool, and his small spare figure contrasted
strongly with those of the tall square-built Yorkshiremen
among whom he lived.

He was a good workman, but his nervous irritability,
his self-assertion, and impatience of orders had lost him
so many places that he had finally determined to become his own master, and, coming into a few pounds at
the death of his father, had wandered away from the
great towns, until, finding in Varley a village without a
smith, he had established himself there, and having
adopted the grievances of the men as his own, had speedily
become a leading figure among them.

A short time after his arrival the old man who had offi-
ciated at Little Bethel had died, and Stukeley, who had

from the first taken a prominent part in the service, and
who possessed the faculty of fluent speech to a degree
rare among the Yorkshiremen, was installed as his successor, and soon filled Little Bethel as it had never been
filled before. In his predecessor's time, small as the meeting-house was, it had been comparatively empty. Two
or three men, half a dozen women, and their children
being the only attendants, but it was now filled to
crowding.

Stukeley's religion was political; his prayers and discourses related to the position of affairs in Varley rather
than to Christianity. They were a down-trodden people
whom he implored to burst the bonds of their Egyptian
task-masters. The strength he prayed for was the
strength to struggle and to fight. The enemy he denounced was the capitalist rather than the devil.

Up to that time "King Lud" had but few followers in
Varley; but the fiery discourses in Little Bethel roused
among the younger men a passionate desire to right their
alleged wrongs, and to take vengeance upon those denounced as their oppressors, so the society recruited its
numbers fast. Stukeley was appointed the local secretary,
partly because he was the leading spirit, partly because
he alone among its members was able to write, and under
his vigorous impulsion Varley became one of the leading
centres of the organization in West Yorkshire.

It was on a Saturday evening soon after Bill Swinton
had become convalescent. The parlour of the "Brown
Cow" was filled with its usual gathering; a peat-fire glowed

upon the hearth, and two tallow-candles burned somewhat faintly in the dense smoke. Mugs of beer stood on
the tables, but they were seldom applied to the lips of
the smokers, for they had to do service without being refilled through the long evening. The silence was broken
only by the short puffs at the pipes. All were thinking
over the usual topic, when old Gideon Jones unexpectedly
led their ideas into another channel.

"Oive heern," he said slowly, taking his pipe from his
mouth, "as how Nance Wilson's little gal is wuss."

"Ay, indeed!" "So oi've heern;" "Be she now?" and
various other exclamations arose from the smokers.

Gideon was pleased with the effect he had produced,
and a few minutes later continued the subject.

"It be the empty coopbud more nor illness, I expect."
There was another chorus of assent, and a still heartier one
when he wound up the subject: "These be hard toimes
surelye."

Thinking that he had now done sufficient to vindicate
his standing as one of the original thinkers of the village
Gideon relapsed into silence and smoked away gravely
with his eyes fixed on the fire in the post of honour on
one side of which was his regular seat. The subject, however, was too valuable to be allowed to drop altogether,
and Luke Marner brought it into prominence again by
remarking:

"They tell oi as how Nance has asked Bet Collins to
watch by the rood soide to catch doctor as he droives
whoam. He went out this arternoon to Retlow."

" Oi doubt he woant do she much good; it be food, and
not doctor's stuff as the child needs," another remarked.

" That be so, surelye," went up in a general chorus, and
then a new-comer who had just entered the room said:

" Oi ha' joost coom vrom Nance's and Bill Swinton ha'
sent in a basin o' soup as he got vrom the feyther o' that
boy as broke his leg. Nance war a feeding the child wi'
it, and maybe it will do her good. He ha' been moighty
koind to Bill, that chap hav."

" He ha' been that," Gideon said after the chorus of approval had died away.

" Oi seed t' young un to-day a-sitting in front o' th' cottage, a-talking and laughing wi' Bill."

" They be good uns, feyther and son, though they tells
oi as neither on them bain't Yaarkshire."

The general feeling among the company was evidently
one of surprise that any good thing should be found outside Yorkshire. But further talk on the subject was in-
terrupted by a slight exclamation at the door.

" O what a smoke, feyther! I can't see you, but I suppose you're somewhere here. You're wanted at home."

Although the speaker was visible to but few in the
room there was no doubt as to her identity, or as to
the person addressed as feyther. Mary Powlett was indeed the niece and not the daughter of Luke Marner,
but as he had brought her up from childhood she looked
upon him as her father. It was her accent and the tone of
her voice which rendered it unnecessary for any of those
present to see her face.

Luke was a bachelor when the child had arrived fifteen years before in the carrier's cart from Marsden, having made the journey in a similar conveyance to that town from Sheffield, where her father and mother had died within a week of each other, the last request of her mother being that little Polly should be sent off to the care of Luke Marner at Varley.

Luke had not then settled down into the position of one of the elders of the village, and he had been somewhat embarrassed by the arrival of the three-year-old girl. He decided promptly, however, upon quitting the lodgings which he had as a single man occupied and taking a cottage by himself. His neighbours urged upon him that so small a child could not remain alone all day while he was away at Marsden at work—a proposition to which he assented; but to the surprise of everyone, instead of placing her during the day under the care of one of the women of the place, he took her down with him to Marsden and placed her under the care of a respectable woman there who had children of her own.

Starting at five every morning from his cottage with Polly perched on his shoulder he tramped down to the town, leaving her there before going to work, and calling for her in the evening. A year later he married, and the village supposed that Polly would now be left behind. But they were mistaken. When he became engaged he had said:

" Now Loiza, there's one point as oi wish settled. As oi have told ye, oi ha' partly chosen ye becos oi knowed as how ye would maake a good mother to my little Polly; but oi doan't mean to give up taking her down with me o' days to the town. Oi likes to ha' her wi' me on the roade—it makes it shorter loike. As thou knowest thyself, oi ha' bin a chaanged man sin she coom There warn't a cropper in the village drank harder nor oi; but oi maad oop moi moind when she came to gi' it up, and oi have gi'd it up."

"I know, Luke," the girl said. "I wouldna have had ye, hadn't ye doon so, as I told ye two years agone. I know the child ha' done it, and I loves her for it and will be a good mother to her."

"Oi knows you will, Loiza, and oi bain't feared as ye'll be jealous if so be as ye've children o' your own. Oi sha'n't love 'em a bit the less coss oi loves little Polly. She be just the image o' what moi sister Jane was when she war a little thing and oi used to take care o' her. Mother she didn't belong to this village, and the rough ways of the men and the drink frightened her. She war quiet and tidy and neat in her ways, and Jane took arter her, and glad she was when the time came, to marry and get away from Varley. Oi be roight sure if she knows owt what's goin' on down here, she would be glad to know as her child ain't bein' brought oop in Varley ways. I ha' arranged wi' the woman where she gets her meals for her to go to school wi' her own children. Dost thee object to that, lass?—if so, say so noo afore it's too late, but doon't thraw it in moi face arterwards. Ef thou'st children they shall go to school too. Oi don't want to do more for Polly nor oi'd do for moi own."

"I ha' no objection, Luke. I remembers your sister, how pretty and quiet she wor; and thou shalt do what you likest wi' Polly, wi'out no grumble from me."

Eliza Marner kept the promise she had made before marriage faithfully. If she ever felt in her heart any jealousy as she saw Polly growing up a pretty bright little maiden, as different to the usual child product of Varley as could well be, she was wise enough never to express her thoughts, and behaved with motherly kindness to her in the evening hours spent at home. She would perhaps have felt the task a harder one had her own elder children been girls; but three boys came first, and a girl was not born until she had been married eleven years. Polly, who was now fourteen, had just come home from her schooling at Marsden for good, and was about to go out into service there. But after the birth of her little girl Mrs. Marner, who had never for a Varley girl been strong, faded rapidly away; and Polly's stay at home, intended at first to last but a few weeks until its mother was about again, extended into months.

The failing woman reaped now the benefit of Polly's training. Her gentle quiet way, her soft voice, her neatness and tidiness, made her an excellent nurse, and she devoted herself to cheer and brighten the sick-room of the woman who had made so kind an adopted mother to her. Her influence kept even the rough boys quiet; and all Varley, which had at first been unanimous in its condemnation of the manner in which Luke Marner was bringing up that "gal" of his, just as if the place was

not good enough for her, were now forced to confess that
the experiment had turned out well.

"Polly, my dear," the sick woman said to her one afternoon when the girl had been reading to her for some
time, and was now busy mending some of the boys'
clothes, while baby, nearly a year old, was gravely amusing herself with a battered doll upon the floor, "I used
to think, though I never said so, as your feyther war
making a mistake in bringing you up different to other
gals here; but I see as he was right. There ain't one of
them as would have been content to give up all their
time and thoughts to a sick woman as thou hast done.
There ain't a house in the village as tidy and comfortable
as this, and the boys mind you as they never minded me.
When I am gone Luke will miss me, but thar won't be
no difference in his comfort, and I know thou'lt look
arter baby and be a mother to her. I don't suppose as
thou wilt stay here long; thou art over fifteen now, and
the lads will not be long afore they begin to come a-coort-
ing of thee. But doan't ee marry in Varley, Polly. My
Luke's been a good husband to me. But thou know'st
what the most of them be—they may do for Varley-bred
gals, but not for the like of thee. And when thou goest
take baby wi' thee and bring her up like thysel till she
be old enough to coom back and look arter Luke and the
house."

Polly was crying quietly while the dying woman was
speaking. The doctor, on leaving that morning, had told
her that he could do no more and that Mrs. Marner was

sinking rapidly. Kneeling now beside the bed she promised to do all that her adopted mother asked her, adding, "and I shall never, never leave feyther as long as he lives." The woman smiled faintly.

"Many a girl ha' said that afore now, Polly, and ha' changed her moind when the roight man asked her. Don't ee make any promises that a-way, lass. 'Tis natural that, when a lassie's time comes, she should wed; and if Luke feels loanly here, why he's got it in his power to get another to keep house for him. He be but a little over forty now; and as he ha' lived steady and kept hisself away from drink, he be a yoonger man now nor many a one ten year yoonger. Don't ye think to go to sacrifice your loife to hissen. And now, child, read me that chapter over agin, and then I think I could sleep a bit."

Before morning Eliza Marner had passed away, and Polly became the head of her uncle's house. Two years had passed, and so far Mary Powlett showed no signs of leaving the house, which, even the many women in the village, who envied her for her prettiness and neatness and disliked her for what they called her airs, acknowledged that she managed well. But it was not from lack of suitors. There were at least half-a-dozen stalwart young croppers who would gladly have paid court to her had there been the smallest sign on her part of willingness to accept their attentions; but Polly, though bright and cheerful and pleasant to all, afforded to none of them an opportunity for anything approaching intimacy.

On Sundays, the times alone when their occupations

enabled the youth of Varley to devote themselves to attentions to the maidens they favoured, Mary Powlett was not to be found at home after breakfast, for, having set everything in readiness for dinner, she always started for Marsden, taking little Susan with her, and there spent the day with the woman who had even more than Eliza Marner been her mother. She had, a month after his wife's death, fought a battle with Luke and conquered. The latter had, in pursuance of the plans he had originally drawn up for her, proposed that she should go into service at Marsden.

"Oi shall miss thee sorely, Polly," he said; "and oi doan't disguise it from thee, vor the last year, lass, thou hast been the light o' this house, and oi couldna have spared ye. But oi ha' always fixed that thou shouldst go into service at Marsden—Varley is not fit vor the loikes o' ye. We be a rough lot here, and a drunken; and though oi shall miss thee sorely for a while, oi must larn to do wi'out thee."

Polly heard him in silence, and then positively refused to go. "You have been all to me, feyther, since I was a child, and I am not going to leave you now. I don't say that Varley is altogether nice, but I shall be very happy here with you and the boys and dear little Susan, and I am not going to leave, and so—there!"

Luke knew well how great would be the void which her absence would make, but he still struggled to carry out his plans. "But, Polly, oi should na loike to see thee marry here, and thy mother would never ha' loiked it, and thou wilt no chance of seeing other men here."

"Why I am only sixteen, feyther, and we need not talk of my marriage for years and years yet, and I promise you I sha'n't think of marrying in Varley when the time comes; but there is one thing I should like, and that is to spend Sundays, say once a fortnight, down with Mrs. Mason; they were so quiet and still there, and I did like so much going to the church; and I hate that Little Bethel, especially since that horrible man came there; he is a disgrace, feyther, and you will see that mischief will come out of his talk."

"Oi don't like him myself, Polly, and maybe me and the boys will sometoimes come down to the church thou art so fond of. However, if thou wilt agree to go down every Sunday to Mrs. Mason, thou shalt stay here for a bit till oi see what can best be done."

And so it was settled, and Polly went off every Sunday morning, and Luke went down of an evening to fetch her back.

"Well, what is't, lass?" he asked as he joined her outside the "Brown Cow."

"George has scalded his leg badly, feyther. I was just putting Susan to bed, and he took the kettle off the fire to pour some water in the tea-pot, when Dick pushed him, or something, and the boiling water went over his leg."

"Oi'll give that Dick a hiding," Luke said wrathfully as he hastened along by her side. "Why didn't ye send him here to tell me instead of cooming thyself?"

"It was only an accident, feyther, and Dick was so

frightened when he saw what had happened and heard George cry out that he ran out at once. I have put some flour on George's leg; but I think the doctor ought to see him, that's why I came for you."

"It's no use moi goaing voor him now, lass, he be expected along here every minute. Jack Wilson, he be on the look-out by the roadside vor to stop him to ask him to see Nance, who be taken main bad. I will see him and ask him to send doctor to oor house when he comes, and tell Jarge I will be oop in a minute."

Upon the doctor's arrival he pronounced the scald to be a serious one, and Dick, who had been found sobbing outside the cottage and had been cuffed by his father, was sent down with the doctor into the town to bring up some lint to envelop the leg. The doctor had already paid his visit to Nance Wilson, and had rated her father soundly for not procuring better food for her.

"It's all nonsense your saying the times are bad," he said in reply to the man's excuses. "I know the times are bad; but you know as well as I do that half your wages go at the public-house; your family are starving while you are squandering money in drink. That child is sinking from pure want of food, and I doubt if she would not be gone now if it hadn't have been for that soup your wife tells me Bill Swinton sent in to her. I tell you, if she dies you will be as much her murderer as if you had chopped her down with a hatchet."

The plain speaking of the doctor was the terror of his parish patients, who nevertheless respected him for the

honest truths he told them.   He himself used to say that
his plain speaking saved him a world of trouble, for that
his patients took good care never to send for him except
when he was really wanted.

The next day Mary Powlett was unable to go off as
usual to Marsden as George was in great pain from his
scald. She went down to church, however, in the evening
with her father, Bill Swinton taking her place by the
bedside of the boy.

"Thou hast been a-sitting by moi bedside hours every
day, Polly," he said, "and it's moi turn now to take thy
place here. Jack ha' brought over all moi books, for oi
couldn't maake a shift to carry them and use moi crutches,
and oi'll explain all the pictures to Jarge jest as Maister
Ned explained 'em to oi."

The sight of the pictures reconciled George to Polly's
departure, and seeing the lad was amused and comfortable
she started with Luke, Dick taking his place near the
bed, where he could also enjoy a look at the pictures.

"Did you notice that pretty girl with the sweet voice
in the aisle in a line with us, father," Ned asked that
evening, "with a great, strong, quiet-looking man by the
side of her?"

"Yes, lad, the sweetness of her singing attracted my
attention, and I thought what a bright pretty face it was!"

"That's Mary Powlett and her uncle. You have heard
me speak of her as the girl who was so kind in nursing
Bill."

"Indeed, Ned! I should scarcely have expected to find

so quiet and tidy looking a girl at Varley, still less to meet her with a male relation in church."

"She lives at Varley, but she can hardly be called a Varley girl," Ned said. "Bill was telling me about her. Her uncle had her brought up down here. She used to go back to sleep at night, but otherwise all her time was spent here. It seems her mother never liked the place, and married away from it, and when she and her husband died and the child came back to live with her uncle he seemed to think he would be best carrying out his dead sister's wishes by having her brought up in a different way to the girls at Varley. He has lost his wife now, and she keeps house for him, and Bill says all the young men in Varley are mad about her, but she won't have anything to say to them."

"She is right enough there," Captain Sankey said smilingly. "They are mostly croppers, and rightly or wrongly—rightly, I am afraid—they have the reputation of being the most drunken and quarrelsome lot in York-shire. Do you know the story that is current among the country people here about them?"

"No, father, what is it?"

"Well, they say that no cropper is in the place of punish-ment. It was crowded with them at one time, but they were so noisy and troublesome that his infernal majesty was driven to his wits' end by their disputes. He offered to let them all go. They refused. So one day he struck upon a plan to get rid of them. Going outside the gates he shouted at the top of his voice, 'Beer, beer, who wants beer?' every cropper in the place rushed out, and he then slipped in again and shut the gates, and has taken good care ever since never to admit a cropper into his territory."

Ned laughed at the story. "It shows at any rate, father, what people think of them here; but I don't think they are as bad as that, though Bill did say that there are awful fights and rows going on there of an evening, and even down here if there is a row there is sure to be a cropper in it. Still you see there are some good ones; look at Luke Marner, that's the man we saw in church, see how kind he has been to his niece."

"There are good men of all sorts, and though the croppers may be rough and given to drink, we must not blame them too severely; they are wholly uneducated men, they work hard, and their sole pleasure is in the beer-shop. At bottom they are no doubt the same as the rest of their countrymen, and the Yorkshire men, though a hard-headed, are a soft-hearted race; the doctor tells me that except that their constitutions are ruined by habitual drinking he has no better patients; they bear pain un-flinchingly, and are patient, and even-tempered. I know he loves them with all their faults, and I consider him to be a good judge of character."

CHAPTER IV.

THE WORMS TURN.

"I SAY, it's a shame, a beastly shame!" Ned Sankey exclaimed passionately as the boys came out from school one day.

Generally they poured out in a confused mass, eager for the fresh air and anxious to forget in play the remembrance of the painful hours in school; but to-day they came out slowly and quietly, each with a book in his hand, for they had tasks set them which would occupy every moment till the bell sounded again.

"Every one says they know nothing about the cat. I don't know whether it's true or not, for I am sorry to say some of the fellows will tell lies to escape the cane, but whether it is so or not he's no right to punish us all for what can only be the fault of one or two."

That morning the cat, which was the pet of Mr. Hathorn and his wife, had been found dead near the door of the school-house. It had been most brutally knocked about. One of its eyes had been destroyed, its soft fur was matted with blood, and it had evidently been beaten to death. That the cat was no favourite with the boys was certain. The door between the school-room and the house was unfastened at night, and the cat, in her pursuit of mice not unfrequently knocked over ink-stands, and the ink, penetrating into the desks, stained books and papers, and more than one boy had been caned severely for damage due to the night prowlings of the cat.

Threats of vengeance against her had often been uttered, and when the cat was found dead it was the general opinion in the school that one or other of their comrades had carried out his threats, but no suspicion fell upon anyone in particular. The boys who were most likely to have done such a thing declared their innocence stoutly. Mr. Hathorn had no doubt on the subject. The cane had been going all the morning, and he had told them that extra tasks would be given which would occupy all their playtime until the offender was given up to judgment.

In point of fact the boys were altogether innocent of the deed. Pussy was a noted marauder, and having been caught the evening before in a larder, from which she had more than once stolen tit-bits, she had been attacked by an enraged cook with a broomstick, and blows had been showered upon her until the woman, believing that life was extinct, had thrown her outside into the road; but the cat was not quite dead, and had, after a time, revived sufficiently to drag her way home, only, however, to die.

"I call it a shame!" Ned repeated. "Mind, I say it's a brutal thing to ill-treat a cat like that. If she did knock down inkstands and get fellows into rows it was not her fault. It's natural cats should run after mice, and the wainscotting of the school-room swarmed with them. One can hear them chasing each other about and squeaking all day. If I knew any of the fellows had killed the cat I should go straight to Hathorn and tell him.

"You might call it sneaking if you like, but I would do it, for I hate such brutal cruelty. I don't see how it could have been any of the fellows, for they would have had to get out of the bed-room and into it again; besides, I don't see how they could have caught the cat if they did get out; but whether it was one of the fellows or not makes no difference. I say it's injustice to punish every one for the fault of one or two fellows.

"I suppose he thinks that in time we shall give up the names of the fellows who did it. As far as I am concerned, it will be just the other way. If I had known who had done it this morning, when he accused us, I should have got up and said so, because I think fellows who treat dumb animals like that are brutes that ought to be punished, but I certainly would not sneak because Hathorn punished me unjustly. I vote we all refuse to do the work he has set us."

This bold proposition was received with blank astonishment.

"But he would thrash us all fearfully," Tompkins said.

"He daren't if we only stuck together. Why, he wouldn't have a chance with us if we showed fight. If we were to say to him, 'We won't do these extra tasks, and if you touch one of us the whole lot will pitch into you,' what could he do then?"

"I will tell you what he could do, Sankey," Tom Room, a quiet, sensible boy, replied. "If we were in a desert island it would be all well enough, he could not tyrannize over us then; but here it is different. He would just put on his hat and go into the town, and in ten minutes he would be back again with the six constables, and if that wasn't enough he could get plenty of other men, and where would our fighting be then? We should all get the most tremendous licking we have ever had, and get laughed at besides through the town for a pack of young fools."

Ned broke into a good-tempered laugh.

"Of course you are right, Room. I only thought about Hathorn himself. Still, it is horribly unfair. I will do it to-day. But if he goes on with it, as he threatens, I won't do it, let him do what he likes."

For some days this state of things continued. There was no longer any sound of shouting and laughter in the playground. The boys walked about moody and sullen, working at their lessons. They were fast becoming desperate. No clue had been obtained as to the destroyer of the cat, and the schoolmaster declared that if it took him months to break their spirits he would do it. Ned Sankey had said nothing at home as to his troubles. His father noticed that he ran off again as soon as his dinner was over, and that he no longer said anything as to the sports in which he was engaged in playtime; also, that his lessons occupied him from tea-time until he went up to bed.

"Anything is better than this," Ned said one day to some of the boys of his own age. "In my opinion it's better to have a regular row. What Room said was quite true, we shall get the worst of it; but the story will then come out, and it will be seen what a beastly tyranny we have been undergoing. I tell you, I for one will not stand it any longer, so here goes," and he threw his book up into a tree, in whose branches it securely lodged.

His comrades followed his example, and the news that Sankey and some of the other fellows were determined to put up with it no longer soon spread, and in five minutes not a book was to be seen in the playground. The spirit of resistance became strong and general, and when the bell rang the boys walked into the school-room silent and determined, but looking far less moody and downcast than usual. Mr. Hathorn took his seat at his desk.

"The first class will come up and say their tasks."

Not a boy moved in his seat.

"The first class will come up and say their tasks," the master repeated, bringing his cane down with angry emphasis on the desk.

Still no one moved.

"What does this mean?" he shouted, rising from his seat.

"It means, sir," Ned Sankey said, rising also, "that we

are determined, all of us, that we will learn no more extra tasks. None of us, so far as we know, ever touched your cat, and we are not going to submit to be punished any longer for a fault which none of us have committed."

"No, no," rose in a general chorus through the school-room, "we will do no more tasks."

Mr. Hathorn stood petrified with astonishment and white with anger.

"So you are at the bottom of this, Sankey. I will make an example of you."

So saying, he took a stride forward towards Ned. In an instant a shower of books flew at him from all parts of the room. Infuriated by the attack, he rushed forward with his cane raised. Ned caught up a heavy inkstand.

"If you touch me," he shouted, "I will fling this at your head."

Mr. Hathorn hesitated. The shower of books had not affected him, but the heavy missile in Ned's hand was a serious weapon. In another moment he sprang forward and brought his cane down with all his force upon Ned's back.

Ned at once hurled the heavy inkstand at him. The schoolmaster sprang on one side, but it struck him on the shoulder, and he staggered back.

"You have broken my shoulder, you young scoundrel!" he exclaimed.

"I shouldn't care if I had broken your head," Ned retorted, white with passion; "it would have served you right if I had killed you, you tyrant."

NED HEADS A REBELLION AGAINST THE TYRANT.

"One of you go and fetch a constable," Mr. Hathorn said to the boys.

"Let him send his servant. He will find me at home. Mr. Hathorn, I am not going to run away, you need not think it. Give me in charge if you dare; I don't care what they do to me, but the whole country shall know what a tyrant you are."

So saying, he collected his books, put his cap on his head, and walked from the school-room, the boys cheering him loudly as he went. On reaching home he went at once to his father's study.

"I am sorry to say, sir, that there has been a row in the school, and Hathorn has threatened to send a constable here after me for throwing an inkstand at him."

"Throwing an inkstand!" Captain Sankey exclaimed. "Is it possible?"

"It is quite possible and quite true; he has been treating us shamefully for the last ten days; he has been always a cruel brute all along, though I never wanted to make a fuss about it, but it has been getting worse and worse. Ten days ago some one killed his cat, and I am almost sure it was none of the boys, but he chose to believe it was, and because he couldn't find out who, he has punished the whole school, and all our play hours have been taken up with lessons ever since, and he said he would keep on so till he found out who did it, if it was months.

"So at last we could not stand it any longer, and we all agreed that we wouldn't do the extra tasks, and that we would stick together when we told him so. He rushed at me with his cane, and gave me one with all his might, and I threw an inkstand at him, and it caught him on the shoulder, and he says it has broken it, and that he would send for a constable. So I told him to do so if he dared, and here I am."

"This is a very serious business, Ned," his father said gravely. "In the first place, there is something like a rebellion in the school, of which, I suppose, you were one of the leaders or he would not have singled you out. In the second place, you threw a missile at him, which has broken his shoulder, and might have killed him had it struck him on the head. I have warned you, my boy, over and over again against giving way to that passionate temper of yours, and have told you that it would lead you into serious trouble."

"I can't help it, sir," Ned said doggedly. "I've put up with a tremendous lot there, and have said nothing about it, because I did not wish to give you trouble; but when it came to downright tyranny like this I would rather be killed than put up with it. I warned him fairly that if he struck me I would throw the inkstand at him, and he brought it on himself."

Captain Sankey seeing that in his son's present state of mind talking would be useless to him, ordered him to remain in his study till his return, and putting on his hat went towards the school. Ned's temper had always been a source of anxiety to him. The boy was, no doubt, of a passionate nature, but had he had the advantage of a proper supervision and care when he was a child the tendency might have been overcome. Unfortunately this had not been the case. His mother had left the children entirely to the care of ayahs, he himself had been far too occupied with his regimental duties to be able to superintend their training, while Abijah's hands had been too full with the management of the house, which entirely devolved upon her, and with the constant attention demanded by Mrs. Sankey, to give them any close superintendence. Thus like most children born in India and left entirely in the charge of coloured nurses, Ned had acquired the habit of giving way to bursts of ungovernable passion; for the black nurses have no authority over their young charges, unless seconded and supported by the firmness of their mothers. In this case no such support had been forthcoming.

Mrs. Sankey hated being troubled, and the ayahs always found that any complaints to her recoiled upon themselves, for she always took the part of her children, and insisted that the fault lay on the side of the nurses and not on them. The natural result was, that the ayahs ceased to trouble her, and found it easier to allow the children to do as they chose, and to give way quietly to Ned's outbursts of passion.

Captain Sankey knew nothing of all this. Ned was very fond of him, and was always bright and good-tempered when with his father, and it was not until he left India and was thrown more with him that Captain Sankey discovered how grievously Ned's disposition, which was in other respects a fine one, was marred by the habit which had been encouraged by indulgence and want of control. Then he set to work earnestly to remedy the mischief, but the growth of years is hard to eradicate, and although under the influence of the affection for his father and his own good sense Ned had so far conquered himself that his fits of passion were few and far between, the evil still existed, and might yet, as his father felt, lead to consequences which would mar his whole life.

Thinking the matter sadly over, Captain Sankey was proceeding towards the school when he met one of the constables. The man touched his hat and stopped.

"This be a moighty oonpleasant business, Captain," he said; "your boy, he ha' been and battered school maister; and t' doctor says he ha' broke his collar-bone. Oi ha' got to take him afore t' magistrate."

"Very well, Harper," Captain Sankey said quietly; "of course you must do your duty. It is a sad business, and I was on my way to the school to see if the matter could not be arranged; however, as it has been put in your hands it is now too late, and things must take their course; the magistrates are not sitting to-day. I will guarantee that my son shall be present at the sitting on Thursday, I suppose that will be sufficient?"

"Yes, oi supposes if you promises to produce him, that ull do," the constable said. "Oi doan't suppose as nought will come o't; these schoolmaister chaps does thrash t' boys cruel, and oi ain't surprised as t' little chaps roises agin' it soometoimes. T'others all seem moighty glad o' it:

oi heard 'em shouting and cheering in t' yard as if they was all mad."

Captain Sankey shook his head. "I'm afraid the magistrates won't see it in that light, Harper; discipline is discipline. However, we must hope for the best."

The story that there had been a rebellion among the boys at Hathorn's, that the schoolmaster had his shoulder broken, and that Captain Sankey's son was to go before the magistrates, spread rapidly through Marsden, and the court-house was crowded at the sitting of the magistrates on Thursday.

There were two magistrates on the bench, Mr. Thompson the local banker, and Squire Simmonds of Lathorpe Hall, three miles from the town. Several minor cases were first disposed of, and then Ned's name was called. Captain Sankey had been accommodated with a seat near the magistrates, with both of whom he had some personal acquaintance. Ned was sitting by the side of the lawyer whom his father had retained to defend him; he now moved quietly into the dock, while Mr. Hathorn, with his arm in a sling, took his place in the witness-box.

Ned had recovered now from his fit of passion, and looked amused rather than concerned as the schoolmaster gave his evidence as to the fray in the school-room.

" I have a few questions to ask you, Mr. Hathorn," Mr. Wakefield, Ned's lawyer, said. " Had you any reason for expecting any outbreak of this kind among your boys?"

" None whatever," Mr. Hathorn said.

" You use the cane pretty freely, I believe, sir."

" I use it when it is necessary," Mr. Hathorn replied.

" Ah! and how often do you consider it necessary?"

" That must depend upon circumstances."

" You have about thirty boys, I think?"

" About thirty."

" And you consider it necessary that at least fifteen out of that thirty should be caned every day. You must have got a very bad lot of boys, Mr. Hathorn?"

" Not so many as that," the schoolmaster said, flushing.

" I shall be prepared to prove to your worships," the lawyer said, " that for the last six months the average of boys severely caned by this man has exceeded sixteen a day, putting aside such minor matters as one, two, or three vicious cuts with the cane given at random. It fortunately happened, as I find from my young friend in the dock, that one of the boys has, from motives of curiosity, kept an account for the last six months of the number of boys thrashed every day. I have sent round for him, and he is at present in court."

Mr. Hathorn turned pale, and he began to think that it would have been wiser for him to have followed Ned's advice, and not to have brought the matter into court.

" Your worships," the lawyer said, " you have been boys, as I have, and you can form your own ideas as to the wretchedness that must prevail among a body of lads of whom more than half are caned daily. This, your worships, is a state of tyranny which might well drive any boys to desperation. But I have not done with Mr. Hathorn yet.

"During the ten days previous to this affair things were even more unpleasant than usual in your establishment, were they not, sir? I understand that the whole of the boys were deprived of all play whatever, and that every minute was occupied by extra tasks, and moreover the prospect was held out to them that this sort of thing would continue for months."

There had already been several demonstrations of feeling in court, but at this statement by the lawyer there was a general hiss. The schoolmaster hesitated before replying.

"Now, Mr. Hathorn," the lawyer said briskly, "we want neither hesitation nor equivocation. We may as well have it from you, because if you don't like telling the truth I can put the thirty miserable lads under your charge into the box one after the other."

"They have had extra tasks to do during their playtime," Mr. Hathorn said, "because they refused to reveal which among them brutally murdered my cat."

"And how do you know they murdered your cat?"

"I am sure they did," the schoolmaster said shortly.

"Oh! you are sure they did! And why are you so sure? Had they any grudge against your cat?"

"They pretended they had a grudge."

"What for, Mr. Hathorn?"

"They used to accuse her of upsetting the ink-bottles when they did it themselves."

"You did not believe their statements, I suppose?"

"Not at all."

"You caned them just the same as if they had done it themselves. At least I am told so."

"Of course I caned them, especially as I knew that they were telling a lie."

"But if it was a lie, Mr. Hathorn, if this cat did not upset their ink, why on earth should these boys have a grudge against her and murder her?"

The schoolmaster was silent.

"Now I want an answer, sir. You are punishing thirty boys in addition to the sixteen daily canings divided among them; you have cut off all their play-time, and kept them at work from the time they rise to the time they go to bed. As you see, according to your own statement, they could have had no grudge against the cat, how are you sure they murdered her?"

"I am quite sure," Mr. Hathorn said doggedly. "Boys have always a spite against cats."

"Now, your honours, you hear this," Mr. Wakefield said. "Now I am about to place in the witness-box a very respectable woman, one Jane Tytler, who is cook to our esteemed fellow-townsman Mr. Samuel Hawkins, whose residence is, as you know, not far from this school. She will tell you that, having for some time been plagued by a thieving cat which was in the habit of getting into her larder and carrying off portions of food, she, finding it one day there in the act of stealing a half-chicken, fell upon it with a broom-stick and killed it, or as she thought killed it, and I imagine most cooks would have acted the same under the circumstances.

"She thought no more about it until she heard the reports in the town about this business at the school, and then she told her master. The dates have been compared, and it is found that she battered this cat on the evening before the Hathorn cat was found dead in the yard. Furthermore, the cat she battered was a white cat with a black spot on one side, and this is the exact description of the Hathorn cat; therefore, your honours, you will see that the assumption, or pretence, or excuse, call it what you will, by which this man justifies his tyrannical treatment of these unfortunate boys has no base or foundation whatever. You can go now, Mr. Hathorn; I have nothing further to say to you."

A loud hiss rose again from the crowded court as the schoolmaster stepped down from the witness-box, and Jane Tytler took his place. After giving her evidence she was succeeded by Dick Tompkins in much trepidation. Dick was a most unwilling witness, but he produced the note-book in which he had daily jotted down the number of boys caned, and swore to the general accuracy of the figures.

Mr. Wakefield then asked the magistrates if they would like to hear any further witnesses as to the state of things in the school-room. They said that what they had heard was quite sufficient. He then addressed them on the merits of the case, pointing out that although in this case one of the parties was a master and the other a pupil this in no way removed it in the eye of the law from the category of other assaults. "In this case," he said, "your worships, the affair has arisen out of a long course of tyranny and provocation on the part of one of the parties, and you will observe that this is the party who first commits the assault, while my client was acting solely in self-defence.

"It is he who ought to stand in the witness-box, and the complainant in the dock, for he is at once the aggressor and the assailant. The law admits any man who is assaulted to defend himself, and there is, so far as I am aware, no enactment whatever to be found in the statute-book placing boys in a different category to grown-up persons. When your worships have discharged my client, as I have no doubt you will do at once, I shall advise him to apply for a summons for assault against this man Hathorn."

The magistrates consulted together for some time; then the squire, who was the senior, said:

"We are of opinion that Master Sankey, by aiding this rebellion against his master, has done wrongly, and that he erred grievously in discharging a heavy missile at his master; at the same time we think that the provocation that he received by the tyranny which has been proved to have been exercised by Mr. Hathorn towards the boys under his charge, and especially by their unjust punishment for an offence which the complainant conceived without sufficient warrant, or indeed without any warrant at all, that they had committed, to a great extent justifies and excuses the conduct of Master Sankey. Therefore, with a reprimand as to his behaviour, and a caution as to the consequences which might have arisen from his allowing his temper to go beyond bounds, we discharge him.

"As to you, sir," he said to the schoolmaster, "we wish to express our opinion that your conduct has been cruel and tyrannical in the extreme, and we pity the unfortunate boys who are under the care of a man who treats them with such cruel harshness as you are proved to have done."

The magistrates now rose, and the court broke up. Many of those present crowded round Ned and shook his hand, congratulating him on the issue; but at a sign from his father the boy drew himself away from them, and joining Captain Sankey, walked home with him.

"The matter has ended better than I expected, Ned," he said gravely; "but pray, my boy, do not let yourself think that there is any reason for triumph. You have been gravely reprimanded, and had the missile you used struck the schoolmaster on the head, you would now be in prison awaiting your trial for a far graver offence, and that before judges who would not make the allowances for you that the magistrates here have done.

"Beware of your temper, Ned, for unless you overcome it, be assured that sooner or later it may lead to terrible consequences." Ned, who had in fact been inclined to feel triumphant over his success, was sobered by his father's grave words and manner; and resolved that he would try hard to conquer his fault; but evil habits are hard to overcome, and the full force of his father's words was still to come home to him.

He did not, of course, return to Mr. Hathorn's, and indeed the disclosures of the master's severity made at the examination before the magistrates obtained such publicity that several of his pupils were removed at once, and notices were given that so many more would not return after the next holidays that no one was surprised to hear that the schoolmaster had arranged with a successor in the school, and that he himself was about to go to America.

The result was that after the holidays his successor took his place, and many of the fathers who had intended to remove their sons decided to give the new-comer a trial. The school opened with nearly the original number of pupils. Ned was one of those who went back. Captain Sankey had called on the new master, and had told him frankly the circumstances of the fracas between Ned and Mr. Hathorn.

"I will try your son at any rate, Mr Sankey," the master said. "I have a strong opinion that boys can be managed without such use of the cane as is generally adopted; that, in my opinion, should be the last resort. Boys are like other people, and will do more for kindness than for blows. By what you tell me, the circumstances of your son's bringing up in India among native servants, have encouraged the growth of a passionate temper, but I trust that we may be able to overcome that; at any rate I will give him a trial." And so it was settled that Ned should return to Porson's, for so the establishment was henceforth to be known.

CHAPTER V.

THE NEW MASTER.

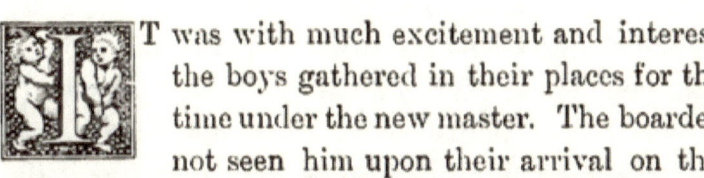T was with much excitement and interest that the boys gathered in their places for the first time under the new master. The boarders had not seen him upon their arrival on the previous evening, but had been received by an old housekeeper, who told them Mr. Porson would not return until the coach came in from York that night.

All eyes were turned to the door as the master entered. The first impression was that he was a younger man than they had expected. Mr. Hathorn had been some five-and-forty years old; the new-comer was not over thirty. He was a tall loosely made man, with somewhat stooping shoulders; he had heavy eyebrows, gray eyes, and a firm mouth. He did not look round as he walked straight to his desk; then he turned, and his eyes travelled quietly and steadily round the room as if scanning each of the faces directed towards him.

"Now, boys," he said in a quiet voice, "a few words before we begin. I am here to teach, and you are here to learn. As your master I expect prompt obedience. I shall look to see each of you do your best to acquire the knowledge which your parents have sent you here to obtain. Above all I shall expect that every boy here will be straightforward, honourable, and truthful. I shall not expect to find that all are capable of making equal progress; there are clever boys and stupid boys, just as there are clever men and stupid men, and it would be unjust to expect that one can keep up to the other; but I do look to each doing his best according to his ability. On my part I shall do my best to advance you in your studies, to correct your faults, and to make useful men of you.

"One word as to punishments. I do not believe that knowledge is to be thrashed into boys, or that fear is the best teacher. I shall expect you to learn, partly because you feel that as your parents have paid for you to learn it is your duty to learn, partly because you wish to please me. I hope that the cane will seldom be used in this school. It will be used if any boy tells me a lie, if any boy does anything which is mean and dishonourable, if any boy is obstinately idle, and when it is used it will be used to a purpose, but I trust that the occasion for it will be rare.

"I shall treat you as friends whom it is my duty to instruct. You will treat me, I hope, as a friend whose duty it is to instruct you, and who has a warm interest in your welfare; if we really bear these relations to each other there should be seldom any occasion for punishment. And now as a beginning to-day, boys, let each come up to my desk, one at a time, with his books. I shall examine you separately, and see what each knows and is capable of doing. I see by the report here that there are six boys in the first class. As these will occupy me all the morning the rest can go into the playground. The second class will be taken this afternoon."

The boys had listened with astonished silence to this address, and so completely taken aback were they that all save those ordered to remain rose from their seats and went out in a quiet and orderly way, very different from the wild rush which generally terminated school-time.

Ned being in the second class was one of those who went out. Instead of scattering into groups, the boys gathered in a body outside.

"What do you think of that, Sankey?" Tompkins said. "It seems almost too good to be true. Only fancy, no more thrashing except for lying and things of that sort, and treating us like friends! and he talked as if he meant it too."

"That he did," Ned said gravely; "and I tell you, fellows, we shall have to work now, and no mistake. A fellow who will not work for such a man as that deserves to be skinned."

"I expect," said James Mathers, who was one of the biggest boys in the school though still in the third class, "that it's all gammon, just to give himself a good name, and to do away with the bad repute the school has got into for Hathorn's flogging. You will see how long it will last! I ain't going to swallow all that soft soap."

Ned, who had been much touched at the master's address, at once fired up:

"Oh! we all know how clever you are, Mathers—quite a shining genius, one of the sort who can see through a stone wall. If you say it's gammon, of course it must be so."

There was a laugh among the boys.

"I will punch your head if you don't shut up, Sankey," Mather said angrily; "there's no ink-bottle for you to shy here."

Ned turned very white, but he checked himself with an effort.

"I don't want to fight to-day—it's the first day of the half-year, and after such a speech as we've heard I don't want to have a row on this first morning. But you had better look out; another time you won't find me so patient. Punch my head, indeed! Why, you daren't try it."

But Mathers would have tried it, for he had for the last year been regarded as the cock of the school. However, several of the boys interfered.

"Sankey is right, Mathers; it would be a beastly shame to be fighting this morning. After what Porson said there oughtn't to be any rows to-day. We shall soon see whether he means it."

Mathers suffered himself to be dissuaded from carrying his threat into execution, the rather that in his heart of hearts he was not assured that the course would have been a wise one. Ned had never fought in the school, but Tompkins' account of his fight on the moor with Bill

Swinton, and the courage he had shown in taking upon himself the office of spokesman in the rebellion against Hathorn, had given him a very high reputation among the boys; and in spite of Mather's greater age and weight there were many who thought that Ned Sankey would make a tough fight of it with the cock of the school.

So the gathering broke up and the boys set to at their games, which were played with a heartiness and zest all the greater that none of them were in pain from recent punishments, and that they could look forward to the afternoon without fear and trembling.

When at twelve o'clock the boys of the first class came out from school the others crowded round to hear the result of the morning's lessons. They looked bright and pleased.

"I think he is going to turn out a brick," Ripon, the head of the first class, said. "Of course one can't tell yet. He was very quiet with us and had a regular examination of each of us. I don't think he was at all satisfied, though we all did our best, but there was no shouting or scolding. We are to go in again this afternoon with the rest. He says there's something which he forgot to mention to us this morning."

"More speeches!" Mathers grumbled. "I hate all this jaw."

"Yes," Ripon said sharply; "a cane is the thing which suits your understanding best. Well, perhaps he will indulge you; obstinate idleness is one of the things he mentioned in the address."

When afternoon school began Mr. Porson again rose.

"There is one thing I forgot to mention this morning. I understand that you have hitherto passed your play-time entirely in the playground, except on Saturday afternoons, when you have been allowed to go where you like between dinner and tea-time. With the latter regulation I do not intend to interfere, or at any rate I shall not do so so long as I see that no bad effects come of it; but I shall do so only with this proviso, I do not think it good for you to be going about the town. I shall therefore put Marsden out of bounds. You will be free to ramble where you like in the country, but any boy who enters the town will be severely punished. I am not yet sufficiently acquainted with the neighbourhood to draw the exact line beyond which you are not to go, but I shall do so as soon as I have ascertained the boundaries of the town.

"I understand that you look forward to Saturday for making such purchases as you require. Therefore each Saturday four boys, selected by yourselves, one from each class, will be allowed to go into the town to make purchases for the rest, but they are not to be absent more than an hour.

"In the second place, I do not think that the playground affords a sufficient space for exercise, and being gravelled, it is unsuitable for many games. Therefore I have hired a field, which I dare say you all know; it is called 'The Four-acre Field,' about a hundred yards down the road on the left-hand side. This you will use as your playground during the six summer months. I have brought with me from York a box which I shall place under the charge of Ripon and the two next senior to him. It contains bats, wickets, and a ball for cricket; a set of quoits; trap-bat and ball for the younger boys; leaping-bars, and some other things. These will give you a start. As they become used-up or broken they must be replaced by yourselves; and I hope you will obtain plenty of enjoyment from them. I shall come and play a game of cricket with you myself sometimes.

"You will bear in mind that it is my wish that you should be happy. I expect you to work hard, but I wish you to play hard too. Unless the body works the brain will suffer, and a happy and contented boy will learn as easily again as a discontented and miserable one. I will give you the box after tea, so that you can all examine them together. The second and third classes will now stay in; the fourth class can go out in the playground with the first. I shall have time to examine them while the others are doing their work to-morrow."

There was a suppressed cheer among the boys, and Ripon, as the senior, said:

"I am sure, sir, we are all very much obliged to you for your kindness, and we will do our best to deserve it."

There was a chorus of assent, and then the elder and younger boys went out into the playground while the work of examination of the second and third classes began.

On the following day lessons began in earnest, and the

boys found their first impressions of the new master more than justified. A new era had commenced. The sound of the cane was no longer heard, and yet the lessons were far better done than had been the case before. Then the whole work had fallen on the boys; the principal part of the day's lessons had been the repeating of tasks learned by heart, and the master simply heard them and punished the boys who were not perfect.

There was comparatively little of this mechanical work now; it was the sense and not the wording which had to be mastered. Thus geography was studied from an atlas and not by the mere parrot-like learning of the names of towns and rivers. In grammar the boys had to show that they understood a rule by citing examples other than those given in their books. History was rather a lecture from the master than a repetition of dry facts and dates by the boys. Latin and mathematics were made clear in a similar way. "It was almost too good to last," the boys said after the first day's experience of this new method of teaching; but it did last. A considerable portion of the work out of school was devoted to the keeping up the facts they had learned, for Mr. Porson was constantly going back and seeing that their memories retained the facts they had acquired, and what they called examinations were a part of the daily routine.

In some points upon which Mr. Hathorn had laid the greatest stress Mr. Porson was indifferent—dates, which had been the bane of many a boy's life and an unceasing source of punishment, he regarded but little, insisting only that the general period should be known, and his questions generally took the form of, "In the beginning or at the end of such and such a century, what was the state of things in England or in Rome?" A few dates of special events, the landmarks of history, were required to be learned accurately, all others were passed over as unimportant.

It was not that the boys worked fewer hours than before, but that they worked more intelligently, and therefore more pleasantly to themselves. The boys—and there were some—who imagined that under this new method of teaching they could be idle, very soon found out their mistake, and discovered that in his way Mr. Porson was just as strict as his predecessor. He never lost his temper; but his cold displeasure was harder to bear than Mr. Hathorn's wrath; nor were punishments wanting. Although the cane was idle, those who would not work were kept in the school-room during play hours; and in cases where this was found to be ineffectual Mr. Porson coldly said:

"Your parents pay me to teach you, and if you do not choose to be taught I have only to write home to them and request them to take you away. If you are one of those boys who will only learn from fear of the cane you had better go to some school where the cane is used."

This threat, which would have been ineffective in Mr. Hathorn's time, never failed to have an effect now; for even Mather, the idlest and worst boy there, was able to appreciate the difference between the present regime and the last. In a marvellously short time Mr. Porson seemed to have gauged the abilities of each of the boys,

and while he expected much from those who were able
to master easily their tasks, he was content with less
from the duller intellects, providing they had done their
best. After a week's experience of Mr. Porson, Ned gave
so glowing an account to his father of the new master
and his methods that Captain Sankey went down to the
school and arranged that Charlie, now ten years old,
should accompany his brother. There were several boys
no older than he; but Charlie differed widely from his
elder brother, being a timid and delicate child, and ill-
fitted to take care of himself. Captain Sankey felt, however, after what Ned had told him of Mr. Porson, that
he could trust to him during the school hours, and Ned
would be an active protector in the playground.

It was not until a fortnight after the school began
that the Four-acre Field was ready. By that time a flock
of sheep had been turned into it, and had eaten the grass
smooth, and a heavy horse-roller had been at work for a
day making a level pitch in the centre. It was a Saturday afternoon when the boys took possession of it for the
first time. As they were about to start in the highest
glee, Mr. Porson joined them. Some of their faces fell a
little; but he said cheerfully:

"Now, boys, I am going with you; but not, you know,
to look after you or keep you in order. I want you all to
enjoy yourselves just in your own way, and I mean to
enjoy myself too. I have been a pretty good cricketer
in my time, and played in the York Eleven against
Leeds, so I may be able to coach you up to a little, and I

hope after a bit we may be able to challenge some of the village elevens round here. I am afraid Marsden will be too good for us for some time; still, we shall see."

On reaching the field Mr. Porson saw the ground measured and the wickets erected, and then said:

"Now I propose we begin with a match. There are enough of us to make more than two elevens; but there are the other games. Would any of the bigger boys like to play quoits better than cricket?"

Mather, who felt much aggrieved at the master's presence, said he should prefer quoits; and Williamson, who always followed his lead, agreed to play with him.

"Now," Mr. Porson said, "do you, Ripon, choose an eleven. I will take the ten next best. The little ones who are over can play at trap-bat, or bowls, as they like." There was a general approval of the plan. Ripon chose an eleven of the likeliest boys, selecting the biggest and most active; for as there had been no room for cricket in the yard their aptitude for the game was a matter of guess-work, though most of them had played during the holidays. Mr. Porson chose the next ten, and after tossing for innings, which Ripon won, they set to work. Mr. Porson played for a time as long-stop, putting on two of the strongest of his team as bowlers, and changing them from time to time to test their capacity. None of them turned out brilliant, and the runs came fast, and the wickets taken were few and far between, until at last Mr. Porson himself took the ball.

"I am not going to bowl fast," he said, "just straight

easy lobs;" but the boys found that the straight lobs were not so easy after all, and the wickets of the boys who had made a long score soon fell. Most of those who followed managed to make a few runs as well off Mr. Porson's bowling as from that at the other end; for the master did not wish to discourage them, and for a few overs after each batsman came to the wicket aimed well off it so as to give them a chance of scoring.

The last wicket fell for the respectable score of fifty-four. The junior eleven then went in, the master not going in until the last. Only twenty runs had been made when he took the bat. In the five balls of the over which were bowled to him he made three fours; but before it came to his turn again his partner at the other end was out, and his side were twenty-two behind on the first innings. The other side scored thirty-three for the first four wickets before he again took the ball, and the remaining six went down for twelve runs. His own party implored him to go in first, but he refused.

"No, no, boys," he said; "you must win the match, if you can, without much aid from me."

The juniors made a better defence this time and scored forty before the ninth wicket fell. Then Mr. Porson went in and ran the score up to sixty before his partner was out, the seniors winning the match by nine runs. Both sides were highly pleased with the result of the match. The seniors had won after a close game. The juniors were well pleased to have run their elders so hard. They all gathered round their master and thanked him warmly.

THE OLD CAKE-WOMAN DUNS MASTER MATHER FOR HER MONEY.

"I am glad you are pleased, my boys," he said; "I will come down two or three times a week and bowl to you for an hour and give you a few hints, and you will find that you get on fast. There is plenty of promise among you, and I prophesy that we shall turn out a fair eleven by the end of the season."

The younger boys had also enjoyed themselves greatly, and had been joined by many of the elders while waiting for their turn to go in Altogether the opening day of the Four-acre Field had been a great success.

The old cake-woman who had previously supplied the boys still came once a week, her usual time being Wednesday evening, when, after tea, the boys played for half an hour in the yard before going in to their usual lessons. Ned was not usually present, but he one evening went back to fetch a book which he needed. As he came in at the gate of the yard Mather was speaking to the woman.

"No, I won't let you have any more, Master Mather. You have broken your promises to me over and over again. That money you owed me last half ain't been paid yet. If it had only been the money for the cakes and sweets I shouldn't ha' minded so much, but it's that ten shillings you borrowed and promised me solemn you would pay at end of the week and ain't never paid yet. I have got to make up my rent, and I tell ye if I don't get the money by Saturday I shall speak to t' maister about it and see what he says to such goings on."

"Don't talk so loud," Mather said hurriedly, "and I will get you the money as soon as I can."

"I don't care who hears me," the woman replied in a still louder voice, "and as soon as you can won't do for I. I have got to have it on Saturday, so that's flat. I will come up to the field, and you'll best have it ready for me."

Ned did not hear the last few words, but he had heard enough to know that Mather owed ten shillings which he had borrowed, besides a bill for cakes. Mather had not noticed him come into the yard, for his back was towards the gate, and the noise which the boys made running about and shouting prevented him hearing the gate open and close.

"It's a beastly shame," Ned muttered to himself as he went off to school, " to borrow money from an old woman like that. Mather must have known he couldn't pay it, for he has only a small allowance, and is always short of money, and of course he could not expect a tip before the holidays. He might have paid her when he came back, but as he didn't I don't see how he is to do so now, and if the old woman tells Porson there will be a row. It's just the sort of thing would rile him most."

On the next Saturday he watched with some curiosity the entry of the old woman into the field. Several of the boys went up and bought sweets. When she was standing alone Mather strolled up to her. After a word or two he handed her something. She took it, and said a few words. Mather shook his head positively, and in a minute or two walked away, leaving her apparently satisfied.

"I suppose he has given her something on account," Ned said to himself. "I wonder where he got it. When

Ripon asked him last Monday for a subscription to buy another set of bats and wickets, so that two lots could practise at once, he said he had only sixpence left, and Mather would not like to seem mean now, for he knows he doesn't stand well with any one except two or three of his own set, because he is always running out against everything that Porson does."

A week later Mr. Porson said, at the end of school:

"By the way, boys, have any of you seen that illustrated classical dictionary of mine. I had it in school about ten days ago when I was showing you the prints of the dress and armour of the Romans, and I have not seen it since. I fancy I must have left it on my table, but I cannot be sure. I looked everywhere in my library for it last night and cannot find it. Perhaps if I left it on the desk one of you has taken it to look at the pictures."

There was a general silence.

"I think it must be so," Mr. Porson went on more gravely. "If the boy who has it will give it up I shall not be angry, as, if I left it on the desk, there would be no harm in taking it to look at the pictures."

Still there was silence.

"I value the book," Mr. Porson went on, "not only because it is an expensive work, but because it is a prize which I won at Durham."

He paused a moment, and then said in a stern voice: "Let every boy open his desk."

The desks were opened, and Mr. Porson walked round and glanced at each.

"This is a serious matter now," he said. "Ripon, will you come to the study with me and help me to search again. It is possible it may still be there and I may have overlooked it. The rest will remain in their places till I return."

There was a buzz of conversation while the master was absent. On his return he said:

"The book is certainly not there. The book-shelves are all so full that it could only have been put in its own place or laid upon the table. Ripon and I have searched the room thoroughly and it is certainly not there. Now, boys, this is a serious business. In the first place, I will give a last chance to whoever may have taken it to rise in his place and confess it."

He paused, and still all were silent.

"Now mind," he said, "I do not say that any of you have taken it—I have no grounds for such an accusation. It may have been taken by a servant. A tramp may have come in at the back gate when you were all away and have carried it off. These things are possible. And even were I sure that it had been done by one of you I should not dream of punishing all; therefore for the present we will say no more about it. But in order to assure myself and you I must ask you for the keys of your boxes. The servants' boxes will also be searched, as well as every nook and corner of the house; and then, when we have ascertained for a certainty that the book is not within these four walls, I shall go on with a lighter heart."

The boys all eagerly opened their trunks and play-boxes, searched under the beds, in the cupboards, and in every nook and corner of their part of the house, and an equally minute search was afterwards made in the other apartments; but no trace of the book was discovered. For days the matter was a subject of conversation among the boys, and endless were the conjectures as to what could have become of the dictionary. Their respect and affection for their master were greatly heightened by the fact that his behaviour towards them was in no way altered by the circumstances. His temper was as patient and equable as before in the school-room; he was as cheerful and friendly in the cricket-field. They could see, however, that he was worried and depressed, though he strove to appear the same as usual. Often did they discuss among themselves how different the state of things would have been had the loss happened to Mr. Hathorn, and what a life they would have led under those circumstances.

At the end of a week the happy thought struck Ripon that a subscription should be made to buy a new dictionary. The amount was a serious one, as they found that the book could not be purchased under two guineas; but every boy subscribed to his last farthing. Some promised their pocket-money for weeks in advance; others wrote home to their parents to ask for money, and in ten days the boys had the satisfaction of seeing Ripon at the commencement of school walk up to Mr. Porson's desk and present him with the handsome volume in the name of all the boys. Ripon had taken some pains in getting up an appropriate speech, and it was voted a great success.

"Mr. Porson," he said, "in the name of all the boys in the school I beg to ask your acceptance of this volume. It cannot have the value to you of that which you have lost, as that was a prize; but we hope, that as a proof of the respect and affection which we all have for you, and as a token of our appreciation of your very great kindness towards us, you will accept it in place of the other."

Mr. Porson's face lit up with pleasure.

"My boys," he said, "I am very highly gratified at this proof that I have succeeded in my endeavour to make you feel that I am your friend as well as your master, and I shall value your gift far more highly than my college prize. That was simply the result of my own labour; this is a proof of kindness and affection on your parts. I shall value it very greatly all my life. And now, as I don't think you will be able to pay much attention to your work this morning, and as I have been for some days awaiting an opportunity to go over to York, where I have some pressing business, I shall start at once, and can just catch the stage, and shall get back in time for school to-morrow morning, so you will have the day to yourselves."

With a shout of pleasure the boys started off for a long day in the cricket-field, while Mr. Porson hurried away to catch the stage-coach for York.

CHAPTER VI.

THE THIEF DETECTED.

MR. PORSON was in his place next morning having returned only half an hour before school began; he looked fagged, and he was scarcely so attentive as usual to the lessons, his thoughts seeming to be elsewhere.

"He seems regularly done up with his journey," Ripon said as the boys came out of school.

"I think he is upset about something," Ned remarked. "Sometimes he hardly seemed paying attention to what was going on, and he did not speak as cheerfully as usual. I noticed a sort of change in his voice directly he began. I hope nothing wrong has occurred, we were getting on so jollily."

When afternoon school began Mr. Porson placed on the desk before him a packet done up in brown paper.

"Boys," he said, "I have got my book again."

An exclamation of surprise and pleasure burst from the boys. The mystery had weighed heavily on the school, and a look of eager curiosity came over every face to hear how the book had been recovered. "It was found in a book-seller's shop in York," Mr. Porson went on. "I myself had inquired at Leighton's here, but with little hope of finding it, for no one who stole it would have disposed of it so near home. I then wrote to several friends in the large towns, and one of them, a clergyman at York, wrote to me two days ago to say that just such a book as I had described was on sale in the window of one of the book-sellers there. It was a second-hand copy, but in excellent preservation. The fly-leaf was missing. On going over yesterday I found that it was my book, and was able to prove it by several marginal notes in my handwriting.

"The bookseller said at once that it was sent him by a general dealer at Marsden who was in the habit of picking up books at sales in the neighbourhood and send-ing them to him; he had given eighteen shillings for it. This morning I have called upon the man, whose name is White, accompanied by a constable. He admitted at once that he had sent the book to York, and said that he bought it from some one about a month ago. His customer came late, and as White is short-sighted, and there was only a tallow-candle burning in the shop, he said that he should not know him again, and could say nothing about his age; however, I shall call him in; he is now outside with the constable. I am sure that for your own sakes you will not object to his taking a look at you."

Mr. Porson went to the door, and the constable and White entered. The chief constable, when Mr. Porson had called upon him to ask for one of his men to accompany

him to the dealer's, had told him that White bore a very
bad reputation. He was suspected of being the medium
through whom stolen goods in that part of Yorkshire were
sent up to London for disposal. A highwayman who had
been caught and executed at York, had in his confession
stated that this man had acted as his go-between for the
disposal of the watches and other articles he took from
travellers, and White's premises had then been thoroughly
searched by the constables; but as nothing suspicious
was found, and there was only the unsupported confes-
sions of the highwayman against him, he had got off
scot-free. "I don't think you will get anything out of
him, Mr. Porson," the constable said. "The fact that he has
been trusted by these fellows shows that he is not a man
to peach upon those with whom he deals; and in the next
place he would know well enough that if any one were
convicted of stealing this book he would be liable to a
prosecution as receiver; and though we could scarcely
get a conviction against him, as we could not prove that
he knew that it was stolen, it would do him no good."

The boys all stood up in a line. "I will look at 'em,
sir," White said; "but, as I have told you, I should not
know the man as I bought that book from, from Adam.
Anyhow none of these little ones couldn't be he. If it
weren't a man, he were as big as a man. You don't suppose an honest tradesman would buy an expensive book
like that from a kid."

So saying he placed a pair of horn spectacles on his
nose and walked round the line.

" I don't see any one here whose face I ever see before
as far as I knows; but bless you, the man as I bought it
of, might have had hair all over his face, and I be none
the wiser looking at him across that counter of mine in
the dark."

" Thank you," Mr. Porson said; " then it is of no use
troubling you further. I have got my book back; but
I confess that this affords me but small gratification in
comparison to that which I should feel if I could unravel
this mystery."

The discovery of the book reopened the interest in the
matter, and nothing else was talked of that evening in the
playground.

" Ripon," Ned said, putting his arm in that of the head-
boy, " I want to tell you a thing that has been in my mind
for the last three weeks; mind, I don't say that there's anything in it, and I hate to think harm of any one.   There
is another thing; he and I ain't good friends. If it hadn't
been for that I should have spoken to you before; but I
was afraid that it would look like a piece of dirty spite
on my part; but I do think now that as head-boy you
ought to know, and I want your advice whether I ought
to say anything about it or not."

" What a long-winded chap you are, Sankey!   What is
it all about?"

" Well, you know, Ripon, when we got up that subscription for the cricket things, Mather didn't give anything.
He said he had no money."

" No; and he hadn't any," Ripon said, " for I had only

the day before lent him twopence to buy some string, and he paid me when he got his allowance on Saturday."

"Well, a day or two after that I came back after tea for a book that I had left behind me, and as I came in at the gate there Mather was standing at the corner talking to Mother Brown. He had his back to the door, and they didn't see me. She was talking loud and angry and I couldn't help hearing what she said."

"Well, what did she say?" Ripon said rather impatiently.

"She said, 'You have disappointed me over and over again, and if you don't pay me that ten shillings you borrowed of me last half, and the bill for the cakes, by Saturday, I will see the master and tell him all about it.' I didn't hear any more; but on the Saturday I saw him go up to her in the field and pay her something. Of course I don't know what it was; not all, I think, by the manner in which she took it; still, I suppose it was enough to content her. About ten days afterwards we heard the book was missing. It didn't strike me at the time; but afterwards, when I thought of it, I remembered that the last time Porson brought it out was on the Thursday, which was the day after Mather had been speaking to Mother Brown. Now, of course, Ripon, I don't actually suspect Mather of taking the book; still it is curious its being missing just at the time he wanted money so badly. He may have got the money from home, or he may have borrowed it from some other fellow."

"No," Ripon said positively, "I am sure Mather has

had no letter, because I always distribute the letters, and Mather's people never write to him; and I am sure there was no fellow in the school had more than a shilling or two at the outside at that time. Why didn't you tell me before, Sankey?"

"I didn't like to, because everyone knows Mather and I are not good friends; then I thought perhaps Mather might be able to explain it all right, and I should have cut a nice figure if he could; then at the time when I thought of it, and had got the dates right, the first excitement had died out and I thought we might hear no more of it and it would be forgotten; but now that the book has been found and the whole thing has come up fresh again I thought it better to tell you all about it and ask you what you would advise me to do."

Ripon did not answer for some time; then he said:

"I am sure I don't know, Ned; I will think it over till to-morrow. You have not said anything about it to any-one else?"

"Not to a soul. I hesitated whether I should tell you or father, but he wouldn't understand how boys think of these things so well as you do; so I thought as you were head of the school it was best you should know."

"I wish you hadn't told me," Ripon grumbled. "I am sure I don't know what's best to do;" and he turned away and began to pace the yard moodily up and down.

"The only thing I have decided," he said to Ned the next day, "is to ask Mother Brown myself how much Mather paid her. We may as well settle that question first."

As this was Wednesday and the cake-woman was coming that evening there was not long to wait. Ripon chose a time when most of the boys had made their purchases and the old woman was alone.

"Don't you give too much tick to any of the fellows, Mother Brown," he began. "You know it isn't always easy to get money that's owing."

"I should think not, Master Ripon; I wish they would always pay money down as you do. There's Master Mather, he been owing me money ever since last half. He borrowed ten shillings of me and promised solemn he would pay at the end of the week, and he has only paid five shillings yet, a month ago, and that was only 'cause I told him I would tell the master about him; there's that five shillings, and seven shillings and eightpence for cakes and things; but I have been giving him a piece of my mind this afternoon; and if I don't get that other five shillings by Saturday, sure enough I will speak to t'maister about it. No one can say as Mother Brown is hard on boys, and I am always ready to wait reasonable; but I can't abear lies, and when I lent that ten shillings I expected it was going to be paid punctual."

"Then he knows you are going to speak to Mr. Porson on Saturday if he doesn't pay up another five shillings?"

"He knows it," the old woman said nodding. "When I says a thing I mean it. So he had best pay up."

When Ripon met Ned next day he said: "I talked to her last night. Mather paid her five shillings, and she has told him if he doesn't pay her the other five by

Saturday she will speak to Porson; so I think the best plan is to wait till then and see what comes of it. She will tell the whole story and Porson will learn it without our interference, and can think what he likes about it."

Relieved in mind at finding that there was a prospect of his avoiding the decision whether or not to inform the master of his suspicions, Ned went to his desk. When afternoon school began Mr. Porson said gravely:

"Boys, when you came back from the field did you all go straight to the washing-room to wash your hands before dinner?"

There was a chorus of surprised assent.

"I am sorry to tell you that another theft has been committed. A gold pencil-case has disappeared from my study table. I was using it after school. I left it on the table when I went for a stroll before dinner. I remember most distinctly laying it down among the pens. I went into my study ten minutes ago, and wanting to make a note as to this afternoon's work looked for the pencil and it was gone. The window was open as usual, and it is possible that tramps passing along the road may have come into the garden and have got in at the window. As in the case of the book I suspect no one, but two such occurrences as these are very uncomfortable for us all. I shall not propose any search this time, for had any of you taken it, which I cannot for a moment believe, he would not have been careless enough to put it in his pocket, or conceal it in his desk or boxes, but would have stowed it away somewhere where there would be no chance whatever of its being found. Now let us dismiss the subject and go on with our lessons."

While the master was speaking Ripon and Sankey had glanced for a moment at each other; the same thought was in both their minds. After school was over they joined each other in the yard.

"Was Mather in the washing-room with the others?" Sankey asked eagerly.

"He was, but he came up last," Ripon replied. "You know he generally saunters along in a lazy way and is the last to get in. So he was to-day, but I don't know that he was later than usual."

"I think, Ripon, we ought to speak to Porson."

"I think so too," Ripon rejoined gravely; "it is too serious to keep to ourselves. Any ordinary thing I would not peach about on any account, but a disgraceful theft like this, which throws a doubt over us all, is another thing; the honour of the whole school is at stake. I have been thinking it over. I don't want Mather to suspect anything, so I will go out at the back gate with you, as if I was going to walk part of the way home with you, and then we will go round to the front door and speak to Porson."

The master was sitting on a low seat in the window of his study. Hearing footsteps coming up from the front gate he looked round.

"Do you want to speak to me, boys?" he asked in some surprise through the open window. "What makes you come round the front way?"

" We want to see you privately, sir," Ripon said.

" Very well, boys, I will open the door for you. Now, what is it?" he asked as the boys followed him into the study.

" Well, sir, it may be nothing, I am sure I hope so," Ripon said; " but Sankey and I thought you ought to know and then it will be off our minds, and you can do as you like about it. Now, Sankey, tell what you know first, then I will tell what Mother Brown said to me on Wednesday."

Ned told the story in the same words in which he had related it to Ripon; and Ripon then detailed his conversation with the cake-woman, and her threats of reporting Mather on Saturday were the debt not paid. Ned had already given his reason for keeping silence in the matter hitherto, and Ripon now explained that they had determined to wait till Saturday to see what came of it, but that after that new theft they deemed it their duty to speak at once. Mr. Porson sat with his face half shaded with his hand and without speaking a single word until the boys had concluded.

" It is a sad business," he said in a low tone, " a very sad business. It is still possible that you may have come to false conclusions; but the circumstances you have related are terribly strong. I am grieved, indeed, over the business, and would rather have lost a hundred books and pencil-cases than it should have happened. You have done quite right, boys; I am greatly obliged to you both, and you have acted very well. I know how painful it must be to you both to have been obliged to bring so grave a matter to my ears. Thank you; I will consider what is the best course to adopt. If it can be avoided, I shall so arrange that your names do not appear in the matter."

For some little time after the boys had left him Mr. Porson remained in deep thought; then he rose, put on his hat, and went out, first inquiring of the servant if she knew where the woman who sold cakes to the boys lived.

"Yes, sir; she lives in a little house in Mill Street; it's not a regular shop, but there are a few cakes in one of the windows; I have bought things there for the kitchen, knowing that she dealt with the young gentlemen."

Mr. Porson made his way to Mill Street and easily found the house he was in search of. On being questioned the old woman at first showed some reluctance in answering his questions, but Mr. Porson said sharply:

"Now, dame, I want no nonsense; I am acquainted with the whole affair, but wish to have it from your own lips. Unless you tell me the whole truth not a cake will you sell my boys in future."

Thus pressed Mrs. Brown at once related the story of Mather having borrowed some money of her; of her threats to report him unless he paid, and of his having given her five shillings on the following Saturday, saying that he would give her the rest in a few days but could pay no more then; and how, after repeated disappointments, she had now given him till Saturday to settle the debt.

"If he didn't pay, sir, I meant to have come to ye and telled ye all about it, for I hate lies, and Master Mather has lied to me over and over again about it; but seeing that Saturday hasn't come I don't like telling ye the story, as he may have meant to keep his word to me this time."

"Here are the five shillings which he borrowed of you; as to the other money, you will never get it, and I hope it will be a lesson to you; and mind, if I find that you ever allow the boys to run an account with you further than the following Saturday after it is incurred, you will never come into my field or playground again."

Mr. Porson then went to the chief constable's, and after a short conversation with him a constable was told off to accompany him. He and the master took their station at a short distance from the shop of the man White and waited quietly. A little after nine a figure was seen coming down the street from the other end. He passed quickly into the shop.

"That is the boy," Mr. Porson said.

"Wouldn't it be better, sir," the constable asked, "to wait till the deed is completed, then we can lay our hands on White as a receiver?"

"No," Mr. Porson replied, "for in that case the boy would have to appear with him in the dock, and that I wish of all things to avoid."

So saying he walked quickly on and entered the shop. Mather was leaning across the counter while the man was examining the pencil-case by the light of the candle.

"Five shillings," the man said, "and no more. I was nearly getting into trouble over that last job of yours."

"But it's worth a great deal more than that," Mather said. "You might give me ten."

"Well, take it back then," the man said, pushing it across the counter.

"Thank you, I will take it myself," Mr. Porson said quietly, as he advanced and stretched out his hand.

Mather turned round with a sudden cry, and then stood the picture of silent terror.

"As for you," the master said indignantly to the dealer, "you scoundrel, if you had your deserts I would hand you over to the constable, who is outside the door, as a receiver of stolen goods, and for inciting this boy to theft. I heard you offer him a sum of money for it which shows that you knew it was stolen; but your time will come, sir, and you will hang over the gate of York prison as many a poor wretch far less guilty than yourself has done;" for in those days death was the punishment of receivers of stolen goods, as well as of those convicted of highway robbery and burglary.

"Have mercy, sir, oh, spare me!" Mather exclaimed, falling on his knees. "Don't give me in charge."

"I am not going to do so," the master said. "Get up and come with me." Not a word was spoken on the way back to the school.

Mr. Porson then took Mather into his study, where they remained for half an hour. What passed between them was never known. In the morning the boys who

slept in the room with Mather were surprised to find that
his bed was empty and the window open. He had gone to
bed at half-past eight as usual, and saying he was sleepy
had threatened to punch the head of any boy who spoke,
so that all had gone off to sleep in a very short time. A
stout ivy grew against the wall, and some fallen leaves on
the ground showed them that he had climbed down with
the assistance of its stem. But why he should have gone,
and what on earth possessed him to run away, none could
imagine. The news ran rapidly through the other bed-
rooms, and brimful of excitement all went down when
the bell rang for prayers before breakfast. The list of
names was called out by the master as usual, and the excitement grew breathless as the roll of the third class was
called; but to the astonishment of all, Mather's name was
omitted. When the list was concluded Mr. Porson said:

" Mather has left; I grieve to say that I have discovered
that it was he who stole the book and pencil-case. He
has confessed the whole to me, and he is, I trust, sincerely
penitent. He slept last night on the sofa in my study,
and has gone off this morning by the coach. I may tell
you that I have written to his parents stating the whole
circumstances under which he was driven to commit the
theft, and that although I could not permit him to remain
here I trusted and believed that his repentance was sin-
cere, and that it would be a lesson to him through life,
and I urged them to give him a further trial, and not to
drive him to desperation by severity.

" There is a lesson which you may all learn from this.

Mather committed these crimes because he had borrowed money which he could not repay. Most foolishly and mistakenly the woman who supplies you with cakes had lent him money, and when he could not repay it according to his promise to her, threatened to report the case to me, and it was to prevent the matter coming to my ears that he took these things. Let this be a warning to you, boys, through life. Never borrow money, never spend more than your means afford. An extravagance may seem to you but a small fault, but you see crime and disgrace may follow upon it. Think this well over, and be lenient in your hearts to your late schoolfellow. He was tempted, you see, and none of us can tell what we may do when temptation comes, unless we have God's help to enable us to withstand it, and to do what is right. Now let us fall to at our breakfast."

It was a strangely silent meal. Scarce a word was spoken, even in a whisper. It came as a shock to everybody there, that after all the dictionary should have been taken by one of their number, and that the master's kindness on that occasion should have been requited by another robbery seemed a disgrace to the whole school. That Mather, too, always loud, noisy, and overbearing, should have been the thief was surprising indeed. Had it been some quiet little boy, the sort of boy others are given to regard as a sneak, there would have been less surprise, but that Mather should do such a thing was astounding. These were probably the first reflections which occurred to every boy as he sat down to breakfast.

The next impression was how good Mr. Porson had been about it. He might have given Mather in charge, and had him punished by law. He might have given him a terrific flogging and a public expulsion before all the school. Instead of that he had sent him quietly away, and seemed sorry for rather than angry with him. By the time the meal was finished there was probably not a boy but had taken an inward resolution that there was nothing he would not do for his master, and although such resolutions are generally but transient, Mr. Porson found that the good effect of his treatment of Mather was considerable and permanent. Lessons were more carefully learned, obedience was not perhaps more prompt, but it was more willing, and the boys lost no opportunity of showing how anxious they were to please in every respect.

Ned and his brother were not present when Mr. Porson explained the cause of Mather's absence to the others, but they were surrounded by their schoolfellows, all eager to tell the news upon their arrival in the playground a few minutes before the school began.

Before breaking up in June, Porson's played their first cricket-match with a strong village team, and beat them handsomely, although, as the boys said, it was to their master's bowling that their success was due. Still the eleven all batted fairly, and made so long a score that they won in one innings; and Mr. Porson promised them that before the season ended they should have a whole holiday, and play the Marsden Eleven.

Ned enjoyed his holiday rambles, taking several long

walks across the moors accompanied by Bill Swinton, who had now perfectly recovered. The discontent among the croppers, and indeed among the workers in the mills generally through the country was as great as ever; but the season was a good one; bread had fallen somewhat in price, and the pinch was a little less severe than it had been. The majority of the masters had been intimidated by the action of their hands from introducing the new machinery, and so far the relations between master and men in that part of Yorkshire at any rate remained unchanged. But although Ned enjoyed his rambles he was glad when the holidays were over. He had no friends of his own age in Marsden; his brother was too young to accompany him in his long walks, and Bill obtained a berth in one of the mills shortly after the holidays began, and was no longer available. Therefore Ned looked forward to meeting his schoolfellows again, to the fun of the cricket-field and playground, and even to lessons, for these were no longer terrible.

The school reopened with largely increased numbers. The reports which the boys had taken home of the changed conditions of things and of their master's kindness excited among all their friends an intense longing to go to a school where the state of things was so different to that which prevailed elsewhere; and the parents were equally satisfied with the results of the new master's teaching. Such as took the trouble to ask their boys questions found that they had acquired a real grasp of the subjects, and that they were able to answer clearly and intelligently.

The consequence was, the house was filled with its full complement of fifty boarders, and indeed Mr. Porson was obliged to refuse several applications for want of room. As he had not the same objection as his predecessor to receive home boarders, the numbers were swelled by eighteen boys whose parents resided in Marsden.

To meet the increased demands upon his teaching powers Mr. Porson engaged two ushers, both of them young men who had just left Durham. They were both pleasant and gentlemanly young fellows; and as Mr. Porson insisted that his own mode of teaching should be adopted, the change did not alter the pleasant state of things which had prevailed during the past half year. Both the ushers were fond of cricket, and one turned out to be at least equal to Mr. Porson as a bowler. Therefore the boys looked forward to their match with Marsden with some confidence.

Captain Sankey saw with great pleasure the steady improvement which was taking place in Ned's temper. It was not to be expected that the boy would at once overcome a fault of such long standing, but the outbursts were far less frequent, and it was evident that he was putting a steady check upon himself; so that his father looked forward to the time when he would entirely overcome the evil consequences engendered by his unchecked and undisciplined childhood.

CHAPTER VII.

A TERRIBLE SHOCK.

NED had been looking forward with great anticipations to Michaelmas day, upon which the great match was to take place; for he was one of the eleven, being the youngest of the boys included in it. An event, however, happened which deprived him of his share in the match, and caused the day to pass almost unnoticed. On the 20th of September the servant came in to Mr. Porson during morning school to say that he was wanted. A minute or two later she again re-entered and said that Ned and his brother were to go to the master's study. Much surprised at this summons they followed her. Mr. Porson was looking exceedingly grave.

"My dear boys," he said, "I have bad news for you. Very bad news. You must bear it bravely, looking for support and consolation to Him who alone can give it. Dr. Green's boy has just been here. He was sent down by his master to say that there has been a serious accident in the town."

The commencement of the master's speech and the graveness of his tone sent a serious thrill through the hearts of the boys. Mr. Porson would never have spoken thus had not the news been serious indeed.

When he paused Ned gave a little gasp and exclaimed, "My father!"

"Yes, Ned, I am grieved to say that it is your brave father who has suffered from the accident. It seems that as he was walking down the High Street one of Ramsay's heavy waggons came along. A little girl ran across the street ahead, but stumbled and fell close to the horses. Your father, forgetful of the fact of his wooden leg, rushed over to lift her; but the suddenness of the movement, he being a heavy man, snapped the wooden leg in sunder, and he fell headlong in the street. He was within reach of the child, and he caught her by the clothes and jerked her aside; but before he could, in his crippled condition, regain his feet, the wheel was upon him, and he has suffered very serious injuries."

"He is not dead, sir!" Ned gasped, while his brother began to cry piteously.

"No, Ned, he is not dead," Mr. Porson said; "but I fear, my dear boy, that it would be a cruel kindness did I not tell you to prepare yourself for the worst. I fear from what I hear that he is fatally injured, and that there is but little hope. Get your hats, my boys, and I will walk home with you at once."

There were but few words exchanged during that dismal walk, and these were addressed by Mr. Porson to

Ned. "Try to calm yourself, my boy," he said, putting his hand on his shoulder, which was shaking with the boy's efforts to keep down his convulsive sobs; "try and nerve yourselves for the sake of your father himself, of your mother, and the little ones. The greatest kindness you can show to your father now is by being calm and composed."

"I will try, sir," Ned said as steadily as he could; "but you don't know how I loved him!"

"I can guess it, my boy; for I, too, lost my father when I was just your age. God's ways are not our ways, Ned; and be sure, although you may not see it now, that he acts for the best."

A little crowd stood gathered near the door. They were talking in low tones of the gallant way in which the crippled officer had sacrificed himself to save the child. They made way silently for the boys to pass. Ned opened the door and entered.

Abijah was in the hall. She was tearless, but her face was white and set. "My poor boy," she said to Ned, "he is in the parlour; he has just been asking for you. I am glad you have come. Your mother is in hysterics in her bed-room, and is going on like a mad woman. You must be calm, dear, for your father's sake."

Ned gave a little nod, and, taking his brother's hand, opened the door of the parlour.

Captain Sankey was lying on the hearth-rug, his head propped up with pillows from the sofa; his face was an ashen pallor, and his eyes were closed. The doctor was kneeling beside him, pouring some liquid from a glass between his lips. A strong friendship had sprung up between the two men, and tears were running fast down the doctor's cheeks. He motioned to the boys to approach. They fell on their knees by their father's side.

"Sankey," the doctor said in a steady voice, "here are your boys, Ned and Charlie." The eyes of the dying man opened slowly, and he looked at his sons, and Ned felt a slight pressure of the hand which he had taken in his own.

" God bless you, my boys!" he said, in a faint whisper. " Ned, be kind to your mother; care for her always. She will need all your kindness."

" I will, father," the boy said steadily. "I will take care of mother, I promise you."

A faint smile passed over the pale face; then the eyes closed again, and there was silence for five minutes, broken only by the sobbing of the younger boy. The doctor, who had his fingers on the pulse of Captain Sankey, leaned closely over him; then he laid his arm gently down, and putting his hand on Ned's shoulder said softly:

" Come, my boy, your father is out of pain now."

Ned gave one loud and bitter cry, and threw himself down by the side of the corpse, and gave way to his pent-up emotion.

The doctor led the younger boy from the room, and gave him into the care of Abijah. Then he returned and stood for a while watching Ned's terrible outburst of grief;

"THE BOYS FELL ON THEIR KNEES BY THEIR FATHER'S SIDE."

281

then he poured some wine into a glass. "My boy," he said tenderly, "you must not give way like this or you will make yourself ill. Drink this, Ned, and then go up and lie down on your bed until you feel better. Remember you must be strong for the sake of the others. You know you will have to bear your mother's burdens as well as your own."

He helped Ned to his feet and neld the glass to his lips, for the boy's hand was shaking so that he could not have held it. After drinking it Ned stumbled up-stairs and threw himself on the bed, and there cried silently for a long time; but the first passion of grief had passed, and he now struggled with his tears, and in an hour rose, bathed his flushed and swollen face, and went downstairs.

"Abijah," he said, in a voice which he struggled in vain to steady, "what is there for me to do? How is my mother?"

"She has just cried herself off to sleep, Master Ned, and a mercy it is for her, poor lady, for she has been going on dreadful ever since he was brought in here; but if you go in to Master Charlie and Miss Lucy and try and comfort them it would be a blessing. I have not been able to leave your mother till now, and the poor little things are broken-hearted. I feel dazed myself, sir. Think of the captain, who went out so strong and well this morning, speaking so kind and bright just as usual, lying there!" and here Abijah broke down, and for the first time since Captain Sankey was carried into the house tears came to her relief, and throwing her arms round Ned's neck she wept passionately.

Ned's own tears flowed too fast for him to speak for some time. At last he said quietly, "Don't cry so, Abijah. It is the death of all others that was fitted for him, he, so brave and unselfish, to die giving his life to save a child. You told me to be brave; it is you who must be brave, for you know that you must be our chief dependence now."

"I know, Master Ned; I know, sir," the woman said, choking down her sobs, and wiping her eyes with her apron, "and I will do my best, never fear. I feel better now I have had a good cry. Somehow I wasn't able to cry before. Now, sir, do you go to the children and I will look after things."

A fortnight passed. Captain Sankey had been laid in his grave, after such a funeral as had never been seen in Marsden, the mills being closed for the day, and all the shutters up throughout the little town, the greater part of the population attending the funeral as a mark of respect to the man who, after fighting the battles of his country, had now given his life for that of a child. The great cricket-match did not come off, it being agreed on all hands that it had better be postponed. Mr. Porson had called twice to see Ned, and had done much by his comforting words to enable him to bear up. He came again the day after the funeral.

"Ned," he said, "I think that you and Charlie had better come to school again on Monday. The sooner you fall into your regular groove the better. It would only do you both harm to mope about the house here; and although the laughter and noise of your schoolfellows will jar upon you for a while, it is better to overcome the feeling at once; and I am sure that you will best carry out what would have been his wishes by setting to your work again instead of wasting your time in listless grieving."

" I think so too, sir," Ned said, " but it will be awfully hard at first, and so terrible to come home and have no one to question one on the day's work, and to take an interest in what we have been doing."

" Very hard, Ned; I thoroughly agree with you, but it has to be borne, and remember there is One who will take interest in your work. If I were you I should take your brother out for walks this week. Get up into the hills with him, and try and get the colour back into his cheeks again. He is not so strong as you are, and the confinement is telling upon him—the fresh air will do you good too."

Ned promised to take his master's advice, and the next morning started after breakfast with Charlie. His mother had not yet risen, and indeed had not been down-stairs since the day of the accident, protesting that she was altogether unequal to any exertion whatever. Ned had sat with her for many hours each day, but he had indeed found it hard work. Sometimes she wept, her tears being mingled with self-reproaches that she had not been able to do more to brighten her husband's life.

Sometimes she would break off and reproach the boy bitterly for what she called his want of feeling. At other times her thoughts seemed directed solely towards the fashion of her mourning garments, and after the funeral she drove Ned almost to madness by wanting to know all the details of who was there and what was done, and was most indignant with him because he was able to tell her nothing, the whole scene having been as a mist to him, absorbed as he was in the thought of his father alone.

But Ned had never showed the least sign of impatience or hastiness, meeting tears, reproaches, and inquiries with the same stoical calmness and gentleness. Still it was with a sigh of relief that he took a long breath of fresh air as he left the house and started for a ramble on the moor with his brother. He would have avoided Varley, for he shrank even from the sympathy which Bill Swinton would give; but Bill would be away, so as it was the shortest way he took that road. As he passed Luke Marner's cottage the door opened and Mary came down to the gate. One of the little ones had seen Ned coming along the road and had run off to tell her. Little Jane Marner trotted along by Polly's side.

"Good morning, Polly!" Ned said, and walked on. He dreaded speech with anyone. Polly saw his intention and hesitated; then she said:

"Good morning, Master Ned! One moment, please sir."
Ned paused irresolutely.

" Please don't say anything," he began.

" No, sir, I am not agoing to—at least—" and then she

hesitated, and lifted up the child, who was about four years old, a soft-eyed, brown-haired little maiden. "It's little Jenny," she said; "you know sir, you know;" and she looked meaningly at the child as the tears stood in her eyes.

Ned understood at once.

"What!" he said; "was it her? I did not know; I had not heard."

"Yes, sir; she, and all of us owe her life to him. Feyther wanted to come down to you, but I said better not yet awhile, you would understand."

"How did it happen?" Ned said, feeling that here at least his wound would be touched with no rough hand.

"She went down to the town with Jarge, who was going to fetch some things I wanted. He left her looking in at a shop window while he went inside. They were some time serving him as there were other people in the shop. Jenny got tired, as she says, of waiting, and seeing some pictures in a window on the other side of the street started to run across, and her foot slipped, and—and—"

"I know," Ned said. "I am glad you have told me, Polly. I am glad it was someone one knows something about. Don't say anything more now, I cannot bear it."

"I understand, sir," the girl said gently. "God bless you!"

Ned nodded. He could not trust himself to speak, and turning he passed on with Charlie through the village, while Mary Powlett, with the child still in her arms, stood looking sorrowfully after him as long as he was in sight.

"So thou'st seen the boy?" Luke said, when on his return from work Polly told him what had happened. "Thou told's him, oi hope, how we all felt about it, and how grateful we was?"

"I didn't say much, feyther, he could not bear it; just a word or two; if I had said more he would have broken out crying, and so should I."

"Thou hast cried enoo, lass, the last ten days. Thou hast done nowt but cry," Luke said kindly, "and oi felt sore inclined to join thee. Oi ha' had hard work to keep back the tears, old though oi be, and oi a cropper."

"You are just as soft-hearted as I am, feyther, every bit, so don't pretend you are not;" and indeed upon the previous day Luke Marner had broken down even more completely than Mary. He had followed the funeral at a short distance, keeping with Mary aloof from the crowd; but when all was over, and the church-yard was left in quiet again, Luke had gone and stood by the still open grave of the man who had given his life for his child's, and had stood there with the tears streaming down his cheeks, and his strong frame so shaken by emotion that Polly had been forced to dry her own eyes and stifle her sobs, and to lead him quietly away.

"Strange, bain't it, lass; feyther and son seem mixed up with Varley. First the lad has a foight wi' Bill Swinton, and braakes the boy's leg; then t' feyther sends oop all sorts o' things to Bill, and his son comes up here and gets as friendly with Bill as if he were his brother, and gets to know you, and many another in the village.

Then our Jane goes down into t' town and would ha'
lost her life if Captain he hadn't been passing by and
saaved her. Then he gets killed. Just gived his life for
hearn. Looks loike a fate aboot it; may be it ool be our
toorn next, and if ever that lad waants a man to stand
beside him Luke Marner will be there. And there's
Bill too—oi believe that boy would lay down his life for
him. He's very fond of our Janey—fonder nor her own
brothers. He ain't got no sister of his own, and he's
took to t' child wonderful since he got ill. He thowt a
soight o' Ned Sankey afore; I doan't know what he
wouldn't do for him now."

"I don't suppose, feyther, as any of us will be able to
do anything for him; but we may do, who knows?"

"Ay, who knows, lass? toimes is main bad, and oi doot
there will be trouble, but oi doan't see as that can affect
him no ways, being as he is a lad, and having nowt
to do with the mills—but oi do hoape as the time may
come, lass, as we can show un as we knows we owes a
loife to him."

On the Monday following Ned and Charlie returned to
school, and found it less painful than Ned had expected.
Mr. Porson had taken Ripon aside and had told him that
the kindest way to treat the boys would be to avoid all
allusion to their loss or anything like a show of open
sympathy, but to let them settle quietly into their places.
"Sankey will know you all feel for him, Ripon, he will
need no telling of that."

Ripon passed the word round the school, and accordingly when the boys came into the playground, two or three minutes before the bell rang, Ned, to his great relief, found that with the exception of a warm silent wring of the hand from a few of those with whom he was most intimate, and a kindly nod from others, no allusion was made to his fortnight's absence or its cause.

For the next month he worked hard and made up the time he had lost, running straight home when he came out from school, and returning just in time to go in with the others; but gradually he fell into his former ways, and by the time the school broke up at Christmas was able to mix with the boys and take part in their games. At home he did his best to make things bright, but it was uphill work. Mrs. Sankey was fretful and complaining. Their income was reduced by the loss of Captain Sankey's half-pay, and they had now only the interest of the fortune of four thousand pounds which Mrs. Sankey had brought to her husband on her marriage. This sum had been settled upon her, and was entirely under her own control. The income was but a small one, but it was sufficient for the family to live upon with care and prudence.

Captain Sankey had made many friends since the time when he first settled at Marsden, and all vied with each other in their kindness to his widow. Presents of game were constantly left for her; baskets of chickens, eggs, and fresh vegetables were sent down by Squire Simmonds and other county magnates, and their carriages often stopped at the door to make inquiries.

Many people who had not hitherto called now did so, and all Marsden seemed anxious to testify its sympathy with the widow of the brave officer. Ned was touched with these evidences of respect for his father's memory. Mrs. Sankey was pleased for herself, and she would of an evening inform Ned with much gratification of the visits she had received.

Ned was glad that anything should occur which could rouse his mother, and divert her from her own grievances; but the tone in which she spoke often jarred painfully upon him, and he wondered how his mother could find it in her heart to receive these people and to talk over his father's death. But Mrs. Sankey liked it. She was conscious she looked well in her deep mourning, and that even the sombre cap was not unbecoming with her golden hair peeping out beneath it. Tears were always at her command, and she had ever a few ready to drop upon her dainty embroidered handkerchief when the occasion commanded it; and her visitors, when they agreed among themselves, what a soft gentle woman that poor Mrs. Sankey was, but sadly delicate you know—had no idea of the querulous complaining and fretfulness whose display was reserved for her own family only. To this Ned was so accustomed that it passed over his head almost unheeded; not so her constant allusions to his father. Wholly unconscious of the agony which it inflicted upon the boy, Mrs. Sankey was incessantly quoting his opinions or utterances.

"Ned, I do wish you would not fidget with your feet.

(251)   I

You know your dear father often told you of it;" or, "As your dear father used to say, Ned;" until the boy in despair would throw down his book and rush out of the room to calm himself by a run in the frosty night air; while Mrs. Sankey would murmur to herself, "That boy's temper gets worse and worse, and with my poor nerves how am I to control him?"

Mr. Porson was very kind to him in those days. During that summer holiday he had very frequently spent the evening at Captain Sankey's, and had formed a pretty correct idea of the character of Ned's mother. Thus when he saw that Ned, when he entered the school after breakfast or dinner, had an anxious hunted look, and was clearly in a state of high tension, he guessed he was having a bad time of it at home.

Charlie had fast got over the shock of his father's death; children quickly recover from a blow, and, though delicate, Charlie was of a bright and gentle disposition, ready to be pleased at all times, and not easily upset.

One morning when Ned came in from school looking pale and white, gave random answers to questions, and even, to the astonishment of the class, answered Mr. Porson himself snappishly, the master, when school was over and the boys were leaving their places, said:

"Sankey, I want to have a few words with you in the study."

Ned followed his master with an air of indifference. He supposed that he was going to be lectured for the way he had spoken, but as he said to himself, "What did it

matter! what did anything matter!" Mr. Porson did not
sit down on entering the room, but when Ned had closed
the door after him took a step forward and laid his hand
on his shoulder.

"My boy," he said, "what is it that is wrong with you?
I fear that you have trouble at home."

Ned stood silent, but the tears welled up into his eyes.

"It can't be helped, sir," he said in a choking voice,
and then with an attempt at gaiety: "it will be all the
same fifty years hence, I suppose."

"That is a poor consolation, Ned," Mr. Porson rejoined.
"Fifty years is a long time to look forward to. Can't we
do anything before that?"

Ned was silent.

"I do not want you to tell me, Ned, anything that happens at home—God forbid that I should pry into matters
so sacred as relations between a boy and a parent!—but
I can see, my boy, that something is wrong. You are not
yourself. At first when you came back I thought all was
well with you; you were, as was natural, sad and depressed, but I should not wish it otherwise. But of late
a change has come over you; you are nervous and excited;
you have gone down in your class, not, I can see, because
you have neglected your work, but because you cannot
bring your mind to bear upon it. Now all this must have
a cause. Perhaps a little advice on my part might help
you. We shall break up in a week, Ned, and I shall be
going away for a time. I should like to think before I
went that things were going on better with you."

"I don't want to say anything against my mother,"
Ned said in a low voice. "She means kindly, sir; but, oh!
it is so hard to bear. She is always talking about father,
not as you would talk, sir, but just as if he were alive and
might come in at any moment, and it seems sometimes
as if it would drive me out of my mind."

"No doubt it is trying, my boy," Mr. Porson said; "but
you see natures differ, and we must all bear with each
other and make allowances. Your mother's nature, as far
as I have seen of her, is not a deep one. She was very fond
of your father, and she is fond of you; but you know, just
as still waters run deep, shallow waters are full of ripples,
and eddies, and currents. She has no idea that what
seems natural and right to her should jar upon you. You
upon your part can scarcely make sufficient allowance
for her different treatment of a subject which is to you
sacred. I know how you miss your father, but your
mother must miss him still more. No man ever more
lovingly and patiently tended a woman than he did her
so far as lay in his power. She had not a wish ungratified.
You have in your work an employment which occupies
your thoughts and prevents them from turning constantly
to one subject; she has nothing whatever to take her
thoughts from the past. It is better for her to speak of
him often than to brood over him in silence. Your tribute
to your father's memory is deep and silent sorrow, hers
is frequent allusion. Doubtless her way jars upon you;
but, Ned, you are younger than she, and it is easier for
you to change. Why not try and accept her method as

being a part of her, and try, instead of wincing every time that she touches the sore, to accustom yourself to it. It may be hard at first, but it will be far easier in the end."

Ned stood silent for a minute or two; then he said:

"I will try, sir. My father's last words to me were to be kind to mother, and I have tried hard, and I will go on trying."

"That is right, my boy; and ask God to help you. We all have our trials in this life, and this at present is yours; pray God to give you strength to bear it."

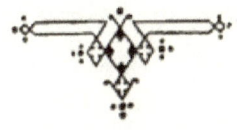

CHAPTER VIII.

NED IS SORELY TRIED.

MONG the many who called upon Mrs. Sankey after the death of her husband was Mr. Mulready, the owner of a mill near Marsden. He was one of the leading men in the place, although his mill was by no means a large one. He took rank in the eyes of the little town with men in a much larger way of business by means of a pushing manner and a fluent tongue. He had come to be considered an authority upon most subjects. He paid much attention to his dress, and drove the fastest horse and the best got-up gig in that part of the country; but it was Mr. Mulready's manner which above all had raised him to his present position in the esteem of the good people of Marsden. He had the knack of adapting himself to the vein of those he addressed.

With the farmers who came into market he was bluff and cordial; with people in general he was genial and good-tempered. At meetings at which the county gentry were present he was quiet, business-like, and a trifle deferential, showing that he recognized the difference between his position and theirs. With ladies he was gay when they were gay, sympathetic when sympathy was expected. With them he was even more popular than with the men, for the latter, although they admired and somewhat envied his varied acquirements, were apt in the intimacy of private conversation to speak of him as a humbug.

There was one exception, however, to his general popularity. There was no mill-owner in the neighbourhood more heartily detested by his workpeople; but as these did not mingle with the genteel classes of Marsden their opinion of Mr. Mulready went for nothing. The mill-owner was a man of three or four and forty, although when dressed in his tightly-fitting brown coat with its short waist, its brass buttons, and high collar, and with a low hat with narrow brim worn well forward and coming down almost to the bridge of his nose, he looked seven or eight years younger.

His hair was light, his trimly cut mutton-chop whiskers were sandy, he had a bright fresh complexion, a large mouth, and good teeth, which he always showed when he smiled, and in public he was always smiling; his eyes were light in colour, very close together, and had a somewhat peculiar appearance. Indeed there were men who hinted that he had a slight cast, but these were, no doubt, envious of his popularity. Mrs. Sankey had been flattered by his visit and manner; indeed it could hardly have been otherwise, for he had expressed a sympathy and deference which were very soothing to her.

"It is indeed kind of you to receive me," he had said. "I know, of course, that it is not usual for a man who has the misfortune to be unmarried to make a call upon a lady, but I could not help myself. William Mulready is not a man to allow his feelings to be sacrificed to the cold etiquette of the world. I had not the pleasure of the acquaintance of that most brave and distinguished officer your late husband. I had hoped that some day circumstances might throw me in contact with him, but it was not for me, a humble manufacturer, to force my acquaintance upon one socially my superior; but, my dear madam, when I heard of that terrible accident, of that noble self-devotion, I said to myself, 'William Mulready, when a proper and decent time elapses you must call upon the relict of your late noble and distinguished townsman, and assure her of your sympathy and admiration, even if she spurns you from the door.'"

"You could not think I should do that, Mr. Mulready," Mrs. Sankey said. "It is most gratifying to me to receive this mark of sympathy in my present sad position;" and she sighed deeply.

"You are good indeed to say so," Mr. Mulready said in a tone of deep gratitude; "but I might have been sure that my motives at least would not be misunderstood by a high-bred and delicate lady like yourself. I will not now trespass on your time, but hope that I may be permitted to call again. Should there be anything in which so humble an individual could be in the slightest degree useful to you pray command my services. I know the responsibility which you must feel at being left in charge of those two noble boys and your charming little daughter must be well-nigh overwhelming, and if you would not think it presumption I would say that any poor advice or opinion which I, who call myself in some degree a man of the world, can give, will be always at your service."

"You are very good," Mrs. Sankey murmured. "It is indeed a responsibility. My younger boy and girl are all that I could wish, but the elder is already almost beyond me;" and by the shake of her head she testified that her troubles on that score approached martyrdom.

"Never fear, my dear madam," Mr. Mulready said heartily. "Boys will be boys, and I doubt not that he will grow up everything that you could desire. I may have heard that he was a little passionate. There was a trifling affair between him and his schoolmaster, was there not? But these things mend themselves, and doubtless all will come well in time; and now I have the honour of wishing you good-morning."

"Charming manners!" Mrs. Sankey said to herself when her visitor had left. "A little old-fashioned, perhaps, but so kind and deferential. He seemed to understand my feelings exactly."

That evening when they were at tea Mrs. Sankey mentioned the agreeable visitor who had called in the afternoon.

"What! William Mulready!" Ned exclaimed; "Foxey, as his hands call him. I have heard Bill speak of him

often.   His men hate him.   They say he is a regular
tyrant.   What impudence his coming here!"

"Ned, I am surprised at you," his mother said angrily.
"I am sure Mr. Mulready is nothing of the sort.   He is
a most kind and considerate gentleman, and I will not
allow you to repeat these things you hear from the low
companions whom your father permitted you to associate
with."

"Bill is not a low companion, mother," Ned exclaimed
passionately.   "A better fellow never stood, and Foxey is
not kind and considerate.   He is a brutal tyrant, and I
am sure my father, if you will quote his opinion, would
not have had such a man inside his doors."

"Leave the room, Ned, this moment," his mother exclaimed, more angry than he had ever seen her before.
"I am ashamed of you speaking to me in that way.   You
would not have dared to do it had your father been alive."

Ned dashed down his scarcely-begun bread and butter
and flung himself out of the room, and then out of the
house, and it was some hours before he returned.   Then
he went straight up to his mother's room.

"I beg your pardon, mother," he said quietly.   "I am
very sorry I spoke as I did.   I ought not to have
done so."

"Very well," Mrs. Sankey said coldly; "then don't do it
again, Ned."

Without another word Ned went off to his books.   He
was grieved and sore at heart.   He had during his walk
fought a hard battle with himself, and had conquered.

As his temper cooled down he had felt that he had broken his promise, that he had not been kind to his mother; felt, too, that her accusation was a true one—he would not have dared to speak so to her had his father been alive.

"But it was so different then," he had said to himself as the tears chased each other down his cheeks. "Father understood me, and cared for me, and made allowances. It was worth while fighting against one's temper just to have him put his hand on my shoulder and say, 'Well done, my boy.' Now it is so different. I will go on trying for his sake; but I know it's no good. Do what I will, I can't please her. It's my fault, I dare say, but I do try my best. I do, indeed, father," he said, speaking out loud; "if you can hear me, I do, indeed, try to be kind to mother, but she won't let me. I do try to make allowances, that is, when I am not in a passion, and then I go and spoil it all, like a beast, just as I did to-night. Anyhow," he said to himself as he turned his face homeward again, "I will go and tell her I am sorry, and beg her pardon. I don't suppose she will be nice, but I can't help that. It's my duty anyhow, and I will try and not say anything against Foxey next time she speaks of him."

The latter part of his resolution Ned found it very hard to maintain, for Mr. Mulready became a not unfrequent visitor. He had always some excuse for calling, either to bring in a basket of fresh trout, some game, or hot-house fruit, for, as he said, he knew her appetite was delicate and needed tempting, or some book newly issued from the London press which he was sure she would appreciate.

After a short time Mrs. Sankey ceased to speak of these visits, perhaps because she saw how Ned objected to the introduction of Mr. Mulready's name, perhaps for some other reason, and a year passed without Ned's being seriously ruffled on the subject.

Ned was now nearly sixteen. He had worked hard, and was the head boy at Porson's. It had always been regarded as a fixed thing that he should go into the army. As the son of an officer who had lost his leg in the service it was thought that he would be able to obtain a commission without difficulty, and Squire Simmonds, who had been a kind friend since his father's death, had promised to ask the lord-lieutenant of the county to interest himself in the matter, and had no doubt that the circumstances of Captain Sankey's death would be considered as an addition to the claim of his services in the army.

Captain Sankey had intended that Ned should have gone to a superior school to finish his education, but the diminished income of the family had put this out of the question, and the subject had never been mooted after his death. Ned, however, felt that he was making such good progress under Mr. Porson that he was well content to remain where he was.

His struggle with his temper had gone on steadily, and he hoped he had won a final victory over it. Mr. Porson

had been unwearied in his kindnesses, and often took
Ned for an hour in the evening in order to push him forward, and although he avoided talking about his home
life the boy felt that he could, in case of need, pour out
his heart to him; but, indeed, things had gone better at
home. Mrs. Sankey was just as indisposed as ever to
take any share whatever in the trouble of housekeeping,
but as Abijah was perfectly capable of keeping the house
in order without her instructions things went on smoothly
and straightly in this respect.

In other matters home life was more pleasant than it
had been. Mrs. Sankey was less given to querulous
complaining, more inclined to see things in a cheerful
light, and Ned especially noticed with satisfaction that
the references to his father which had so tried him had
become much less frequent of late.

One day in September, when his father had been dead
just a year, one of the town boys, a lad of about Ned's
age, said to him as they were walking home from school
together:

"Well, Ned, I suppose I ought to congratulate you,
although I don't know whether you will see it in that
light."

"What do you mean?" Ned said. "I don't know that
anything has happened on which I should be particularly
congratulated, except on having made the top score against
the town last week."

"Oh! I don't mean that," the boy said. "I mean
about Mulready."

"What do you mean?" Ned said, stopping short and turning very white.

"Why," the lad said laughing, "all the town says he is going to marry your mother."

Ned stood as if stupefied. Then he sprang upon his companion and seized him by the throat.

"It's a lie," he shouted, shaking him furiously. "It's a lie, I say, Smithers, and you know it. I will kill you if you don't say it's a lie."

With a great effort Smithers extricated himself from Ned's grasp.

"Don't choke a fellow," he said. "It may be a lie if you say it is, but it is not my lie anyhow. People have been talking about it for some time. They say he's been down there nearly every day. Didn't you know it?"

"Know it?" Ned gasped. "I have not heard of his being in the house for months, but I will soon find out the truth."

And without another word he dashed off at full speed up the street. Panting and breathless he rushed into the house, and tore into the room where his mother was sitting trifling with a piece of fancy-work.

"I do wish, Edward, you would not come into the room like a whirlwind. You know how any sudden noise jars upon my nerves. Why, what is the matter?" she broke off suddenly, his pale, set face catching her eye, little accustomed as she was to pay any attention to Ned's varying moods.

NED'S HORROR AT THE DREADFUL NEWS.

"Mother," he panted out, "people are saying an awful thing about you, a wicked, abominable thing. I know, of course, it is not true, but I want just to hear you say so, so that I can go out and tell people they lie. How dare they say such things!"

"Why, what do you mean, Edward?" Mrs. Sankey said, almost frightened at the boy's vehemence.

"Why, they say that you are going to marry that horrible man Mulready. It is monstrous, isn't it? I think they ought to be prosecuted and punished for such a wicked thing, and father only a year in his grave."

Mrs. Sankey was frightened at Ned's passion. Ever since the matter had first taken shape in her mind she had felt a certain uneasiness as to what Ned would say of it, and had, since it was decided, been putting off from day to day the telling of the news to him. She had, in his absence, told herself over and over again that it was no business of his, and that a boy had no right to as much as question the actions of his mother; but somehow when he was present she had always shrunk from telling him. She now took refuge in her usual defence—tears.

"It is shameful," she said, sobbing, as she held her handkerchief to her eyes, "that a boy should speak in this way to his mother; it is downright wicked."

"But I am not speaking to you, mother; I am speaking of other people—the people who have invented this horrible lie—for it is a lie, mother, isn't it? It is not possible it can be true?"

"It is true," Mrs. Sankey said, gaining courage from

her anger; "it is quite true. And you are a wicked and
abominable boy to talk in that way to me. Why shouldn't
I marry again? Other people marry again, and why
shouldn't I? I am sure your poor father would never
have wished me to waste my life by remaining single,
with nothing to do but to look after you children.
And it is shameful of you to speak in that way of Mr.
Mulready."

Ned stopped to hear no more. At her first words he
had given a low gasping cry, as one who has received a
terrible wound. The blood flew to his head, the room
swam round, and he seemed to feel the veins in his
temples swell almost to bursting. The subsequent words
of his mother fell unheeded on his ears, and turning round
he went slowly to the door, groping his way as one half-
asleep or stupefied by a blow. Mechanically he opened the
door and went out into the street; his cap was still on
his head, but he neither thought of it one way or the
other.

Almost without knowing it he turned from the town
and walked towards the hills. Had anyone met him by
the way they would assuredly have thought that the boy
had been drinking, so strangely and unevenly did he
walk. His face was flushed almost purple, his eyes were
bloodshot; he swayed to and fro as he walked, sometimes
pausing altogether, sometimes hurrying along for a few
steps. Passing a field where the gate stood open he
turned into it, kept on his way for some twenty yards
further, and then fell at full length on the grass. There

he lay unconscious for some hours, and it was not until the evening dews were falling heavily that he sat up and looked round.

For some time he neither knew where he was nor what had brought him there. At last the remembrance of what had passed flashed across him, and with a cry of "Father! father!" he threw himself at full length again with his head on his arm; but this time tears came to his relief, and for a long time he cried with a bitterness of grief even greater than that which he had suffered at his father's death. The stars were shining brightly when he rose to his feet, his clothes were soaked with dew, and he trembled with cold and weakness.

"What am I to do?" he said to himself; "what am I to do?" He made his way back to the gate and leaned against it for some time; then, having at last made up his mind, he turned his back on the town and walked towards Varley, moving more slowly and weariedly than if he was at the end of a long and fatiguing day's walk. Slowly he climbed the hill and made his way through the village till he reached the Swintons' cottage. He tapped at the door with his hand, and lifting the latch he opened the door a few inches.

"Bill, are you in?" There was an exclamation of surprise.

"Why, sure-ly, it's Maister Ned!" and Bill came to the door.

"Come out, Bill, I want to speak to you."

Much surprised at the low and subdued tone in which

K

Ned spoke, Bill snatched down his cap from the peg by the door and joined him outside.

"What be't, Maister Ned? what be t' matter with thee? Has owt gone wrong?"

Ned walked on without speaking. In his yearning for sympathy, in his intense desire to impart the miserable news to some one who would feel for him, he had come to his friend Bill. He had thought first of going to Mr. Porson. But though his master would sympathize with him he would not be able to feel as he did; he would no doubt be shocked at hearing that his mother was so soon going to marry again, but he would not be able to understand the special dislike to Mr. Mulready, still less likely to encourage his passionate resentment. Bill would, he knew, do both, for it was from him he had learned how hated the mill-owner was among his people. But at present he could not speak. He gave a short wave of his hand to show that he heard, but could not answer yet, and with his head bent down made his way out through the end of the village on to the moor—Bill following him, wondering and sympathetic, unable to conjecture what had happened. Presently, when they had left the houses far behind them, Ned stopped.

"What be't, Maister Ned?" Bill again asked, laying his strong hand upon Ned's shoulder; "tell oi what it be. Hast got in another row with t' maister? If there be owt as oi can do, thou knowest well as Bill Swinton be with thee heart and soul."

"I know, Bill—I know," Ned said in a broken voice,

"but you can do nothing; I can do nothing; no one can. But it's dreadful to think of. It's worse than if I had killed twenty masters. Only think—only think, Bill, my mother's going to marry Mulready!"

"Thou doesn't say so, lad! What! thy mother marry Foxey! Oi never heer'd o' such a thing. Well, that be bad news, surely! Well, well, only to think, now! Poor lad! Well, that beats all!"

The calamity appeared so great to Bill that for some time no idea occurred to him which could, under the circumstances, be considered as consolatory. But Ned felt the sympathy conveyed in the strong grasp of his shoulder, and in the muttered "Well, well, now!" to which Bill gave vent at intervals.

"What bee'st going to do vor to stop it?" he asked at last.

"What can I do, Bill? She won't listen to me—she never does. Anything I say always makes her go the other way. She wouldn't believe anything I said against him. It would only make her stick to him all the more."

"Do'st think," Bill suggested after another long pause, "that if we got up a sort of depitation—Luke Marner and four or five other steady chaps as knows him; yes, and Polly Powlett, she could do the talking—to go to her and tell her what a thundering bad un he is—dost think it would do any good?"

Even in his bitter grief Ned could hardly help smiling at the thought of such a deputation waiting upon his mother.

" No, it wouldn't do, Bill."

Bill was silent again for some time.

" Dost want un killed, Maister Ned?" he said in a low voice at last; " 'cause if ye do oi would do it for ye. Oi would lay down my life for ye willing, as thou knowest; and hanging ain't much, arter all. They say 'tis soon over. Anyhow oi would chance it, and perhaps they wouldn't find me out."

Ned grasped his friend's hand.

" I could kill him myself!" he exclaimed passionately. " I have been thinking of it; but what would be the good? I know what my mother is — when once she has made up her mind there's no turning her; and if this fellow were out of the way, likely enough she would take up with another in no time."

" But it couldn't been as bad as if it wur Foxey," Bill urged, " he be the very worsest lot about Marsden."

" I would do it," Ned said passionately; " I would do it over and over again, but for the disgrace it would bring on Charlie and Lucy."

" But there would be no disgrace if oi was to do it, Maister Ned."

'Yes, there would, Bill—a worse disgrace than if I did it myself. It would be a nice thing to let you get hanged for my affairs; but let him look out—let him try to ill-treat Charlie and Lucy, and he will see if I don't get even with him. I am not so much afraid of that—it's the shame of the thing. Only to think that all Marsden should know my mother is going to be married again within a year of my father's death, and that after being his wife she was going to take such a man as this! It's awful, downright awful, Bill!"

"Then what art thou going to do, Maister Ned—run away and 'list for a soldier, or go to sea?"

"I wish I could," Ned exclaimed. "I would turn my back on Marsden and never come back again, were it not for the little ones. Besides," he added after a pause, "father's last words were, 'Be kind to mother;' and she will want it more than he ever dreamt of."

"She will that," Bill agreed; "leastways unless oi be mistaken. And what be'st going to do now, lad? Be'st agoing whoam?"

"No, I won't go home to-night," Ned replied. "I must think it over quietly, and it would be worse to bear there than anywhere else. No, I shall just walk about."

"Thou canst not walk abowt all night, Maister Ned," Bill said positively; "it bain't to be thowt of. If thou don't mind thou canst have moi bed and oi can sleep on t' floor."

"No, I couldn't do that," Ned said, "though I do feel awfully tired and done up; but your brothers would be asking me questions and wondering why I didn't go home. I could not stand that."

"No, Maister Ned, oi can see that wouldn't do; but if we walk about for an hour or two, or—no, I know of a better plan. We can get in at t' window of the school; it bain't never fastened, and bain't been for years, seeing as thar bain't been neither school nor schoolers since auld

Mother Brown died. Oi will make a shift to loight a fire there. There be shutters, so no one will see the loight. Then oi will bring ee up some blankets from our house, and if there bain't enough Polly will lend me some when oi tell her who they are for. She bain't a one to blab. What dost thou say?"

Ned, who felt utterly worn out, assented gladly to the proposal, and an entrance was easily effected into the desolate cottage formerly used as a day-school. Bill went off at once and soon returned with a load of firewood; the shutters were then carefully closed, and a fire quickly blazed brightly on the hearth. Bill then went away again, and in a quarter of an hour returned with Mary Powlett. He carried a bundle of rugs and blankets, while she had a kettle in one hand and a large basket in the other.

"Good-evening! Master Sankey," she said as she entered. "Bill has told me all about it, and I am sorry indeed for you and for your mother. It is worse for her, poor lady, than for you. You will soon be old enough to go out into the world if you don't like things at home; but she will have to bear what trouble comes to her. And now I thought you would like a cup of tea, so I have brought the kettle and things up. I haven't had tea yet, and they don't have tea at Bill's; but I like it, though feyther grumbles sometimes, and says it's too expensive for the likes of us in sich times as these; but he knows I would rather go without meat than without tea, so he lets me have it. Bill comes in for a cup sometimes, for he likes it better than beer, and it's a deal better for him to be sitting taking a cup of tea with me than getting into the way of going down to the 'Spotted Dog,' and drinking beer there. So we will all have a cup together. No one will disturb us. Feyther is down at the 'Brown Cow;' and when I told the children I had to go out on special business they all promised to be good, and Jarge said he would see them all safely into bed. I told him I should be back in an hour."

While Polly was speaking she was bustling about the room, putting things straight; with a wisp of heather she swept up the dust which had accumulated on the floor, in a semicircle in front of the fire, and laid down the rugs and blankets to form seats. Three cups and saucers, a little jug of milk, a tea-pot, and basin of sugar were placed in the centre, and a pile of slices of bread and butter beside them, while from a paper-bag she produced a cake which she had bought at the village shop on her way up.

Ned watched her preparations listlessly.

"You are very good, Polly," he said, "and I shall be very glad of the cup of tea, but I cannot eat anything."

"Never mind," she said cheerfully. "Bill and I can do the eating, and perhaps after you have had a cup of tea you will be able to, for Bill tells me you have had nothing to eat since breakfast."

Ned felt cheered by the warm blaze of the fire and by the cheerful sound of the kettle, and after taking a cup of tea found that his appetite was coming, and was soon able to eat his share. Mary Powlett kept up a

cheerful talk while the meal was going on, and no allusion
was made to the circumstances which had brought Ned
there.   After it was done she sat and chatted for an hour.
Then she said:

"I must be off now, and I think, Bill, you'd best be
going soon too, and let Master Ned have a good night of
it.   I will make him up his bed on the rugs; and I will
warrant, after all the trouble he has gone through, he will
sleep like a top."

CHAPTER IX.

A PAINFUL TIME.

HEN Ned was left alone he rolled himself up in the blankets, placed a pillow which Polly had brought him under his head, and lay and looked at the fire; but it was not until the flames had died down, and the last red glow had faded into blackness that he fell off to sleep. His thoughts were bitter in the extreme. He pictured to himself the change which would take place in his home life with Mulready the manufacturer, the tyrant of the workmen, ruling over it. For himself he doubted not that he would be able to hold his own.

"He had better not try on his games with me," he muttered savagely. "Though I am only sixteen he won't find it easy to bully me; but of course Charlie and Lucy can't defend themselves. However, I will take care of them. Just let him be unkind to them, and see what comes of it! As to mother, she must take what she gets, at least she deserves to. Only to think of it! only to think of it! Oh, how bitterly she will come to repent! How could she do it!

"And with father only dead a year! But I must stand by her too. I promised father to be kind to her, though he could never have guessed how she would need it. He meant that I would only put up, without losing my temper, with her way of always pretending to be ill, and never doing anything but lie on the sofa and read poetry. Still, of course it meant I was to be kind anyhow whatever happened, and I will try to be so, though it is hard when she has brought such trouble upon us all.

"As for Mulready I should like to burn his mill down, or to break his neck. I hate him; it's bad enough to be a tyrant; but to be a tyrant and a hypocrite too, is horrible. Well, at any rate he sha'n't lord it over me;" and so at last Ned dropped off to sleep. He was still soundly asleep when Bill Swinton came in to wake him. It was half-past six, a dull October morning with a dreary drizzling rain. Bill brought with him a mug of hot tea and some thick slices of bread and butter. Ned got up and shook himself.

"What o'clock is it, Bill?"

"Half-past six; the chaps went off to t' mill an hour gone; oi've kept some tea hot for ee."

"Thank you, Bill, my head aches, and so do all my bones, and I feel as if I hadn't been asleep all night, although, indeed, I must have slept quite as long as usual. Can't I have a wash?"

"Yes," Bill said, "thou canst come to our place; but thou hadst best take thy breakfast whilst it be hot. It ull waken thee up loike."

Ned drank the tea and ate a slice of bread and butter, and felt refreshed thereat. Then he ran with Bill to his cottage and had a wash, and then started for the town. It was eight o'clock when he reached home. Abijah was at the door, looking down the road as he came up.

"Oh! Master Ned, how can you go on so? Not a bit of sleep have I had this blessed night, and the mistress in strong hystrikes all the evening. Where have you been?" Ned gave a grunt at the news of his mother's hysterics— a grunt which clearly expressed "served her right," but he only answered the last part of the question.

"I have been up at Varley, and slept at the school-house. Bill Swinton and Polly Powlett made me up a bed and got me tea and breakfast. I am right enough."

"But you shouldn't have gone away, Master Ned, in that style, leaving us to wait and worry ourselves out of our senses."

"Do you know what she told me, Abijah? Wasn't it enough to make any fellow mad?"

"Ay, ay," the nurse said. "I know. I have see'd it coming months ago; but it wasn't no good for me to speak. Ay lad, it's a sore trouble for you, sure-ly a sore trouble for you, and for us all; but it ain't no manner of use for you to set yourself agin it. Least said sooner mended, Master Ned; in a case like this it ain't no good your setting yourself up again the missis. She ain't strong in some things, but she's strong enough in her will, and you ought to know by this time that what she sets her mind on she gets. It were so allus in the captain's time, and

if he couldn't change her, poor patient lamb—for if ever
there were a saint on arth he was that—you may be sure
that you can't. So try and take it quietly, dearie. It be
main hard for ye, and it ain't for me to say as it isn't; but
for the sake of peace and quiet, and for the sake of the
little ones, Master Ned, it's better for you to take it
quiet. If I thought as it would do any good for you to
make a fuss I wouldn't be agin it; but it ain't, you know,
and it will be worse for you all if you sets him agin you to
begin with. Now go up and see your mother, dearie, afore
you goes off to school. I have just taken her up her tea."

"I have got nothing to say to her," Ned growled.

"Yes, you have, Master Ned; you have got to tell her
you hopes she will be happy. You can do that, you know,
with a clear heart, for you do hope so. Fortunately she
didn't see him yesterday; for when he called I told him
she was too ill to see him, and a nice taking she was in
when I told her he had been and gone; but I didn't mind
that, you know, and it was better she shouldn't see him
when she was so sore about the words you had said to
her. It ain't no use making trouble aforehand, or setting
him agin you. He knows, I reckon, as he won't be wel-
comed here by you. The way he has always come when
you would be out showed that clear enough. But it ain't
no use making matters worse. It's a pretty kettle of fish
as it stands. No, go up, dearie, like a good boy, and
make things roight."

Ned lingered irresolute for a little time in the hall, and
then his father's words, "Be kind to her," came strongly

in his mind, and he slowly went upstairs and knocked at
his mother's door.

"Oh! here you are again!" she said in querulous tones
as he entered, "after being nearly the death of me with
your wicked goings on! I don't know what you will come
to, speaking to me as you did yesterday, and then running away and stopping out all night."

"It was wrong, mother," Ned said quietly, "and I have
come to tell you I am sorry; but you see the news was
very sudden, and I wasn't prepared for it. I did not
know that he had been coming here, and the news took
me quite by surprise. I suppose fellows never do like
their mothers marrying again. It stands to reason they
wouldn't; but, now I have thought it over, I am sorry I
spoke as I did, and I do hope, mother, you will be happy
with him."

Mrs. Sankey felt mollified. She had indeed all along
dreaded Ned's hearing the news, and had felt certain it
would produce a desperate outbreak on his part. Now
that it was over she was relieved. The storm had been
no worse than she expected, and now that Ned had so
speedily come round, and was submissive, she felt a load
off her mind.

"Very well, Ned," she said more graciously than usual,
"I am glad that you have seen the wickedness of your
conduct. I am sure that I am acting for the best, and
that it will be a great advantage to you and your brother
and sister having a man like Mr. Mulready to help you
push your way in life. I am sure I am thinking of

your interest as much as my own; and I have spoken to him over and over again about you, and he has promised dozens of times to do his best to be like a father to you all." Ned winced perceptibly.

"All right, mother! I do hope you will be happy; but, please, don't let us talk about it again till — till it comes off; and, please, don't let him come here in the evening. I will try and get accustomed to it in time; but you see it's rather hard at first, and you know I didn't expect it."

So saying Ned left the room, and collecting his books made his way off to school, leaving his mother highly satisfied with the interview.

His absence from afternoon school had, of course, been noticed, and Smithers had told his friends how Ned had flown at him on his speaking to him about the talk of his mother and Mulready. Of course before afternoon school broke up every boy knew that Ned Sankey had cut up rough about the report; and although the great majority of the boys did not know Mr. Mulready by name there was a general feeling of sympathy with Ned. The circumstances of his father's death had, of course, exalted him greatly in the eyes of his school-fellows, and it was the unanimous opinion, that after having had a hero for his father, a fellow would naturally object to having a stepfather put over him.

Ned's absence was naturally associated with the news, and caused much comment and even excitement. His attack upon Mr. Hathorn had become a sort of historical incident in the school, and the younger boys looked up with a sort of respectful awe upon the boy who had defied a head-master. There were all sorts of speculations rife among them as to what Ned had done, there being a general opinion that he had probably killed Mr. Mulready, and the debate turning principally upon the manner in which this act of righteous vengeance had been performed.

There was, then, a feeling almost of disappointment when Ned walked into the playground looking much as usual, except that his face was pale and his eyes looked heavy and dull. No one asked him any questions; for although Ned was a general favourite, it was generally understood that he was not the sort of fellow to be asked questions that might put him out. When they went in school, and the first class was called up, Ned, who was always at its head, took his place at the bottom of the class, saying quietly to the master:

"I have not prepared my lesson to-day, sir, and I have not done the exercises."

Mr. Porson made no remark; he saw at once by Ned's face that something was wrong with him. When several questions went round, which Ned could easily have answered without preparation, the master said:

"You had better go to your desk, Sankey; I see you are not well. I will speak to you after school is over."

Ned sat down and opened a book, but he did not turn a page until school was over; then he followed his master to the study.

"Well, my boy," he asked kindly, "what is it?"

"My mother is going to marry Mr. Mulready," Ned said shortly. The words seemed to come with difficulty from his lips.

"Ah! it is true, then. I heard the report some weeks ago, but hoped that it was not true. I am sorry for you, Ned. I know it must be a sore trial for you; it is always so when anyone steps into the place of one we have loved and lost."

"I shouldn't care so much if it wasn't him," Ned said in a dull voice.

"But there's nothing against the man, is there?" Mr. Porson asked. "I own I do not like him myself; but I believe he stands well in the town."

"Only with those who don't know him," Ned replied; "his work-people say he is the worst master and the biggest tyrant in the district."

"We must hope it's not so bad as that, Ned; still, I am sorry—very sorry, at what you tell me; but, my boy, you must not take it to heart. You see you will be going out into the world before long. Your brother will be following you in a few years. It is surely better that your mother should marry again and have someone to take care of her."

"Nice care of her he is likely to take!" Ned laughed bitterly. "You might as well put a fox to take care of a goose."

"You are severe on both parties," Mr. Porson said with a slight smile; "but I can hardly blame you, my boy, for feeling somewhat bitter at first; but I hope that, for your own sake and your mother's, you will try and conquer this feeling and will make the best of the circumstances. It is worse than useless to kick against the pricks. Any show of hostility on your part will only cause unhappiness, perhaps between your mother and him—almost certainly between you and her. In this world, my boy, we have all our trials. Some are very heavy ones. This is yours. Happily, so far as you are concerned, you need only look forward to its lasting eighteen months or so. In that time you may hope to get your commission; and as the marriage can hardly take place for some little time to come, you will have but a year or so to bear it."

"I don't know, sir," Ned said gloomily; "everything seems upset now. I don't seem to know what I had best do."

"I am sure at present, Ned," Mr. Porson said kindly—for he saw that the boy was just now in no mood for argument—"the best is to try and think as little of it as possible. Make every allowance for your mother; as you know, my boy, I would not speak disrespectfully to you of her on any account; but she is not strong-minded. She has always been accustomed to lean upon someone, and the need of someone to lean on is imperative with her. Had you been a few years older, and had you been staying at home, it is probable that you might have taken your place as her support and strength. As it is, it was almost inevitable that something of this sort would happen.

(251) L

"But you know, Ned, where to look for strength and support. You have fought one hard battle, my boy, and have well-nigh conquered; now you have another before you. Seek for strength, my boy, where you will assuredly find it, and remember that this discipline is doubtless sent you for your good, and that it will be a preparation for you for the struggle in after life. I don't want you to be a thoughtless careless young officer, but a man earnest in doing his duty, and you cannot but see that these two trials must have a great effect in forming your character. Remember, Ned, that if the effect be not for good, it will certainly be for evil."

"I will try, sir," Ned said; "but I know it is easy to make good resolutions, and how it will be when he is in the house as master I can't trust myself even to think."

"Well, let us hope the best, Ned," Mr. Porson said kindly; "things may turn out better than you fear."

Then seeing that further talking would be useless now, he shook Ned's hand and let him go.

The next three or four months passed slowly and heavily. Ned went about his work again quietly and doggedly; but his high spirits seemed gone. His mother's engagement with Mr. Mulready had been openly announced, directly after he had first heard of it. Charlie had, to Ned's secret indignation, taken it quietly. He knew little of Mr. Mulready, who had, whenever he saw him, spoken kindly to him, and who now made him frequent presents of books and other things dear to schoolboys. Little Lucy's liking he had, however, failed to gain, although in his frequent visits he had spared no pains to do so, seldom coming without bringing with him cakes or papers of sweets. Lucy accepted the presents, but did not love the donor, and confided to Abijah that his teeth were exactly like those of the wolf who ate Little Red Riding Hood.

Ned found much more comfort in her society during those dull days than in Charlie's. He had the good sense, however, never to encourage her in her expressions of dislike to Mr. Mulready, and even did his best to combat her impression, knowing how essential it was for her to get on well with him. Ned himself did not often see Mr. Mulready during that time. The first time that they met, Ned had, on his return from school, gone straight up into the drawing-room, not knowing that Mr. Mulready was there. On opening the door and seeing him he paused suddenly for a moment and then advanced. For a moment neither of them spoke, then Mr. Mulready said in his frankest manner:

"Ned, you have heard I am going to marry your mother. I don't suppose you quite like it; it wouldn't be natural if you did; I know I shouldn't if I were in your place. Still you know your disliking it won't alter it, and I hope we shall get on well together. Give me your hand, my lad, you won't find me a bad sort of fellow."

"I hope not," Ned said quietly, taking Mr. Mulready's hand and continuing to hold it while he went on: "I don't pretend I like it, and I know it makes no difference whether I do or not; the principal point is, that my mother should be happy, and if you make her happy I have no doubt we shall, as you say, get on well together; if you don't, we sha'n't."

There was no mistaking the threat conveyed in Ned's steady tones, and Mr. Mulready, as Ned dropped his hand, felt that he should have more trouble with the boy than he had expected. He gave a forced laugh.

"One would think, Ned, that you thought it likely I was going to be unkind to your mother."

"No," Ned said quietly, "I don't want to think about it one way or the other, only I promised my father I would be kind to my mother; that means that I would look after her, and I mean to. Well, mother," he said in his usual tone, turning to Mrs. Sankey, "and how are you this morning?"

"I was feeling better, Ned," she said sharply; "but your unpleasant way of talking, and your nonsense about taking care of me, have made me feel quite ill again. Somehow you always seem to shake my nerves. You never seem to me like other boys. One would think I was a child instead of being your mother. I thought after what you said to me that you were going to behave nicely."

"I am trying to behave nicely," Ned said. "I am sure I meant quite nicely, just as Mr. Mulready does; I think he understands me."

"I don't understand that boy," Mrs. Sankey said plaintively when Ned had left the room, "and I never have understood him. He was dreadfully spoilt when he was

in India, as I have often told you; for in my weak state
of health I was not equal to looking after him, and his
poor father was sadly over-indulgent. But he has certainly
been much better as to his temper lately, and I do hope,
William, that he is not going to cause trouble."

" Oh, no!" Mr. Mulready said lightly, " he will not cause
trouble; I have no doubt we shall get on well together.
Boys will be boys, you know; I have been one myself,
and of course they look upon stepfathers as natural
enemies; but in this case, you see, we shall not have to
put up with each other long, as he will be getting his
commission in a year or so. Don't trouble yourself
about it, love; in your state of health you ought really
not to worry yourself, and worry, you know, spoils the
eyes and the complexion, and I cannot allow that, for
you will soon be my property now."

The wedding was fixed for March. It was to be perfectly quiet, as Mrs. Sankey would, up to the day, be still
in mourning. A month before the time Ned noticed that
his mother was more uncertain in her temper than usual,
and Abijah confided to him in secret that she thought
things were not going on smoothly between the engaged
couple.

Nor were they. Mr. Mulready had discovered, to his
surprise, that, indolent and silly as Mrs. Sankey was in
many respects, she was not altogether a fool, and was
keen enough where her own interests were concerned.
He had suggested something about settlements, hoping
that she would at once say that these were wholly un-

necessary; but to his surprise she replied in a manner which showed that she had already thought the matter over, and had very fixed ideas on the subject.

" Of course," she said, " that will be necessary. I know nothing about business, but it was done before, and my poor husband insisted that my little fortune should be settled so as to be entirely at my own disposal."

But this by no means suited Mr. Mulready's views. Hitherto want of capital had prevented his introducing the new machinery into his mills, and the competition with the firms which had already adopted it was injuring him seriously, and he had reckoned confidently upon the use of Mrs. Sankey's four thousand pounds. Although he kept his temper admirably under the circumstances, he gave her distinctly to understand, in the pleasantest way, that an arrangement which was most admirably suitable in every respect in the case of a lady marrying an officer in the army, to whom her capital could be of no possible advantage, was altogether unsuitable in the case of a manufacturer.

" You see, my love," he argued, " that it is for your benefit as well as mine that the business should grow and flourish by the addition of the new machinery which this little fortune of yours could purchase. The profits could be doubled and trebled, and we could look forward ere long to holding our heads as high as the richest manufacturers at Leeds and Bradford—while the mere interest of this money invested in consols as at present would be absolutely useless to us."

Mrs. Sankey acknowledged the force of his argument, but was firm in her determination to retain her hold of her money, and so they parted, not in anger, for Mr. Mulready altogether disclaimed the possibility of his being vexed, but with the sense that something like a barrier had sprung up between them.

This went on for a few days, and although the subject was not mooted, Mrs. Sankey felt that unless some concession on her part was made it was likely that the match would fall through. This she had not the slightest idea of permitting, and rather than it should happen she would have married without any settlement at all, for she really loved, in her weak way, the man who had been so attentive and deferential to her.

So one day the subject was renewed, and at last an understanding was arrived at. Mrs. Sankey's money was to be put into the business in her own name. Should she not survive her husband, he was to have the option of paying the money to her children or of allowing them the sum of eighty pounds a year each from the business. Should he not survive her the mill was to be settled upon any children she might have after her marriage; should there be no children it was to be hers absolutely.

All this was only arrived at after several long discussions, in all of which Mrs. Sankey protested that she knew nothing of business, that it was most painful to her to be thus discussing money matters, and that it would be far better to leave it in the hands of a solicitor to arrange in a friendly manner with him. She never-

theless stuck to her views, and drove a bargain as keenly
and shrewdly as any solicitor could have done for her,
to the surprise and exasperation of Mr. Mulready. Had
he known that she really loved him, and would, if she
had been driven to it, have sacrificed everything rather
than lose him, he could have obtained very different terms;
but having no heart to speak of, himself, he was ignorant
of the power he possessed over her.

Bankruptcy stared him in the face unless he could
obtain this increase of capital, and he dared not, by
pressing the point, risk its loss. The terms, he told himself, were not altogether unsatisfactory; it was not likely
that she would survive him. They were of about the same
age; he had never known what it was to be ill, and she,
although not such an invalid as she fancied herself, was
still not strong. If she did not survive him he would
have the whole business, subject only to the paltry
annuity of two hundred and forty pounds a year to the
three children. If, the most unlikely thing in the world,
she did survive him—well, it mattered not a jot in that
case who the mill went to.

So the terms were settled, the necessary deeds were
drawn up by a solicitor, and signed by both parties.
Mrs. Sankey recovered her spirits, and the preparations
for the wedding went on. Ned had intended to absent
himself from the ceremony, but Mr. Porson, guessing that
such might be his intention, had talked the matter gravely
over with him. He had pointed out to Ned that his
absence would in the first place be an act of great disre-

spect to his mother; that in the second place it would cause general comment, and would add to the unfavourable impression which his mother's early re-marriage had undoubtedly created; and that, lastly, it would justify Mr. Mulready in regarding him as hostile to the marriage, and, should trouble subsequently arise, he would be able to point to it in self-justification, and as a proof that Ned had from the first determined to treat him as an enemy.

So Ned was present at his mother's marriage. Quiet as the wedding was, for only two or three acquaintances were asked to be present, the greater part of Marsden were assembled in the church.

The marriage had created considerable comment. The death of Captain Sankey in saving a child's life had rendered his widow an object of general sympathy, and people felt that not only was this marriage within eighteen months of Captain Sankey's death almost indecent, but that it was somehow a personal wrong to them, and that they had been defrauded in their sympathy.

Therefore the numerous spectators of the marriage were critical rather than approving. They could find nothing to find fault with, however, in the bride's appearance. She was dressed in a dove-coloured silk, and with her fair hair and pale complexion looked quite young, and, as everyone admitted, pretty. Mr. Mulready, as usual, was smiling, and seemed to convey by the looks which he cast round that he regarded the assemblage as a personal compliment to himself.

Lucy and Charlie betrayed no emotion either way; they were not pleased, but the excitement of the affair amused and interested them, and they might be said to be passive spectators. Ned, however, although he had brought himself to be present, could not bring himself to look as if the ceremony had his approval or sanction. He just glared, as Abijah, who was present, afterwards confided to some of her friends, as if he could have killed the man as he stood. His look of undisguised hostility was indeed noticed by all who were in church, and counted heavily against him in the days which were to come.

CHAPTER X.

TROUBLES AT HOME.

IT was not one of the least griefs of the young Sankeys connected with their mother's wedding that Abijah was to leave them. It was she herself who had given notice to Mrs. Sankey, saying that she would no longer be required. The first time that she had spoken of her intention, Mrs. Sankey vehemently combated the idea, saying that neither she nor Lucy could spare her; but she did not afterwards return to the subject, and seemed to consider it a settled thing that Abijah intended to leave. Mrs. Sankey had, in fact, spoken to Mr. Mulready on the subject, but instead of taking the view she had expected he had said cheerfully:

"I am glad that she has given notice. I know that she is a valuable woman and much attached to you. At the same time these old servants always turn out a mistake under changed circumstances. She would never have been comfortable or contented. She has, my dear, if I may say so, been mistress too long, and as I intend you to be mistress of my house, it is much better that she should go."

As Mrs. Sankey had certain doubts herself as to whether Abijah would be a success in the new home, the subject was dropped, and it became an understood thing that Abijah would leave after the wedding.

The newly married couple were absent for three weeks. Until two days before their return Abijah remained in the old house with the young Sankeys; then they moved into their new home, and she went off to her native village ten miles distant away on the moors. The next day there was a sale at the old house. A few, a very few, of the things had been moved. Everything else was sold, to the deep indignation of Ned, who was at once grieved and angry that all the articles of furniture which he associated with his father should be parted with. Abijah shared the boy's feelings in this respect, and at the sale all the furniture and fittings of Captain Sankey's study were bought by a friendly grocer on her behalf, and the morning after the sale a badly written letter, for Abijah's education had been neglected, was placed in Ned's hand.

"My dear Master Ned,—Knowing as it cut you to the heart that everything should go away into the hands of strangers, I have made so bold as to ask Mr. Willcox for to buy all the furniter and books in maister's study. He is agoing to stow them away in a dry loft, and when so bee as you gets a home of your own there they is for you; they are sure not to fetch much, and when you gets a rich man you can pay me for them; not as that matters at all one way or the other. I have been a saving up pretty nigh all my wages from the day as you was born, and is quite comfortable off. Write me a letter soon, dearie, to tell me as how things is going on. Your affectionate nurse—Abijah Wolf."

Although Ned was a lad of sixteen, he had a great cry over this letter, but it did him good, and it was with a softer heart that he prepared to receive his mother and her husband that evening.

The meeting passed off better than he had anticipated. Mrs. Mulready was really affected at seeing her children again, and embraced them, Ned thought, with more fondness than she had done when they went away. Mr. Mulready spoke genially and kindly, and Ned began to hope that things would not be so bad after all.

The next morning, to his surprise, his mother appeared at breakfast, a thing which he could not remember that she had ever done before, and yet the hour was an early one, as her husband wanted to be off to the mill. During the meal Mr. Mulready spoke sharply two or three times, and it seemed to Ned that his mother was nervously anxious to please him.

"Things are not going on so well after all," he said to himself as he walked with his brother to school. "Mother has changed already; I can see that she isn't a bit like herself. There she was fussing over whether he had enough sugar with his tea, and whether the kidneys were done enough for him; then her coming down to breakfast was wonderful. I expect she has found already that

somebody else's will besides her own has got to be consulted; it's pretty soon for her to have begun to learn the
lesson."

It was very soon manifest that Mr. Mulready was
master in his own house. He still looked pleasant and
smiled, for his smile was a habitual one; but there was a
sharpness in the ring of his voice, an impatience if everything was not exactly as he wished. He roughly silenced
Charlie and Lucy if they spoke when he was reading his
paper at breakfast, and he spoke snappishly to his wife
when she asked him a question on such occasions. Ned
felt his face burn as with his eyes on his plate he continued his meal. To him Mr. Mulready seldom spoke
unless it was absolutely necessary.

Ned often caught himself wondering over the change
which had taken place in his mother. All the ways and
habits of an invalid had disappeared. She not only gave
directions for the management of the house, but looked
after everything herself, and was for ever going up stairs
and down seeing that everything was properly done.
However sharply Mr. Mulready spoke she never replied
in the same tone. A little flush of colour would come
into her cheek, but she would pass it off lightly, and at
all times she appeared nervously anxious to please him.
Ned wondered much over the change.

" He is a tyrant," he said, " and she has learned it already;
but I do think she loves him. Fancy my mother coming
to be the slave of a man like this! I suppose," he laughed
bitterly, " it's the story of 'a woman, a dog, and a walnut

tree, the more you thrash them the better they will be.'
My father spent his whole life in making hers easy, and
in sparing her from every care and trouble, and I don't
believe she cared half as much for him as she does for this
man who is her master."

For some months Mr. Mulready was very busy at his
mill. A steam-engine was being erected, new machinery
brought in, and he was away the greater part of his time
superintending it.

One day at breakfast, a short time before all was in
readiness for a start with the new plant, Mr. Mulready
opened a letter directed in a sprawling and ill-written
hand which lay at the top of the pile by his plate. Ned
happened to notice his face, and saw the colour fade out
from it as he glanced at the contents. The mouth remained as usual, set in a smile, but the rest of the face
expressed agitation and fear. The hand which held the
letter shook. Mrs. Mulready, whose eyes seldom left her
husband's face when he was in the room, also noticed the
change.

" Is anything the matter, William?"

" Oh! nothing," he said with an unnatural laugh, " only
a little attempt to frighten me."

" An attempt which has succeeded," Ned said to himself,
" whatever it is."

Mr. Mulready passed the letter over to his wife. It
was a rough piece of paper; at the top was scrawled the
outline of a coffin, underneath which was written:

" Mr. Mulready,—Sir, this is to give you warning that if

you uses the new machinery you are a dead man. You have been a marked man for a long time for your tyrannical ways, but as long as you didn't get the new machinery we let you live; but we has come to the end of it now; the day as you turns on steam we burns your mill to the ground and shoots you, so now you knows it."

At the bottom of this was signed the words " Captain Lud."

" Oh! William," Mrs. Mulready cried, " you will never do it! You will never risk your life at the hands of these terrible people!"

All the thin veneer of politeness was cracked by this blow, and Mr. Mulready said sullenly:

" Nice thing indeed; after I have married to get this money, and then not to be able to use it!"

His wife gave a little cry.

" It's a shame to say so," Charlie burst out sturdily.

Mr. Mulready's passion found a vent. He leaped up and seized the boy by the collar and boxed his ears with all his force.

In an instant the fury which had been smouldering in Ned's breast for months found a vent. He leaped to his feet and struck Mr. Mulready a blow between the eyes which sent him staggering back against the wall; then he caught up the poker. The manufacturer with a snarl like that of an angry wild beast was about to rush at him, but Ned's attitude as he stood, poker in hand, checked him.

" Stand back," Ned said threateningly, " or I will strike you. You coward and bully; for months I have put up

NED DEFENDS LITTLE CHARLIE AGAINST THEIR STEPFATHER.

with your tyrannizing over Charlie and Lucy, but touch either of them again if you dare. You think that you are stronger than I am—so you are ever so much; but you lay a finger on them or on me, and I warn you, if I wait a month for an opportunity I will pay you for it, if you kill me afterwards."

Mrs. Mulready's screams had by this time brought the servants into the room, and they stood astonished at the spectacle.

Lucy crying bitterly had run to Ned and thrown her arms round him, begging him to be quiet. Charlie, hardly recovered from the heavy blows he had received, was crying too. Mr. Mulready as pale as death was glaring at Ned, while his wife had thrown herself between them. Mr. Mulready was the first to recover himself.

"This is a nice spectacle," he said to the servants. "You see that boy has attacked me with the poker and might have murdered me. However, you can go now, and mind, no chattering about what you have seen. And now," he continued to Ned as the door closed behind the servants, "out of this house you go this day."

"You don't suppose I want to stay in your house," Ned said passionately. "You don't suppose that it's any pleasure to me to stop here, seeing you play the tyrant over my mother."

"Oh, Ned, Ned," Mrs. Mulready broke in, "how can you talk so!"

"It is true, mother, he is a tyrant to you as well as to everyone else; but I don't mean to go, I mean to stop here to protect you and the children. He daren't turn me out; if he did, I would go and work in one of the mills, and what would the people of Marsden say then? What would they think of this popular pleasant gentleman then, who has told his wife before her children that he married her for her money? They shall all know it, never fear, if I leave this house. I would have gone to Mr. Simmonds and asked him to apply for a commission for me before now, for other fellows get it as young as I am; but I have made up my mind that it's my duty not to do so. I know he has been looking forward to my being out of the way, and his being able to do just what he likes with the others, but I ain't going to gratify him. It's plain to me that my duty at present is to take care of you all, and though God knows how I set my mind upon going into the army and being a soldier like my father, I will give it up if it means leaving Charlie here under him."

"And do you suppose, sir," Mr. Mulready asked with intense bitterness, "that I am going to keep you here doing nothing all your life, while you are pleased to watch me?"

"No, I don't," Ned replied. "I shall get a clerkship or something in one of the mills, and I shall have Charlie to live with me until he is old enough to leave school, and then I will go away with him to America or some-where. As to mother, I can do nothing for her. I think my being here makes it worse for her, for I believe you tyrannize over her all the more because you think it hurts me. I know you hated me from the first, just as I hated you. As for Lucy, mother must do the best she can for her. Even you daren't hit a girl."

"Oh Ned, how can you go on so!" Mrs. Mulready wailed. "You are a wicked boy to talk so."

"All right, mother," Ned replied recklessly; "if I am, I suppose I am. I know in your eyes he can do no wrong. And I believe if he beat you, you would think that you deserved it." So he flung himself down in his chair and continued his breakfast.

Mr. Mulready drank off his tea without sitting down, and then left the room without another word; in fact, as yet he did not know what to say.

Almost speechless with passion as he was he restrained himself from carrying out his threat and turning Ned at once from the house. Above all things he prized his position and popularity, and he felt that, as Ned had said, he would indeed incur a heavy odium by turning his wife's son from his doors. Captain Sankey's death had thrown almost a halo over his children. Mr. Mulready knew that he was already intensely unpopular among the operative class, but he despised this so long as he stood well with the rest of the townsmen; but he dared not risk Ned's going to work as an ordinary hand in one of the factories; public opinion is always against stepfathers, and assuredly this would be no exception. Hating him as he did, he dared not get rid of this insolent boy, who had struck and defied him. He cursed himself now with his rashness in letting his temper get the best of him and telling his wife

openly that he had married her for her money; for this
in Ned's hands would be a serious weapon against him.

That his wife's feelings were hurt he cared not a jot,
but it would be an awkward thing to have it repeated in
the town. Then there was this threatening letter; what
was he to do about that? Other men had had similar
warnings. Some had defied Captain Lud, and fortified
their mills and held them. Many had had their property
burned to the ground; some had been murdered. It
wouldn't be a pleasant thing to drive about in the country
knowing that at any moment he might be shot dead. His
mill was some little distance out of the town; the road was
dark and lonely. He dared not risk it.

Mr. Mulready was, like all tyrants, a coward at heart,
and his face grew white again as he thought of the
letter in his pocket. In the meantime Mrs. Mulready was
alternately sobbing and upbraiding Ned as he quietly
finished his breakfast. The boy did not answer, but continued his meal in dogged silence, and when it was over
collected his books and without a word went off to school.

Weeks went on, and no outward change took place. Ned
continued to live at home. Mr. Mulready never addressed
him, and beyond helping him to food entirely ignored
his presence. At meal-times when he opened his lips it
was either to snap at Charlie or Lucy, or to snarl at his
wife, whose patience astonished Ned, and who never
answered except by a smile or murmured excuse. The lad
was almost as far separated from her now as from his stepfather. She treated him as if he only were to blame for

the quarrel which had arisen. They had never understood each other, and while she was never weary of making excuses for her husband, she could make none for her son. In the knowledge that the former had much to vex him she made excuses for him even in his worst moods. His new machinery was standing idle, his business was getting worse and worse, he was greatly pressed and worried, and it was monstrous, she told herself, that at such a time he should be troubled with Ned's defiant behaviour.

A short time before the school Christmas holidays Ned knocked at the door of Mr. Porson's study. Since the conversation which they had had when first Ned heard of his mother's engagement Mr. Porson had seen in the lad's altered manner, his gloomy looks, and a hardness of expression which became more and more marked every week, that things were going on badly. Ned no longer evinced the same interest in his work, and frequently neglected it altogether; the master, however, had kept silence, preferring to wait until Ned should himself broach the subject.

"Well, Sankey, what is it?" he asked kindly as the boy entered.

"I don't think it's any use my going on any longer, Mr. Porson."

"Well, Sankey, you have not been doing yourself much good this half, certainly. I have not said much to you about it, for it is entirely your own business: you know more than nineteen out of twenty of the young fellows who get commissions, so that if you choose to give up work it is your own affair."

"I have made up my mind not to go into the army," Ned said quietly. Mr. Porson was silent a minute.

"I hope, my dear lad," he said, "you will do nothing hastily about this. Here is a profession open to you which is your own choice and that of your father, and it should need some very strong and good reason for you to abandon it. Come let us talk the matter over together, my boy, not as a master and his pupil, but as two friends.

"You know, my boy, how thoroughly I have your interest at heart. If you had other friends whom you could consult I would rather have given you no advice, for there is no more serious matter than to say anything which might influence the career of a young fellow just starting in life. Terrible harm often results from well-intentioned advice or opinions carelessly expressed to young men by their elders; it is a matter which few men are sufficiently careful about; but as I know that you have no friends to consult, Ned, and as I regard you with more than interest, I may say with affection, I think it would be well for you to tell me all that there is in your mind before you take a step which may wreck your whole life.

" I have been waiting for some months in hopes that you would open your mind to me, for I have seen that you were unhappy; but it was not for me to force your confidence."

"I don't know that there's much to tell," Ned said wearily. "Everything has happened just as it was certain it would do. Mulready is a brute; he ill-treats my mother, he ill-treats Charlie and Lucy, and he would ill-treat me if he dared."

"All this is bad, Ned," Mr. Porson said gravely; "but of course much depends upon the amount of his ill-treatment. I assume that he does not actively ill-treat your mother."

"No," Ned said with an angry look in his face; "and he'd better not."

"Yes, Ned, he had better not, no doubt," Mr. Porson said soothingly; "but what I want to know, what it is essential I should know if I am to give you any advice worth having, is what you mean by ill-treatment—is he rough and violent in his way with her? does he threaten her with violence? is he coarse and brutal?"

"No," Ned said somewhat reluctantly; "he is not that, sir; he is always snapping and snarling and finding fault."

"That is bad, Ned, but it does not amount to ill-treatment. When a man is put out in business and things go wrong with him it is unhappily too often his custom to vent his ill-temper upon innocent persons; and I fancy from what I hear—you know in a little place like this everyone's business is more or less known—Mr. Mulready has a good deal to put him out. He has erected new machinery and dare not put it to work, owing, as I hear —for he has laid the documents before the magistrates— to his having received threatening letters warning him against doing so. This is very trying to the man. Then, Ned, you will excuse my saying that perhaps he is some-

what tried at home. It is no pleasant thing for a man
to have a young fellow like yourself in the house taking
up an attitude of constant hostility. I do not say that
his conduct may or may not justify it; but you will not
deny that from the first you were prepared to receive
him as an enemy rather than as a friend. I heard a story
some weeks ago in the town, which emanated no doubt
from the servants, that you had actually struck him."

"He hit Charlie, sir," Ned exclaimed.

"That may be," Mr. Porson went on gravely; "and I
have no doubt, Ned, that you considered then, and that
you consider now, that you were acting rightly in interfering on behalf of your brother. But I should question
much whether in such a matter you are the best judge.
You unfortunately began with a very strong prejudice
against this man; you took up the strongest attitude of
hostility to him; you were prepared to find fault with
everything he said and did; you put yourself in the position of the champion of your mother, brother, and sister
against him. Under such circumstances it was hardly
possible that things could go on well. Now I suppose,
Ned, that the idea which you have in your mind in deciding to give up the profession you have chosen, is that you
may remain as their champion and protector here."

"Yes, sir," Ned said. "Father told me to be kind to
mother, whatever happened."

"Quite so, my boy; but the question is, Are you being
kind ?"

Ned looked surprised.

"That you intend to be so, Ned, I am sure. The question is, Are you going the right way to work? Is this championship that you have taken upon yourself increasing her happiness, or is it not?"

Ned was silent.

"I do not think that it is, Ned. Your mother must be really fond of this man or she would not have married him. Do you think that it conduces to the comfort of her home to see the constant antagonism which prevails between you and him? Is it not the fact that this ill-temper under which she suffers is the result of the irritation caused to him by your attitude? Do you not add to her burden rather than relieve it?"

Ned was still silent. He had so thoroughly persuaded himself that he was protecting his mother, his brother, and sister from Mr. Mulready that he had never considered the matter in this light.

"Does your mother take his part or yours in these quarrels, Ned?"

"She takes his part, sir," said Ned indignantly.

"Very well, Ned; that shows in itself that she does not wish for your championship, that in her eyes the trouble in the house is in fact caused by you. You must remember that when a woman loves a man she makes excuses for his faults of temper; his irritable moods, sharp expressions, and what you call snapping and snarling do not seem half so bad to her as they do to a third person, especially when that third person is her partisan. Instead of your adding to her happiness by renouncing your idea of going into the army, and of deciding to remain here in some position or other to take care of her, as, I suppose, is your intention, the result will be just the contrary. As to your sister, 1 think the same thing would happen.

"Your mother is certainly greatly attached to her; and owing to her changed habits—for I understand that she is now a far more active, and I may say, Ned, a more sensible woman than before her marriage—I see no reason why Lucy should not be happy with her, especially if the element of discord—I mean yourself—were out of the way. As to Charlie, at the worst I don't think that he would suffer from your absence. His stepfather's temper will be less irritable; and as Charlie is away at school all day, and has to prepare his lessons in the evening, there is really but slight opportunity for his stepfather treating him with any active unkindness, even should he be disposed to do so.

"Did I think, my boy, that your presence here would be likely to benefit your family I should be the last person to advise you to avoid making a sacrifice of your private wishes to what you consider your duty; but upon the contrary I am convinced that the line which you have, with the best intention, taken up has been altogether a mistake, that your stay at home does vastly more harm than good, and that things would go on very much better in your absence."

This was a bitter mortification for Ned, who had hitherto nursed the idea that he was performing rather a heroic part, and was sacrificing himself for the sake of his mother.

"You don't know the fellow as I do," he said sullenly at last.

"I do not, Ned; but I know human nature, and I know that any man would show himself at his worst under such circumstances as those in which you have placed him. It is painful to have to say, but I am sure that you have done harm rather than good, and that things will get on much better in your absence."

"I believe he is quite capable of killing her," Ned said passionately, "if he wanted her out of the way."

"That is a hard thing to say, Ned; but even were it so, we have no reason for supposing that he does want her out of the way. Come, Sankey, I am sure you have plenty of good sense. Hitherto you have been acting rather blindly in this matter. You have viewed it from one side only, and with the very best intentions in the world have done harm rather than good.

"I am convinced that when you come to think it over you will see that, in following out your own and your father's intentions and wishes as to your future career you will really best fulfil his last injunctions and will show the truest kindness to your mother. Don't give me any answer now, but take time to think it over. Try and see the case from every point of view, and I think you will come to the conclusion that what I have been saying, although it may seem rather hard to you at first, is true, and that you had best go into the army, as you had intended. I am sure in any case you will know that what I have said, even if it seems unkind, has been for your good."

"Thank you, Mr. Porson," Ned replied; "I am quite sure of that. Perhaps you are right, and I have been making a fool of myself all along. But anyhow I will think it over."

CHAPTER XI.

THE NEW MACHINERY.

T is rather hard for a lad who thinks that he has been behaving somewhat as a hero to come to the conclusion that he has been making a fool of himself; but this was the result of Ned Sankey's cogitation over what Mr. Porson had said to him. Perhaps he arrived more easily at that conclusion because he was not altogether unwilling to do so. It was very mortifying to allow that he had been altogether wrong; but, on the other hand, there was a feeling of deep pleasure at the thought that he could, in Mr. Porson's deliberate opinion, go into the army and carry out all his original hopes and plans. His heart had been set upon this as long as he could remember, and it had been a bitter disappointment to him when he had arrived at the conclusion that it was his duty to abandon the idea. He did not now come to the conclusion hastily that Mr. Porson's view of the case was the correct one; but after a fortnight's consideration he went down on New Year's-day to the school, and told his master that he had made up his mind.

"I see, sir," he said, "now that I have thought it all over, that you are quite right, and that I have been behaving like an ass, so I shall set to work again and try and make up the lost time. I have only six months longer, for Easter is the time when Mr. Simmonds said that I should be old enough, and he will write to the lord-lieutenant, and I suppose that in three months after that I should get my commission."

"That is right, Ned. I am exceedingly glad you have been able to take my view of the matter. I was afraid you were bent upon spoiling your life, and I am heartily glad that you have been able to see the matter in a different light."

A day or two afterwards Ned took an opportunity of telling his mother that he intended at Easter to remind Mr. Simmonds of his promise to apply for a commission for him; and had he before had any lingering doubt that the decision was a wise one it would have been dissipated by the evident satisfaction and relief with which the news was received; nevertheless, he could not help a feeling of mortification at seeing in his mother's face the gladness which the prospect of his leaving occasioned her.

It was some time since Ned had seen his friend Bill Swinton, for Bill was now regularly at work in Mr. Mulready's factory and was only to be found at home in the evening, and Ned had been in no humour for going out. He now, however, felt inclined for a friendly talk again, and the next Sunday afternoon he started for Varley.

"Well, Maister Ned," Bill said as he hurried to the

door in answer to his knock, "it be a long time surely sin oi saw thee last—well-nigh six months, I should say."

"It is a long time, Bill, but I haven't been up to anything, even to coming up here. Put on your cap and we will go for a walk across the moors together."

In a few seconds Bill joined him, and they soon left the village behind.

"Oi thought as how thou didn't feel oop to talking loike, Maister Ned. Oi heared tell as how thou did'st not get on well wi' Foxey; he be a roight down bad un, he be; it were the talk of the place as how you gived him a clout atween t' eyes, and oi laughed rarely to myself when oi seed him come through t' mill wi' black and blue all round 'em. There warn't a hand there but would have given a week's pay to have seen it done."

"I am afraid I was wrong, Bill," Ned said, feeling ashamed rather than triumphant at the thought. "I oughtn't to have done it, but my beastly temper got the best of it."

"Doan't say that, Maister Ned; he deserves ten toimes worse nor you gived him, and he will get it some time if he doan't mind. Oi tell ee there be lots of talk of him, and Captain Lud's gang be a getting stronger and stronger. Oi tell ye, t' maisters be agoing to have a bad time on it afore long, and Foxey be sure to be one of the first served out."

"Well, don't you have anything to do with it, Bill. You know I have told you over and over again that no good can come of such bad doings, and that the men will only make matters much worse for themselves. My father used to say that no good ever came of mob violence. They may do some harm for a time, but it is sure to recoil on their own heads."

"Oi doan't ha' nowt to do wi' it," Bill replied, "cause oi told yer oi wouldn't; but oi've some trouble to keep oot o't. Ye see oi am nointeen now, and most o' t' chaps o' moi age they be in't; they meet at the 'Dog' nigh every noight, and they drills regular out on t' moor here, and it doan't seem natural for oi not to be in it, especial as moi brothers be in it. They makes it rough for me in t' village, and says as how I ain't got no spirit, and even t' girls laughs at me."

"Not Polly Powlett, I am sure, Bill."

"No, not Polly," Bill replied. "She be a different sort. A' together it be a bit hard, and it be well for me as oi'm main strong and tough, for oi ha' to fight pretty nigh every Saturday. However, oi ha' thrashed pretty nigh every young chap in Varley, and they be beginning now to leave oi alone."

"That's right, Bill; I am sure I have no right to preach to you when I am always doing wrong myself; still I am quite sure you will be glad in the long run that you had nothing to do with King Lud. I know the times are very hard, but burning mills and murdering masters are not the way to make them better; you take my word for that. And now how are things going on in Varley?"

"No great change here," Bill replied. "Polly Powlett

bain't made up her moind yet atween t' chaps as is arter her. They say as she sent John Stukeley, the smith, to the roight about last Sunday; he ha' been arter her vor the last year. Some thowt she would have him, some didn't. He ha' larning, you see, can read and wroite foine, and ha' got a smooth tongue, and knows how to talk to gals, so some thought she would take him; oi knew well enough she wouldn't do nowt of the koind, for oi ha' heard her say he were a mischievous chap, and a cuss to Varley. Thou know'st, Maister Ned, they do say, but in course oi knows nowt about it, as he be the head of the Luddites in this part of Yorkshire.

"Luke Marner he be dead against King Lud, he be, and so be many of the older men here; it's most the young uns as takes to them ways; and nateral, Polly she thinks as Luke does, or perhaps," and Bill laughed, "it's Polly as thowt that way first, and Luke as thinks as she does. However it be, she be dead set agin them, and she's said to me jest the same thing as thou'st been a-saying; anyhow, it be sartin as Polly ha' said no to John Stukeley, not as she said nowt about it, and no one would ha' known aboot it ef he hadn't gone cussing and swearing down at the 'Dog.'

"I thinks, Maister Ned, as we shall ha' trouble afore long. The men ha' been drilling four or five years now, and oi know as they ha' been saying, What be the good of it when nowt be done and the wages gets lower and lower? They have preachments now out on t' moor on Sundays, and the men comes from miles round, and they tells me as Stukeley and others, but him chiefly, goes on awful agin t' maisters, and says, There's Scripture vor it as they owt to smite 'em, and as how tyrants owt vor to be hewed in pieces."

"The hewing would not be all on one side, Bill, you will see, if they begin it. You know how easily the soldiers have put down riots in other places."

"That be true," Bill said; " but they doan't seem vor to see it. Oi don't say nowt one way or t' other, and oi have had more nor half a mind to quit and go away till it's over. What wi' my brothers and all t' other young chaps here being in it, it maaks it moighty hard vor oi to stand off; only as oi doan't know what else vor to do, oi would go. Oi ha' been a-thinking that when thou get'st to be an officer oi'll list in the same regiment and go to the wars wi' thee. Oi am sick of this loife here."

" Well, Bill, there will be no difficulty about that if you really make up your mind to it when the time comes. Of course I should like to have you very much. I have heard my father say that each officer has a soldier as his special servant; and if you would like that, you see, when we were alone together we should be able to talk about Varley and everything here just as we do now. Then I suppose I could help you on and get you made first a corporal and then a sergeant."

" Very well, Maister Ned, then we will look on that as being as good as settled, and as soon as thou gets to be an officer oi will go as one of your soldiers."

For an hour they walked across the moor, talking about

a soldier's life, Ned telling of the various parts of the world in which England was at that time engaged in war, and wondering in which of them they would first see service. Then they came back to the village and there parted, and Ned, feeling in better spirits than he had been from the day when he first heard of his mother's engagement to Mr. Mulready, walked briskly down to Marsden.

For a time matters went on quietly. Few words were exchanged between Ned and Mr. Mulready; and although the latter could not but have noticed that Ned was brighter and more cheerful in his talk, he was brooding over his own trouble, and paid but little heed to it.

The time was fast approaching when he could no longer go on as at present. The competition with the mills using the new machinery was gradually crushing him, and it was necessary for him to come to a determination either to pluck up heart and to use his new machines, or to close his mill.

At last he determined to take the former course and to defy King Lud. Other manufacturers used steam, and why should not he? It was annoying to him in the extreme that his friends and acquaintances, knowing that he had fitted the mill with the new plant, were always asking him why he did not use it.

A sort of uneasy consciousness that he was regarded by his townsmen as a coward was constantly haunting him. He knew in his heart that his danger was greater than that of others, because he could not rely on his men. Other masters had armed their hands, and had turned their fac-

tories into strong places, some of them even getting down
cannon for their defence; for, as a rule, the hands employed
with the new machinery had no objection to it, for they
were able to earn larger wages with less bodily toil than
before.

The hostility was among the hands thrown out of employment, or who found that they could now no longer
make a living by the looms which they worked in their
own houses. Hitherto Mr. Mulready had cared nothing
for the good-will of his hands. He had simply regarded
them as machines from whom the greatest amount of
work was to be obtained at the lowest possible price.
They might grumble and curse him beneath their breaths;
they might call him a tyrant behind his back, for this he
cared nothing; but he felt now that it would have been
better had their relations been different; for then he could
have trusted them to do their best in defence of the mill.

Having once determined upon defying King Lud, Mr.
Mulready went before the magistrates, and laying before
them the threatening letters he had received, for the first
had been followed by many others, he asked them to
send for a company of infantry, as he was going to set his
mill to work. The magistrates after some deliberation
agreed to do so, and wrote to the commanding officer of
the troops at Huddersfield asking him to station a detach-
ment at Marsden for a time.

The request was complied with. A company of infantry marched in and were billeted upon the town. A
room was fitted up at the mill, and ten of them were

quartered here, and upon the day after their arrival the new machinery started.

Now that the step was taken, Mr. Mulready's spirits rose. He believed that the presence of the soldiers was ample protection for the mill, and he hoped that ere they left the town the first excitement would have cooled down, and the Luddites have turned their attention to other quarters

Ned met Bill on the following Sunday.

"I suppose, Bill," he said, "there is a rare stir about Foxey using his new machinery?"

"Ay, that there be, and no wonder," Bill said angrily, "there be twenty hands turned adrift. Oi bee one of them myself."

"You, Bill! I had no idea you had been discharged."

"Ay; oi have got the sack, and so ha' my brother and young Jarge Marner, and most o' t' young chaps in the mill. Oi suppose as how Foxey thinks as the old hands will stick to t' place, and is more afeerd as the young uns might belong to King Lud, and do him a bad turn with the machinery. Oi tell ye, Maister Ned, that the sooner as you goes as an officer the better, vor oi caan't bide here now and hold off from the others. Oi have had a dog's loife for some time, and it ull be worse now. It would look as if oi hadn't no spirit in the world, to stand being put upon and not join the others. T' other chaps scarce speak to me, and the gals turn their backs as oi pass them. Oi be willing vor to be guided by you as far as oi can; but it bain't in nature to stand this. Oi'd as lief go and hang myself. Oi would go and list to-morrow, only oi don't know what regiment you are going to."

"Well, Bill, it is hard," Ned said, "and I am not surprised that you feel that you cannot stand it; but it won't be for long now. Easter will be here in a fortnight, and then I shall see Mr. Simmonds and get him to apply at once. I met him in the street only last week, and he was talking about it then. He thinks that it will not be long after he sends in an application before I get my commission. He says he has got interest in London at the Horse Guards, and will get the application of the lord lieutenant backed up there; so I hope that in a couple of months at latest it will all be settled."

"Oi hope so, oi am sure, vor oi be main sick of this. However, oi can hold on for another couple of months; they know anyhow as it ain't from cowardice as I doan't join them. I fowt Jack Standfort yesterday and licked un; though, as you see, oi 'ave got a rare pair of black eyes to-day. If oi takes one every Saturday it's only eight more to lick, and oi reckon oi can do that."

"I wish I could help you, Bill," Ned said; "if father had been alive I am sure he would have let you have a little money to take you away from here and keep you somewhere until it is time for you to enlist; but you see I can do nothing now."

"Doan't you go vor to trouble yourself aboot me, Maister Ned. Oi shall hold on roight enow. The thought as it is for two months longer will keep me up. Oi can spend moi evenings in at Luke's. He goes off to the 'Coo;' but

Polly doan't moind moi sitting there and smoking moi pipe, though it bain't every one as she would let do that."

Ned laughed. " It's a pity, Bill, you are not two or three years older, then perhaps Polly mightn't give you the same answer she gave to the smith."

" Lor' bless ee," Bill said seriously, "Polly wouldn't think nowt of oi, not if oi was ten years older. Oi bee about the same age as she; but she treats me as if I was no older nor her Jarge. No, when Polly marries it won't be in Varley. She be a good many cuts above us, she be. Oi looks upon her jest as an elder sister, and oi doan't moint how much she blows me up—and she does it pretty hot sometimes, oi can tell ee; but oi should just loike to hear anyone say a word agin her; but theere no one in Varley would do that. Every one has a good word for Polly; for when there's sickness in the house, or owt be wrong, Polly's always ready to help. Oi do believe that there never was such a gal. If it hadn't been for her oi would ha' cut it long ago. Oi wouldn't go agin what ye said, Maister Ned; but oi am danged if oi could ha' stood it ef it hadn't been for Polly."

" I suppose," Ned said, "that now they have got the soldiers down in Marsden it will be all right about the mill."

" Oi caan't say," Bill replied; "nateral they doan't say nowt to me; but oi be sure that some'ats oop. They be a-drilling every night, and there will be trouble avore long. Oi doan't believe as they will venture to attack the mill as long as the sojers be in Marsden; but oi wouldn't give the price of a pint of ale for Foxey's loife ef they could lay their hands on him. He'd best not come up this way arter dark."

"He's not likely to do that," Ned said. "I am sure he is a coward or he would have put the mill to work weeks ago."

Secure in the protection of the troops, and proud of the new machinery which was at work in his mill, Mr. Mulready was now himself again. His smile had returned. He carried himself jauntily, and talked lightly and contemptuously of the threats of King Lud. Ned disliked him more in this mood than in the state of depression and irritation which had preceded it. The tones of hatred and contempt in which he spoke of the starving workmen jarred upon him greatly, and it needed all his determination and self-command to keep him from expressing his feelings. Mr. Mulready was quick in perceiving, from the expression of Ned's face, the annoyance which his remarks caused him, and reverted to the subject all the more frequently. With this exception, the home life was more pleasant than it had been before.

Mr. Mulready, in his satisfaction at the prospect of a new prosperity, was far more tolerant with his wife, and her spirits naturally rose with his. She had fully shared his fears as to the threats by the Luddites, and now agreed cordially with his diatribes against the workpeople, adopting all his opinions as her own.

Ned's acquaintance with Bill Swinton had long been a

grievance to her, and her constant complainings as to his love for low company had been one of the afflictions to which Ned had long been accustomed. Now, having her husband by her side, it was a subject to which she frequently reverted.

"Why can't you leave me alone, mother?" Ned burst out one day when Mr. Mulready had left the room. "Can't you leave me in quiet as to my friends, when in two or three months I shall be going away? Bill Swinton is going to enlist in the same regiment in which I am, so as to follow me all over the world.

"Would any of the fine friends you would like me to make do that? I like all the fellows at school well enough, but there is not one of them would do a fiftieth part as much for me as Bill would. Even you, mother, with all your prejudices, must allow that it will be a good thing for me to have some one with me who will really care for me, who will nurse me if I am sick or wounded, who would lay down his life for mine if necessary. I tell you there isn't a finer fellow than Bill living. Of course he's rough, and he's had no education, I know that; but it's not his fault. But a truer or warmer-hearted fellow never lived. He is a grand fellow. I wish I was only half as true and as honest and manly as he is. I am proud to have Bill as a friend. It won't be long before I have gone, mother. I have been fighting hard with myself so that there shall be peace and quietness in the house for the little time I have got to be here, and you make it harder for me."

"It's ridiculous your talking so," Mrs. Mulready said peevishly, "and about a common young fellow like this. I don't pretend to understand you, Ned. I never have, and never shall do. But I am sure the house will be much more comfortable when you have gone. Whatever trouble there is with my husband is entirely your making. I only wonder that he puts up with your ways as he does. If his temper was not as good as yours is bad he would not be able to do so."

"All right, mother," Ned said. "He is an angel, he is, we all know, and I am the other thing. Well, if you are contented, that's the great thing, isn't it? I only hope you will always be so; but there," he said, calming himself with a great effort as his father's last words again came into his mind, "don't let's quarrel, mother. I am sorry for what I have said. It's quite right that you should stick up for your husband, and I do hope that when I go you will, as you say, be more comfortable and happy. Perhaps you will. I am sure I hope so. Well, I know I am not nice with him. I can't help it. It's my beastly temper, I suppose. That's an old story. Come, mother, I have only a short time to be at home now. Let us both try and make it as pleasant as we can, so that when I am thousands of miles away, perhaps in India, we may have it to look back upon. You try and leave my friends alone and I will try and be as pleasant as I can with your husband."

Mrs. Mulready was crying now.

"You know, Ned, I would love you if you would let

me, only you are so set against my husband. I am sure
he always means kindly. Look how he takes to little
Lucy, who is getting quite fond of him."

"Yes, I am very glad to think that he is, mother,"
Ned said earnestly. "You see Lucy is much younger, and
naturally remembers compaiatively little about her father,
and has been able to take to Mr. Mulready without our
prejudices. I am very glad to see that he really does like
her—in fact I do think he is getting quite fond of her.
I shall go away feeling quite easy about her. I wish I
could say as much about Charlie. He is not strong, like
other boys, and feels unkindness very sharply. I can see
him shrink and shiver when your husband speaks to him,
and am afraid he will have a very bad time of it when I
am gone."

"I am sure, Ned, he will get on very well," Mrs. Mulready said. "I have no doubt that when he gets rid of
the example you set him—I don't want to begin to quarrel
again—but of the example you set him of dislike and
disrespect to Mr. Mulready, that he will soon be quite
different. He will naturally turn to me again instead of
looking to you for all his opinions, and things will go on
smoothly and well."

"I am sure I hope so, mother. Perhaps I have done
wrong in helping to set Charlie against Mulready. Perhaps when I have gone, too, things will be easier for him.
If I could only think so I should go away with a lighter
heart. Well, anyhow, mother, I am glad we have had this
talk. It is not often we get a quiet talk together now."

"I am sure it is not my fault," Mrs. Mulready said in a slightly injured tone.

"Perhaps not, mother," Ned said kindly. "With the best intentions, I know I am always doing things wrong. It's my way, I suppose. Anyhow, mother, I really have meant well, and I hope you will think of me kindly after I have gone."

"You may be sure I shall do that, Ned," his mother said, weeping again. "I have no doubt the fault has been partly mine too, but you see women don't understand boys, and can't make allowances for them."

And so Ned kissed his mother for the first time since the day when she had returned home from her wedding tour, and mother and son parted on better terms than they had done for very many months, and Ned went with a lightened heart to prepare his lessons for the next day.

CHAPTER XII.

MURDERED!

IN spite of Ned's resolutions that he would do nothing to mar the tranquillity of the last few weeks of his being at home, he had difficulty in restraining his temper the following day at tea. Never had he seen his stepfather in so bad a humour. Had he known that things had gone wrong at the mill that day, that the new machine had broken one of its working parts and had brought everything to a standstill till it could be repaired, he would have been able to make allowances for Mr. Mulready's ill-humour.

Not knowing this he grew pale with the efforts which he made to restrain himself as his stepfather snarled at his wife, snapped at Lucy and Charlie, and grumbled and growled at everything throughout the meal. Everything that was said was wrong, and at last, having silenced his wife and her children, the meal was completed in gloomy silence. The two boys went into the little room off the hall which they used of an evening to prepare their lessons for next day. Charlie, who came in last, did not shut the door behind him.

"That is a nice man, our stepfather," Ned said in a cold fury. "His ways get more and more pleasant every day; such an amiable, popular man, so smiling and pleasant!"

"Oh! it's no use saying anything," Charlie said in an imploring voice, "it only makes things worse."

"Worse!" Ned exclaimed indignantly; "how could they be worse? Well may they call him Foxey, for foxey he is, a double-faced snarling brute."

As the last word issued from Ned's lips he reeled under a tremendous box on the ear from behind. Mr. Mulready was passing through the hall—for his gig was waiting at the door to take him back to the mill, where some fitters would be at work till late, repairing the damages to the machine—when he had caught Ned's words, which were spoken at the top of his voice.

The smouldering anger of months burst at once into a flame heightened by the ill-humour which the day's events had caused, and he burst into the room and almost felled Ned to the ground with his swinging blow. Recovering himself, Ned flew at him, but the boy was no match for the man, and Mr. Mulready's passion was as fierce as his own; seizing his throat with his left hand and forcing him back into a corner of the room, his stepfather struck him again and again with all his force with his right.

Charlie had run at once from the room to fetch his mother, and it was scarcely a minute after the commence-

MR. MULREADY'S ATTACK UPON HIS STETSON.

ment of the outbreak that she rushed into the room, and with a scream threw her arms round her husband.

"The young scoundrel!" Mr. Mulready exclaimed panting, as he released his hold of Ned; "he has been wanting a lesson for a long time, and I have given him one at last. He called me Foxey, the young villain, and said I was a double-faced snarling brute; let him say so again and I will knock his head off."

But Ned just at present was not in a condition to repeat his words; breathless and half stunned he leaned in the corner, his breath came in gasps, his face was as pale as death, his cheek was cut, there were red marks on the forehead which would speedily become black, and the blood was flowing from a cut on his lip, his eyes had a dazed and half-stupid look.

"Oh! William!" Mrs. Mulready said as she looked at her son, "how could you hurt him so!"

"Hurt him, the young reptile!" Mr. Mulready said savagely. "I meant to hurt him. I will hurt him more next time."

Mrs. Mulready paid no attention to his words, but went up to Ned.

"Ned, my boy," she said tenderly, "what is it? Don't look like that, Ned; speak to me."

His mother's voice seemed to rouse Ned into consciousness. He drew a long breath, then slowly passed his hand across his eyes, and lips, and mouth. He looked at his mother and seemed about to speak, but no sound came from his lips. Then his eye fell on his stepfather, who, rather alarmed at the boy's appearance, was standing near the door. The expression of Ned's face changed, his mouth became set and rigid, his eyes dilated, and Mr. Mulready, believing that he was about to spring upon him, drew back hastily half a step and threw up his hands to defend himself. Mrs. Mulready threw herself in Ned's way; the boy made no effort to put her aside, but kept his eyes fixed over her shoulder at his stepfather.

"Take care!" he said hoarsely, "it will be my turn next time, and when it comes I will kill you, you brute."

"Oh, go away, William!" Mrs. Mulready cried; "oh! do go away, or there will be more mischief. Oh! Ned, do sit down, and don't look so dreadful; he is going now."

Mr. Mulready turned and went with a laugh which he intended to be scornful, but in which there was a strong tinge of uneasiness. He had always in his heart been afraid of this boy with his wild and reckless temper, and felt that in his present mood Ned was capable of anything. Still as Mr. Mulready took his seat in his gig his predominant feeling was satisfaction.

"I am glad I have given him a lesson," he muttered to himself, "and have paid him off for months of insolence. He won't try it on again, and as for his threats, pooh! he'll be gone in a few weeks, and there will be an end of it."

After he had gone Mrs. Mulready tried to sooth Ned, but the boy would not listen to her, and in fact did not seem to hear her.

"Don't you mind, mother," he said in a strange quiet

voice, "I will pay him off;" and muttering these words over and over again he went out into the hall, took down his cap in a quiet mechanical sort of way, put it on, opened the door, and went out.

"Oh! Charlie," Mrs. Mulready said to her second son, who, sobbing bitterly, had thrown himself down in a chair by the table, and was sitting with his head on his hands, "there will be something terrible come of this! Ned's temper is so dreadful, and my husband was wrong, too. He should never have beaten him so, though Ned did say such things to him. What shall I do? these quarrels will be the death of me. I suppose Ned will be wandering about all night again. Do put on your cap, Charlie, and go out and see if you can find him, and persuade him to come home and go to bed; perhaps he will listen to you."

Charlie was absent an hour, and returned saying that he could not find his brother.

"Perhaps he's gone up to Varley as he did last time," Mrs. Mulready said. "I am sure I hope he has, else he will be wandering about all night, and he had such a strange look in his face that there's no saying where he might go to, or what he might do."

Charlie was almost heart-broken, and sat up till long past his usual time waiting for his brother's return. At last his eyes would no longer keep open, and he stumbled up stairs to bed, where he fell asleep almost as his head touched the pillow, in spite of his resolution to be awake until Ned returned.

Down stairs Mrs. Mulready kept watch. She did not

(251)   o

expect Ned to return, but she was listening for the wheels of her husband's gig. It was uncertain at what time he would return; for when he rose from the tea-table she had asked him what time he expected to be back, and he had replied that he could not say; he should stop until the repairs were finished, and she was to go to bed and not bother.

So at eleven o'clock she went up stairs, for once before when he had been out late and she had sat up he had been much annoyed; but after she got in bed she lay for hours listening for the sound of the wheels. At last she fell asleep and dreamed that Ned and her husband were standing at the end of a precipice grappling fiercely together in a life-and-death struggle. She was awaked at last by a knocking at the door; she glanced at her watch, which hung above her head; it was but half-past six.

"What is it, Mary?"

"Please, mum, there's a constable below, and he wants to speak to you immediate."

Mrs. Mulready sprang from the bed and began to dress herself hurriedly. All sorts of mischief that might have come to Ned passed rapidly through her mind; her husband had not returned, but no doubt he had stopped at the mill all night watching the men at work. His absence scarcely occasioned her a moment's thought. In a very few minutes she was down stairs in the kitchen, where the constable was standing waiting for her. She knew him by sight, for Marsden possessed but four constables, and they were all well-known characters.

"What is it?" she asked; "has anything happened to my son?"

"No, mum," the constable said in a tone of surprise, "I didn't know as he wasn't in bed and asleep, but I have some bad news for you, mum; it's a bad job altogether."

"What is it?" she asked again; "is it my husband?"

"Well, mum, I am sorry to say as it be. A chap came in early this morning and told me as summat had happened, so I goes out, and half a mile from the town I finds it just as he says."

"But what is it?" Mrs. Mulready gasped.

"Well, mum, I am sorry to have to tell you, but there was the gig all smashed to atoms, and there was the little black mare lying all in a heap with her neck broke, and there was ——," and he stopped.

"My husband!" Mrs. Mulready gasped.

"Yes, marm, I be main sorry to say it were. There, yards in front of them, were Mr. Mulready just stiff and cold. He'd been flung right out over the hoss's head. I expect he had fallen on his head and must have been killed roight out; and the worst of it be, marm, as it warn't an accident, for there, tight across the road, about eighteen inches above the ground, was a rope stretched tight atween a gate on either side. It was plain enough to see what had happened. The mare had come tearing along as usual at twelve mile an hour in the dark, and she had caught the rope, and in course there had been a regular smash."

The pretty colour had all gone from Mrs. Mulready's

face as he began his story, but a ghastly palor spread over her face, and a look of deadly horror came into her eyes as he continued.

"Oh, Ned, Ned," she wailed, "how could you!" and then she fell senseless to the ground.

The constable raised her and placed her in a chair.

"Are you sure the master's dead?" the servant asked, wiping her eyes.

"Sure enough," the constable said. "I have sent the doctor off already, but it's no good, he's been dead hours and hours. But," he continued, his professional instincts coming to the surface, "what did she mean by saying, 'Oh, Ned, how could you!' She asked me, too, first about him; ain't he at home?"

"No, he ain't," the servant said, "and ain't been at home all night; there were a row between him and maister last even; they had a fight. Maister Charlie he ran into the parlour as I was a clearing away the tea-things, hallowing out as maister was a killing Ned. Missis she ran in and I heard a scream, then maister he drove off, and a minute or two later Maister Ned he went out, and he ain't come back again. When I went in with the candles I could see missis had been a crying. That's all I know about it."

"And enough too," the constable said grimly "This here be a pretty business. Well, you had best get your missis round and see about getting the place ready for the corpse. They have gone up with a stretcher to bring him back. They will be here afore long. I must go up to Justice Thompson's and tell him all about it. This be a pretty kittle of fish, surely. I be main sorry, but I have got my duty to do."

An hour later Williams the constable with a companion started out in search of Ned Sankey, having a warrant in his pocket for his arrest on the charge of wilful murder.

The excitement in Marsden when it became known that Mr. Mulready had been killed was intense, and it was immensely heightened when it was rumoured that a warrant had been issued for the arrest of his stepson on the charge of murder. Quite a little crowd hung all day round the house with closed blinds, within which their so lately active and bustling townsman was lying.

All sorts of conjectures were rife, and there were many who said that they had all along expected harm would come of the marriage which had followed so soon after the death of Captain Sankey. The majority were loud in expression of their sympathy with the dead mill-owner, recalling his cheery talk and general good temper. Others were disposed to think that Ned had been driven to the act: but among very few was there any doubt as to his guilt. It was recalled against him that he had before been in the dock for his assault upon Mr. Hathorn, and that it had been proved that he had threatened to kill his master. His sullen and moody demeanour at the marriage of his mother told terribly against him, and the rumours of the previous quarrel when Ned had assaulted his stepfather, and which, re-lated with many exaggerations, had at the time furnished a subject of gossip in the town, also told heavily to his disadvantage.

Williams having learned from the servant that Ned was in the habit of going up to Varley had first made his inquiries there; but neither Bill nor Luke Marner, who were, the constable speedily learned, his principal friends there, had seen him. Varley was greatly excited over the news of the murder. Many of the men worked at Mulready's mill, and had brought back the news at an early hour, as all work was of course suspended.

There was no grief expressed in Varley at Mr. Mulready's death, indeed the news was received with jubilant exultation. "A good job too," was the general verdict; and the constable felt that were Ned in the village he would be screened by the whole population. He was convinced, however, that both Bill Swinton and Luke Marner were ignorant of his whereabouts, so genuine had been their astonishment at his questions, and so deep their indignation when they learned his errand.

"Thou duss'n't believe it, Luke?" Bill Swinton said as he entered the latter's cottage.

" No, lad, oi duss'n't," Luke said; "no more does Polly here, but it looks main awkward," he said, slowly stroking his chin, "if as how what the constable said is right, and there was a fight atween them that evening."

" Maister Ned were a hot 'un," Bill said; " he allus said as how he had a dreadful temper, though oi never seed nowt of it in him, and he hated Foxey like poison; that oi allow; but unless he tells me hisself as he killed him nowt will make me believe it. He might ha picked up summat handy when Foxey hit him and smashed him, but oi don't believe it of Maister Ned as he would ha done it arterwards."

"He war a downright bad 'un war Foxey," Luke said, "vor sure. No worse in the district, and there's many a one as would rejoice as he's gone to his account, and oi believe as whoever's done it has saved Captain Lud from a job; but there, it's no use a talking of that now. Now, look here, Bill, what thou hast got to do be this. Thou hast got to find the boy; oi expect he be hiding somewheres up on t' moors. Thou knowst better nor oi wheere he be likely vor to be. Voind him out, lad, an tell him as they be arter him. Here be ten punds as oi ha had laying by me for years ready in case of illness; do thou give it to him and tell him he be heartily welcome to it, and can pay me back agin when it suits him. Tell him as he'd best make straight for Liverpool and git aboard a ship there for 'Merikee—never moind whether he did the job or whether he didn't. Things looks agin him now, and he best be on his way."

"Oi'll do't," Bill said, "and oi'll bid thee good-bye, Luke, and thee too, Polly, for ye won't see me back agin. Of course I shall go wi' him. He havn't got man's strength yet, and oi can work for us both. I bain't a going to let him go by hisself, not loikely."

"Thou art roight, lad," Luke said heartily. "Dang it all, lad, thou speak'st loike a man. Oi be sorry thou art going, Bill, for oi loike thee; but thou be right to go wi'

this poor lad. Good-bye, lad, and luck be wi' ye;" and
Luke wrung Bill's hand heartily.

"I sha'n't say good-bye, Bill," Mary Powlett said quietly.
"I don't think Ned Sankey can have done this thing,
and if he hasn't you will find that he will not run away,
but will stay here and face it out."

"Then he will be a fool," Luke Marner said. "I tell ee
the evidence be main strong agin him, and whether he
be innocent or not he will find it hard to clear hisself.
Oi don't think much the worst of him myself if he
done it, and most in Varley will be o' my way o' thinking.
Foxey war a tyrant if ever there war one, and the man
what was so hard a maister to his hands would be loike
to be hard to his wife's children."

"Don't speak like that, feyther," Polly said; "murder is
murder, you know."

"Ay, lass, and human natur be human natur, and it
be no use your going agin it. If he ha been and ill-
treated the boy, and I don't doubt as he has, thou may'st
argue all noight, but thou won't get me to say as oi blames
him much if he has done it. Oi don't suppose as he meant
to kill him—not vor a moment. I should think hard
of him if oi thowt as how he did. He meant, oi reckon,
vor to throw his horse down and cut his knees, knowing,
as every one did, as Mulready were moighty proud of his
horse, and he may have reckoned as Foxey would git a
good shake, and some bruises as well, as a scare, but oi
doan't believe, not vor a moment, as he meant vor to kill
him. That's how oi reads it, lass."

" Well, it may be so," Mary assented. "It is possible he may have done it, meaning really only to give him a fright and a shake; but I hope he didn't. Still if that was how it happened I will shake hands, Bill, and wish you good-bye and good luck, for it would be best for him to get away, for I am afraid that the excuse that he only meant to frighten and not to kill him will not save him. I am sorry you are going, Bill, very sorry; but if you were my own brother I would not say a word to stop you. Didn't his feyther give up his life to save little Janey? and I would give mine to save his. But I do think it will be good for you, Bill; times are bad, and it has been very hard for you lately in Varley. I know all about it, and you will do better across the seas. You will write, won't you, sometimes?"

" Never fear," Bill said huskily, " oi will wroite, Polly; good-bye, and God bless you all; but it mayn't be good-bye, for oi mayn't foind him;" and wringing the hands of Luke and Polly Bill returned to his cottage, hastily packed up a few things in a kit, slung it over his shoulder on a stick, and started out in search of Ned.

Late that evening there came a knock at the door of Luke's cottage. On opening it he found Bill standing there.

" Back again, Bill!—then thou hasn't found him?"

" No," Bill replied in a dejected voice. " Oi ha' hoonted high and low vor him; oi ha' been to every place on the moor wheer we ha' been together, and wheer oi thowt as he might be a-waiting, knowing as oi should set out to look for him as soon as oi heard the news. Oi doin't think he be nowhere on the moor. Oi have been a-tramping ever sin' oi started this mourning. Twice oi ha' been down Maarston to see if so be as they've took him, but nowt ain't been seen of him. Oi had just coom from there now. Thou'st heerd, oi suppose, as the crowner's jury ha found as Foxey wer murdered by him; but it bain't true, you know, Luke—be it ?"

Bill made the assertion stoutly, but there was a tremulous eagerness in the question which followed it. He was fagged and exhausted. His faith in Ned was strong, but he had found the opinion in the town so unanimous against him that he longed for an assurance that some-one beside himself believed in Ned's innocence.

" Oi doan't know, Bill," Luke Marner said, stroking his chin as he always did when he was thinking; " oi doan't know, Bill—oi hoape he didn't do it, wi' all my heart. But oi doan't knaw aboot it. He war sorely tried—that be sartain. But if he did it, he did it; it makes no differ to me. It doan't matter to me one snap ov the finger whether the lad killed Foxey or whether he didn't—that bain't my business or yours. What consarns me is, as the son of the man as saved my child's loife at t' cost of his own be hunted by the constables and be in risk of his loife. That's t' question as comes home to me—oi've had nowt else ringing in my ears all day. Oi ha' been oot too a sarching high and low. Oi ain't a found him, but oi ha made oop moi moind whaat I be agoing to do."

They had moved a little away from the cottage now, but Luke lowered his voice:

"Oi be a-going down to t' town in the morning to give moiself oop vor the murder of Foxey."

Bill gave an exclamation of astonishment:

"But thou didn'st do it, Luke?"

"I moight ha' done it for owt thou knaw'st, Bill. He wer the worst of maisters, and, as thou knaw'st, Bill, oi hated him joost as all the country-side did. He's been warned by King Lud and ha' been obliged to get the sojers at his factory. Well, thou knowest it was nateral as he would drive down last noight to see how t' chaps at t' engine was a-getting on, and it coomed across my moind as it wer a good opportunity vor to finish un; so ther thou hast it."

Bill gazed in astonishment through the darkness at his companion.

"But it bain't true, Luke? Thou wast talking to me arter thou coom'd out of the Coo at noine o'clock, and thou saidst as thou was off to bed."

"Nowt of the koind," Luke replied. "Oi told ye, thou knaw'st, as I wer a-going down to t' toon and oi had got a job in hand. Oi spoke mysterous loike, and you noticed as how oi had got a long rope coiled up in moi hand."

Bill gave a gasp of astonishment.

"That's what thou hast got to say," Luke said doggedly; "only astead o' its being at noine o'clock it war at ten. Oi were just a-slipping owt of the cottage, t' others were all asleep and knew nowt aboot moi having goone out."

Bill was silent now.

"Oi wish oi had a-thowt of it," he said at last; "oi would ha' doon it moiself."

"Oi wouldn't ha' let thee, Bill," Luke said quietly. "He be a friend of thine, and oi knaw thou lovest him loike a brother, and a soight mor'n most brothers; but it be moi roight. The captain gave his loife vor moi child's, and oi bee a going vor to give mine for his. That will make us quits. Beside, thou art young; oi be a-getting on. Jarge, he will be a-arning money soon; and Polly, she can get a place in sarvice, and 'ul help t' young uns. They will manage. Oi ha' been thinking it over in all loites, and ha' settled it all in moi moind."

Bill was silent for a time and then said:

"Ther be one thing agin' it, Luke, and it be this: As we can't hear nowt of Maister Ned, oi be a thinking as he ha' made straight vor Liverpool or Bristol or London, wi' a view to going straight across the seas or of 'listing, or doing somewhat to keep out of t' way. He be sure to look in t' papers to see how things be a-going on here; and as sure as he sees as how you've gived yourself up and owned up as you ha' done it, he will coom straight back again and say as how it were him.

"Maister Ned might ha' killed Foxey in a passion, but not loike this. He didn't mean to kill him, but only vor to give him a shaake and frighten him. But oi be sartin sure as he wouldn't let another be hoonged in his place. So ye see thou'd do more harm nor good, vor you might bring him back just when he had gone safe away."

"Oi didn't think of that," Luke said, rubbing his chin. "That be so, sure-ly. He'd be bound to coom back agin. Well, lad, oi will think it over agin avore moorning, and do thou do t' same. Thou knaw'st moi wishes now. We ha' got atween us to get Maister Ned off—that be the thing as be settled. It doan't matter how it's done, but it's got to be done soomhow; and oi rely on thee to go into the box and sweer sommat as 'ull maake moi story good, whatever it be.

"There can't be nowt wrong about it—a loife vor a loife be fair, anyway. There be more nor eno' in Yorkshire in these toimes, and one more or less be of no account to anyone."

"Oi be thy man, Luke," Bill said earnestly. "Whatever as thou sayest oi will sweer to; but I would reyther change places."

"That caan't be, Bill, so it bain't no use thinking aboot it. Oi knaw thou wilt do thy best vor Polly and t' young uns. It 'ull be rough on her, but it bain't to be helped; and as she will be going away from Varley and settling elsewhere, it wouldn't be brought up agin her as she had an uncle as were a Luddite and got hoong for killing a bad maister. Good-noight, lad! oi will see thee i' t' morning."

CHAPTER XIII.

COMMITTED FOR TRIAL.

FTER a talk with Luke Marner early in the morning Bill Swinton went down into Marsden to hear if there was any news of Ned. He was soon back again. "Maister Ned's took," he said as he met Luke, who was standing in front of his cottage awaiting his return before starting out to renew his search for Ned. "Oi hear, at noine o'clock last noight he walked in to Justice Thompson's and said as he had coom to give hisself up. He said as how he had been over at Painton, where the old woman as was his nurse lives; and directly as the news coom in t' arternoon as Foxey had been killed and he was wanted for the murder, he coom straight over."

"That's roight," Luke said heartily; "that settles it. He must ha' been innocent or he would ha' bolted straight away, and not coom back and gi'd hisself oop to justice. It were only his hiding away as maade oi think as he moight ha' done it. Noo in course he will be able to clear hisself; for if he was over at Painton, why, he couldn't be here—that be plain to anyone."

"Oi be aveared, by what t' constable told me, as he won't be able vor to prove it. It seems as how he didn't get to Painton till t' morning. He says as how he were awalking aboot on t' moor all night. So you see he will have hard work vor to clear hisself."

"Then I shall ha' to give meself up," Luke said quietly. "Ye see as it can't do him harm now, 'cause he ha' coom back; and ef oi says as I killed the man they will open the doors, and he will only have to walk out."

"Oi ha' been athinking of that as I coom back," Bill said, "and oi doan't think as oi see my way clear through it now. Firstly, if Maister Ned did it, of course he will hold his tongue and leave 'em to prove it, which maybe they can't do; so he has a chance of getting off. But if you cooms forward and owns up, he will be saaf, if he did it, to say so at once; and so you will have done him harm rather nor good. Vor of course he will be able to prove his story better nor you will yourn, and you will have put the noose round his neck instead of getting it put round yourn. In the second place, it be loike enough as they lawyer chaps moight find out as your story weren't true when they coom to twisting me inside owt in the box. They might foind as oi war a-swearing false. There be never no saying. They moight prove as that bit of rope warn't yourn. Polly moight swear as she hadn't been asleep till arter the time you said you went out, and that you never moved as long as she war awake. Lots of unexpected things moight turn up to show it war a lie and then you know they'd drop onto Maister Ned wourse nor ever."

"I doan't believe they would ask you any questions, Bill. When a man cooms and says, 'Oi did a murder,' they doan't want to ask many questions aboot it. They takes it vor granted as he wouldn't be such a fool as vor to say he did it when he didn't. But th' other point be more sarous. It be loike enough as t' lad did it, and if he did he will out wi' it when oi cooms forward. If oi could get to see him first oi moight argue him into holding his tongue by pointing owt that moi loife bain't of so much valley as hissen, also that I owe a debt to his feyther."

"Well, oi ha' been thinking it over," Bill said, "and moi opinion is thou had best hold thy tongue till the trial. Thou can'st be in the court. Ef the jury foind him innocent, of course thou will't hold thy tongue; ef they foind him guilty, then thou'lt get up in the court, and thou'lt say to the joodge, civil loike:

"Moi lord, the gentlemen of the jury have made a mistake; oi am the chap as killed Foxey, and oi ha' got a young man here as is a witness as moi words is true."

"Perhaps that will be the best way, Bill," Luke said thoughtfully. "Oi ha' bin thinking how we moight get over Polly's evidence agin me; every noight oi will get up regular and coom and ha' a talk wi' you; oi will coom out wi'out my shoes as quiet as a cat, and then if Polly sweers as oi didn't leave t' house that noight thou can'st sweer as she knaws nothing at all aboot it, as oi ha' been out every noight to see thee."

So the matter was allowed to stand for the time; and Bill and Luke, when they had had their break-fast, went down again to Marsden to hear what was going on.

Marsden was greatly excited. The sensation caused by the news of the murder scarcely exceeded that which was aroused when it was heard that Ned Sankey had come in and given himself up. Some thought that at the exami-nation which was to take place at noon he would at once confess his guilt, while others believed that he would plead not guilty, and would throw the burden of proving that he killed his stepfather upon the prosecution.

All through the previous day Mrs. Mulready had been the central object of interest to the town gossips pending the capture of her son. Dr. Green had been in and out of the house all day. It was known that she had passed from one fit of hysterics into another, and that the doctor was seriously alarmed about her state. Rumours were about that the servants, having been interviewed at the back gate, said, that in the intervals of her screaming and wild laughter she over and over again accused Ned as the murderer of her husband. Dr. Green, when questioned, peremptorily refused to give any information whatever as to his patient's opinions or words.

"The woman is well-nigh a fool at the best of times," he said irritably, "and at present she knows no more what she is saying than a baby. Her mind is thrown completely off any little balance that it had, and she is to all intents and purposes a lunatic."

Only with his friend Mr. Porson, who called upon him after the first visit had been paid to Mrs. Mulready immediately after her husband's body had been brought in. did Dr. Green discuss in any way what had happened.

"I agree with you, Porson, in doubting whether the poor boy had a hand in this terrible business. We both know, of course, that owing to the bad training and total absence of control when he was a child in India his temper was, when he first came here, very hot and ungovernable. His father often deplored the fact to me, blaming himself as being to a great extent responsible for it, through not having had time to watch and curb him when he was a child; but he was, as you say, an excellently disposed boy, and your testimony to the efforts which he has made to overcome his faults is valuable. But I cannot conceal from you, who are a true friend of the boy's, what I should certainly tell to no one else, namely, that I fear that his mother's evidence will be terribly against him.

"She has always been prejudiced against him. She is a silly selfish woman. So far as I could judge she cared little for her first husband, who was a thousand times too good for her; but strangely enough she appears to have had something like a real affection for this man Mulready, who, between ourselves, I believe, in spite of his general popularity in the town, to have been a bad fellow. One doesn't like to speak ill of the dead under ordinary circumstances, but his character is an important element in the question before us. Of course among my poorer patients I hear things of which people in general are ignorant, and it is certain that there was no employer in this part of the country so thoroughly and heartily detested by his men."

"I agree with you cordially," Mr. Porson said. "Unfortunately I know from Ned's own lips that the lad hated his stepfather; but I can't bring myself to believe that he has done this."

"I hope not," the doctor said gravely, "I am sure I hope not; but I have been talking with his brother, who is almost heart-broken, poor boy, and he tells me that there was a terrible scene last night. It seems that Mulready was extremely cross and disagreeable at tea-time; nothing, however, took place at the table; but after the meal was over, and the two boys were alone together in that little study of theirs, Ned made some disparaging remarks about Mulready. The door, it seems, was open. The man overheard them, and brutally assaulted the boy, and indeed Charlie thought that he was killing him. He rushed in and fetched his mother, who interfered, but not before Ned had been sadly knocked about. Mulready then drove off to his factory, and Ned, who seems to have been half stunned, went out almost without saying a word, and, as you know, hasn't been heard of since.

"It certainly looks very dark against him. You and I, knowing the boy, and liking him, may have our doubts, but the facts are terribly against him, and unless he is absolutely in the position to prove an alibi, I fear that it will go hard with him."

"I cannot believe it," Mr. Porson said, "although I admit that the facts are terribly against him. Pray, if you get an opportunity urge upon his mother that her talk will do Ned horrible damage and may cost him his life. I shall at once go and instruct Wakefield to appear for him, if he is taken, and to obtain the best professional assistance for his defence. I feel completely unhinged by the news, the boy has been such a favourite of mine ever since I came here; he has fought hard against his faults, and had the makings of a very fine character in him. God grant that he may be able to clear himself of this terrible accusation!"

Ned's first examination was held on the morning after he had given himself up, before Mr. Simmonds and Mr. Thompson. The sitting was a private one. The man who first found Mr. Mulready's body testified to the fact that a rope had been laid across the road. Constable Williams proved that when he arrived upon the spot nothing had been touched. Man and horse lay where they had fallen, the gig was broken in pieces, a strong rope was stretched across the road. He said that on taking the news to Mrs. Mulready he had learned from the servants that the prisoner had not slept at home that night, and that there had been a serious quarrel between him and the deceased the previous evening.

After hearing this evidence Ned was asked if he was in a position to account for the time which had elapsed between his leaving home and his arrival at his nurse's cottage.

He replied that he could only say that he had been wandering on the moor.

The case was remanded for a week, as the evidence of Mrs. Mulready and the others in the house would be necessary, and it was felt that a mother could not be called upon to testify against her son with her husband lying dead in the house.

"I am sorry indeed to see you in this position," Mr. Simmonds said to Ned. "My friendship for your late father, and I may say for yourself, makes the position doubly painful to me, but I can only do my duty. I should advise you to say nothing at this period of the proceedings; but if there is anything which you think of importance to say, and which will give another complexion to the case, I am ready to hear it."

"I have nothing to say, sir," Ned said quietly, "except that I am wholly innocent of the affair. As you may see by my face I was brutally beaten by my stepfather on the evening before his death. I went out of the house scarce knowing what I was doing. I had no fixed intention of going anywhere or of doing anything, I simply wanted to get away from home. I went up onto the moors and wandered about, I suppose for some hours. Then I threw myself down under the shelter of a pile of stones and lay there awake till it was morning. Then I determined to go to the house of my old nurse and to stop there until I was fit to be seen. In the afternoon

I heard what had taken place here, and that I was accused of the murder, and I at once came over here and gave myself up."

"As you are not in a position to prove what you state," Mr. Simmonds said, "we have nothing to do but to remand the case until this day week. I may say that I have received a letter from Dr. Green saying that he and Mr. Porson are ready to become your bail to any amount; but we could not think of accepting bail in a charge of murder."

Ned bowed and followed the constable without a word to the cells. His appearance had not been calculated to create a favourable impression. His clothes were stained and muddy; his lips were swollen, his eyes were discoloured and so puffed that he could scarcely see between the lids, his forehead was bruised and cut in several places. He had passed two sleepless nights; his voice had lost its clearness of ring and was low and husky. Mr. Simmonds shook his head to his fellow magistrate.

"I am afraid it's a bad case, Thompson, but the lad has been terribly ill-used, there is no doubt about that. It's a thousand pities he takes up the line of denying it altogether. If he were to say, what is no doubt the truth, that having been brutally beaten he put the rope across the road intending to punish and even injure his stepfather, but without any intention of killing him, I think under the circumstances of extreme provocation, and what interest we could bring to bear on the matter, he would get off the capital punishment, for the jury would be sure to recommend him to mercy. I shall privately let Green and Porson, who are evidently acting as his friends in the matter, know that I think it would be far better for him to tell the truth and throw himself on the mercy of the crown."

"They may not find him guilty," Mr. Thompson said. "The jury will see that he received very strong provocation; and after all, the evidence is, so far as we know at present, wholly circumstantial, and unless the prosecution can bring home to him the possession of the rope, it is likely enough they will give him the benefit of the doubt."

"His life is ruined anyhow," Mr. Simmonds said. "Poor lad! poor lad! Another fortnight and I was going to apply for a commission for him. I wish to Heavens I had done so at Christmas, and then all this misery would have been spared."

As soon as Ned had been led back to the cell Mr. Porson obtained permission to visit him. He found him in a strange humour.

"Well, my poor boy," he began, "this is a terrible business."

"Who do you mean it is a terrible business for, Mr. Porson, me or him?"

Ned spoke in a hard unnatural voice, without the slightest tone of trouble or emotion. Mr. Porson perceived at once that his nerves were brought up to such a state of tension by the events of the preceding forty-eight hours that he was scarce responsible for what he was saying.

"I think I meant for you, Ned. I cannot pretend to

have any feeling for the man who is dead, especially when
I look at your face."

"Yes, it is not a nice position for me," Ned said coldly,
"just at the age of seventeen to be suspected of the
murder of one's stepfather, and such a nice stepfather
too, such a popular man in the town! And not only
suspected, but with a good chance of being hung for it!"

"Ned, my dear boy," Mr. Porson said kindly, "don't
talk in that way. You know that we, your friends, are
sure that you did not do it."

"Are you quite sure, sir?" Ned said. "I am not quite
sure myself. I know I should have done it if I had had
the chance. I thought over all sorts of ways in which
I might kill him, and I wouldn't quite swear that I did
not think of this plan and carry it out, though it doesn't
quite seem to me that I did. I have no very definite
idea what happened that night, and certainly could give
but a vague account of myself from the time I left the
house till next morning, when I found myself lying stiff
and half frozen on the moor. Anyhow, whether I killed
him or not it's all the same. I should have done so if I
could. And if some one else has saved me the trouble I
suppose I ought to feel obliged to him."

Mr. Porson saw that in Ned's present state it was useless to talk to him. Two nights without sleep, together
with the intense excitement he had gone through, had
worked his brain to such a state of tension that he was
not responsible for what he was saying. Further conversation would do him harm rather than good. What

he required was rest and, if possible, sleep. Mr. Porson therefore only said quietly:

"We will not talk about it now, Ned; your brain is over-excited with all you have gone through. What you want now is rest and sleep."

"I don't feel sleepy, Mr. Porson. I don't feel as if I should ever get to sleep again. I don't look like it, do I?"

"No, Ned, I don't think you do at present; but I wish you did, my boy. Well, remember that we, your old friends, all believe you innocent of this thing, and that we will spare no pains to prove it to the world. I see," he said, looking at the table, "that you have not touched your breakfast. I am not surprised that you could not eat it. I will see that you have a cup of really good tea sent you in."

"No," Ned said with a laugh which it pained Mr. Porson to hear, "I have not eaten since I had tea at home. It was only the day before yesterday, but it seems a year."

On leaving the cell Mr. Porson went to Dr. Green, who lived only three or four doors away, told him of the state in which he had found Ned, and begged him to give him a strong and, as far as possible, a tasteless sedative, and to put it in a cup of tea.

"Yes, that will be the best thing," the doctor replied. "I had better not go and see him, for talking will do him harm rather than good. We shall be having him on our hands with brain-fever if this goes on. I will go round with the tea myself to the head constable and tell him that no one must on any account be permitted to see

Ned, and that rest and quiet are absolutely necessary for him. I will put a strong dose of opium into the tea."

Ten minutes later Dr. Green called upon the chief constable and told him that he feared from what he had heard from Mr. Porson that Ned was in a very critical state, and that unless he got rest and sleep he would probably have an attack of brain-fever, even if his mind did not give way altogether.

"I was intending to have him removed at once," the officer said, "to a comfortable room at my own house. He was only placed where he is temporarily. I exchanged a few words with him after the examination and was struck myself with the strangeness of his tone. Won't you see him?"

"I think that any talk is bad for him," the doctor said. "I have put a strong dose of opium in this tea, and I hope it will send him off to sleep. When he recovers I will see him."

"I think, doctor," the constable said significantly, "it would be a good thing if you were to see him at once. You see, if things go against him, and between ourselves the case is a very ugly one, if you could get in the box and say that you saw him here, and that, in your opinion, his mind was shaken, and that as likely as not he had not been responsible for his actions from the time he left his mother's house, it might save his life."

"That is a capital idea," Dr. Green said, "and Porson's evidence would back mine. Yes, I will go in and see him even if my visit does do him harm."

"I will move him into his new quarters first," the officer said; "then if he drinks the tea he may, if he feels sleepy, throw himself on the bed and go off. He will be quiet and undisturbed there."

Two or three minutes later the doctor was shown into a comfortable room. A fire was burning brightly, and the tea was placed on a little tray with a new roll and a pat of butter.

Ned's mood had somewhat changed. He received the doctor with a boisterous laugh.

"How are you, doctor? Here I am, you see, monarch of all I survey. This is the first time you have visited me in a room which I could consider entirely my own. Not a bad place either."

"I hope you will not be here long, Ned," Dr. Green said, humouring him. "We shall all do our best to get you out as soon as we can."

"I don't think your trying will be of much use, doctor; but what's the odds as long as you are happy!"

"That's right, my boy, nothing like looking at matters cheerfully. You know, lad, how warmly all your old friends are with you. Would you like me to bring Charlie next time I come?"

"No, no, doctor," Ned said almost with a cry. "No. I have thought it over, and Charlie must not see me. It will do him harm and I shall break down. I shall have to see him at the trial—of course he must be there—that will be bad enough."

"Very well," the doctor said quietly, "just as you like,

Ned. I shall be seeing you every day, and will give him news of you. I am going to see him now."

"Tell him I am well and comfortable and jolly," Ned said recklessly.

"I will tell him you are comfortable, Ned, and I should like to tell him that you had eaten your breakfast."

"Oh, yes! Tell him that. Say I ate it voraciously." And he swallowed down the cup of tea and took a bite at the roll.

"I will tell him," Dr. Green said. "I will come in again this evening, and will perhaps bring in with me a little medicine. You will be all the better for a soothing draught."

"I want no draughts," Ned said. "Why should I? I am as right as ninepence."

"Very well. We will see," the doctor said. "Now I must be going my rounds."

As soon as he had gone Ned began pacing up and down the room, as he had done the whole of the past night without intermission. Gradually, however, the powerful narcotic began to take effect. His walk became slower, his head began to droop, and at last he stumbled towards the bed in the corner of the room, threw himself heavily down, and was almost instantly sound asleep. Five minutes later the door opened quietly and Dr Green entered.

He had been listening outside the door, had noticed the change in the character of Ned's walk, and having heard the fall upon the bed, and had no fear of his rousing himself at his entrance. The boy was lying across the bed, and the doctor, who was a powerful man, lifted him gently and laid him with his head upon the pillow. He felt his pulse, and lifted his eyelid.

"It was a strong dose," he said to himself, "far stronger than I should have dared give him at any other time, but nothing less would have acted, with his brain in such an excited state. I must keep in the town to-day and look in from time to time and see how he is going on. It may be that I shall have to take steps to rouse him."

At the next visit Dr. Green looked somewhat anxious as he listened to the boy's breathing and saw how strongly he was under the influence of the narcotic. "Under any other circumstances," he said to the chief constable, who had entered the room with him, "I should take strong measures to arouse him at once, but as it is I will risk it. I know it is a risk both for him and me, for a nice scrape I should get in if he slipped through my fingers; but unless he gets sleep I believe his brain will go, and anything is better than that."

"Yes, poor lad," the officer said. "When I look at his face I confess my sympathies are all with him rather than with the man he killed."

"I don't think he killed him," the doctor said quietly. "I am almost sure he didn't."

"You don't say so!" the chief constable said, surprised. "I had not the least doubt about it."

"No. Nobody seems to have the least doubt about it," the doctor said bitterly. "I am almost sure that he had nothing to do with it; but if he did it it was when he was in a state of such passion that he was practically irresponsible for his actions. At any rate, I am prepared to swear that his mind is unhinged at present. I will go back now and fetch two or three books and will then sit by him. He needs watching."

For several hours the doctor sat reading by Ned's bedside. From time to time he leant over the lad, listened to his breathing, felt his pulse, and occasionally lifted his eyelid. After one of these examinations, late in the afternoon, he rose with a sigh of relief, pulled down the blind, gently drew the curtains, and then, taking his books, went down and noiselessly closed the door after him.

"Thank God! he will do now," he said to the chief constable; "but it has been a very near squeak, and I thought several times I should have to take immediate steps to wake him. However, the effects are passing off, and he will soon be in a natural sleep. Pray let the house be kept as quiet as possible, and let no one go near him. The chances are he will sleep quietly till morning."

The doctor called again the last thing that evening, but was told that no stir had been heard in Ned's room, and the same report met him when he came again next morning.

"That is capital," he said. "Let him sleep on. He has a long arrears to make up. I shall not be going out to-day; please send in directly he wakes."

"Very well," the officer replied. "I will put a man outside his door, and the moment a move is heard I will let you know."

CHAPTER XIV.

COMMITTED FOR TRIAL.

T was not until after mid-day that the message arrived, and Dr. Green at once went in. Ned was sitting on the side of the bed, a constable having come off with the message as soon as he heard him make the first move.

"Well, Ned, how are you now?" Dr. Green asked cheerfully as he went to the window and drew back the curtains. "Had a good sleep, my boy, and feel all the better for it, I hope."

"Yes, I think I have been asleep," Ned said in a far more natural voice than that of the previous day. "How did the curtains get drawn?"

"I drew them, Ned. I looked in in the afternoon, and found you fast asleep, so I darkened the room."

"Why, what time is it now?" Ned asked.

"Half-past twelve, Ned."

"Half-past twelve! Why, how can that be?"

"Why, my boy, you have had twenty-two hours' sleep."

Ned gave an exclamation of astonishment.

"You had two nights' arrears to make up for, and Nature is not to be outraged in that way with impunity. I am very thankful that you had a good night, for I was really anxious about you yesterday."

"I feel rather heavy and stupid now," Ned said, "but I am all the better for my sleep. Let me think," he began, looking round the room, for up till now remembrance of the past had not come back again, "what am I doing here? Oh! I remember now."

"You are here, my boy, on a charge of which I have no doubt we shall prove you innocent. Of course Porson and I and all your friends know you are innocent, but we have got to prove it to the world, and we shall want all your wits to help us. But we needn't talk about that now. The first thing for you to do is to put your head in a basin of water. By the time you have had a good wash your breakfast will be here. I told my old cook to prepare it when I came out, and as you are a favourite of hers I have no doubt it will be a good one. After you have discussed that we can talk matters over. I sent my boy down to the school just now to ask Porson to come up here in half an hour. Then we three can lay our heads together and see what are the best steps to take."

"Let me see," Ned said thoughtfully "Was I dreaming, or have I seen Mr. Porson since I came here?"

"You are not dreaming, Ned; but the fact is, you were not quite yourself yesterday. The excitement you had gone through had been too much for you."

"It all seems a dream to me," Ned said in a hopeless tone, "a confused, muddled sort of dream."

"Don't think about it now, Ned," the doctor said cheerfully, "but get off your things at once, and set to and sluice your head well with water. I will be back in a quarter of an hour with the breakfast."

At the end of that time the doctor returned, his boy carrying a tray. The constable on duty took it from him, and would have carried it into Ned's room, but the doctor said:

"Give it me, Walker. I will take it in myself. I don't want him to see any of you just at present. His head's in a queer state, and the less he is impressed with the fact that he is in charge the better."

Dr. Green found Ned looking all the better for his wash. The swelling of his face had now somewhat abated, but the bruises were showing out in darker colours than before; still he looked fresher and better.

"Here is your breakfast, Ned, and if you don't enjoy it Jane will be terribly disappointed."

"I shall enjoy it, doctor. I feel very weak; but I do think I am hungry."

"You ought to be, Ned, seeing that you have eaten nothing for two days."

The doctor removed the cloth which covered the tray. The meal consisted of three kidneys and two eggs, and a great pile of buttered toast. The steam curled out of the spout of a dainty china teapot, and there was a small jug brimful of cream.

The tears came into Ned's eyes.

"Oh! how good you are, doctor!"

"Nonsense, good?" the doctor said; "come, eat away, that will be the best thanks to Jane and me."

Ned needed no pressing. He ate languidly at first; but his appetite came as he went on, and he drank cup after cup of the fragrant tea, thick with cream. With the exception of one egg, he cleared the tray.

"There, doctor!" he said, as he pushed back his chair; "if you are as satisfied as I am you must be contented indeed."

"I am, Ned; that meal has done us both a world of good. Ah! here is Porson, just arrived at the right moment."

"How are you, Ned?" the master asked heartily.

"I am quite well, sir, thank you. Sleep and the doctor, and the doctor's cook, have done wonders for me. I hear you came yesterday, sir, but I don't seem to remember much about it."

"Yes, I was here, Ned," Mr. Porson said, "but you were pretty well stupid from want of sleep. However, I am glad to see you quite yourself again this morning."

"And now," the doctor said, "we three must put our heads together and see what is to be done. You understand, Ned, how matters stand, don't you?"

"Yes, sir," Ned said after a pause; "I seem to know that someone said that Mr. Mulready was dead, and someone thought that I had killed him, and then I started to come over to give myself up. Oh! yes, I remember that, and then there was an examination before the magistrates. I remember it all; but it seems just as if it had been a dream."

"Yes, that is what happened, Ned, and naturally it seems a dream to you, because you were so completely overcome by excitement and want of food and sleep that you were scarcely conscious of what was passing. Now we want you to think over quietly, as well as you can, what you did when you left home."

Ned sat for a long time without speaking. "It seems all confused," he said at last. "I don't even remember going out of the house. I can remember his striking me in the face again and again, and then I heard my mother scream, and everything seems to have become misty. But I know I was walking about; I know that I was worrying to get at him, and that if I had met him I should have attacked him, and if I had had anything in my hand I should have killed him."

"But you don't remember doing anything, Ned? You cannot recall that you went anywhere and got a rope and fastened it across the road with the idea of upsetting his gig on the way back from the mill?"

"No, sir," Ned said decidedly; "I can't recollect anything of that at all. I am quite sure if I had done that I should remember it; for I seem to remember, now I think of it, a good deal of what I did. Yes, I went up through Varley; the lights weren't out, and I wondered what Bill would say if I were to knock at his door and he opened it and saw what a state my face was in. Then

I went out on the moor, and it seems to me that I walked about for hours, and the longer I walked the more angry I was. At last—it could not have been long before morning, I think—I lay down for a time, and then when it was light I made up my mind to go over and see Abijah. I knew she would be with me. That's all I remember about it. Does my mother think I did it?"

Dr. Green hesitated a moment.

"Your mother is not in a state to think one way or the other, Ned; she is in such a state of grief that she hardly knows what she is saying or doing."

In fact Mrs. Mulready entertained no doubt whatever upon the subject, and had continued to speak of Ned's wickedness until Dr. Green that morning had lost all patience with her, and told her she ought to be ashamed of herself to be the first to accuse her son, and that if he was hung she would only have herself to blame for it.

Ned guessed by the doctor's answer that his mother was against him.

"It is curious," he said, "she did not take on so after my father's death, and he was always kind and good to her, while this man was just the reverse."

"There's never any understanding women," Dr. Green said testily, "and your mother is a singularly inconsequent and weak specimen of her sex. Well, Ned, and so that is all you can tell us about the way you passed that unfortunate evening. What a pity it is, to be sure, that you did not rouse up your friend Bill. His evidence would probably have cleared you at once. As it is, of course we believe your story, my boy. The question is, will the jury believe it?"

"I don't seem to care much whether they do or not," Ned said sadly, "unless we find the man who did it. Every one will think me guilty even if I am acquitted. Fancy going on living all one's life and knowing that everyone one meets is thinking to himself, 'That is the man who killed his stepfather'—it would be better to be hung at once."

"You must look at it in a more hopeful way than that, Ned," Mr. Porson said kindly; "many will from the first believe, with us, that you are innocent. You will live it down, my boy, and sooner or later we may hope and believe that God will suffer the truth to be known. At the worst, you know you need not go on living here. The world is wide, and you can go where your story is unknown.

"Do not look on the darkest side of things. And now, for the present, I have brought you down a packet of books. If I were you I would try to read—anything is better than going on thinking. You will want all your wits about you, and the less you worry your mind the better. Mr. Wakefield will represent you at the examination next week; but I do not see that there will be much for him to do, as I fear there is little doubt that you will be committed for trial, when of course we shall get the best legal assistance for you. I will tell him exactly what you have said to me, and he can then come and see you or not as he likes. I shall come in every day. I have already obtained permission from the magistrates to do so. I shall go now and see Charlie and tell him all about it. It will cheer him very much, poor boy. You may be sure he didn't think you guilty; still, your assurance that you know nothing whatever about it will be a comfort to him."

"Yes," Ned said, "Charlie knows that I would not tell a lie to save my life, though he knows that I might possibly kill anyone when I am in one of my horrible tempers; and I did think I was getting over them, Mr. Porson!" he broke out with a half sob. "I have really tried hard."

"I know you have, Ned. I am sure you have done your best, my boy, and you have been sorely tried; but, now, I must be off. Keep up your spirits, hope for the best, and pray God to strengthen you to bear whatever may be in store for you, and to clear you from this charge."

That evening when Mr. Porson was in his study the servant came in and said that a young man wished to speak to him.

"Who is it, Mary?"

"He says his name is Bill Swinton, sir."

"Oh! I know," the master said; "show him in."

Bill was ushered in.

"Sit down, Bill," Mr. Porson said; "I have heard of you as a friend of Sankey's. I suppose you have come to speak to me about this terrible business?"

"Ay," Bill said, "that oi be, sir, seeing as how Ned always spake of you as a true friend, and loiked you hearty. They say too as you ha' engaged lawyer Wakefield to defend him."

"That is so, Bill. I am convinced of the boy's innocence. He has always been a favourite of mine. He has no relations to stand by him now, poor boy, so we who are his friends must do our best for him."

"Surely," Bill said heartily; "and dost really think as he didn't do it?"

"I may say I am quite sure he did not, Bill. Didn't you think so too?"

"No, sir," Bill said; "it never entered my moind as he didn't do it. Oi heard as how t' chap beat Maister Ned cruel, and it seemed to me natural loike as he should sarve him out. Oi didn't suppose as how he meant vor to kill him, but as everyone said as how he did the job it seemed to me loike enough; but of course it didn't make no differ to oi whether so be as he killed un or not. Maister Ned's moi friend, and oi stands by him; still oi be main glad to hear as you think he didn't do it; but will the joodge believe it?"

"Ah! that I cannot say," Mr. Porson replied. "I know the lad and believe his word; but at present appearances are sadly against him. That unfortunate affair that he had with my predecessor induced a general idea that he was very violent-tempered. Then it has been notorious that he and his stepfather did not get on well together, and this terrible quarrel on the evening of Mr. Mulready's death seems only too plainly to account for the affair; still, without further evidence, I question if a jury will find him guilty. It is certain he had no rope when he went out, and unless the prosecution can prove that he got possession of a rope they cannot bring the guilt home to him."

"No, surely," Bill assented, and sat for some time without further speech; then he went on, "now, sir, what oi be come to thee about be this. Thou bee'st his friend and knaw'st best what 'ould be a good thing for him. Now we ha' been a-talking aboot a plan, Luke Marner and oi, as is Maister's Ned's friends, and we can get plenty of chaps to join us. We supposes as arter the next toime as they has him up in coort they will send him off to York Castle to be tried at the 'sizes."

"Yes; I have no doubt he will be committed after his next appearance, Bill; but what is the plan that you and your friend Luke were thinking of?"

"Well, we was a-thinking vor twenty or so on us to coom down at noight and break open t' cells. There be only t' chief constable and one other, and they wouldn't be no good agin us, and we could get Maister Ned owt and away long afore t' sojers would have toime to wake up and coom round; then we could hide un up on t' moor till there was toime to get un away across the seas. Luke he be pretty well bent on it, but oi says as before we did nothing oi would coom and ax thee, seeing as how thou bee'st a friend of his."

"No, Bill," Mr. Porson said gravely. "It would not do at all, and I am glad you came to ask me. If I thought it certain that the jury would find a verdict of guilty, and that Ned, innocent as I believe him of the crime, would be hung, I should say that your plan might be worth thinking of; for in that case Ned might possibly be got away till we his friends here could get at the bottom of the matter. Still it would be an acknowledgment for the time of his guilt, and I am sure that Ned himself would not run away without standing his trial even if the doors of his cell were opened. I shall see him to-morrow morning, and will tell him of your scheme on his behalf. I am sure he will be grateful, but I am pretty certain that he will not avail himself of it. If you will come down to-morrow evening I will let you know exactly what he says."

As Mr. Porson expected, Ned, although much moved at the offer of his humble friends to free him by force, altogether declined to accept it.

"It is just like Bill," he said, "ready to get into any scrape himself to help me; but I must stand my trial. I know that even if they cannot prove me guilty I cannot prove I am innocent; still, to run away would be an acknowledgment of guilt, and I am not going to do that."

On the day appointed Ned was again brought up before the magistrates. The examination was this time in public, and the justice-room was crowded. Ned, whose face was now recovering from the marks of ill usage, was pale and quiet. He listened in silence to the evidence proving the finding of Mr. Mulready's body. The next witness put into the box was one of the engineers at the factory; he proved that the rope which had been used in upsetting the gig had been cut from one which he had a short time before been using for moving a portion of the machinery. He had used the rope about an hour before Mr. Mulready came back in the evening, and it was then whole. After it had been done with it was thrown outside the mill to be out of the way, as it would not be required again.

After he had given his evidence Mr. Wakefield asked:

"Did you hear any one outside the mill when Mr. Mulready was there?"

"No, sir; I heard nothing."

"Anyone might have entered the yard, I suppose, and found the rope?"

"Yes; the gates were open, as we were at work."

"Would the rope be visible to anyone who entered the yard?"

"It would not be seen plainly, because it was a dark night; but anyone prowling about outside the mill might have stumbled against it."

"You have no reason whatever for supposing that it was Mr. Edward Sankey who cut this rope more than anyone else?"

"No, sir."

Charlie was the next witness. The boy was as white as a sheet, and his eyes were swollen with crying. He glanced piteously at his brother, and exclaimed with a sob, "Oh! Ned."

"Don't mind, Charlie," Ned said quietly. "Tell the

LITTLE CHARLIE GIVES HIS EVIDENCE.

whole story exactly as it happened. You can't do me any harm, old boy."

So encouraged Charlie told the whole story of the quarrel arising in the first place from his stepfather's ill temper at the tea-table.

"Your brother meant nothing specially unpleasant in calling your stepfather Foxey?" Mr. Wakefield asked.

"No, sir; he had always called him so even before he knew that he was going to marry mother. It was a name, I believe, the men called him, and Ned got it from them."

"I believe that your stepfather had received threatening letters, had he not?"

"Yes, sir, several; he was afraid to put his new machines to work because of them."

"Thank you, that will do," Mr. Wakefield said. "I have those letters in my possession," he went on to the magistrates. "They are proof that the deceased had enemies who had threatened to take his life. Shall I produce them now?"

"It is hardly worth while, Mr. Wakefield, though they can be brought forward at the trial. I may say, indeed, that we have seen some of them already, for it was on account of these letters that we applied for the military to be stationed here."

It was not thought necessary to call Mrs. Mulready; but the servant gave her evidence as to what she had heard of the quarrel, and as to the absence of Ned from home that night.

"Unless you are in a position to produce evidence, Mr. Wakefield, proving clearly that at the time the murder was committed the prisoner was at a distance from the spot, we are prepared to commit him for trial."

Mr. Wakefield intimated that he should reserve his evidence for the trial itself, and Ned was then formally committed.

The examination in no way altered the tone of public opinion. The general opinion was that Ned had followed his stepfather to the mill, intending to attack him, that he had stumbled onto the coil of rope, and the idea occurred to him of tying it across the road and upsetting the gig on its return. Charlie's evidence as to the savage assault upon his brother had created a stronger feeling of sympathy than had before prevailed, and had the line of defence been, that, smarting under his injuries, Ned had suddenly determined to injure his stepfather by upsetting the gig, but without any idea of killing him, the general opinion would have been that under such provocation as Ned had received a lengthened term of imprisonment would have been an ample punishment. More than one, indeed, were heard to say, "Well, if I were on the jury, my verdict would be, Served him right." Still, although there was greater sympathy than before with Ned, there were few, indeed, who doubted his guilt.

After Ned was removed from court he was taken back by the chief constable to his house, and ten minutes later he was summoned into the parlour, where he found Charlie and Lucy waiting him. Lucy, who was now ten years old, sprang forward to meet him; he lifted her, and for a while she lay with her head on his shoulder and her arms round his neck, sobbing bitterly, while Charlie clung to his brother's disengaged hand.

"Don't cry, Lucy, don't cry, little woman; it will all come right in the end;" but Lucy's tears were not to be staunched. Ned sat down, and after a time soothed her into stillness, but she still lay nestled up in his arms.

"It was dreadful, Ned," Charlie said, "having to go into court as a witness against you. I had thought of running away, but did not know where to go to, and then Mr. Porson had a talk with me and told me that it was of the greatest importance that I should tell everything exactly word for word, just as it happened. He said every one knew there had been a quarrel, and that if I did not tell everything it would seem as if I was keeping something back in order to screen you, and that would do you a great deal of harm, and that, as really you were not to blame in the quarrel, my evidence would be in your favour rather than against you. He says he knew that you would wish me to tell exactly what took place."

"Certainly, Charlie; there is nothing I could want hid. I was wrong to speak of him as Foxey, and to let fly as I did about him; but there was nothing intended to offend him in that, because, of course, I had no idea that he could hear me. The only thing I have to blame myself very much for is for getting into a wild passion. I don't think any one would say I did wrong in going out of the house after being knocked about so; but if I had not got into a passion, and had gone straight to Bill's, or to Abijah, or to Mr. Porson, which would have been best of all, to have stopped the night, all this would not have come upon me; but I let myself get into a blind passion and stopped in it for hours, and I am being punished for it."

"It was natural that you should get in a passion," Charlie said stoutly. "I think any one would have got in a passion."

"I don't think you would, Charlie," Ned said, smiling.

"No," Charlie replied; "but then you see that is not my way. I should have cried all night; but then I am not a great, strong fellow like you, and it would not be so hard to be knocked about."

"It's no use making excuses, Charlie. I know I ought not to have given way to my temper like that. Now, Lucy dear, as you are feeling better, you must sit up and talk to me. How is mother?"

"Mother is in bed," Lucy said. "She's always in bed now; the house is dreadful, Ned, without you, and they say you are not to come back yet," and the tears came very near to overflowing again.

"Ah! well, I hope I shall be back before long, Lucy."

"I hope so," Lucy said; "but you know you will soon be going away again to be a soldier."

"I shall not go away again now, Lucy," Ned said quietly. "When I come back it will be for good."

"Oh! that will be nice," Lucy said joyously, "just as it used to be, with no one to be cross and scold about everything."

"Hush! little woman, don't talk about that. He had his faults, dear, as we all have, but he had a great deal to worry him, and perhaps we did not make allowances enough for him, and I do think he was really fond of you, Lucy, and when people are dead we should never speak ill of them."

"I don't want to," Lucy said, "and I didn't want him to be fond of me when he wasn't fond of you and Charlie or mother. It seems to me he wasn't fond of mother, and yet she does nothing but cry; I can't make that out, can you?"

Ned did not answer; his mother's infatuation for Mr. Mulready had always been a puzzle to him, and he could at present think of no reply which would be satisfactory to Lucy.

A constable now came in and said that there were other visitors waiting to see Ned. He then withdrew, leaving the lad to say good-bye to his brother and sister alone. Ned kept up a brave countenance, and strove to make the parting as easy as possible for the others, but both were crying bitterly as they went out.

Ned's next visitors were Dr. Green and Mr. Porson.

"We have only a minute or two, my boy," Mr. Porson said, "for the gig is at the door. The chief constable is going to drive you to York himself. You will go half-way and sleep on the road to-night. It is very good of him, as in that way no one will suspect that you are any but a pair of ordinary travellers. Keep up your spirits, my boy. We have sent to London for a detective from

Bow Street to try and ferret out something of this mysterious business; and even if we do not succeed, I have every faith that it will come right in the end. And now good-bye, my boy, I shall see you in a fortnight, for of course I shall come over to York to the trial to give evidence as to character."

"And so shall I, Ned, my patients must get on without me for a day or two," the doctor said. "Mr. Wakefield is waiting to see you. He has something to tell you which may help to cheer you. He says it is of no legal value, but it seems to me important."

CHAPTER XV.

NOT GUILTY.

AS soon as Mr. Porson and the doctor had left him, Mr. Wakefield appeared.

"Well, Sankey, I hope you are not downcast at the magistrates' decision. It was a certainty that they would have to commit you, as we could not prove a satisfactory alibi. Never mind, I don't think any jury will find against you on the evidence they have got, especially in the face of those threatening letters and the fact that several men in Mulready's position have been murdered by the Luddites."

"It won't be much consolation to me, sir, to be acquitted if it can't be proved to the satisfaction of everyone that I am innocent."

"Tut, tut! my boy; the first thing to do is to get you out of the hands of the law. After that we shall have time to look about us and see if we can lay our hands on the right man. A curious thing has happened to-day while I was in court. A little boy left a letter for me at

R

my office here; it is an ill-written scrawl, as you see, but certainly important."

Ned took the paper, on which was written in a scrawling hand:

"Sir, Maister Sankey be innocent of the murder of Foxey. I doan't want to put my neck in a noose, but if so be as they finds him guilty in coort and be a-going to hang him, I shall come forward and say as how I did it. I bean't agoing to let him be hung for this job. A loife for a loife, saes oi; so tell him to keep up his heart."

There was no signature to the paper.

Ned looked up with delight in his face.

"But won't the letter clear me, Mr. Wakefield? It shows that it was not me, but someone else who did it."

"No, Sankey, pray do not cherish any false hopes on that ground. The letter is valueless in a legal way. To you and to your friends it may be a satisfaction; but it can have no effect on the court. There is nothing to prove that it is genuine. It may have been written by any friend of yours with a view of obtaining your acquittal. Of course we shall put it in at the trial, but it cannot be accepted as legal evidence in any way. Still a thing of that sort may have an effect upon some of the jury."

Ned looked again at the letter, and a shade came over his face now that he looked at it carefully. He recognized in a moment Bill's handwriting. He had himself instructed him by setting him copies at the time he was laid up with the broken leg, and Bill had stuck to it so far that he was able to read and write in a rough way.

Ned's first impulse was to tell Mr. Wakefield who had written the note, but he thought that it might get Bill into a scrape. It was evidently written by his friend, solely to create an impression in his favour, and he wondered that such an idea should have entered Bill's head, which was by no means an imaginative one. As to the young fellow having killed Mr. Mulready it did not even occur to Ned for a moment.

As, seated by the side of the chief constable, he drove along that afternoon, Ned turned it over anxiously in his mind whether it would be honest to allow this letter to be produced in court, knowing that it was only the device of a friend. Finally he decided to let matters take their course.

" I am innocent," he said to himself, " and what I have got to live for is to clear myself from this charge. Mr. Wakefield said this letter would not be of value one way or the other, and if I were to say Bill wrote it he might insist upon Bill's being arrested, and he might find it just as hard to prove his innocence as I do."

The assizes were to come on in three weeks. Ned was treated with more consideration than was generally the case with prisoners in those days, when the jails were terribly mismanaged; but Mr. Simmonds had written to the governor of the prison asking that every indulgence that could be granted should be shown to Ned, and Mr. Porson had also, before the lad left Marsden, insisted on his accepting a sum of money which would enable him to purchase such food and comforts as were permitted to be bought by prisoners, able to pay for them, awaiting their trial.

Thus Ned obtained the boon of a separate cell, he was allowed to have books and writing materials, and to have his meals in from outside the prison.

The days, however, passed but slowly, and Ned was heartily glad when the time for the assizes was at hand and his suspense was to come to an end. His case came on for trial on the second day of the sessions. On the previous evening he received a visit from Mr. Wakefield, who told him that Mr. Porson, Dr. Green and Charlie had come over in the coach with him.

"You will be glad to hear that your mother will not be called," the lawyer said. "The prosecution, I suppose, thought that it would have a bad effect to call upon a mother to give evidence against her son; besides, she could prove no more than your brother will be able to do. If they had called her, Green would have given her a certificate that she was confined to her bed and could not possibly attend. However I am glad they did not call her, for the absence of a witness called against the prisoner, but supposed to be favourable to him, always counts against him."

"And you have no clue as to who did it, Mr. Wakefield?"

"Not a shadow," the lawyer replied. "We have had a man down from town ever since you have been away, but we have done no good. He went up to Varley and tried to get into the confidence of the croppers, but somehow they suspected him to be a spy sent down to inquire into the Luddite business, and he had a pretty narrow escape of his life. He was terribly knocked about before he could get out of the public-house, and they chased him all the way down into Marsden. Luckily he was a pretty good runner, and had the advantage of having lighter shoes on than they had, or they would have killed him to a certainty. No, my lad, we can prove nothing; we simply take the ground that you didn't do it; that he was a threatened man and unpopular with his hands; and there is not a shadow of proof against you except the fact that he had ill-treated you just before."

"And that I was known to bear him ill-will," Ned said sadly.

"Yes, of course that's unfortunate," the lawyer said uneasily. "Of course they will make a point of that, but that proves nothing. Most boys of your age do object to a stepfather. Of course we shall put it to the jury that there is nothing uncommon about that. Oh! no, I do not think they have a strong case; and Mr. Grant, who is our leader, and who is considered the best man on the circuit, is convinced we shall get a verdict."

"But what do people think at Marsden, Mr. Wakefield? Do people generally think I am guilty?"

"Pooh! pooh!" Mr. Wakefield said hastily. "What does it matter what people think? Most people are fools. The question we have to concern ourselves with is what do the jury think, or at any rate with what they think is proved, and Mr. Grant says he does not believe any jury could find you guilty upon the evidence. He will work them up. I know he is a wonderful fellow for working up."

Mr. Grant's experience of juries turned out to be well founded. Ned, as he stood pale but firm and composed in the dock, felt that his case was well-nigh desperate when he heard the speech for the prosecution. His long and notorious ill-will against the deceased, "one of the most genial and popular gentlemen in that part of the great county of Yorkshire," was dwelt upon. Evidence would be brought to show that even on the occasion of his mother's marriage the happiness of the ceremonial was marred by the scowls and menacing appearance of this most unfortunate and ill-conditioned lad; how some time after the marriage this young fellow had violently assaulted his stepfather, and had used words in the hearing of the servants which could only be interpreted as a threat upon his life. This, indeed, was not the first time that this boy had been placed in the dock as a prisoner. Upon a former occasion he had been charged with assaulting and threatening the life of his schoolmaster, and although upon that occasion he had escaped the consequences of his conduct by what must now be considered as the ill-timed leniency of the magistrates, yet the facts were undoubted and undenied.

Then the counsel proceeded to narrate the circumstances of the evening up to the point when Mr. Mulready left the house.

"Beyond that point, gentlemen of the jury," the counsel

said, "nothing certain is known. The rest must be mere conjecture; and yet it is not hard to imagine the facts. The prisoner was aware that the deceased had gone to the mill, which is situated a mile and a half from the town. You will be told the words which the prisoner used: 'It will be my turn next time, and when it comes I will kill you, you brute.'

"With these words on his lips, with this thought in his heart, he started for the mill. What plan he intended to adopt, what form of vengeance he intended to take, it matters not, but assuredly it was with thoughts of vengeance in his heart that he followed that dark and lonely road to the mill. Once there he would have hung about waiting for his victim to issue forth. It may be that he had picked up a heavy stone, maybe that he had an open knife in his hand, but while he was waiting, probably his foot struck against a coil of rope, which, as you will hear, had been carelessly thrown out a few minutes before.

"Then doubtless the idea of a surer method of vengeance than that of which he had before thought came into his mind. A piece of the rope was hastily cut off, and with this the prisoner stole quietly off until he reached the spot where two gates facing each other on opposite sides of the lane afforded a suitable hold for the rope. Whether after fastening it across the road he remained at the spot to watch the catastrophe which he had brought about, or whether he hurried away into the darkness secure of his vengeance we cannot tell, nor does it matter. You will understand, gentlemen, that we are not in a position to

prove these details of the tragedy. I am telling you the
theory of the prosecution as to how it happened. Murders
are not generally done in open day with plenty of trustworthy witnesses looking on. It is seldom that the act
of slaying is witnessed by human eye. The evidence
must therefore to some extent be circumstantial. The
prosecution can only lay before juries the antecedent circumstances, show ill-will and animus, and lead the jury
step by step up to the point when the murderer and the
victim meet in some spot at some time when none but
the all-seeing eye of God is upon them. This case is, as
you see, no exception to the general rule.

"I have shown you that between the prisoner and the
deceased there was what may be termed a long-standing
feud, which came to a climax two or three hours before
this murder. Up to that fatal evening I think I shall
show you that the prisoner was wholly in fault, and that
the deceased acted with great good temper and self-command under a long series of provocations; but upon this
evening his temper appears to have failed, and I will
admit frankly that he seems to have committed a very
outrageous and brutal assault upon the prisoner. Still,
gentlemen, such an assault is no justification of the crime
which took place. Unhappily it supplies the cause, but
it does not supply an excuse for the crime.

"Your duty in the case will be simple. You will have
to say whether or not the murder of William Mulready
is accounted for upon the theory which I have laid down
to you and on no other. Should you entertain no doubt

upon the subject it will be your duty to bring in a verdict of guilty; if you do not feel absolutely certain you will of course give the prisoner the benefit of the doubt."

The evidence called added nothing to what was known at the first examination. The two servants testified to the fact of the unpleasant relations which had from the first existed between the deceased and the prisoner, and detailed what they knew of the quarrel. Charlie's evidence was the most damaging, as he had to state the threat which Ned had uttered before he went out.

The counsel for the defence asked but few questions in cross-examination. He elicited from the servants, however, the fact that Mr. Mulready at home was a very different person from Mr. Mulready as known by people in general. They acknowledged that he was by no means a pleasant master, that he was irritable and fault-finding, and that his temper was trying in the extreme. He only asked one or two questions of Charlie.

" You did not find your stepfather a very pleasant man to deal with, did you?"

" Not at all pleasant," Charlie replied heartily.

" Always snapping and snarling and finding fault, wasn't he?"

" Yes, sir, always."

" Now about this threat of which we have heard so much on the part of your brother, did it impress you much? Were you frightened at it? Did you think that your brother intended to kill your stepfather?"

" No, sir, I am sure he didn't; he just said it in a passion.

He had been knocked about until he could hardly stand, and he just said the first thing that came into his head, like fellows do."

"You don't think that he went out with any deliberate idea of killing your stepfather?"

"No, sir; I am sure he only went out to walk about till he got over his passion, just as he had done before."

"It was his way, was it, when anything put him out very much, to go and walk about till he got cool again?"

"Yes, sir."

For the defence Mr. Simmonds was called, and produced the threatening letters which Mr. Mulready had laid before him. He stated that that gentleman was much alarmed, and had asked that a military force should be called into the town, and that he himself and his colleague had considered the danger so serious that they had applied for and obtained military protection.

Luke Marner and several of the hands at the mill testified to the extreme unpopularity of their employer among his men, and said that they should never have been surprised any morning at hearing that he had been killed.

Dr. Green and Mr. Porson testified very strongly in favour of Ned's character. This was all the evidence produced. Mr. Grant then addressed the jury, urging that beyond the fact of this unfortunate quarrel, in which the deceased appeared to have been entirely to blame and to have behaved with extreme brutality, there was nothing whatever to associate the prisoner with the crime. The young gentleman before them, as they had heard from the testimony of gentlemen of the highest respectability, bore an excellent character. That he had faults in temper he admitted, such faults being the result of the lad having been brought up among Indian servants; but Dr. Green and Mr. Porson had both told them that he had made the greatest efforts to master his temper, and that they believed that no ordinary provocation could arouse him. But after all what did what they had heard amount to? simply this, the lad's mother had been married a second time to a man who bore the outward reputation of being a pleasant, jovial man, a leading character among his townsmen, a popular fellow in the circle in which he moved.

It had been proved, however, by the evidence of those who knew him best, of his workpeople, his servants, of this poor lad whom the prosecution had placed in the box as a witness against his brother, that this man's life was a long lie; that, smiling and pleasant as he appeared, he was a tyrant, a petty despot in his family, a hard master to his hands, a cruel master in his house. What wonder that between this lad and such a stepfather as this there was no love lost. There were scores, aye and thousands of boys in England who similarly hated their stepfathers, and was it to be said that, if any of the men came to a sudden and violent death, these boys were to be suspected of their murder. But in the present case, although he was not in a position to lay his finger upon the man who perpetrated this crime, they need not go far to look for him. Had they not heard that he was hated by his workpeople?

Evidence had been laid before them to show that he was a marked man, that he had received threatening letters from secret associations which had, as was notorious, kept the south of Yorkshire, and indeed all that part of the country which was the seat of manufacture, in a state of alarm. So imminent was the danger considered that the magistrates had requested the aid of an armed force, and at the time this murder was committed there were soldiers actually stationed in the mill, besides a strong force in the town for the protection of this man from his enemies.

The counsel for the prosecution had given them his theory as to the actions of the prisoner, but he believed that that theory was altogether wide of the truth. It was known that an accident had taken place to the machinery, for the mill was standing idle for the day. It would be probable that the deceased would go over late in the evening to see how the work was progressing, as every effort was being made to get the machinery to run on the following morning. "What so probable, then, that the enemies of the deceased—and you know that he had enemies, who had sworn to take his life—should choose this opportunity for attacking him as he drove to or from the town. That an enemy was prowling round the mill, as has been suggested to you, I admit readily enough. That he stumbled upon the rope, that the idea occurred to him of upsetting the gig on its return, that he cut off a portion of the rope and fixed it between the two gate-posts across the road, and that this rope caused the death of William Mulready. All this I allow; but I submit to you that the man who did this was a member of the secret association which is a terror to the land, and was the terror of William Mulready, and there is no proof whatever, not even the shadow of a proof, to connect this lad with the crime.

" I am not speaking without a warrant when I assert my conviction that it was an emissary of the association known as the Luddites who had a hand in this matter, for I am in possession of a document, which unfortunately I am not in a position to place before you, as it is not legal evidence, which professes to be written by the man who perpetrated this deed, and who appears, although obedient to the behests of this secret association of which he is a member, to be yet a man not devoid of heart, who says that if this innocent young man is found guilty of this crime he will himself come forward and confess that he did it.

"Therefore, gentlemen of the jury, there is every reason to believe that the slayer of William Mulready is indeed within these walls, but assuredly he is not the most unfortunate and ill-treated young man who stands in the dock awaiting your verdict to set him free."

The summing up was brief. The judge commenced by telling the jury that they must dismiss altogether from their minds the document of which the counsel for the defence had spoken, and to which, as it had not been put into court, and indeed could not be put into court, it was highly irregular and improper for him to have alluded. They must, he said, dismiss it altogether from their minds. Their duty was simple, they were to consider the evidence before them. They had heard of the quarrel which had taken place between the deceased and the prisoner. They had heard the threat used by the prisoner that he would kill the deceased if he had an opportunity, and they had to decide whether he had, in accordance with the theory of the prosecution, carried that threat into effect; or whether on the other hand, as the defence suggested, the deceased had fallen a victim to the agent of the association which had threatened his life. He was bound to tell them that if they entertained any doubt as to the guilt of the prisoner at the bar they were bound to give him the benefit of the doubt.

The jury consulted together for a short time, and then expressed their desire to retire to consider their verdict. They were absent about half an hour, and on their return the foreman said in reply to the question of the judge that they found the prisoner "Not Guilty."

A perfect silence reigned in the court when the jury entered the box, and something like a sigh of relief followed their verdict. It was expected, and indeed there was some surprise when the jury retired, for the general opinion was that whether guilty or innocent the prosecution had failed to bring home unmistakably the crime to the prisoner. That he might have committed it was certain, that he had committed it was probable, but it was assuredly not proved that he and none other had been the perpetrator of the crime.

Of all the persons in the court the accused had appeared the least anxious as to the result. He received almost with indifference the assurances which Mr. Wakefield, who was sitting at the solicitor's table below him, rose to give him, that the jury could not find a verdict against him, and the expression of his face was unchanged when the foreman announced the verdict.

He was at once released from the dock. His solicitor, Dr. Green, and Mr. Porson warmly shook his hand, and Charlie threw his arms round his neck and cried in his joy and excitement.

"It is all right, I suppose," Ned said as, surrounded by his friends, he left the court, "but I would just as lief the verdict had gone the other way."

"Oh! Ned, how can you say so?" Charlie exclaimed.

"Well, no, Charlie," Ned corrected himself. "I am glad for your sake and Lucy's that I am acquitted; it would have been awful for you if I had been hung—it is only for myself that I don't care. The verdict only means that they have not been able to prove me guilty, and I have got to go on living all my life knowing that I am suspected of being a murderer. It is not a nice sort of thing, you know," and he laughed drearily.

"Come, come, Ned," Mr. Porson said cheerily, "you mustn't take too gloomy a view of it. It is natural enough that you should do so now, for you have gone through a great deal, and you are overwrought and worn out; but this will pass off, and you will find things are not as bad as you think. It is true that there may be some, not many, I hope, who will be of opinion that the verdict was like the Scotch verdict 'Not Proven,' rather than 'Not Guilty;' but I am sure the great majority will believe you innocent. You have got the doctor here on your side, and he is a host in himself. Mr. Simmonds told me when the jury were out of the court that he was convinced you were innocent, and his opinion will go a long way in Marsden, and you must hope and trust that the time will come when your innocence will be not only believed in, but proved to the satisfaction of all by the discovery of the actual murderer."

"Ah!" Ned said, "if we ever find that out it will be all right; but unless we can do so I shall have this dreadful thing hanging over me all my life."

They had scarcely reached the hotel where Mr. Porson, the doctor, and Charlie were stopping, when Mr. Simmonds arrived.

"I have come to congratulate you, my boy," he said, shaking hands with Ned. "I can see that at present the verdict does not give so much satisfaction to you as to your friends, but that is natural enough. You have been unjustly accused and have had a very hard time of it, and you are naturally not disposed to look at matters in a cheerful light; but this gives us time, my boy, and time is everything. It is hard for you that your innocence has not been fully demonstrated, but you have your life before you, and we must hope that some day you will be triumphantly vindicated."

"That is what I shall live for in future," Ned said. "Of

course now, Mr. Simmonds, there is an end of all idea of my going into the army. A man suspected of a murder, even if they have failed to bring it home to him, cannot ask for a commission in the army. I know there's an end to all that."

"No," Mr. Simmonds agreed hesitatingly, "I fear that for the present that plan had better remain in abeyance; we can take it up again later on when this matter is put straight."

"That may be never," Ned said decidedly, "so we need say no more about it."

"And now, my boy," Mr. Porson said, "try and eat some lunch. I have just ordered a post-chaise to be round at the door in half an hour. The sooner we start the better. The fresh air and the change will do you good, and we shall have plenty of time to talk on the road."

CHAPTER XVI.

LUKE MARNER'S SACRIFICE.

NOT until they had left York behind them did Ned ask after his mother. He knew that if there had been anything pleasant to tell about her he would have heard it at once, and the silence of his friends warned him that the subject was not an agreeable one.

"How is my mother?" he asked at last abruptly.

"Well, Ned," Dr. Green replied, "I have been expecting your question, and I am sorry to say that I have nothing agreeable to tell you."

"That I was sure of," Ned said with a hard laugh. "As I have received no message from her from the day I was arrested I guessed pretty well that whatever doubt other people might feel, my mother was positive that I had murdered her husband."

"The fact is, Ned," Dr. Green said cautiously, "your mother is not at present quite accountable for her opinions. The shock which she has undergone has, I think, unhinged her mind. Worthless as I believe him to have been, this man had entirely gained her affections. She has not risen from her bed since he died.

"Sometimes she is absolutely silent for hours, at others she talks incessantly; and painful as it is to tell you so, her first impression that you were responsible for his death is the one which still remains fixed on her mind. She is wholly incapable of reason or of argument. At times she appears sane and sensible enough and talks of other matters coherently; but the moment she touches on this topic she becomes excited and vehement. It has been a great comfort to me, and I am sure it will be to you, that your old servant Abijah has returned and taken up the position of housekeeper.

"As soon as your mother's first excitement passed away I asked her if she would like this, and she eagerly assented. The woman was in the town, having come over on the morning after you gave yourself up, and to my great relief she at once consented to take up her former position. This is a great thing for your sister, who is, of course, entirely in her charge, as your mother is not in a condition to attend to anything. I was afraid at first that she would not remain, so indignant was she at your mother's believing your guilt; but when I assured her that the poor lady was not responsible for what she said, and that her mind was in fact unhinged altogether by the calamity, she overcame her feelings; but it is comic to see her struggling between her indignation at your mother's irresponsible talk and her consciousness that it is necessary to abstain from exciting her by contradiction."

Dr. Green had spoken as lightly as he could, but he knew how painful it must be to Ned to hear of his mother's conviction of his guilt, and how much it would add to the trials of his position.

Ned himself had listened in silence. He sighed heavily when the doctor had finished.

"Abijah will be a great comfort," he said quietly, "a wonderful comfort; but as to my poor mother, it will of course be a trial. Still, no wonder that, when she heard me say those words when I went out, she thinks that I did it. However, I suppose that it is part of my punishment."

"Have you thought anything of your future plans, Ned?" Mr. Porson asked after they had driven in silence for some distance.

"Yes, I have been thinking a good deal," Ned replied, "all the time I was shut up and had nothing else to do. I did not believe that they would find me guilty, and of course I had to settle what I should do afterwards. If it was only myself I think I should go away and take another name; but in that case there would be no chance of my ever clearing myself, and for father's sake and for the sake of Charlie and Lucy I must not throw away a chance of that. It would be awfully against them all their lives if people could say of them that their brother was the fellow who murdered their stepfather. Perhaps they will always say so now; still it is evidently my duty to stay, if it were only on the chance of clearing up the mystery.

" In the next place I feel that I ought to stay for the sake of money matters. I don't think, in the present state of things, with the Luddites burning mills and threatening masters, any one would give anything like its real value for the mill now. I know that it did not pay with the old machinery, and it is not every one who would care to run the risk of working with the new. By the terms of the settlement that was made before my mother married again the mill is now hers, and she and Charlie and Lucy have nothing else to depend upon. As she is not capable of transacting business it falls upon me to take her place, and I intend to try, for a time at any rate, to run the mill myself. Of course I know nothing about it, but as the hands all know their work the foreman will be able to carry on the actual business of the mill till I master the details.

"As to the office business, the clerk will know all about it. There was a man who used to travel about to buy wool. I know my mother's husband had every confidence in him, and he could go on just as before. As to the sales, the books will tell the names of the firms who dealt with us, and I suppose the business with them will go on as before. At any rate I can but try for a time. Of course I have quite made up my mind that I shall have no personal interest whatever in the business. They may think that I murdered Mulready, but they shall not say that I have profited by his death. I should suppose that my mother can pay me some very small salary, just sufficient to buy my clothes. So I shall go on till Charlie

gets to an age when he can manage the business as its
master; then if no clue has been obtained as to the murder
I shall be able to give it up and go abroad, leaving him
with, I hope, a good business for himself and Lucy."

"I think that is as good a plan as any," Mr. Porson
said; "but, however, there is no occasion to come to any
sudden determination at present. I myself should advise
a change of scene and thought before you decide anything finally. I have a brother living in London, and he
would, I am sure, very gladly take you in for a fortnight
and show you the sights of London."

"Thank you, sir, you are very kind," Ned said quietly;
"but I have got to face it out at Marsden, and I would
rather begin at once."

Mr. Porson saw by the set steady look upon Ned's face
that he had thoroughly made up his mind as to the part
he had to play, and that any further argument would be
of no avail. It was not until the post-chaise was approaching Marsden that any further allusion was made
to Ned's mother. Then the doctor, after consulting Mr.
Porson by various upliftings of the eyebrows, returned to
the subject.

"Ned, my boy, we were speaking some little time ago
of your mother. I think it is best that I should tell you
frankly that I do not consider her any longer responsible
for her actions. I tell you this in order that you may not
be wounded by your reception.

"Since that fatal day she has not left her bed. She
declares that she has lost all power in her limbs. Of

course that is nonsense, but the result is the same. She keeps her bed, and, as far as I can see, is likely to keep it. This is perhaps the less to be regretted, as you will thereby avoid being thrown into contact with her; for I tell you plainly such contact, in her present state of mind, could only be unpleasant to you. Were you to meet, it would probably at the least bring on a frightful attack of hysterics, which in her present state might be a serious matter. Therefore, my boy, you must make up your mind not to see her for a while. I have talked the matter over with your old nurse, who will remain with your mother as housekeeper, with a girl under her. You will, of course, take your place as master of the house, with your brother and sister with you, until your mother is in a position to manage—if ever she should be. But I trust at any rate that she will ere long so far recover as to be able to receive you as the good son you have ever been to her."

"Thank you," Ned said quietly. "I understand, doctor."

Ned did understand that his mother was convinced of his guilt and refused to see him; it was what he expected, and yet it was a heavy trial. Very cold and hard he looked as the post-chaise drove through the streets of Marsden. People glanced at it curiously, and as they saw Ned sitting by the side of the men who were known as his champions they hurried away to spread the news that young Sankey had been acquitted.

The hard look died out of Ned's face as the door opened and Lucy sprang out and threw her arms round his neck and cried with delight at seeing him; and Abijah, crying too, greeted him inside with a motherly welcome. A feeling of relief came across his mind as he entered the sitting-room. Dr. Green, who was one of the trustees in the marriage settlement, had, in the inability of Mrs. Mulready to give any orders, taken upon himself to dispose of much of the furniture, and to replace it with some of an entirely different fashion and appearance. The parlour was snug and cosy; a bright fire blazed on the hearth; a comfortable arm-chair stood beside it; the room looked warm and homely. Ned's two friends had followed him in, and tears stood in both their eyes.

"Welcome back, dear boy!" Mr. Porson said, grasping his hand. "God grant that better times are in store for you, and that you may outlive this trial which has at present darkened your life! Now we will leave you to your brother and sister. I am sure you will be glad to be alone with them."

And so Ned took to the life he had marked out for himself. In two months he seemed to have aged years. The careless look of boyhood had altogether disappeared from his face. Except from his two friends he rejected all sympathy. When he walked through the streets of Marsden it was with a cold stony face, as if he were wholly unaware of the existence of passers-by. The thought that as he went along men drew aside to let him pass and whispered after he had gone, "That is the fellow who murdered his stepfather, but escaped because they could not bring it home to him," was ever in his mind. His friends in vain argued with him against his thus shutting himself off from the world. They assured him that there were very many who, like themselves, were perfectly convinced of his innocence, and who would rally round him and support him if he would give them the least encouragement, but Ned shook his head.

"I dare say what you say is true," he would reply; "but I could not do it—I must go on alone. It is as much as I can bear now."

And his friends saw that it was useless to urge him further.

On the day after his return to Marsden Luke Marner and Bill Swinton came back on the coach from York, and after it was dark Ned walked up to Varley and knocked at Bill's door.

On hearing who it was Bill threw on his cap and came out to him. For a minute the lads stood with their hands clasped firmly in each other's without a word being spoken.

"Thank God, Maister Ned," Bill said at last, "we ha' got thee again!"

"Thank God too!" Ned said; "though I think I would rather that it had gone the other way."

They walked along for some time without speaking again, and then Ned said suddenly:

"Now, Bill, who is the real murderer?"

Bill stopped his walk in astonishment.

"The real murderer!" he repeated; "how ever should oi know, Maister Ned?"

"I know that you know, Bill. It was you who wrote that letter to Mr. Wakefield saying that the man who did it would be at the trial, and that if I were found guilty he would give himself up. It's no use your denying it, for I knew your handwriting at once."

Bill was silent for some time. It had never occurred to him that this letter would be brought home to him.

"Come, Bill, you must tell me," Ned said. "Do not be afraid. I promise you that I will not use it against him. Mind, if I can bring it home to him in any other way I shall do so; but I promise you that no word shall ever pass my lips about the letter. I want to know who is the man of whose crime the world believes me guilty. The secret shall, as far as he is concerned, be just as much a secret as it was before."

"But oi dunno who is the man, Maister Ned. If oi did oi would ha' gone into the court and said so, even though oi had been sure they would ha' killed me for 'peaching when oi came back. Oi dunno no more than a child."

"Then you only wrote that letter to throw them on to a false scent, Bill? Who put you up to that, for I am sure it would never have occurred to you?"

"No," Bill said slowly, "oi should never ha' thought of it myself; Luke told oi what to wroit, and I wroited it."

"Oh, it was Luke! was it?" Ned said sharply. "Then the man who did it must have told him."

"Oi didn't mean to let out as it waar Luke," Bill said in confusion; "and oi promised him solemn to say nowt about it."

NED QUESTIONS LUKE MARNER.

"Well," Ned said, turning sharp round and starting on his way back to the village, "I must see Luke himself."

Bill in great perplexity followed Ned, muttering: "Oh Lor'! what ull Luke say to oi? What a fellow oi be to talk, to be sure!"

Nothing further was said until they reached Luke's cottage. Ned knocked and entered at once, followed sheepishly by Bill.

"Maister Ned, oi be main glad to see thee," Luke said as he rose from his place by the fire; while Polly with a little cry, "Welcome!" dropped her work.

"Thanks, Luke—thanks for coming over to York to give evidence. How are you, Polly? There! don't cry— I ain't worth crying over. At any rate, it is a satisfaction to be with three people who don't regard me as a murderer. Now, Polly, I want you to go into the other room, for I have a question which I must ask Luke, and I don't want even you to hear the answer."

Polly gathered her work together and went out. Then Ned went over to Luke, who was looking at him with surprise, and laid his hand on his shoulder.

"Luke," he said, "I want you to tell me exactly how it was that you came to tell Bill to write that letter to Mr. Wakefield?"

Luke started and then looked savagely over at Bill, who stood twirling his cap in his hand.

"Oi couldn't help it, Luke," he said humbly. "Oi didn't mean vor to say it, but he got it out of me somehow. He knawed my fist on the paper, and, says he,

sudden loike, 'Who war the man as murdered Foxey?'
'What was oi vor to say? He says at once as he knowed
the idea of writing that letter would never ha' coom into
my head; and so the long and short of it be, as your name
slipped owt somehow, and there you be."

"Now, Luke," Ned said soothingly, "I want to know
whether there was a man who was ready to take my
place in the dock had I been found guilty, and if so, who
he was. I shall keep the name as a secret. I give you
my word of honour. After he had promised to come
forward and save my life that is the least I can do,
though, as I told Bill, if I could bring it home to him in
any other way I should feel myself justified in doing so.
It may be that he would be willing to go across the seas,
and when he is safe there to write home saying that he
did it."

"Yes, oi was afraid that soom sich thawt might be in
your moind, Maister Ned, but it can't be done that way.
But oi doan't know," he said thoughtfully, "perhaps it
moight, arter all. Perhaps the chap as was a-coomin' forward moight take it into his head to go to Ameriky. Oi
shouldn't wonder if he did. In fact, now oi thinks on't,
oi am pretty sure as he will. Yes. Oi can say for sartin
as that's what he intends. A loife vor a loife, you know,
Maister Ned, that be only fair, bean't it?"

"And you think he will really go?" Ned asked eagerly.

"Ay, he will go," Luke said firmly, "it's as good as
done; but," he added slowly, "I dunno as he's got money
vor to pay his passage wi'. There's some kids as have

to go wi' him. He would want no more nor just the fare. But oi doan't see how he can go till he has laid that by, and in these hard toimes it ull take him some time to do that."

"I will provide the money," Ned said eagerly. "Abijah would lend me some of her savings, and I can pay her back some day."

"Very well, Maister Ned. Oi expect as how he will take it as a loan. Moind, he will pay it back if he lives, honest. Oi doan't think as how he bain't honest, that chap, though he did kill Foxey. Very well," Luke went on slowly, "then the matter be as good as settled. Oi will send Bill down to-morrow, and he will see if thou canst let un have the money. A loife vor a loife, that's what oi says, Maister Ned. That be roight, bain't it?"

"That's right enough, Luke," Ned replied, "though I don't quite see what that has to do with it, except that the man who has taken this life should give his life to make amends."

"Yes, that be it, in course," Luke replied. "Yes; just as you says, he ought vor to give his loife to make amends."

That night Ned arranged with Abijah, who was delighted to hand over her savings for the furtherance of any plan that would tend to clear Ned from the suspicion which hung over him. Bill came down next morning, and was told that a hundred pounds would be forthcoming in two days.

Upon the following evening the servant came in and told Ned that a young woman wished to speak to him.

He went down into the study, and, to his surprise, Mary Powlett was shown in. Her eyes were swollen with crying.

"Master Ned," she said, "I have come to say good-bye."

"Good-bye, Polly! Why, where are you going?"

"We are all going away, sir, to-morrow across the seas, to Ameriky I believe. It's all come so sudden it seems like a dream. Feyther never spoke of such a thing afore, and now all at once we have got to start. I have run all the way down from Varley to say good-bye. Feyther told me that I wasn't on no account to come down to you. 'Not on no account,' he said. But how could I go away and know that you had thought us so strange and ungrateful as to go away without saying good-bye after your dear feyther giving his life for little Jenny. I couldn't do it, sir. So when he started off to spend the evening for the last time at the 'Cow' I put on my bonnet and ran down here. I don't care if he beats me—not that he ever did beat me, but he might now—for he was terrible stern in telling me as I wasn't to come and see you."

Ned heard her without an interruption. The truth flashed across his mind. It was Luke Marner himself who was going to America, and was going to write home to clear him. Yet surely Luke could never have done it —Luke, so different from the majority of the croppers— Luke, who had steadily refused to have anything to say to General Lud and his schemes against the masters. Mary's last words gave him a clue to the mystery—"Your dear feyther gave his life for little Jenny." He coupled it with Luke's enigmatical words, "A loife for a loife."

For a minute or two he sat absolutely silent. Mary was hurt at the seeming indifference with which he received her news. She drew herself up a little, and said, in an altered voice:

"I will say good-bye, sir. I hope you won't think I was taking a liberty in thinking you would be sorry if we were all to go without your knowing it."

Ned roused himself at her words.

"It is not that, Polly. It is far from being that. But I want to ask you a question. You remember the night of Mr. Mulready's murder? Do you remember whether your father was at home all that evening?"

Polly opened her eyes in surprise at a question which seemed to her so irrelevant to the matter in hand.

"Yes, sir," she replied, still coldly. "I remember that night. We are not likely any of us to forget it. Feyther had not gone down to the 'Cow.' He sat smoking at home. Bill had dropped in, and they sat talking of the doings of the Luddites till it was later than usual. Feyther was sorry afterwards, because he said if he had been down at the 'Cow' he might have noticed by the talk if any one had an idea that anything was going to take place."

"Then he didn't go out at all that night, Polly?"

"No, sir, not at all that night; and now, sir, I will say good-bye."

"No, Polly, you won't, for I shall go back with you, and I don't think that you will go to America."

"I don't understand," the girl faltered.

"No, Polly, I don't suppose you do; and I have not understood till now. You will see when you get back."

"If you please," Mary said hesitatingly, "I would rather that you would not be there when feyther comes back. Of course I shall tell him that I have been down to see you, and I know he will be very angry."

"I think I shall be able to put that straight. I can't let your father go. God knows I have few enough true friends, and I cannot spare him and you; and as for Bill Swinton, he would break his heart if you went."

"Bill's only a boy, he will get over it," Polly said in a careless tone, but with a bright flush upon her cheek.

"He is nearly as old as you are, Polly, and he is one of the best fellows in the world. I know he's not your equal in education, but a steadier, better fellow, never was."

Mary made no reply, and in another minute the two set out together for Varley. In spite of Ned's confident assurance that he would appease Luke's anger, Mary was frightened when, as they entered the cottage, she saw Luke standing moodily in front of the fire.

"Oi expected this," he said in a tone of deep bitterness. "Oi were a fool vor to think as you war different to other gals, and that you would give up your own wishes to your feyther's."

"Oh, feyther!" Polly cried, "don't speak so to me. Beat me if you like, I deserve to be beaten, but don't speak to me like that. I am ready to go anywhere you like, and to be a good daughter to you; forgive me for this once disobeying you."

" Luke, old friend," Ned said earnestly, putting his hand on the cropper's shoulder, "don't be angry with Polly, she has done me a great service. I have learned the truth, and know what you meant now by a life for a life. You were going to sacrifice yourself for me. You were going to take upon yourself a crime which you never committed, to clear me. You went to York to declare yourself the murderer of Mulready, in case I had been found guilty. You were going to emigrate to America to send home a written confession."

" Who says as how oi didn't kill Foxey?" Luke said doggedly. "If oi choose to give myself oop now who is to gainsay me?"

" Mary and Bill can both gainsay you," Ned said. "They can prove that you did not stir out of the house that night. Come, Luke, it's of no use I feel with all my heart grateful to you for the sacrifice you were willing to make for me. I thank you as deeply and as heartily as if you had made it. It was a grand act of self-sacrifice, and you must not be vexed with Polly that she has prevented you carrying it out. It would have made me very unhappy had she not done so. When I found that you were gone I should certainly have got out from Bill the truth of the matter, and when your confession came home I should have been in a position to prove that you had only made it to screen me. Besides, I cannot spare you. I

have few friends, and I should be badly off indeed if the
one who has proved himself the truest and best were to
leave me. I am going to carry on the mill, and I must
have your help. I have relied upon you to stand by me,
and you must be the foreman of your department. Come,
Luke, you must say you forgive Polly for opening my
eyes just a little sooner than they would otherwise have
been, to the sacrifice you wanted to make for me."

Luke, who was sorely shaken by Mary's pitiful sobs,
could resist no longer, but opened his arms, and the girl
ran into them.

"There, there," he said, "doan't ee go on a crying, girl.
thou hasn't done no wrong, vor indeed it must have
seemed to thee flying in the face of natur to go away
wi'out saying good-bye to Maister Ned. Well, sir, oi be
main sorry as it has turned out so. Oi should ha' loiked
to ha' cleared thee; but if thou won't have it oi caan't
help it. Oi think thou beest wrong, but thou know'st best."

"Never mind, Luke, I shall be cleared in time, I trust,"
Ned said. "I am going down to the mill to-morrow for
the first time, and shall see you there. You have done me
good, Luke. It is well, indeed, for a man to know that he
has such a friend as you have proved yourself to be."

CHAPTER XVII.

A LONELY LIFE.

THE machinery had not started since the death of Mr. Mulready, the foreman having received several letters threatening his life if he ventured to use the new machinery; and the works had therefore been carried on on their old basis until something was settled as to their future management.

The first few days after his return Ned spent his time in going carefully through the books with the clerk, and in making himself thoroughly acquainted with the financial part of the business. He was assisted by Mr. Porson, who came every evening to the house, and went through the accounts with him. The foreman and the men in charge of the different rooms were asked to give their opinion as to whether it was possible to reduce expenses in any way, but they were unanimous in saying that this could not be done. The pay was at present lower than in any other mill in the district, and every item of expenditure had been kept down by Mr. Mulready to the lowest point.

"It is clear," Ned said at last, "that if the mill is to be kept on we must use the new machinery. I was afraid it would be so, for he would never have taken to it and risked his life unless it had been absolutely necessary. I don't like it, for I have strong sympathies with the men, and although I am sure that in the long run the hands will benefit by the increased trade, it certainly causes great suffering at present. So if it had been possible I would gladly have let the new machinery stand idle until the feeling against it had passed away; but as I see that the mill has been running at a loss ever since prices fell, it is quite clear that we must use it at once."

The next morning Ned called the foreman into his office at the mill, and told him that he had determined to set the new machinery at work at once.

"I am sorry to be obliged to do so," he said, "as it will considerably reduce the number of hands at work; but it cannot be helped, it is either that or stopping altogether, which would be worse still for the men. Be as careful as you can in turning off the hands, and as far as possible retain all the married men with families. The only exception to that rule is young Swinton, who is to be kept on whoever goes."

That evening Luke Marner called at the house to see Ned.

"Be it true, Maister Ned, as the voreman says, the new machines is to be put to work?"

"It is true, Luke, I am sorry to say. I would have avoided it if possible; but I have gone into the matter with Mr. Porson, and I find I must either do that or shut up the mill altogether, which would be a good deal worse for you all. Hand-work cannot compete with machinery, and the new machines will face a dozen yards of cloth while a cropper is doing one, and will do it much better and more evenly."

"That be so, surely, and it bain't no use my saying as it ain't, and it's true enough what you says, that it's better half the hands should be busy than none; but those as gets the sack won't see it, and oi fears there will be mischief. Oi don't hold with the Luddites, but oi tell ye the men be getting desperate, and oi be main sure as there will be trouble afore long. Your loife won't be safe, Maister Ned."

"I don't hold much to my life," Ned laughed bitterly, "so the Luddites won't be able to frighten me there."

"I suppose thou wilt have some of the hands to sleep at the mill, as they do at some of the other places. If thou wilt get arms those as is at work will do their best to defend it. Cartwright has got a dozen or more sleeping in his mill."

"I will see about it," Ned said, "but I don't think I shall do that. I don't want any men to get killed in defending our property."

"Then they will burn it, thou wilt see if they doan't," Luke said earnestly.

"I hope not, Luke. I shall do my best to prevent it anyhow."

"Oi will give ee warning if a whisper of it gets to

moi ears, you may be sure, but the young uns doan't say much to us old hands, who be mostly agin them, and in course they will say less now if oi be one of those kept on."

"We must chance it, Luke; but be sure, whatever I do I sha'n't let the mill be destroyed if I can help it."

And so on the Monday following the water-wheel was set going and the new machinery began to work. The number of hands at the mill was reduced by nearly one-half, while the amount of cloth turned out each week was quadrupled.

The machinery had all the latest improvements, and was excellently arranged. Mr. Mulready had thoroughly understood his business, and Ned soon saw that the profits under the new system of working would be fully as great as his stepfather had calculated.

A very short time elapsed before threatening letters began to come in. Ned paid no heed to them, but quietly went on his way. The danger was, however, undoubted. The attitude of the Luddites had become more openly threatening. Throughout the whole of the West Riding open drilling was carried on.

The mills at Marsden, Woodbottom, and Ottewells were all threatened. In answer to the appeals of the mill-owners the number of troops in the district was largely increased. Infantry were stationed in Marsden, and the 10th King's Bays, the 15th Hussars, and the Scots Greys were alternately billeted in the place. The roads to Ottewells, Woodbottom, and Lugards Mill were patrolled regularly, and the whole country was excited and alarmed by constant rumours of attacks upon the mills.

Ned went on his way quietly, asking for no special protection for his mill or person, seemingly indifferent to the excitement which prevailed. Except to the workmen in the mill, to the doctor, and Mr. Porson he seldom exchanged a word with anyone during the day.

Mr. Simmonds and several of his father's old friends had on his return made advances towards him, but he had resolutely declined to meet them. Mr. Porson and the doctor had remonstrated with him.

"It is no use," he replied. "They congratulated me on my acquittal, but I can tell by their tones that there is not one of them who thoroughly believes in his heart that I am innocent."

The only exception which Ned made was Mr. Cartwright, a mill-owner at Liversedge. He had been slightly acquainted with Captain Sankey; and one day soon after Ned's return as he was walking along the street oblivious, as usual, of every one passing, Mr. Cartwright came up and placing himself in front of him, said heartily:

"I congratulate you with all my heart, Sankey, on your escape from this rascally business. I knew that your innocence would be proved. I would have staked my life that your father's son never had any hand in such a black affair as this. I am heartily glad."

There was no withstanding the frank cordiality of the Yorkshireman's manner. Ned's reserve melted at once before it.

"Thank you very much," he said, returning the grasp of his hand; "but I am afraid that though I was acquitted my innocence wasn't proved, and never will be. You may think me innocent, but you will find but half a dozen people in Marsden to agree with you."

"Pooh! pooh!" Mr. Cartwright said. "You must not look at things in that light. Most men are fools, you know; never fear. We shall prove you innocent some day. I have no doubt these rascally Luddites are at the bottom of it. And now, look here, young fellow, I hear that you are going to run the mill. Of course you can't know much about it yet. Now I am an old hand and shall be happy to give you any advice in my power, both for your own sake and for that of your good father. Now I mean what I say, and I shall be hurt if you refuse. I am in here two or three times a week, and my road takes me within five hundred yards of your mill, so it will be no trouble to me to come round for half an hour as I pass, and give you a few hints until you get well into harness. There are dodges in our trade, you know, as well as in all others, and you must be put up to them if you are to keep up in the race. There is plenty of room for us all, and now that the hands are all banding themselves against us, we mill-owners must stand together too."

Ned at once accepted the friendly offer, and two or three times a week Mr. Cartwright came round to the mill, went round the place with Ned, and gave him his advice as to the commercial transactions. Ned found this of inestimable benefit. Mr. Cartwright was acquainted with all the buyers in that part of Yorkshire, and was able several times to prevent Ned from entering into transactions with men willing to take advantage of his inexperience.

Sometimes he went over with Mr. Cartwright to his mill at Liversedge and obtained many a useful hint there as to the management of his business. Only in the matter of having some of his hands to sleep at the mill Ned declined to act on the advice of his new friend.

"No," he said; "I am determined that I will have no lives risked in the defence of our property. It has cost us dearly enough already."

But though Ned refused to have any of his hands to sleep at the mill, he had a bed fitted up in his office, and every night at ten o'clock, after Charlie had gone to bed, he walked out to the mill and slept there. Heavy shutters were erected to all the lower windows and bells were attached to these, and to the doors, which would ring at the slightest motion.

A cart one evening arrived from Huddersfield after the hands had left the mill, and under Ned's direction a number of small barrels were carried up to his office.

Although three months had now elapsed since his return home he had never once seen his mother, and the knowledge that she still regarded him as the murderer of her husband greatly added to the bitterness of his life. Of an evening after Lucy had gone to bed he assisted Charlie with his lessons, and also worked for an hour with Bill Swinton, who came regularly every evening to be taught.

Bill had a strong motive for self-improvement. Ned had promised him that some day he should be foreman to the factory, but that before he could take such a position it would, of course, be necessary that he should be able to read and write well. But an even higher incentive was Bill's sense of his great inferiority in point of education to Polly Powlett. He entertained a deep affection for her, but he knew how she despised the rough and ignorant young fellows at Varley, and he felt that even if she loved him she would not consent to marry him unless he were in point of education in some way her equal; therefore he applied himself with all his heart to improving his education.

It was no easy task, for Bill was naturally somewhat slow and heavy; but he had perseverance, which makes up for many deficiencies, and his heart being in his work he made really rapid progress.

Sometimes Ned would start earlier than usual, and walk up with Bill Swinton, talking to him as they went over the subjects on which he had been working, the condition of the villagers, or the results of Bill's Sunday rambles over the moors.

On arriving at Varley Ned generally went in for half an hour's talk with Luke Marner and Mary Powlett before going off for the night to sleep at the mill. With these three friends, who all were passionately convinced of his innocence, he was more at his ease than anywhere else, for at home the thought of the absent figure upstairs was a never-ceasing pain.

"The wind is very high to-night," Ned said one evening as the cottage shook with a gust which swept down from the moor.

"Aye, that it be," Luke agreed; "but it is nowt to a storm oi saw when oi war a young chap on t' coast!"

"I did not not know you had ever been away from Varley," Ned said; "tell me about it, Luke."

"Well, it coomed round i' this way. One of t' chaps from here had a darter who had married and gone to live nigh t' coast, and he went vor a week to see her.

"Theere'd been a storm when he was there, and he told us aboot the water being all broke up into furrowes, vor all the world like a ploughed field, only each ridge wur twice as high as one of our houses, and they came a moving along as fast as a horse could gallop, and when they hit the rocks vlew up into t' air as hoigh as the steeple o' Marsden church. It seemed to us as this must be a lie, and there war a lot of talk oor it, and at last vour on us made up our moinds as we would go over and see vor oursclves.

"It war a longer tramp nor we had looked vor, and though we sometoimes got a lift i' a cart we was all pretty footsore when we got to the end of our journey. The village as we was bound for stood oop on t' top of a flattish hill, one side of which seemed to ha' been cut away by a knife, and when you got to the edge there you were a standing at the end o' the world. Oi know when we got thar and stood and looked out from the top o' that wall o' rock thar warn't a word among us.

"We was a noisy lot, and oi didn't think as nothing would ha' silenced a cropper; but thar we stood a-looking over at the end of the world, oi should say for five minutes, wi'out a word being spoke. Oi can see it now. There warn't a breath of wind nor a cloud i' the sky. It seemed to oi as if the sky went away as far as we could see, and then seemed to be doubled down in a line and to coom roight back agin to our feet. It joost took away our breath, and seemed somehow to bring a lump into the throat. Oi talked it over wi' the others afterwards and we'd all felt just the same.

"It beat us altogether, and you never see a lot of croppers so quiet and orderly as we war as we went up to t' village. Most o' t' men war away, as we arterwards learned, fishing, and t' women didn't knaw what to make o' us, but gathered at their doors and watched us as if we had been a party o' robbers coom down to burn the place and carry 'em away. However, when we found Sally White—that war the name of the woman as had married from Varley—she went round the village and told 'em as we was a party of her friends who had joost walked across Yorkshire to ha' a look at the sea. Another young chap, Jack Purcell war his name, as was Sally's brother, and oi, being his mate, we stopt at Sally's house. The other two got a lodging close handy.

"Vor the vurst day or two vokes war shy of us, but arter that they began to see as we meant no harm. Of course they looked on us as foreigners, just as we croppers do here on anyone as cooms to Varley. Then Sally's

husband coom back from sea and spoke up vor us, and
that made things better, and as we war free wi' our
money the fishermen took to us more koindly.

"We soon found as the water warn't always smooth
and blue like the sky as we had seen it at first. The
wind coom on to blow the vurst night as we war thar,
and the next morning the water war all tossing aboot
joost as Sally's feyther had said, though not so high
as he had talked on. Still the wind warn't a blow-
ing much, as Sally pointed owt to us; in a regular storm
it would be a different sort o' thing altogether. We said
as we should loike to see one, as we had coom all that
way o' purpose. The vorth noight arter we got there
Sally's husband said: 'You be a going vor to have your
wish; the wind be a getting up, and we are loike to have
a big storm on the coast to-morrow.' And so it war. Oi
can't tell you what it war loike, oi've tried over and
over again to tell Polly, but no words as oi can speak can
give any idee of it.

"It war not loike anything as you can imagine. Standing down on the shore the water seemed all broke up
into hills, and as if each hill was a-trying to get at you,
and a-breaking itself up on the shore wi' a roar of rage
when it found as it couldn't reach you. The noise war so
great as you couldn't hear a man standing beside you
speak to you. Not when he hollooed. One's words war
blowed away. It felt somehow as if one war having a
wrastle wi' a million wild beastes. They tells me as the
ships at sea sometoimes floates and gets through a storm

loike that; but oi doan't believe it, and shouldn't if they took their Bible oath to it, it baiant in reason.

"One of them waves would ha' broaked this cottage up loike a egg-shell. Oi do believes as it would ha' smashed Marsden church, and it doan't stand to reason as a ship, which is built, they tells me, of wood and plank, would stand agin waves as would knock doon a church. Arter the storm oi should ha' coom back next morning, vor I felt fairly frighted. There didn't seem no saying as to what t' water moight do next toime. We should ha' gone there and then, only Sally's husband told us as a vessel war expected in two or three days wi' a cargo of tubs and she was to run them in a creek a few miles away.

"He said as loike as not there moight be a foight wi' the officers, and that being so we naterally made up our moinds vor to stop and lend un a hand. One night arter it got dark we started, and arter a tramp of two or three hours cam' to the place. It were a dark noight, and how the ship as was bringing the liquor was to foind oot the place was more nor oi could make oot. Jack he tried to explain how they did it, but oi couldn't make head nor tails on it except that when they got close they war to show a loight twice, and we war to show a loight twice if it war all roight for landing.

"Oi asked what had becoom of the revenue men, and was told as a false letter had been writ saying a landing was to be made fifteen mile away. We went vorward to a place whar there war a break in the rocks and a sort of valley ran down to the sea. There war a lot of men standing aboot, and just as we coom up thar war a move, and we hears as the loights had been shown and the vessel war running in close. Down we goes wi' the others, and soon a boat cooms ashore. As soon as she gets close the men runs out to her; the sailors hands out barrels, and each man shoulders one and trudges off. We does the same and takes the kegs up to t' top, whar carts and horses was waiting for 'em. Oi went oop and down three toimes and began to think as there war moor hard work nor fun aboot it. Oi war a going to knock off when someone says as one more trip would finish the cargo, so down oi goes again. Just when oi gets to t' bottom there war a great shouting oop at top. 'They're just too late,' a man says; 'the kegs be all safe away except this last lot,' for the horses and carts had gone off the instant as they got their loads. 'Now we must run for it, for the revenue men will be as savage as may be when they voinds as they be too late.' 'Where be us to run?' says oi. 'Keep close to me, oi knows the place,' says he.

"So we runs down and voinds as they had tumbled the bar'ls into t' boat again, and t' men war just pushing her off when there war a shout close to us. 'Shove, shove!' shouts the men, and oi runs into t' water loike t' rest and shooved. Then a lot o' men run up shouting, 'Stop! in the king's name!' and began vor to fire pistols.

"Nateral oi wasn't agoing to be fired at for nowt, so oi clutches moi stick and goes at 'em wi' the rest, keeping close to t' chap as told me as he knew the coontry. There was a sharp foight vor a minute. Oi lays aboot me hearty and gets a crack on my ear wi' a cootlas, as they calls theer swords, as made me pretty wild.

"We got the best o't. 'Coom on,' says the man to me, 'there's a lot moor on 'em a cooming.' So oi makes off as hard as oi could arter him. He keeps straight along at t' edge o' t' water. It war soft rowing at first, vor t' place war as flat as a table, but arter running vor a few minutes he says, 'Look owt!' Oi didn't know what to look owt vor, and down oi goes plump into t' water. Vor all at once we had coomed upon a lot o' rocks covered wi' a sort of slimy stuff, and so slippery as you could scarce keep a footing on 'em. Oi picks myself up and vollers him. By this toime, Maister, oi war beginning vor to think as there warn't so mooch vun as oi had expected in this koind o' business. Oi had been working two hours loike a nigger a-carrying tubs. Oi had had moi ear pretty nigh cut off, and it smarted wi' the salt water awful. Oi war wet from head to foot and had knocked the skin off moi hands and knees when oi went down. However there warn't no toime vor to grumble. Oi vollers him till we gets to t' foot o' t' rocks, and we keeps along 'em vor aboot half a mile.

"The water here coombed close oop to t' rocks, and presently we war a walking through it. 'Be'st a going vor to drown us all?' says oi. 'We are jest there,' says he. 'Ten minutes later we couldn't ha' got along.' T' water war a-getting deeper and deeper, and t' loomps of water cooms along and well-nigh took me off my feet. Oi was aboot to turn back, vor it war better, thinks oi, to be took by t' king's men than to be droonded, when he says, 'Here we be.' He climbs oop t' rocks and oi follows him. Arter climbing a short way he cooms to a hole i' rocks, joost big enough vor to squeeze through, but once inside it opened out into a big cave. A chap had struck a loight, and there war ten or twelve more on us thar. 'We had better wait another five minutes,' says one, 'to see if any more cooms along. Arter that the tide ull be too high.'

"We waits, but no one else cooms; me and moi mate war t' last. Then we goes to t' back of the cave, whar 't rock sloped down lower and lower till we had to crawl along one arter t'other pretty nigh on our stomachs, like raats going into a hole. Oi wonders whar on aarth we war agoing, till at last oi found sudden as oi could stand oopright. Then two or three more torches war lighted, and we begins to climb oop some steps cut i' the face of t' rock. A rope had been fastened alongside to hold on by, which war a good job for me, vor oi should never ha' dared go oop wi'out it, vor if oi had missed my foot there warn't no saying how far oi would ha' fallen to t' bottom. At last the man avore me says, 'Here we be!' and grateful oi was, vor what wi' the crawling and the climbing, and the funk as oi was in o' falling, the swaat was a-running down me loike water. The torches war put out, and in another minute we pushes through some bushes and then we war on t' top of the cliff, a hundred yards or so back from t' edge, and doon in a sort of hollow all covered

(251)   U

thickly over wi' bushes. We stood and listened vor a moment, but no sound war to be heard. Then one on 'em says, 'We ha' done 'em agin. Now the sooner as we gets off to our homes the better.' Looky for me, Jack war one of the lot as had coom up through the cave. 'Coom along, Luke,' says he, 'oi be glad thou hast got out of it all roight. We must put our best foot foremost to get in afore day breaks.' So we sets off, and joost afore morning we gets back to village. As to t' other two from Varley, they never coom back agin. Oi heerd as how all as war caught war pressed for sea, and oi expect they war oot in a ship when a storm coom on, when in coorse they would be drownded. Oi started next day vor hoam, and from that day to this oi ha' never been five mile away, and what's more, oi ha' never grudged the price as they asked for brandy. It ud be cheap if it cost voive toimes as much, seeing the trouble and danger as there be in getting it ashore, to say nothing o' carrying it across the sea."

"That was an adventure, Luke," Ned said, "and you were well out of it. I had no idea you had ever been engaged in defrauding the king's revenue. But now I must be off. I shall make straight across for the mill without going into Varley."

One night Ned had as usual gone to the mill, and having carried down the twelve barrels from the office and placed them in a pile in the centre of the principal room of the mill he retired to bed. He had been asleep for some hours when he was awoke by the faint tingle of a bell. The office was over the principal entrance to the mill, and leaping from his bed he threw up the window and looked out. The night was dark, but he could see a crowd of at least two hundred men gathered in the yard. As the window was heard to open a sudden roar broke from the men, who had hitherto conducted their operations in silence.

"There he be, there's the young fox; burn the mill over his head. Now to work, lads, burst in the door."

And at once a man armed with a mighty sledge-hammer began to batter at the door.

Ned tried to make himself heard, but his voice was lost in the roar without. Throwing on some clothes he ran rapidly down-stairs and lighted several lamps in the machine-room. Then he went to the door, which was already tottering under the heavy blows, shot back some of the bolts, and then took his place by the side of the pile of barrels with a pistol in his hand.

In another moment the door yielded and fell with a crash, and the crowd with exultant cheers poured in. They paused surprised and irresolute at seeing Ned standing quiet and seemingly indifferent by the pile of barrels in the centre of the room.

"Hold!" he said in a quiet clear voice, which sounded distinctly over the tumult. "Do not come any nearer, or it will be the worse for you. Do you know what I have got here, lads? This is powder. If you doubt it, one of you can come forward and look at this barrel with the head out by my side. Now I have only got to fire my pistol into it to blow the mill, and you with it, into the air, and I mean to do it. Of course I shall go too; but some of you with black masks over your faces, who, I suppose, live near here, may know something about me, and may know that my life is not so pleasant a one that I value it in the slightest. As far as I am concerned you might burn the mill and me with it without my lifting a finger; but this mill is the property of my mother, brother, and sister. Their living depends upon it, and I am going to defend it. Let one of you stir a single step forward and I fire this pistol into this barrel beside me." And Ned held the pistol over the open barrel.

A dead silence of astonishment and terror had fallen upon the crowd. The light was sufficient for them to see Ned's pale but determined face, and as his words came out cold and steady there was not one who doubted that he was in earnest, and that he was prepared to blow himself and them into the air if necessary.

A cry of terror burst from them as he lowered the pistol to the barrel of powder. Then in wild dismay every man threw down his arms and fled, jostling each other fiercely to make their escape through the doorway from the fate which threatened them. In a few seconds the place was cleared and the assailants in full flight across the country. Ned laughed contemptuously. Then with some difficulty he lifted the broken door into its place, put some props behind it, fetched a couple of blankets from his bed, and lay down near the powder, and there slept quietly till morning.

Luke and Bill Swinton were down at the factory an

hour before the usual time. The assailants had for the most part come over from Huddersfield, but many of the men from Varley had been among them. The terror which Ned's attitude had inspired had been so great that the secret was less well kept than usual, and as soon as people were astir the events of the night were known to most in the village. The moment the news reached the ears of Luke and Bill they hurried down to the mill without going in as usual for their mug of beer and bit of bread and cheese at the "Brown Cow."

The sight of the shattered door at once told them that the rumours they had heard were well founded. They knocked loudly upon it.

"Hullo!" Ned shouted, rousing himself from his slumbers; "who is there? What are you kicking up all this row about?"

"It's oi, Maister Ned, oi and Bill, an glad oi am to hear your voice. It's true, then, they haven't hurt thee?"

"Not a bit of it," Ned said as he moved the supports of the door. "I think they got the worst of it."

"If so be as what oi ha' heard be true you may well say that, Maister Ned. Oi hear as you ha' gived 'em such a fright as they won't get over in a hurry. They say as you was a-sitting on the top of a heap of gunpowder up to the roof with a pistol in each hand."

"Not quite so terrible as that, Luke; but the effect would have been the same. Those twelve barrels of powder you see there would have blown the mill and all in it into atoms."

"Lor, Maister Ned," Bill said, "where didst thou get that powder, and why didn't ye say nowt about it? Oi ha' seen it up in the office, now oi thinks on it. Oi wondered what them barrels piled up in a corner and covered over wi' sacking could be; but it warn't no business o' mine to ax."

"No, Bill, I did not want any of them to know about it, because these things get about, and half the effect is lost unless they come as a surprise; but I meant to do it if I had been driven to it, and if I had, King Lud would have had a lesson which he would not have forgotten in a hurry. Now, Luke, you and Bill had better help me carry them back to their usual place. I don't think they are likely to be wanted again."

"That they won't be," Luke said confidently; "the Luddites ull never come near this mill agin, not if thou hast twenty toimes as many machines. They ha' got a froight they won't get over. They told me as how some of the chaps at Varley was so froighted that they will be a long toime afore they gets round. Oi'll go and ask to-night how that Methurdy chap, the blacksmith, be a feeling. Oi reakon he's at the bottom on it. Dang un for a mischievous rogue! Varley would ha' been quiet enough without him. Oi be wrong if oi sha'n't see him dangling from a gibbet one of these days, and a good riddance too."

The powder was stowed away before the hands began to arrive, all full of wonder and curiosity. They learned little at the mill, however. Ned went about the place as usual with an unchanged face, and the hands were soon at their work; but many during the day wondered how it was possible that their quiet and silent young employer should have been the hero of the desperate act of which everyone had heard reports more or less exaggerated.

A lad had been sent over to Marsden the first thing for some carpenters, and by nightfall a rough but strong door had been hung in place of that which had been shattered. By the next day rumour had carried the tale all over Marsden, and Ned on his return home was greeted by Charlie with:

"Why, Ned, there is all sorts of talk in the place of an attack upon the mill the night before last. Why didn't you tell me about it?"

"Yes, Master Ned," Abijah put in, "and they say as you blew up about a thousand of them."

"Yes, Abijah," Ned said with a laugh, "and the pieces haven't come down yet."

"No! but really, Ned, what is it all about?"

"There is not much to tell you, Charlie. The Luddites came and broke open the door. I had got several barrels of powder there, and when they came in I told them if they came any farther I should blow the place up. That put them in a funk, and they all bolted, and I went to sleep again. That's the whole affair."

"Oh!" Charlie said in a disappointed voice, for this seemed rather tame after the thrilling reports he had heard.

"Then you didn't blow up any of 'em, Maister Ned," Abijah said doubtfully.

"Not a man jack, Abijah. You see I could not very well have blown them up without going up myself too, so I thought it better to put it off for another time."

"They are very wicked bad men," Lucy said gravely.

"Not so very wicked and bad, Lucy. You see they are almost starving, and they consider that the new machines have taken the bread out of their mouths, which is true enough. Now you know when people are starving, and have not bread for their wives and children, they are apt to get desperate. If I were to see you starving, and thought that somebody or something was keeping the bread out of your mouth, I daresay I should do something desperate."

"But it would be wrong all the same," Lucy said doubtfully.

"Yes, my dear, but it would be natural; and when human nature pulls one way, and what is right pulls the other, the human nature generally gets the best of it."

Lucy did not exactly understand, but she shook her head gravely in general dissent to Ned's view.

"Why did you not tell us when you came home to breakfast yesterday?" Charlie asked.

"Because I thought you were sure to hear sooner or later. I saw all the hands in the mill had got to know about it somehow or other, and I was sure it would soon get over the place; and I would rather that I could say, if anyone asked me, that I had not talked about it to anyone, and was in no way responsible for the absurd stories which had got about. I have been talked about

enough in Marsden, goodness knows, and it is disgusting
that just as I should think they must be getting tired of
the subject here is something fresh for them to begin upon
again."

As they were at tea the servant brought in a note which
had just been left at the door. It was from Mr. Thompson, saying that in consequence of the rumours which
were current in the town he should be glad to learn from
Ned whether there was any foundation for them, and
would therefore be obliged if he would call at eight o'clock
that evening. His colleague Mr. Simmonds would be
present.

Ned gave an exclamation of disgust as he threw down
the note.

"Is there any answer, sir?" the servant asked. "The
boy said he was to wait."

"Tell him to say to Mr. Thompson that I will be there
at eight o'clock; but that—no, that will do. It wouldn't
be civil," he said to Charlie as the door closed behind the
servant, "to say that I wish to goodness he would let my
affairs alone and look to his own."

When Ned reached the magistrates at the appointed
hour he found that the inquiry was of a formal character.
Besides the two justices Major Browne, who commanded
the troops at Marsden, was present; and the justices' clerk
was there to take notes.

Mr. Simmonds greeted Ned kindly, Mr. Thompson
stiffly. He was one of those who had from the first been
absolutely convinced that the lad had killed his stepfather.

The officer, who was of course acquainted with the story, examined Ned with a close scrutiny.

"Will you take a seat, Ned?" Mr. Simmonds, who was the senior magistrate, said. "We have asked you here to explain to us the meaning of certain rumours which are current in the town of an attack upon your mill."

"I will answer any questions that you may ask," Ned said quietly, seating himself, while the magistrates' clerk dipped his pen in the ink and prepared to take notes of his statement.

"Is it the case that the Luddites made an attack upon your mill the night before last?"

"It is true, sir."

"Will you please state the exact circumstances."

"There is not much to tell," Ned said quietly. "I have for some time been expecting an attack, having received many threatening letters. I have, therefore, made a habit of sleeping in the mill, and a month ago I got in twelve barrels of powder from Hudderstield. Before going to bed of a night I always pile these in the middle of the room where the looms are, which is the first as you enter. I have bells attached to the shutters and doors to give me notice of any attempt to enter. The night before last I was awoke by hearing one of them ring, and looking out of the window made out a crowd of two or three hundred men outside. They began to batter the door, so, taking a brace of pistols which I keep in readiness by my bed, I went down and took my place by the powder. When they broke down the door and entered I just told them that if they came any farther I should fire my pistol into one of the barrels, the head of which I had knocked out; and, as I suppose they saw that I meant to do it, they went off. That is all I have to tell, so far as I know."

The clerk's pen ran swiftly over the paper as Ned quietly made his statement. Then there was a silence for a minute or two.

"And did you really mean to carry out your threat, Mr. Sankey?"

"Certainly," Ned said.

"But you would, of course, have been killed yourself."

"Naturally," Ned said drily; "but that would have been of no great consequence to me or anyone else. As the country was lately about to take my life at its own expense it would not greatly disapprove of my doing so at my own, especially as the lesson to the Luddites would have been so wholesale a one that the services of the troops in this part of the country might have been dispensed with for some time."

"Did you recognize any of the men concerned?"

"I am glad to say I did not," Ned replied. "Some of them were masked. The others were, so far as I could see among such a crowd of faces in a not very bright light, all strangers to me."

"And you would not recognize any of them again were you to see them?"

"I should not," Ned replied. "None of them stood out prominently among the others."

"You speak, Mr. Sankey," Mr. Thompson said, "as if

your sympathies were rather on the side of these men, who would have burned your mill, and probably have murdered you, than against them."

"I do not sympathize with the measures the men are taking to obtain redress for what they regard as a grievance; but I do sympathize very deeply with the amount of suffering which they are undergoing from the introduction of machinery and the high prices of provisions; and I am not surprised that, desperate as they are, and ignorant as they are, they should be led astray by bad advice. Is there any other question that you wish to ask me?"

"Nothing at present, I think," Mr. Simmonds said after consulting his colleague by a look. "We shall, of course, forward a report of the affair to the proper authorities, and I may say that although you appear to take it in a very quiet and matter-of-fact way, you have evidently behaved with very great courage and coolness, and in a manner most creditable to yourself. I think, however, that you ought immediately to have made a report to us of the circumstances, in order that we might at once have determined what steps should be taken for the pursuit and apprehension of the rioters."

Ned made no reply, but rising, bowed slightly to the three gentlemen and walked quietly from the room.

"A singular young fellow!" Major Browne remarked as the door closed behind him. "I don't quite know what to make of him, but I don't think he could have committed that murder. It was a cowardly business, and although I believe he might have a hand in any desperate

NED IS QUESTIONED BY THE JUSTICES.

affair, as indeed this story he has just told us shows, I would lay my life he would not do a cowardly one."

"I agree with you," Mr. Simmonds said, "though I own that I have never been quite able to rid myself of a vague suspicion that he was guilty."

"And I believe he is so still," Mr. Thompson said. "To me there is something almost devilish about that lad's manner."

"His manner was pleasant enough," Mr. Simmonds said warmly, "before that affair of Mulready. He was as nice a lad as you would wish to see till his mother was fool enough to get engaged to that man, who, by the way, I never liked. No wonder his manner is queer now; so would yours be, or mine, if we were tried for murder and, though acquitted, knew there was still a general impression of our guilt."

"Yes, by Jove," the officer said, "I should be inclined to shoot myself. You are wrong, Mr. Thompson, take my word for it. That young fellow never committed a cowardly murder. I think you told me, Mr. Simmonds, that he had intended to go into the army had it not been for this affair? Well, his majesty has lost a good officer, for that is just the sort of fellow who would lead a forlorn hope though he knew the breach was mined in a dozen places. It is a pity, a terrible pity!"

CHAPTER XVIII.

NED IS ATTACKED.

S Ned had foreseen and resented, the affair at the mill again made him the chief topic of talk in the neighbourhood, and the question of his guilt or innocence of the murder of his stepfather was again debated with as much earnestness as it had been when the murder was first committed. There was this difference, however, that whereas before he had found but few defenders, for the impression that he was guilty was almost universal, there were now many who took the other view.

The one side argued that a lad who was ready to blow himself and two or three hundred men into the air was so desperate a character that he would not have been likely to hesitate a moment in taking the life of a man whom he hated, and who had certainly ill-treated him. The other side insisted that one with so much cool courage would not have committed a murder in so cowardly a way as by tying a rope across the road which his enemy had to traverse. One party characterized his conduct at the mill as that of the captain of a pirate ship, the other likened it to any of the great deeds of devotion told in history—the death of Leonidas and his three hundred, or the devotion of Mutius Scævola.

Had Ned chosen now he might have gathered round himself a strong party of warm adherents, for there were many who, had they had the least encouragement, would have been glad to shake him by the hand and to show their partisanship openly and warmly; but Ned did not choose. The doctor and Mr. Porson strongly urged upon him that he should show some sort of willingness to meet the advances which many were anxious to make.

"These people are all willing to admit that they have been wrong, Ned, and really anxious to atone as far as they can for their mistake in assuming that you were guilty. Now is your time, my boy; what they believe to-day others will believe to-morrow; it is the first step towards living it down. I always said it would come, but I hardly ventured to hope that it would come so soon."

"I can't do it, Mr. Porson; I would if I could, if only for the sake of the others; but I can't talk, and smile, and look pleasant. When a man knows that his mother lying at home thinks that he is a murderer how is he to go about like other people?"

"But I have told you over and over again, Ned, that your mother is hardly responsible for her actions. She has never been a very reasonable being, and is less so than ever at present. Make an effort, my boy, and mix with others. Show yourself at the cricket-match next week.

You know the boys are all your firm champions, and I warrant that half the people there will flock round you and make much of you if you will but give them the chance."

But Ned could not, and did not, but went on his way as before, living as if Marsden had no existence for him, intent upon his work at the mill, and unbending only when at home with his brother and sister.

His new friend, Cartwright, was, of course, one of the first to congratulate him on the escape the mill had had of destruction.

"I was wondering what you would do if they came," he said, "and was inclined to think you were a fool for not following my example and having some of your hands to sleep at the mill. Your plan was best, I am ready to allow; that is to say, it was best for anyone who was ready to carry out his threat if driven to it. I shouldn't be, I tell you fairly. If the mill is attacked I shall fight and shall take my chance of being shot, but I could not blow myself up in cold blood."

"I don't suppose I could have done so either in the old times," Ned said with a faint smile. "My blood used to be hot enough, a good deal too hot, but I don't think anything could get it up to boiling point now, so you see if this thing had to be done at all it must have been in cold blood."

"By the way, Sankey, I wish you would come over one day next week and dine with me; there will be no one else there except my daughter."

Ned hastily muttered an excuse.

"Oh, that is all nonsense!" Mr. Cartwright said good-humouredly; "you are not afraid of me, and you needn't be afraid of my daughter. She is only a child of fifteen, and of course takes you at my estimate, and is disposed to regard you as a remarkable mixture of the martyr and the hero, and to admire you accordingly. Pooh, pooh, lad! you can't be living like a hermit all your life; and at any-rate if you make up your mind to have but a few friends you must be all the closer and more intimate with them. I know you dine with Porson and Green, and I am not going to let you keep me at arm's-length; you must come, or else I shall be seriously offended."

So Ned had no resource left him, and had to consent to dine at Liversedge. Once there he often repeated the visit. With the kind and hearty manufacturer he was perfectly at home, and although at first he was uncomfortable with his daughter he gradually became at his ease with her, especially after she had driven over with her father to make friends with Lucy, and, again, a short time afterwards, to carry her away for a week's visit at Liversedge. For this Ned was really grateful. Lucy's life had been a very dull one. She had no friends of her own age in Marsden, for naturally at the time of Mr. Mulready's death all intimacy with the few acquaintances they had in the place had been broken off, for few cared that their children should associate with a family among whom such a terrible tragedy had taken place.

Charlie was better off, for he had his friends at school,

(281) X

and the boys at Porson's believed in Ned's innocence as a point of honour. In the first place, it would have been something like a reflection upon the whole school to admit the possibility of its first boy being a murderer; in the second, Ned had been generally popular among them, he was their best cricketer, the life and soul of all their games, never bullying himself and putting down all bullying among others with a strong hand. Their championship showed itself in the shape of friendship for Charlie; and at the midsummer following Mr. Mulready's death he had received invitations from many of them to stay with them during the holidays, and had indeed spent that time on a series of short visits among them.

He himself would, had he had his choice, have remained at home with Ned, for he knew how lonely his brother's life was, and that his only pleasure consisted in the quiet evenings; but Ned would not hear of it.

"You must go, Charlie, both for your sake and my own. The change will do you good; and if you were to stop at home and refuse to go out people would say that you were ashamed to be seen, and that you were crushed down with the weight of my guilt. You have got to keep up the honour of the family now, Charlie; I have proved a failure."

It was September now, and six months had elapsed since the death of Mr. Mulready. The getting in of the harvest had made no difference in the price of food, the general distress was as great as ever, and the people shook their heads and said that there would be bad doings when the winter with its long nights was at hand.

The mill was flourishing under its new management. The goods turned out by the new machinery were of excellent quality and finish, and Ned had more orders on hand than he could execute. The profits were large, the hands well paid and contented. Ned had begged Dr. Green and the other trustee of his mother's property to allow him to devote a considerable part of the profits to assist, during the hard time of winter, the numerous hands in Varley and other villages round Marsden who were out of employment; but the trustees said they were unable to permit this. Mrs. Mulready absolutely refused to hear anything about the mill or to discuss any questions connected with money, therefore they had no resource but to allow the profits, after deducting all expenses of living, to accumulate until, at anyrate, Lucy, the youngest of the children, came of age.

Ned, however, was not to be easily thwarted, and he quietly reverted to the old method of giving out a large quantity of work to the men to be performed by the hand-looms in their own cottages, while still keeping his new machinery fully employed. There was, indeed, a clear loss upon every yard of cloth so made, as it had, of course, to be sold at the lower prices which machinery had brought about; still the profits from the mill itself were large enough to bear the drain, and means of support would be given to a large number of families throughout the winter. Ned told Dr. Green what he had done.

"You see, doctor," he said, "this is altogether beyond your province. You and Mr. Lovejoy appointed me, as the senior representative of the family, to manage the mill. Of course I can manage it in my own way, and as long as the profits are sufficient to keep us in the position we have hitherto occupied I don't see that you have any reason to grumble."

"You are as obstinate as a mule, Ned," the doctor said smiling; "but I am glad enough to let you have your way so long as it is not clearly my duty to thwart you; and indeed I don't know how those poor people at Varley and at some of the other villages would get through the winter without some such help."

"I am very glad I hit upon the plan. I got Luke Marner to draw up a list of all the men who had families depending upon them; but indeed I find that I have been able to set pretty nearly all the looms in the neighbourhood at work, and of course that will give employment to the spinners and croppers. I have made a close calculation, and find that with the profit the mill is making I shall just be able to clear our household expenses this winter, after selling at a loss all the cloth that can be made in the looms round."

"At anyrate, Ned," the doctor said, "your plan will be a relief to me in one way. Hitherto I have never gone to bed at night without an expectation of being awakened with the news that you have been shot on your way out to the mill at night. The fellows you frightened away last month must have a strong grudge against you in

addition to their enmity against you as an employer.
You will be safe enough in future, and can leave the mill
to take care of itself at night if you like. You will have
the blessings of all the poor fellows in the neighbourhood, and may henceforth go where you will by night or
day without the slightest risk of danger."

"You are right, no doubt," Ned said, "though that
did not enter my mind. When I took the step my only
fear was that by helping them for a time I might be
injuring them in the future. Hand-weaving, spinning,
and cropping are doomed. Nothing can save them, and
the sooner the men learn this and take to other means of
gaining a livelihood the better. Still the prices that I
can give are of course very low, just enough to keep them
from starvation, and we must hope that ere long new
mills will be erected in which the present hand-workers
will gradually find employment."

Hardly less warm than the satisfaction that the an-
nouncement that Sankey was about to give out work to
all the hand-looms excited in the villages round Marsden,
was that which Abijah felt at the news.

Hitherto she had kept to herself the disapprobation
which she felt at Ned's using the new machinery. She
had seen in her own village the sufferings that had
been caused by the change, and her sympathies were
wholly with the Luddites, except of course when they
attempted anything against the life and property of her
boy. Strong in the prejudices of the class among whom
she had been born and reared, she looked upon the new

machinery as an invention of the evil one to ruin the
working-classes, and had been deeply grieved at Ned's
adoption of its use. Nothing but the trouble in which
he was could have compelled her to keep her opinion on
the subject to herself.

"I am main glad, Maister Ned. I b'lieve now as we may
find out about that other affair. I never had no hope
before, it warn't likely as things would come about as
you wanted, when you was a-flying in the face of providence by driving poor folks to starvation with them
noisy engines of yours; it warn't likely, and I felt as it
was wrong to hope for it. I said my prayers every
night, but it wasn't reasonable to expect a answer as
long as that mill was a-grinding men to powder."

" I don't think it was as bad as all that, Abijah.   In
another ten years there will be twice as many hands
employed as ever there were, and there is no saying how
large the trade may not grow."

Abijah shook her head as if to imply her belief that
an enlargement of trade by means of these new machines
would be clearly flying in the face of providence. However she was too pleased at the news that hand-work
was to be resumed in the district to care about arguing
the question. Even the invalid upstairs took a feeble
interest in the matter, when Abijah told her that Master
Ned had arranged to give work to scores of starving
people through the winter.

As a rule Abijah never mentioned his name to her
mistress, for it was always the signal for a flood of tears,

and caused an excitement and agitation which did not calm down for hours; but lately she had noticed that her mistress began to take a greater interest in the details she gave her of what was passing outside. She spoke more cheerfully when Lucy brought in her work and sat by her bedside, and she had even exerted herself sufficiently to get up two or three times and lie upon the sofa in her room. It was Charlie who, full of the news, had rushed in to tell her about Ned's defence at the mill. She had made no comment whatever, but her face had flushed and her lips trembled, and she had been very silent and quiet all that day. Altogether Abijah thought that she was mending, and Dr. Green was of the same opinion.

Although the setting to work of the hand-looms and spindles relieved the dire pressure of want immediately about Marsden, in other parts things were worse than ever that winter, and the military were kept busy by the many threatening letters which were received by the mill-owners from King Lud.

One day Mr. Cartwright entered Ned's office at the mill.

" Have you heard the news, Sankey?"

" No, I have heard no news in particular."

" Horsfall has been shot."

" You don't say so!" Ned exclaimed.

" Yes, he has been threatened again and again. He was over at Huddersfield yesterday afternoon; he started from the 'George' on his way back at half-past five. It

seems that his friend Eastwood of Slaithwaite, knowing
how often his life had been threatened, offered to ride
back with him, and though Horsfall laughed at the offer
and rode off alone, Eastwood had his horse saddled and
rode after him, but unfortunately did not overtake him.

"About six o'clock Horsfall pulled up his horse at the
Warren-house Inn at Crossland Moor. There he gave a
glass of liquor to two of his old work-people who happened to be outside, drank a glass of rum and water as
he sat in the saddle, and then rode off. A farmer named
Parr was riding about a hundred and fifty yards behind
him. As Horsfall came abreast of a plantation Parr noticed four men stooping behind a wall, and then saw two
puffs of smoke shoot out. Horsfall's horse started round
at the flash, and he fell forward on his saddle.

"Parr galloped up, and jumping off caught him as he
was falling. Horsfall could just say who he was and
ask to be taken to his brother's house, which was near
at hand. There were lots of people in the road, for it
was market-day in Huddersfield, you know, and the folks
were on their way home, so he was soon put in a cart
and taken back to the Warren-house. It was found that
both balls had struck him, one in the right side and one
in the left thigh. I hear he is still alive this morning,
but cannot live out the day."

"That is a bad business indeed," Ned said.

"It is indeed. Horsfall was a fine generous high-
spirited fellow, but he was specially obnoxious to the
Luddites, whose doings he was always denouncing in the

most violent way. Whose turn will it be next, I wonder? The success of this attempt is sure to encourage them, and we may expect to hear of some more bad doings. Of course there will be a reward offered for the apprehension of the murderers. A labourer saw them as they were hurrying away from the plantation, and says he should know them again if he saw them; but these fellows hang together so that I doubt if we shall ever find them out."

After Mr. Cartwright had gone Ned told Luke what had happened. " I hope, Luke, that none of the Varley people have had a hand in this business?"

" Oi hoape not," Luke said slowly, "but ther bain't no saying; oi hears little enough of what be going on. Oi was never much in the way of hearing, but now as I am head of the room, and all the hands here are known to be well contented, oi hears less nor ever. Still matters get talked over at the ' Cow.' Oi hears it said as many of the lads in the village has been wishing to leave King Lud since the work was put out, but they have had messages as how any man turning traitor would be put out of the way. It's been somewhat like that from the first, and more nor half of them as has joined has done so because they was afeard to stand out. They ain't tried to put the screw on us old hands, but most of the young uns has been forced into joining.

" Bill has had a hard toime of it to stand out. He has partly managed because of his saying as how he has been sich good friends with you that he could not join to take

part against the maisters; part, as oi hears, because his
two brothers, who been in the thick of it from the first,
has stuck up agin Bill being forced into it. Oi wish
as we could get that blacksmith out of t' village; he be
at the bottom of it all, and there's nowt would please
me more than to hear as the constables had laid their
hands on him. Oi hear as how he is more violent than ever
at that meeting-house. Of course he never mentions
names or says anything direct, but he holds forth agin
traitors as falls away after putting their hands to the
plough, and as forsakes the cause of their starving
brethren because their own stomachs is full."

"I wish we could stop him," Ned said thoughtfully.
"I might get a constable sent up to be present at the
meetings, but the constables here are too well known,
and if you were to get one from another place the sight
of a stranger there would be so unusual that it would put
him on his guard at once. Besides, as you say, it would
be very difficult to prove that his expressions applied to
the Luddites, although every one may understand what
he means. One must have clear evidence in such a case.
However, I hope we shall catch him tripping one of these
days. These are the fellows who ought to be punished,
not the poor ignorant men who are led away by them."

The feeling of gratitude and respect with which Ned
was regarded by the workpeople of his district, owing to
his action regarding the hand-frames, did something towards lightening the load caused by the suspicion which
still rested upon him. Although he still avoided all inter-

course with those of his own station, he no longer felt the pressure so acutely. The hard set expression of his face softened somewhat, and though he was still strangely quiet and reserved in his manner towards those with whom his business necessarily brought him in contact, he no longer felt absolutely cut off from the rest of his kind.

Ned had continued his practice of occasionally walking up with Bill Swinton to Varley on his way to the mill. There was now little fear of an attempt upon his life by the hands in his neighbourhood; but since the failure on the mill he had incurred the special enmity of the men who had come from a distance on that occasion, and he knew that any night he might be waylaid and shot by them. It was therefore safer to go round by Varley than by the direct road. One evening when he had been chatting rather later than usual at Luke Marner's, Luke said:

"Oi think there's something i' t' wind. Oi heerd at t' Cow this evening that there are some straangers i' the village. They're at t' Dog. Oi thinks there's soom sort ov a council there. Oi heers as they be from Huddersfield, which be the headquarters o' General Lud in this part. However, Maister, oi doan't think as there's any fear of another attack on thy mill; they war too badly scaared t'other noight vor to try that again."

When Ned got up to go Bill Swinton as usual put on his cap to accompany him, as he always walked across the moor with him until they came to the path leading down to the back of the mill, this being the road taken by the hands from Varley coming and going from work.

When they had started a minute or two George, who had been sitting by the fire listening to the talk, got up and stretched himself preparatory to going to bed, and said in his usual slow way:

"Oi wonders what they be adoing to-noight. Twice while ye ha' been a-talking oi ha' seen a chap a-looking in at t' window—"

"Thou hast!" Luke exclaimed, starting up. "Dang thee, thou young fool! Why didn't say so afore? Oi will hoide thee when oi comes back rarely! Polly, do thou run into Gardiner's, and Hoskings', and Burt's; tell 'em to cotch up a stick and to roon for their loives across t' moor towards t' mill. And do thou, Jarge, roon into Sykes' and Wilmot's and tell 'em the same; and be quick if thou would save thy skin. Tell 'em t' maister be loike to be attacked."

Catching up a heavy stick Luke hurried off, running into two cottages near and bringing on two more of the mill hands with him. He was nearly across the moor when they heard the sound of a shot. Luke, who was running at the top of his speed, gave a hoarse cry as of one who has received a mortal wound. Two shots followed in quick succession. A minute later Luke was dashing down the hollow through which the path ran down from the moor. Now he made out a group of moving figures and heard the sounds of conflict. His breath was coming in short gasps, his teeth were set; fast as he was running, he groaned that his limbs would carry him no faster. It was scarce two minutes from

the time when the first shot was fired, but it seemed ages
to him before he dashed into the group of men, knocking
down two by the impetus of his rush. He was but just
in time. A figure lay prostrate on the turf; another
standing over him had just been beaten to his knee. But
he sprang up again at Luke's onward rush. His assailants for a moment drew back.

"Thou'rt joost in toime, Luke," Bill panted out. "Oi
war well-nigh done."

"Be t' maister shot?"

"No, nowt but a clip wi' a stick."

As the words passed between them the assailants again
rushed forward with curses and execrations upon those
who stood between them and their victim.

"Moind, Luke, they ha' got knoives!" Bill exclaimed.
"Oi ha' got more nor one slash already."

Luke and Bill fought vigorously, but they were over-
matched. Anger and fear for Ned's safety nerved Luke's
arm, the weight of the last twenty years seemed to
drop off him, and he felt himself again the sturdy young
cropper who could hold his own against any in the
village. But he had not yet got back his breath, and
was panting heavily. The assailants, six in number,
were active and vigorous young men; and Bill, who was
streaming with blood from several wounds, could only fight
on the defensive. Luke then gave a short cry of relief as
the two men who had started with him, but whom he
had left behind from the speed which his intense eagerness had given him, ran up but a short minute after he

had himself arrived and ranged themselves by him. The assailants hesitated now.

"Ye'd best be off," Luke said; "there ull be a score more here in a minute."

With oaths of disappointment and rage the assailants fell back and were about to make off when one of them exclaimed:

"Ye must carry Tom off wi' thee. It ull never do to let un lay here."

The men gathered round a dark figure lying a few yards away. Four of them lifted it by the hands and feet, and then they hurried away across the moor. As they did so Bill Swinton with a sigh fell across Ned's body.

In two or three minutes four more men, accompanied by George and Polly, whose anxiety would not let her stay behind, hurried up. Luke and his companions had raised Ned and Bill into a sitting posture.

"Are they killed, feyther?" Polly cried as she ran up breathless to them.

"Noa, lass; oi think as t' maister be only stunned, and Bill ha' fainted from loss o' blood. But oi doan't know how bad he be hurted yet. We had best carry 'em back to t' house; we can't see to do nowt here."

"Best let them stay here, feyther, till we can stop the bleeding. Moving would set the wounds off worse."

"Perhaps you are right, Polly. Jarge, do thou run back to t' house as hard as thou canst go. Loight t' lanterns and bring 'em along, wi' a can o' cold water."

Although the boy ran to the village and back at the

top of his speed the time seemed long indeed to those who were waiting. When he returned they set to work at once to examine the injuries. Ned appeared to have received but one blow. The blood was slowly welling from a wound at the back of his head.

"That war maade by a leaded stick, oi guess," Luke said; "it's cut through his hat, and must pretty nigh ha' cracked his skool. One of you bathe un wi' the water while we looks arter Bill."

Polly gave an exclamation of horror as the light fell upon Bill Swinton. He was covered with blood. A clean cut extended from the top of the ear to the point of the chin, another from the left shoulder to the breast, while a third gash behind had cut through to the bone of the shoulder-blade.

"Never moind t' water, lass," Luke said as Polly with trembling hands was about to wash the blood from the cut on the face, "the bluid won't do un no harm, thou must stop t' bleeding."

Polly tore three or four long strips from the bottom of her dress. While she was doing so one of the men by Luke's directions took the lantern and gathered some short dry moss from the side of the slope, and laid it in a ridge on the gaping wound. Then Luke with Polly's assistance tightly bandaged Bill's head, winding the strips from the back of the head round to the chin, and again across the temples and jaw. Luke took out his knife and cut off the coat and shirt from the arms and shoulder, and in the same way bandaged up the other two wounds. After

George had started to fetch the lantern, Luke had at Polly's suggestion sent two men back to the village, and these had now returned with doors they had taken off the hinges. When Bill's wounds were bandaged he and Ned were placed on the doors, Ned giving a faint groan as he was moved.

"That's roight," Luke said encouragingly, "he be a-cooming round."

Two coats were wrapped up and placed under their heads, and they were then lifted and carried off, Polly hurrying on ahead to make up the fire and get hot water.

"Say nowt to no one," Luke said as he started. "Till t' master cooms round there ain't no saying what he'd loike done. Maybe he won't have nowt said aboot it."

The water was already hot when the party reached the cottage; the blood was carefully washed off Ned's head, and a great swelling with an ugly gash running across was shown. Cold water was dashed in his face, and with a gasp he opened his eyes.

"It be all roight, Maister Ned," Luke said soothingly; "it be all over now, and you be among vriends. Ye've had an ugly one on the back o' thy head, but I dowt thou wilt do rarely now."

Ned looked round vaguely, then a look of intelligence came into his face.

"Where is Bill?" he asked.

"He be hurted sorely, but oi think it be only loss o' blood, and he will coom round again; best lie still a few minutes, maister, thou wilt feel better then; Polly she be tending Bill."

In a few minutes Ned was able to sit up; a drink of cold brandy and water further restored him. He went to the bed on which Bill had been placed.

"He's not dead?" he asked with a gasp, as he saw the white face enveloped in bandages.

"No, sure-lie," Luke replied cheerfully; "he be a long way from dead yet, oi hoape, though he be badly cut about."

"Have you sent for the doctor?" Ned asked.

"No!"

"Then send for Dr. Green at once, and tell him from me to come up here instantly."

Ned sat down in a chair for a few minutes, for he was still dazed and stupid; but his brain was gradually clearing. Presently he looked up at the men who were still standing silently near the door.

"I have no doubt," he said, "that I have to thank you all for saving my life, but at present I do not know how it has all come about. I will see you to-morrow. But unless it has already got known, please say nothing about this. I don't want it talked about—at anyrate until we see how Bill gets on. Now, Luke," he continued, when the men had gone, "tell me all about it. My brain is in a whirl, and I can hardly think."

Luke related the incidents of the fight and the flight of the assailants, and said that they had carried off a dead man with them.

Ned sat for some time in silence.

"Yes," he said at last, "I shot one. I was walking along with Bill when suddenly a gun was fired from a bush close by; then a number of men jumped up and rushed upon us. I had my pistol, and had just time to fire two shots. I saw one man go straight down, and then they were upon us. They shouted to Bill to get out of the way, but he went at them like a lion. I don't think any of the others had guns; at anyrate they only attacked us with sticks and knives. I fought with my back to Bill as well as I could, and we were keeping them off, till suddenly I don't remember any more."

"One on them hit ye from behind wi' a loaded stick," Luke said, "and thou must ha' gone doon like a felled ox; then oi expects as Bill stood across thee and kept them off as well as he could, but they war too much for t' lad; beside that cut on the head he ha' one on t' shoulder and one behind. Oi war only joost in toime, another quarter of a minute and they'd ha' got their knives into thee."

"Poor old Bill," Ned said sadly, going up to the bedside and laying his hand on the unconscious figure. "I fear you have given your life to save one of little value to myself or anyone else."

"Don't say that, Master Ned," Polly said softly; "you cannot say what your life may be as yet, and if so be that Bill is to die, and God grant it isn't so, he himself would not think his life thrown away if it were given to save yours."

But few words were spoken in the cottage until Dr. Green arrived. Ned's head was aching so that he was forced to lie down. Polly from time to time moistened Bill's lips with a few drops of brandy. George had been ordered off to bed, and Luke sat gazing at the fire, wishing

that there was something he could do. At last the doctor
arrived; the messenger had told him the nature of the case,
and he had come provided with lint, plaster, and bandages.

"Well, Ned," he asked as he came in, "have you been
in the wars again?"

"I am all right, doctor. I had a knock on the head
which a day or two will put right; but I fear Bill is very
seriously hurt."

The doctor at once set to to examine the bandages.

"You have done them up very well," he said approv-
ingly; "but the blood is still oozing from them. I must
dress them afresh; get me plenty of hot water, Polly, I
have brought a sponge with me. Can you look on without fainting?"

"I don't think I shall faint, sir," Polly said quietly;
"if I do, feyther will take my place."

In a quarter of an hour the wounds were washed,
drawn together, and bandaged. There was but little
fresh bleeding, for the lad's stock of life-blood had nearly
all flowed away.

"A very near case," the doctor said critically; "as close
a shave as ever I saw. Had that wound on the face been
a quarter of an inch nearer the eyebrow it would have
severed the temporal artery. As it is it has merely laid
open the jaw. Neither of the other wounds are serious,
though they might very well have been fatal."

"Then you think he will get round, doctor?" Ned asked
in a low tone.

"Get round! Of course he will," Dr. Green replied

cheerily. "Now that we have got him bound up we will soon bring him round. It is only a question of loss of blood."

"Hullo! this will never do;" he broke off as Ned suddenly reeled and would have fallen to the ground had not Luke caught him. "Pour this cordial down Swinton's throat, Polly, a little at a time, and lift his head as you do it, and when you see him open his eyes, put a pillow under his head; but don't do so till he begins to come round. Now let me look at Ned's head.

"It must have been a tremendous blow, Luke," he said seriously. "I only hope it hasn't fractured the skull. However, all this swelling and suffusion of blood is a good sign. Give me that hot water. I shall put a lancet in here and get it to bleed freely. That will be a relief to him."

While he was doing this an exclamation of pleasure from Polly showed that Bill was showing sign of returning to life. His eyes presently opened. Polly bent over him.

"Lie quiet, Bill, dear; you have been hurt, but the doctor says you will soon be well again. Yes: Master Ned is all right too. Don't worry yourself about him."

An hour later both were sleeping quietly.

"They will sleep till morning," Dr. Green said, "perhaps well on into the day; it is no use my waiting any longer. I will be up the first thing."

So he drove away, while Polly took her work and sat down to watch the sleepers during the night, and Luke, taking his stick and hat, set off to guard the mill till daylight.

Ned woke first just as daylight was breaking; he felt

stupid and heavy, with a splitting pain in his head. He
tried to rise, but found that he could not do so. He
accordingly told George to go down in an hour's time to
Marsden, and to leave a message at the house saying that
he was detained and should not be back to breakfast, and
that probably he might not return that night. The doctor
kept his head enveloped in wet bandages all day, and he
was on the following morning able to go down to Marsden, although still terribly pale and shaken. His appearance excited the liveliest wonder and commiseration on
the part of Charlie, Lucy, and Abijah; but he told them
that he had had an accident, and had got a nasty knock
on the back of his head. He kept his room for a day or
two; but at the end of that time he was able to go to the
mill as usual. Bill Swinton was longer away, but broths
and jellies soon built up his strength again, and in three
weeks he was able to resume work, although it was long
before the ugly scar on his face was healed.

The secret was well kept, and although in time the
truth of the affair became known in Varley it never
reached Marsden, and Ned escaped the talk and comment which it would have excited had it been known,
and, what was worse, the official inquiry which would
have followed. The Huddersfield men naturally kept
their own council. They had hastily buried their dead
comrade on the moor, and although several of them were
so severely knocked about that they were unable to go to
work for some time, no rumour of the affair got about
outside the circle of the conspirators. It need hardly

be said that this incident drew Ned and Bill even more closely together than before, and that the former henceforth regarded Bill Swinton in the light of a brother.

At the end of the Christmas holidays Mr. Porson brought home a mistress to the school-house. She was a bright pleasant woman. and having heard from her husband all the particulars of Ned's case she did her best to make him feel that she fully shared in her husband's welcome whenever he came to the house, and although Ned was some little time in accustoming himself to the presence of one whom he had at first regarded as an intruder in the little circle of his friends, this feeling wore away under the influence of her cordiality and kindness.

"Is it not shocking," she said to her husband one day, "to think that for nearly a year that poor lad should never have seen his own mother, though she is in the house with him, still worse to know that she thinks him a murderer? Do you think it would be of any good if I were to go and see her, and tell her how wicked and wrong her conduct is?"

"No, my dear," Mr. Porson said smiling, "I don't think that course would be at all likely to have a good effect. Green tells me that he is sure that this conviction which she has of Ned's guilt is a deep and terrible grief to her. He thinks that, weak and silly as she is, she has really a strong affection for Ned, as well as for her other children, and it is because this is so that she feels so terribly what she believes to be his guilt. She suffers in her way just as much, or more, than he does in his. He has his business, which occupies his mind and prevents him from brooding over his position; besides, the knowledge that a few of us are perfectly convinced of his innocence enables him to hold up. She has no distraction, nothing to turn her thoughts from this fatal subject.

"Green says she has several times asked him whether a person could be tried twice for the same offence, after he has been acquitted the first time, and he believes that the fear is ever present in her mind that some fresh evidence may be forthcoming which may unmistakably bring the guilt home to him. I have talked it over with Ned several times, and he now takes the same view of it as I do. The idea of his guilt has become a sort of mono-mania with her, and nothing save the most clear and convincing proof of his innocence would have any effect upon her mind. If that is ever forthcoming she may re-cover, and the two may be brought together again. At the same time I think that you might very well call upon her, introducing yourself by saying that as I was a friend of Captain Sankey's and of her son's you were desirous of making her acquaintance, especially as you heard that she was such an invalid. She has no friends whatever. She was never a very popular woman, and the line everyone knows she has taken in reference to the murder of her second husband has set those who would otherwise have been inclined to be kind, against her. Other people may be convinced of Ned's guilt, but you see it seems to everyone to be shocking that a mother should take part against her son."

Accordingly Mrs. Porson called. On the first occasion when she did so Mrs. Mulready sent down to say that she was sorry she could not see her, but that the state of her health did not permit her to receive visitors.

Mrs. Porson, however, was not to be discouraged. First she made friends with Lucy, and when she knew that the girl was sure to have spoken pleasantly of her to her mother she opened a correspondence with Mrs. Mulready. At first she only wrote to ask that Lucy might be allowed to come and spend the day with her. Her next letter was on the subject of Lucy's music. The girl had long gone to a day-school kept by a lady in Marsden, but her music had been neglected, and Mrs. Porson wrote to say that she found that Lucy had a taste for music, and that having been herself well taught she should be happy to give her lessons twice a week, and that if Mrs. Mulready felt well enough to see her she would like to have a little chat with her on the subject.

This broke the ice. Lucy's backwardness in music had long been a grievance with her mother, who, as she lay in bed and listened to the girl practising below had fretted over the thought that she could obtain no good teacher for her in Marsden. Mrs. Porson's offer was therefore too tempting to be refused, and as it was necessary to appear to reciprocate the kindness of that lady, she determined to make an effort to receive her.

The meeting went off well. Having once made the effort Mrs. Mulready found, to her surprise, that it was pleasant to her after being cut off for so many months from all intercourse with the world, except such as she gained from the doctor, her two children, and the old servant, to be chatting with her visitor, who exerted herself to the utmost to make herself agreeable.

The talk was at first confined to the ostensible subject of Mrs. Porson's visit; but after that was satisfactorily arranged the conversation turned to Marsden and the neighbourhood. Many people had called upon Mrs. Porson, and as all of these were more or less known to Mrs. Mulready, her visitor asked her many questions concerning them, and the invalid was soon gossiping cheerfully over the family histories and personal peculiarities of her neighbours.

"You have done me a world of good," she said when Mrs. Porson rose to leave. "I never see anyone but the doctor, and he is the worst person in the world for a gossip. He ought to know everything, but somehow he seems to know nothing. You will come again, won't you? It will be a real kindness, and you have taken so much interest in my daughter that it quite seems to me as if you were an old friend."

And so the visit was repeated; but not too often, for Mrs. Porson knew that it was better that her patient should wait and long for her coming, and now that the ice was once broken, Mrs. Mulready soon came to look forward with eagerness to these changes in her monotonous existence.

For some time Ned's name was never mentioned between them. Then one day Mrs. Porson, in a careless manner, as if she had no idea whatever of the state of the relations between mother and son, mentioned that Ned had been at their house the previous evening, saying: "My husband has a wonderful liking and respect for your son; they are the greatest friends, though of course there is a good deal of difference in age between them. I don't know anyone of whom John thinks so highly."

Mrs. Mulready turned very pale, and then in a constrained voice said:

"Mr. Porson has always been very kind to my sons." Then she sighed deeply and changed the subject of conversation.

"Your wife is doing my patient a great deal more good than I have ever been able to do," Dr. Green said one day to the schoolmaster. "She has become quite a different woman in the last five or six weeks. She is always up and on the sofa now when I call, and I notice that she begins to take pains with her dress again; and that, you know, is always a first-rate sign with a woman. I think she would be able to go down-stairs again soon, were it not for her feeling about Ned. She would not meet him, I am sure. You don't see any signs of a change in that quarter, I suppose?"

"No," Mrs. Porson replied. "The last time I mentioned his name she said: 'My son is a most unfortunate young man, and the subject pains me too much to discuss. Therefore, if you please, Mrs. Porson, I would rather leave it alone.' So I am afraid there is no chance of my making any progress there."

CHAPTER XIX.

THE ATTACK ON CARTWRIGHT'S MILL.

NED still slept at the mill. He was sure that there was no chance of a renewal of the attack by the workpeople near, but an assault might be again organized by parties from a distance. The murder of Mr. Horsfall had caused greater vigilance than ever among the military. At some of the mills the use of the new machinery had been discontinued and cropping by hand resumed. This was the case at the mills at Ottewells and Bankbottom, both of which belonged to Messrs. Abraham & John Horsfall, the father and uncle of the murdered man, and at other mills in the neighbourhood. Mr. Cartwright and some of the other owners still continued the use of the new machinery.

One night Ned had just gone to bed when he was startled by the ringing of the bell. He leapt from his bed. He hesitated to go to the window, as it was likely enough that men might be lying in wait to shoot him when he appeared. Seizing his pistols, therefore, he hurried down below. A continued knocking was going on at the front entrance. It was not, however, the noisy din which would be made by a party trying to force their way in, but rather the persistent call of one trying to attract attention.

"Who is there?" he shouted through the door; "and what do you want?"

"Open the door, please. It is I, Polly Powlett," a voice replied. "I want to speak to you particularly, sir."

"I have come down, sir," she said as Ned threw open the door and she entered, still panting from her long run, "to tell you that Cartwright's mill is going to be attacked. I think some of the Varley men are concerned in it. Anyhow, the news has got about in the village. Feyther and Bill are both watched, and could not get away to give you the news; but feyther told me, and I slipped out at the back-door and made my way round by the moor, for they have got a guard on the road to prevent anyone passing. There is no time to spare, for they were to join a party from Longroyd Bridge, at ten o'clock at the steeple in Sir George Armitage's fields, which ain't more than three miles from the mill. It's half-past ten now, but maybe they will be late. I couldn't get away before, and indeed feyther only learned the particulars just as I started. He told me to come straight to you, as you would know what to do. I said, Should I go and fetch the troops? but he said No—it would be sure to be found out who had brought them, and our lives wouldn't be worth having. But I don't mind risking it, sir, if you think that's the best plan."

"No, Polly; on no account. You have risked quite enough in coming to tell me. I will go straight to Cartwright's. Do you get back as quickly as you can, and get in the same way you came. Be very careful that no one sees you."

So saying he dashed upstairs, pulled on his shoes, and then started at full speed for Liversedge. As he ran he calculated the probabilities of his being there in time. Had the men started exactly at the hour named they would be by this time attacking the mill; but it was not likely that they would be punctual—some of the hands would be sure to be late.

There would be discussion and delay before starting. They might well be half-an-hour after the time named before they left the steeple, as the obelisk in Sir George Armitage's field was called by the country people. He might be in time yet, but it would be a close thing; and had his own life depended upon the result Ned could not have run more swiftly. He had hopes that as he went he might have come across a cavalry patrol and sent them to Marsden and Ottewells to bring up aid; but the road was quiet and deserted. Once or twice he paused for an instant, thinking he heard the sound of distant musketry. He held his breath, but no sound could he hear save the heavy thumping of his own heart.

His hopes rose as he neared Liversedge. He was close now, but as he ran into the yard he heard a confused murmur and the dull tramping of many feet. He had won the race, but by a few seconds only. The great stone-

built building lay hushed in quiet; he could see its outline against the sky, and could even make out the great
alarm-bell which had recently been erected above the
roof. He ran up to the doorway and knocked heavily.
The deep barking of a dog within instantly resounded
through the building. Half a minute later Mr. Cartwright's voice within demanded who was there.

"It is I, Ned Sankey—open at once. The Luddites
are upon you!"

The bolts were hastily undrawn, and Ned rushed in
and assisted to fasten the door behind him.

"They will be here in a minute," he panted out. "They
are just behind."

The noise had already roused the ten men who slept in
the building; five of these were Mr. Cartwright's workmen, the other five were soldiers. Hastily they threw on
their clothes and seized their arms; but they were scarcely
ready when a roar of musketry was heard, mingled with
a clatter of falling glass, nearly every pane in the lower
windows being smashed by the discharge of slugs, buckshot, and bullets.

This was followed by the thundering noise of a score
of sledge-hammers at the principal entrance and the side-
doors. Mr. Cartwright and one of his workmen ran to
the bell-rope, and in a moment its iron tongue was clang-
ing out its summons for assistance to the country round.
A roar of fury broke from the Luddites; many of them
fired at the bell in hopes of cutting the rope, and the
men plied their hammers more furiously than before.

But the doors were tremendously strong and were backed with plates of iron.

The defenders were not idle; all had their allotted places at the windows, and from these a steady return was kept up in answer to the scattering fire without. Ned had caught up the gun which Mr. Cartwright had laid down when he ran to the bell-rope, and with it he kept up a steady fire at the dark figures below. There was a shout of " Bring up Enoch!"

This was a name given to the exceedingly heavy hammers at that time used in the Yorkshire smithies. They were manufactured by the firm of Enoch & James Taylor of Marsden, and were popularly known among the men by the name of their maker. A powerful smith now advanced with one of these heavy weapons and began to pound at the door, which, heavy as it was, shook under his blows. Ned, regardless of the fire of the Luddites, leaned far out of the window so as to be able to aim down at the group round the door, and fired.

The gun was loaded with a heavy charge of buckshot. He heard a hoarse shout of pain and rage, and the hammer dropped to the ground. Another man caught up the hammer and the thundering din recommenced. Mr. Cartwright had now joined Ned, leaving his workman to continue to pull the bell-rope.

"You had better come down, Sankey. The door must give way ere long; we must make a stand there. If they once break in, it will soon be all up with us."

Calling together three or four of the soldiers the manu-

in the mill at the failure of the attack. The defenders gathered in the lower floor.

"I think they are all gone now," Ned said. "Shall we go out, Mr. Cartwright, and see what we can do for the wounded? There are several of them lying round the door and near the windows, I can hear them groaning."

"No, Ned," Mr. Cartwright said firmly, "they must wait a little longer. The others may still be hiding close ready to make a rush if we come out; besides, it would likely enough be said of us that we went out and killed the wounded; we must wait a while." Presently a voice was heard shouting without:

"Are you all right, Cartwright?"

"Yes," the manufacturer replied. "Who are you?"

The questioner proved to be a friend who lived the other side of Liversedge, and who had been aroused by the ringing of the alarm-bell. He had not ventured to approach until the firing had ceased, and had then come on to see the issue. Hearing that the rioters had all departed, Mr. Cartwright ordered the door to be opened. The wounded Luddites were lifted and carried into the mill, and Mr. Cartwright sent at once for the nearest surgeon, who was speedily upon the spot.

Long before he arrived the hussars had ridden up, and had been despatched over the country in search of the rioters, of whom, save the dead and wounded, no signs were visible. As day dawned the destruction which had been wrought was clearly visible. The doors were in splinters, the lower window-frames were all smashed in, scarce a pane of glass remained in its place throughout the whole building, the stonework was dotted and splashed with bullet marks, the angles of the windows were chipped and broken, there were dark patches of blood in many places in the court-yard, and the yard itself, and the roads leading from the mill were strewn with guns, picks, levers, hammers, and pikes, which had been thrown away by the discomfited rioters in their retreat.

"They have had a lesson for once," Mr. Cartwright said as he looked round, "they won't attack my mill again in a hurry. I need not say, Sankey, how deeply I am obliged to you for your timely warning. How did you get to know of it?"

Ned related the story of his being awakened by Mary Powlett. He added, "I don't think, after all, my warning was of much use to you. You could have kept them out anyhow."

"I don't think so," Mr. Cartwright said. "I imagine that your arrival upset all their plans; they were so close behind you that they must have heard the knocking and the door open and close. The appearance of lights in the mill and the barking of the dog would, at anyrate, have told them that we were on the alert, and seeing that they ran on and opened fire. I have no doubt that their plan was to have stolen quietly up to the windows and commenced an attack upon these in several places, and had they done this they would probably have forced an entrance before we could have got together to resist them. No, my lad, you and that girl have saved the mill between you."

"You will not mention, Mr. Cartwright, to anyone how I learned the news. The girl's life would not be safe were it known that she brought me word of the intention of the Luddites."

"You may rely on me for that; and now, if you please, we will go off home at once and get some breakfast. Amy may have heard of the attack and will be in a rare fright until she gets news of me."

Mr. Cartwright's house was about a mile from the mill. When they arrived there it was still closed and quiet, and it was evident that no alarm had been excited. Mr. Cartwright's knocking soon roused the servants, and a few minutes later Amy hurried down.

"What is it, papa? What brings you back so early? it is only seven o'clock now. How do you do, Mr. Sankey? Why, papa, how dirty and black you both look! What have you been doing? And, oh, papa! you have got blood on your hands!"

"It is not my own, my dear, and you need not be frightened. The attack on the mill has come at last, and we have given the Luddites a handsome thrashing. The danger is all over now, for I do not think the mill is ever likely to be attacked again. But I will tell you all about it presently; run and get breakfast ready as soon as you can, for we are as hungry as hunters, I can tell you. We will go and have a wash, and will be ready in ten minutes."

"We can't be ready in ten minutes, papa, for the fires are not lighted yet, but we will be as quick as we can;

and do please make haste and come and tell me all about this dreadful business."

In half an hour the party were seated at breakfast. Amy had already been told the incidents of the fight, and trembled as she heard how nearly the rioters had burst their way into the mill, and was deeply grateful to Ned for the timely warning which had frustrated the plans of the rioters.

In vain did the soldiers scour the country. The Luddites on their retreat had scattered to their villages, the main body returning to Huddersfield and appearing at their work as usual in the morning.

Large rewards were offered for information which would lead to the apprehension of any concerned in the attack, but these, as well as the notices offering two thousand pounds for the apprehension of the murderers of Mr. Horsfall, met with no responses. Scores of men must have known who were concerned in these affairs, but either fidelity to the cause or fear of the consequences of treachery kept them silent.

Mr. Cartwright was anxious to offer a handsome reward to Mary Powlett for the service she had rendered him, but Ned told him that he was sure she would not accept anything. Mr. Cartwright, however, insisting on the point, Ned saw Mary and sounded her upon the subject. She was indignant at the idea.

" No, Master Ned," she said, " I would not take money, not ever so. I came down to tell you because I thought it wicked and wrong of the men to destroy the mill, and because they would no doubt have murdered Mr. Cartwright and the people there; but I would not take money for doing it. Even if nobody ever got to know of it, it would always seem to me as if I had sold the hands, and they have suffered enough, God knows."

" I don't think Mr. Cartwright thought of offering you money. I told him that I was sure that you wouldn't take it, but he hoped that he might be able to do something for you in some other way."

" No, thank you, sir," Mary said with quiet dignity; "there isn't any way that I could take anything for doing what I did."

" Well, Mary, we won't say anything more about it. I only spoke, you know, because Mr. Cartwright insisted, and, of course, as he did not know you he could not tell how different you were from other girls. There is no suspicion, I hope, that you were away from the village."

" No, sir, I don't think so. Two of the men sat here talking with feyther till past eleven o'clock, but they thought that I was in bed, as I had said good-night and had gone into my room an hour before, and I did not see anyone about in the village as I came back over the moor behind."

" None of the hands belonging to the village are missing, I hope, Mary. I was glad to find that none of them were among the killed and wounded round the mill."

" No, sir, except that John Stukeley has not been about since. The smithy was not opened the next morning and the chapel was closed yesterday. They say as he has been taken suddenly ill, but feyther thinks that perhaps he was wounded. Of course men don't speak much before feyther, and I don't talk much to the other women of the village, so we don't know what's going on; anyhow the doctor has not been here to see him, and if he had been only ill I should think they would have had Dr. Green up. Old Sarah James is nursing him. I saw her this morning going to the shop and asked her how he was; she only said it was no business of mine. But she doesn't like me because sometimes I nurse people when they are ill, and she thinks it takes money from her; and so it does, but what can I do if people like me to sit by them better than her? and no wonder, for she is very deaf and horribly dirty."

"I don't think they are to be blamed, Polly," Ned said smiling. "If I were ill I should certainly like you to nurse me a great deal better than that bad-tempered old woman."

The attack on Cartwright's mill made a great sensation through that part of the country. It was the most determined effort which the Luddites had yet made, and although it showed their determination to carry matters to an extremity, it also showed that a few determined men could successfully resist their attacks.

Nothing else was talked about at Marsden, and as Mr. Cartwright everywhere said that the success of the resistance was due entirely to the upsetting of the plans of the rioters by the warning Ned had given him, the latter gained great credit in the eyes of all the peaceful inhabitants. But as it would make Ned still more obnoxious to the Luddites, Major Browne insisted on placing six soldiers permanently at the mill, and on four accompanying him as an escort whenever he went backwards or forwards.

Ned was very averse to these measures, but the magistrates thoroughly agreed with Major Browne as to the danger of assassination to which Ned was exposed from the anger of the croppers at his having twice thwarted their attempts, and he the more readily agreed as the presence of this guard soothed the fears which Charlie and Lucy felt for his safety whenever he was absent from the town. What perhaps most influenced him was a conversation which he had with Mrs. Porson.

" Your mother was speaking of you to me to-day, Ned," she said; "it is the first time she has done so since I made her acquaintance. She began by saying, ' Please, Mrs. Porson, tell me all about this attack on George Cartwright's mill; Abijah and Lucy have been talking about it, but Abijah always gets confused in her stories, and of course Lucy knows only what she is told. I should like to know all about it.' Of course I told her the whole story, and how much Mr. Cartwright says he is indebted to you for the warning you brought him, and how everyone is speaking in praise of your conduct, and what a good effect it has had.

" I told her that of course the Luddites would be very much incensed against you, and that it was adding to the risks that you already ran. She lay on the sofa quietly with her eyes shut all the time I was speaking.

I could see her colour come and go, and some tears fell down her cheeks; then she said in a tone which she tried to make hard and careless, but which really trembled, 'The military ought to put a guard over my son. Why does he go risking his life for other people? What business is it of his whether Cartwright's mill is burned or not?' I said that Mr. Cartwright had been very kind to you, and that I knew that you were much attached to him. I also said that the military were anxious that you should have an escort to and from the mill, but that you objected. I said that I was afraid that your life had not much value in your own eyes, for that it was by no means a happy one. 'It has value in other people's eyes,' she said irritably, 'in Lucy's and in his brother's? What would they do if he was to throw it away? Who would look after the mill and business then? He has no right to run such risks, Mrs. Porson, no right at all. Of course he is unhappy. People who let their tempers master them and do things, are sure to be unhappy, and make other people unhappy too; but that is no reason that he should cause more unhappiness by risking his own life needlessly, so, Mrs. Porson, please talk to your husband and tell him to make my son have an escort. I know he always listens to Mr. Porson.'"

"Naturally my mother is anxious, for the sake of Charlie and Lucy, that I should live to carry on the mill until Charlie is old enough to run it himself," Ned said bitterly.

"I do not think that it is only that, Ned," Mrs. Porson

said kindly. "That was only the excuse that your mother made. I could see that she was deeply moved. I believe, Ned, that at heart she still loves you dearly. She has this unhappy fixed idea in her mind that you killed her husband, and believing this she cannot bear to see you; but I am sure she is most unhappy, most deeply to be pitied. I cannot imagine anything more dreadful than the state of mind of a woman who believes that a son of hers has murdered her husband. I think that if you quite realized what her feelings must be you would feel a little less bitter than you do.

"I know, Ned, how much you have to try you, but I am sure that I would not exchange your position for that of your mother. Her pain must be far greater than yours. You know that you are innocent, and hope that some day you may be able to prove it. She thinks she knows that you are guilty, and is in constant dread that something may occur that may prove your guilt to the world."

"Perhaps you are right, Mrs. Porson," Ned said wearily; "at anyrate I will put up with the nuisance of this escort. I suppose it will not be for very long, for I expect that we shall not hear very much more of the Luddites. The failures upon Cartwright's mill and mine must have disheartened them, and the big rewards that are offered to anyone who will come forward and betray the rest must make them horribly uncomfortable, for no one can be sure that someone may not be tempted to turn traitor."

"What is the matter with Bill?" Ned asked Luke Marner that afternoon. "I see he is away."

"Yes, sir, he be a-sitting with John Stukeley, who they say is main bad.   It seems as how he has taken a fancy to t' lad, though why he should oi dunno, for Bill had nowt to do wi' his lot.   Perhaps he thinks now as Bill were right and he were wrong; perhaps it only is as Bill ha' got a name in the village of being a soft-hearted chap, allas ready to sit up at noight wi' anyone as is ill.   Anyhow he sent last noight to ask him to go and sit wi' him, and Bill sent me word this morning as how he couldn't leave the man."

"Do you know what is the matter with him?"

"I dunno for certain, Maister Ned, but I has my suspicions."

"So have I, Luke.   I believe he got a gunshot wound in that affair at the mill."   Luke nodded significantly.

"Dr. Green ought to see him," Ned said.   "A gunshot wound is not a thing to be trifled with."

"The doctor ha' been up twice a day on the last three days," Luke replied.   "Oi suppose they got frighted and were obliged to call him in."

"They had better have done so at first," Ned said; "they might have been quite sure that he would say nothing about it to the magistrates whatever was the matter with Stukeley.   I thought that fellow would get into mischief before he had done."

"It war a bad day for the village when he coomed," Luke said; "what wi' his preachings and his talk, he ha' turned the place upside down.   I doan't say as Varley had ever a good name, or was a place wheere a quiet chap would have chosen to live. For fighting and drink there weren't a worse place in all Yorkshire, but there weren't no downright mischief till he came. Oi wur afraid vor a bit when he came a-hanging aboot Polly, as the gal might ha' took to him, for he can talk smooth and has had edication, and Polly thinks a wonderful lot of that. Oi were main glad when she sent him aboot his business."

"Well, there is one thing, Luke; if anything happens to him it will put an end to this Luddite business at Varley. Such a lesson as that in their midst would do more to convince them of the danger of their goings-on than any amount of argument and advice."

"It will that," Luke said. "Oi hear as they are all moighty down in the mouth over that affair at Cartwright's. If they could not win there, when they were thirty to one, what chance can they have o' stopping the mills? Oi consider as how that has been the best noight's work as ha' been done in Yorkshire for years and years. There ain't a been anything else talked of in Varley since. I ha' heard a score of guesses as to how you found owt what was a going on in toime to get to the mill—thank God there ain't one as suspects as our Polly brought you the news. My own boys doan't know, and ain't agoing to; not as they would say a word as would harm Polly for worlds, but as they gets a bit bigger and takes to drink, there's no saying what mightn't slip out when they are in liquor. So you and oi and Bill be the only ones as ull ever know the ins and outs o' that there business."

CHAPTER XX.

CLEARED AT LAST.

THE night was a wild one. The weather had changed suddenly, and the rain beat fiercely in the faces of the hands as they made their way back from the mill up to Varley. As the night came on the storm increased. The wind as it swept across the moor swirled down into the hollow in which Varley stood, as if it would scoop the houses out of their foundations, and the drops of rain were driven against roof and wall with the force of hailstones.

Bill Swinton was sitting up again with John Stukeley, and as he bent over the sick man's bed and tenderly lifted his head while he held a cup with some cooling drink to his lips, the contrast between his broad, powerful figure, and his face, marked with the characteristics alike of good-temper, kindness, and a resolute will, and the thin, emaciated invalid was very striking. Stukeley's face was without a vestige of colour; his eyes were hollow and surrounded by dark circles; his cheeks were of an ashen-gray pallor, which deepened almost to a lead colour round his lips.

"Thou ought'st not to talk so much, John," Bill was saying. "Thou know'st the doctor said thou must not excite thyself."

"It makes no difference, Bill, no difference at all, talk or not talk. What does it matter? I am dying, and he knows it, and I know it; so do you. That bit of lead in my body has done its work. Strange, isn't it, that you should be here nursing me when I have thought of shooting you a score of times? A year ago it seemed absurd that Polly Powlett should like a boy like you better than a man like me, and yet I was sure it was because of you she would have nothing to say to me; but she was right, you will make the best husband of the two. I suppose it's because of that I sent for you. I was very fond of Polly, Bill, and when I felt that I was going, and there wasn't any use my being jealous any longer, I seemed to turn to you. I knew you would come, for you have been always ready to do a kindness to a chap who was down. You are different to the other lads here. I do believe you are fond of reading. Whenever you think I am asleep you take up your book."

"Oi am trying to improve myself," Bill said quietly. "Maister Sankey put me in the roight way. He gives me an hour, and sometimes two, every evening. He has been wonderful kind to me, he has; there ain't nothing oi wouldn't do for him."

The sick man moved uneasily.

"No more wouldn't Luke and Polly," Bill went on. "His father gived his loife, you know, for little Jenny. No, there ain't nowt we wouldn't do for him," he continued, glad to turn the subject from that of Stukeley's affection for Polly. "He be one of the best of maisters. Oi would give my life's blood if so be as oi could clear him of that business of Mulready's."

For a minute or two not a word was said. The wind roared round the building, and in the intervals of the gusts the high clock in the corner of the room ticked steadily and solemnly as if distinctly intimating that its movements were not to be hurried by the commotion without. Stukeley had closed his eyes, and Bill began to hope that he was going to doze off, when he asked suddenly:

"Bill, do you know who sent that letter that was read at the trial—I mean the one from the chap as said he done it, and was ready to give himself up if the boy was found guilty?"

Bill did not answer.

"You can tell me, if you know," Stukeley said impatiently. "You don't suppose as I am going to tell now! Maybe I sha'n't see anyone to tell this side of the grave, for I doubt as I shall see the morning. Who wrote it?"

"I wrote it," Bill said; "but it warn't me as was coming forward, it war Luke's idee fust. He made up his moind as to own up as it was he as did it, and to be hung for it to save Maister Ned, acause the captain lost his loife for little Jenny."

" But he didn't do it," Stukeley said sharply.

" No, he didn't do it," Bill replied.

There was a silence again for a long time; then Stukeley opened his eyes suddenly.

" Bill, I should like to see Polly again. Dost think as she will come and say good-bye?"

" Oi am sure as she will," Bill said steadily. "Shall oi go and fetch her?"

" It's a wild night to ask a gal to come out on such an errand," Stukeley said doubtfully.

" Polly won't mind that," Bill replied confidently. " She will just wrap her shawl round her head and come over. Oi will run across and fetch her. Oi will not be gone three minutes."

In little more than that time Bill returned with Mary Powlett.

" I am awfully sorry to hear you are so bad, John," the girl said frankly.

" I am dying, Polly; I know that, or I wouldn't have sent for ye. It was a good day for you when you said no to what I asked you."

" Never mind that now, John; that's all past and gone."

" Ay, that's all past and gone, past and gone. I only wanted to say as I wish you well, Polly, and I hope you will be happy, and I am pretty nigh sure of it. Bill here tells me that you set your heart on having young Sankey cleared of that business as was against him. Is that so?"

"That is so, John; he has been very kind to us all, to feyther and all of us. He is a good master to his men, and has kept many a mouth full this winter as would have been short of food without him; but why do you ask me?"

"Just a fancy of mine, gal, such a fancy as comes into the head of a man at the last. When you get back send Luke here. It is late and maybe he has gone to bed, but tell him I must speak to him. And now, good-bye, Polly, God bless you! I don't know as I hasn't been wrong about all this business, but it didn't seem so to me afore. Just try and think that, will you, when you hear about it. I thought as I was a-acting for the good of the men."

"I will always remember that," Polly said gently.

Then she took the thin hand of the man in hers, glanced at Bill as if she would ask his approval, and reading acquiescence in his eyes she stooped over the bed and kissed Stukeley's forehead. Then without a word she left the cottage and hurried away through the darkness.

A few minutes later Luke Marner came in, and to Bill's surprise Stukeley asked him to leave the room. In five minutes Luke came out again.

"Go in to him, Bill," he said hoarsely. "Oi think he be a-sinking. For God's sake keep him up. Give him that wine and broath stuff as often as thou canst. Keep him going till oi coom back again; thou doan't know what depends on it."

Hurrying back to his cottage Luke threw on a thick coat, and to the astonishment of Polly announced that he was going down into Marsden.

" What! on such a night as this, feyther?"

" Ay, lass, and would if it were ten toimes wurse. Get ye into thy room, and go down on thy knees, and pray God to keep John Stukeley alive and clear-headed till oi coomes back again."

It was many years since Luke Marner's legs had carried him so fast as they now did into Marsden. The driving rain and hail which beat against him seemed unheeded as he ran down the hill at the top of his speed. He stopped at the doctor's and went in. Two or three minutes after the arrival of this late visitor Dr. Green's housekeeper was astonished at hearing the bell ring violently. On answering the bell she was ordered to arouse John, who had already gone to bed, and to tell him to put the horse into the gig instantly.

" Not on such a night as this, doctor! sureley you are not agoing out on such a night as this!"

" Hold your tongue, woman, and do as you are told instantly," the doctor said with far greater spirit than usual, for his housekeeper was, as a general thing, mistress of the establishment.

With an air of greatly offended dignity she retired to carry out his orders. Three minutes later the doctor ran out of his room as he heard the man-servant descending the stairs.

" John," he said, " I am going on at once to Mr. Thompson's; bring the gig round there. I sha'n't want you to go further with me. Hurry up, man, and don't lose a moment, it is a matter of life and death."

A quarter of an hour later Dr. Green, with Mr. Thompson by his side, drove off through the tempest towards Varley.

The next morning, as Ned was at breakfast, the doctor was announced.

"What a pestilently early hour you breakfast at, Ned! I was not in bed till three o'clock, and I scarcely seemed to have been asleep an hour when I was obliged to get up to be in time to catch you before you were off."

"That is hard on you indeed, doctor," Ned said smiling; "but why this haste? Have you got some patient for whom you want my help. You need not have got up so early for that, you know. You could have ordered anything you wanted for him in my name. You might have been sure I should have honoured the bill. But what made you so late last night? You were surely never out in such a gale!"

"I was, Ned, and strange as it seems I never went in answer to a call which gave me so much satisfaction. My dear lad, I hardly know how to tell you. I have a piece of news for you; the greatest, the best news that man could have to tell you."

Ned drew a long breath and the colour left his cheeks. "You don't mean, doctor, you can't mean"—and he paused.

"That you are cleared, my boy. Yes; that is my news. Thank God, Ned, your innocence is proved."

Ned could not speak. For a minute he sat silent and motionless. Then he bent forward and covered his face with his hands, and his lips moved as he murmured a deep thanksgiving to God for this mercy, while Lucy and Charlie, with cries of surprise and delight, leapt from the table, and when Ned rose to his feet, threw their arms round his neck with enthusiastic delight; while the doctor wrung his hand, and then, taking out his pocket-handkerchief, wiped his eyes, violently declaring, as he did so, that he was an old fool.

"Tell me all about it, doctor. How has it happened? What has brought it about?"

"Luke Marner came down to me at ten o'clock last night to tell me that John Stukeley was dying, which I knew very well, for when I saw him in the afternoon I saw he was sinking fast; but he told me, too, that the man was anxious to sign a declaration before a magistrate to the effect that it was he who killed your stepfather. I had my gig got out and hurried away to Thompson's. The old fellow was rather crusty at being called out on such a night, but to do him justice, I must say he went readily enough when he found what he was required for, though it must have given him a twinge of conscience, for you know he has never been one of your partisans. However, off we drove, and got there in time.

"Stukeley made a full confession. It all happened just as we thought. It had been determined by the Luddites to kill Mulready, and Stukeley determined to carry out the business himself, convinced, as he says, that the man was a tyrant and an oppressor, and that his death was not only richly deserved, but that such a blow was necessary to encourage the Luddites. He did not care, however, to run the risk of taking any of the others into his confidence, and therefore carried it out alone, and to this day, although some of the others may have their suspicions, no one knows for certain that he was the perpetrator of the act.

"He had armed himself with a pistol and went down to the mill, intending to shoot Mulready as he came out at night, but, stumbling upon the rope, thought that it was a safer and more certain means. After fastening it across the road he sat down and waited, intending to shoot your stepfather if the accident didn't turn out fatal. After the crash, finding that Mulready's neck was broken and that he was dead, he made off home. He wished it specially to be placed on his deposition that he made this confession not from any regret at having killed Mulready, but simply to oblige Mary Powlett, whose heart was bent upon your innocence being proved. He signed the deposition in the presence of Thompson, myself, and Bill Swinton."

"And you think it is true, doctor, you really think it is true? It is not like Luke's attempt to save me?"

"I am certain it is true, Ned. The man was dying, and there was no mistake about his earnestness. There is not a shadow of doubt. I sent Swinton back in the gig with Thompson and stayed with the man till half-past two. He was unconscious then. He may linger a few hours, but will not live out the day, and there is little chance of his again recovering consciousness. Thompson will to-day send a copy of the deposition to the Home Secretary, with a request that it may be made public through the newspapers. It will appear in all the Yorkshire papers next Saturday, and all the world will know that you are innocent."

"What will my mother say?" Ned exclaimed, turning pale again.

"I don't know what she will say, my lad, but I know what she ought to say. I am going round to Thompson's now for a copy of the deposition, and will bring it for her to see. Thompson will read it aloud at the meeting of the court to-day, so by this afternoon every one will know that you are cleared."

Abijah's joy when she heard that Ned's innocence was proved was no less than that of his brother and sister. She would have rushed upstairs at once to tell the news to her mistress, but Ned persuaded her not to do so until the doctor's return.

"Then he will have to be quick," Abijah said, "for if the mistress's bell rings, and I have to go up before he comes, I shall never be able to keep it to myself. She will see it in my face that something has happened. If the bell rings, Miss Lucy, you must go up, and if she asks for me, say that I am particular busy, and will be up in a few minutes."

The bell, however, did not ring before the doctor's return. After a short consultation between him and Ned, Abijah was called in.

"Mr. Sankey agrees with me, Abijah, that you had better break the news. Your mistress is more accustomed to you than to anyone else, and you understand her ways. Here is the deposition. I shall wait below here till you come down. There is no saying how she will take it. Be sure you break the news gently."

Abijah went upstairs with a hesitating step, strongly in contrast with her usual quick bustling walk. She had before felt rather aggrieved that the doctor should be the first to break the news; but she now felt the difficulty of the task, and would gladly have been spared the responsibility.

"I have been expecting you for the last quarter of an hour, Abijah," Mrs. Mulready said querulously. "You know how I hate to have the room untidy after I have dressed. Why, what's the matter?" she broke off sharply as she noticed Abijah's face! "Why, you have been crying!"

"Yes, ma'am, I have been crying," Abijah said unsteadily, "but I don't know as ever I shall cry again, for I have heard such good news as will last me the rest of my whole life."

"What news, Abijah?" Mrs. Mulready asked quickly. "What are you making a mystery about, and what is that paper in your hand?"

"Well, ma'am, God has been very good to us all. I knew as he would be sooner or later, though sometimes I began to doubt whether it would be in my time, and it did break my heart to see Maister Ned going about so pale and un-

natural loike for a lad like him, and to know as there was
people as thought that he was a murderer. And now,
thank God, it is all over."

"All over! what do you mean, Abijah?" Mrs. Mulready
exclaimed, rising suddenly from her invalid chair. "What
do you mean by saying that it is all over?" and she seized
the old nurse's arm with an eager grasp.

"Don't excite yourself so, mistress. You have been
sore tried, but it is over now, and to-day all the world
will know as Maister Ned is proved to be innocent.
This here paper is a copy of the confession of the man as
did it, and who is, they say, dead by this time. It was
taken all right and proper afore a magistrate."

"Innocent!" Mrs. Mulready gasped in a voice scarcely
above a whisper. "Did you tell me, Abijah, that my
boy, my boy Ned, is innocent?"

"I never doubted as he was innocent, ma'am; but now,
thank God, all the world will know it. There, ma'am, sit
yourself down. Don't look like that. I know as how
you must feel, but for mercy sake don't look like that."

Mrs. Mulready did not seem to hear her, did not seem
to notice, as she passively permitted herself to be seated
in the chair, while Abijah poured out a glass of wine.
Her face was pale and rigid, her eyes wide open, her
expression one of horror rather than relief.

"Innocent! Proved innocent!" she murmured. "What
must he think of me—me, his mother!"

For some time she sat looking straight before her,
taking no notice to the efforts of Abijah to call her

attention, and unheeding the glass of wine which she in vain pressed her to drink.

"I must go away," she said at last, rising suddenly. "I must go away at once. Has he gone yet?"

"Go away, ma'am! Why, what should you go away for, and where are you going?"

"It does not matter; it makes no difference," Mrs. Mulready said feverishly, "so that I get away. Put some of my things together, Abijah. What are you staring there for? Don't you hear what I say? I must go away directly he has started for the mill."

And with trembling fingers she began to open her drawers and pull out her clothes.

"But you can't go away like that, mistress. You can't, indeed," Abijah said aghast.

"I must go, Abijah. There is nothing else for me to do. Do you think I could see him after treating him as I have done? I should fall dead at his feet for shame."

"But where are you going, ma'am?" Abijah said, thinking it better not to attempt to argue with her in her present state.

"I don't know, I don't know. Yes, I do. Do you know whether that cottage you were telling me about, where you lived while you were away from here, is to let? That will do nicely, for there I should be away from every one. Get me a box from the lumber-room, and tell Harriet to go out and get me a post-chaise from the 'Red Lion' as soon as my son has gone to the mill."

"Very well," Abijah said. "I will do as you want

me, 'm, if you will sit down quiet and not excite yourself. You know you have not been out of your room for
a year, and if you go a-tiring yourself like this you will
never be able to stand the journey. You sit down in the
chair and I will do the packing for you. You can tell
me what things you will take with you. I will get the
box down."

So saying, Abijah left the room, and, running hastily
down-stairs, told Ned and the doctor the manner in
which Mrs. Mulready had received the news. Ned would
have run up at once to his mother, but Dr. Green would
not hear of it.

"It would not do, Ned. In your mother's present state
the shock of seeing you might have the worst effect.
Run up, Abijah, and get the box down to her. I will go
out and come back and knock at the door in two or three
minutes, and will go up and see her, and, if necessary, I
will give her a strong soothing draught. You had better
tell her that from what you hear you believe Mr. Sankey
is not going to the mill to-day. That will make her
delay her preparation for moving until to-morrow, and
will give us time to see what is best to be done."

"I have brought the box, mistress," Abijah said as she
entered Mrs. Mulready's room; "but I don't think as you
will want to pack to-day, for I hear as Mr. Ned ain't
agoing to the mill. You see all the town will be coming
to see him to shake hands with him and tell him how
glad they is that he is cleared."

"And only I can't!" Mrs. Mulready wailed. "To think

of it, only I, his mother, can't see him! And I must stop
in the house for another day! Oh! it is too hard! But
I deserve it, and everything else."

"There is Dr. Green's knock," Abijah said.

"I can't see him, Abijah. I can't see him."

"I think you had better see him, ma'am. You always
do see him, you know, and it will look so strange if you
don't. There, I will pop these things into the drawers
again and hide the box."

Abijah bustled about actively, and before Mrs. Mulready had time to take any decided step Dr. Green
knocked at the door and came in.

"How are you to-day, Mrs. Mulready?" he asked
cheerfully. "This is a joyful day indeed for us all. The
whole place is wild with the news, and I expect we shall
be having a deputation presently to congratulate Ned."

"I am not feeling very well," Mrs. Mulready said
faintly. "The shock has been too much for me."

"Very natural, very natural, indeed," Dr. Green said
cheerily. "We could hardly hope it would be otherwise;
but after this good news I expect we shall soon make a
woman of you again. Your son will be the most popular
man in the place. People will not know how to make
enough of him. Porson and I, who have been cheering
him all along, will have to snub him now or his head
will be turned. Now let me feel your pulse. Dear!
dear! this will not do at all; it's going like a mill-engine.
This will never do. If you do not calm yourself we shall
be having you in bed again for a long bout. I will send

you a bottle of soothing medicine. You must take it every two hours, and keep yourself perfectly quiet. There, I will not talk to you now about this good news, for I see that you are not fit to stand it. You must lie down on the sofa at once, and not get off again to-day. I will look in this evening and see how you are."

Frightened at the threat that if she were not quiet she might be confined to her bed for weeks, Mrs. Mulready obeyed orders, took her medicine when it arrived, and lay quiet on the sofa. For a long time the sedative failed to have any effect. Every five minutes throughout the day there were knocks at the door. Every one who knew Ned, and many who did not, called to congratulate him. Some, like Mr. Thompson, made a half apology for having so long doubted him. A few, like Mr. Simmonds, were able heartily to assure him that they had never in their hearts believed it. Ned was too full of gratitude and happiness to cherish the slightest animosity, and he received warmly and thankfully the congratulations which were showered upon him.

"He looks another man," was the universal comment of his visitors; and, indeed, it was so. The cloud which had so long overshadowed him had passed away, and the look of cold reserve had vanished with it, and he was prepared again to receive the world as a friend. He was most moved when, early in the day, Mr. Porson and the whole of the boys arrived. As soon as he had left Mrs. Mulready, Dr. Green had hurried down to the schoolhouse with the news, and Mr. Porson, as soon as he heard

it, had announced it from his desk, adding that after such
news as that he could not expect them to continue their
lessons, and that the rest of the day must therefore be
regarded as a holiday. He yielded a ready assent when
the boys entreated that they might go in a body to congratulate Ned.

Ned was speechless for some time as his old friend
wrung his hand, and his former school-fellows clustered
round him with a very Babel of congratulations and good
wishes. Only the knowledge that his mother was ill
above prevented them from breaking into uproarious
cheering. In the afternoon, hearing that his mother was
still awake, Ned, accompanied by Mr. Porson, went out
for a stroll, telling Harriet that she was to remain at
the open door while he was away, so as to prevent
anyone from knocking. It was something of a trial to
Ned to walk through the street which he had passed
along so many times in the last year oblivious of all
within it. Every man and woman he met insisted on
shaking hands with him. Tradesmen left their shops
and ran out to greet him, and there was no mistaking
the general enthusiasm which was felt on the occasion,
and the desire of every one to atone as far as possible for
the unmerited suffering which had been inflicted on him.

When he returned at six o'clock he found Harriet still
on the watch, and she said in low tones that Abijah had
just come down-stairs with the news that her mistress
had fallen asleep.

"I should not think anyone more will come, Harriet, but

I will get you to stop here for a little longer. Then we must fasten up the knocker and take off the bell. The doctor says that it is all-important that my mother should get a long and undisturbed sleep."

Dr. Green came in again in the evening, and had a long chat with Ned. It was nearly midnight before Mrs. Mulready awoke. On opening her eyes she saw Ned sitting at a short distance from the sofa. She gave a sudden start, and then a look of terror came into her face.

Ned rose to his feet and held out his arms with the one word "Mother!"

Mrs. Mulready slid from the sofa and threw herself on her knees with her hands clasped.

"Oh! my boy, my boy!" she cried, "can you forgive me?" Then, as he raised her in his arms, she fainted.

It was a happy party, indeed, that assembled round the breakfast-table next morning. Mrs. Mulready was at the head of the table making tea, looking pale and weak but with a look of quiet happiness and contentment on her face, such as her children had never seen there before, but which was henceforth to be its habitual expression.

Ned did not carry out his original intention of entering the army. Mr. Simmonds warmly offered to make the application for a commission for him, but Ned declined. He had made up his mind, he said, to stick to the mill; there was plenty of work to be done there, and he foresaw that with a continued improvement of machinery there was a great future for the manufacturing interests of England.

The Luddite movement gradually died out. The high rewards offered for the discovery of the murderers of Mr. Horsfall and of the assailants of Cartwright's mill had their effect. Three croppers, Mellor, Thorpe, and Smith, were denounced and brought to trial. All three had been concerned in the murder, together with Walker, who turned King's evidence for the reward—Mellor and Thorpe having fired the fatal shots. The same men had been the leaders in the attack on Cartwright's mill.

They were tried at the assizes at York on the 2d of January, 1813, with sixty-four of their comrades, before Baron Thomas and Judge Le Blanc, and were found guilty, although they were defended by Henry (afterward Lord) Brougham. Mellor, Thorpe, and Smith were executed three days afterwards. Fourteen of the others were hung, as were five Luddites who were tried before another tribunal.

After this wholesale act of severity the Luddite disturbances soon came to an end. The non-success which had attended their efforts, and the execution of all their leaders, thoroughly cowed the rioters, and their ranks were speedily thinned by the number of hands who found employment in the rapidly-increasing mills in the district. Anyhow from that time the Luddite conspiracy ceased to be formidable.

The Sankeys' mill at Marsden flourished greatly under Ned's management. Every year saw additions to the buildings and machinery until it became one of the largest concerns in Yorkshire. He was not assisted, as he had at one time hoped he should be, by his brother in the management; but he was well contented when Charlie, on leaving school, declared his wish to go to Cambridge, and then to enter the church, a life for which he was far better suited by temperament than for the active life of a man of business.

The trial through which Ned Sankey had passed had a lasting effect upon his character. Whatever afterwards occurred to vex him in business he was never known to utter a hasty word, or to form a hasty judgment. He was ever busy in devising schemes for the benefit of his work-people, and to be in Sankey's mill was considered as the greatest piece of good fortune which could befall a hand.

Four years after the confession of John Stukeley Ned married the daughter of his friend George Cartwright, and settled down in a handsome house which he had built for himself a short distance out of Marsden. Lucy was soon afterwards settled in a house of her own, having married a young land-owner with ample estates.

Mrs. Mulready, in spite of the urgent persuasions of her son and his young wife, refused to take up her residence with them, but established herself in a pretty little house close at hand, spending, however, a considerable portion of each day with him at his home. The trials through which she had gone had done even more for her than for Ned. All her querulous listlessness had disappeared. She was bright, cheerful, and even-tempered. Ned used to tell her that she grew younger looking every day.

Her pride and happiness in her son were unbounded,

and these culminated when, ten years after his accession to the management of the mill, Ned acceded to the request of a large number of manufacturers in the district, to stand for Parliament as the representative of the mill-owning interest, and was triumphantly returned at the head of the poll.

Of the other characters of this story little need be said. Dr. Green and Mr. and Mrs. Porson remained Ned's closest friends to the end of their lives. Mary Powlett did not compel Bill Swinton to wait until the situation of foreman of the mill became vacant, but married him two years after the death of John Stukeley. Bill became in time not only foreman but the confidential manager of the mill, and he and his wife were all their lives on the footing of dear friends with Mr. and Mrs. Sankey.

Luke Marner remained foreman of his room until too old for further work, when he retired on a comfortable pension, and was succeeded in his post by his son George. Ned and Amy Sankey had a large family, who used to listen with awe and admiration to the tale of the terrible trial which had once befallen their father, and of the way in which he had indeed been "tried in the fire."

THE END.

BLACKIE & SON'S
BOOKS FOR YOUNG PEOPLE.

BY G. A. HENTY.

The Tiger of Mysore: A Story of the War with Tippoo Saib. By G. A. HENTY. With 12 Illustrations by W. H. MARGETSON, and a Map. Crown 8vo, cloth elegant, olivine edges, 6s.

Dick Holland's father is supposed to be one of the English captives in the hands of that bloodthirsty tyrant, Tippoo Saib, who is known in history as "The Tiger of Mysore". So Dick, who is a spirited lad, resolves to proceed to India, gain tidings of his father, and help him to escape, if possible. Accordingly he sails for Madras, joins the army under Lord Cornwallis, and takes part in a campaign against Tippoo. Afterwards, he assumes a disguise; enters Seringapatam, the capital of Mysore; rescues Tippoo's harem from a tiger; and is appointed to high office by the tyrant. In this capacity Dick visits the hill fortresses, still in search of his father, and at last he discovers him in the great stronghold of Savandroog. The hazardous rescue which Dick attempts, and the perilous night ride through the enemy's country are at length accomplished, and the young fellow's dangerous mission is done. And the end comes all too soon—so clever, and plucky, and daring are the devices and adventures of gallant Dick Holland.

A Knight of the White Cross: A Tale of the Siege of Rhodes. By G. A. HENTY. With 12 full-page Illustrations by RALPH PEACOCK. Crown 8vo, cloth elegant, olivine edges, 6s.

Gervaise Tresham, the hero of this story, is determined to follow a military career, and from his father's friendship to the Grand Prior of the Knights of St. John, he is enabled to join that famous Order. Leaving England he proceeds to the island stronghold of Rhodes, and becomes a page in the household of the Grand Master. Subsequently, Gervaise is made a Knight of the White Cross for valour in a sea-fight with pirates, while soon afterwards he is appointed commander of a war-galley, and in his first voyage destroys a fleet of Moorish corsairs. During one of his cruises the young knight is attacked on shore, captured after a desperate struggle, and sold into slavery in Tripoli. He succeeds in escaping, however, and returns to Rhodes in time to take part in the splendid defence of that fortress when it was besieged by all the might of the Turks. Altogether a fine chivalrous tale, of varied interest, and full of noble daring.

BY G. A. HENTY.

" Mr. Henty is one of the best of story-tellers for young people."—*Spectator.*

When London Burned: A Story of Restoration Times and the Great Fire. By G. A. HENTY. With 12 page Illustrations by J. FINNEMORE. Crown 8vo, cloth elegant, olivine edges, 6s.

"One of the best stories Mr. Henty has written." —*The Times.*

" No boy needs to have any story of Henty's recommended to him, and parents who do not know and buy him for their boys should be ashamed of themselves. Those to whom he is yet unknown could not make a better beginning than with *When London Burned.*" —*British Weekly.*

Beric the Briton: A Story of the Roman Invasion. By G. A. HENTY. With 12 page Illustrations by W. PARKINSON. Crown 8vo, cloth elegant, olivine edges, 6s.

" We are not aware that any one has given us quite so vigorous a picture of Britain in the days of the Roman conquest. Mr. Henty has done his utmost to make an impressive picture of the haughty Roman character, with its indomitable courage, sternness, and discipline. *Beric* is good all through."—*Spectator.*

Through the Sikh War: A Tale of the Conquest of the Punjaub. By G. A. HENTY. With 12 page Illustrations by HAL HURST, and a Map. Crown 8vo, cloth elegant, olivine edges, 6s.

" The picture of the Punjaub during its last few years of independence, the description of the battles on the Sutlej, and the portraiture generally of native character, seem admirably true. . . . On the whole, we have never read a more vivid and faithful narrative of military adventure in India."—*The Academy.*

With Lee in Virginia: A Story of the American Civil War. By G. A. HENTY. With 10 page Illustrations by GORDON BROWNE, and 6 Maps. Crown 8vo, cloth elegant, olivine edges, 6s.

" The story is a capital one and full of variety, and presents us with many picturesque scenes of Southern life. Young Wingfield, who is conscientious, spirited, and 'hard as nails', would have been a man after the very heart of Stonewall Jackson."—*Times.*

With Wolfe in Canada: Or, The Winning of a Continent. By G. A. HENTY. With 12 page Illustrations by GORDON BROWNE. Crown 8vo, cloth elegant, olivine edges, 6s.

"A model of what a boys' story-book should be. Mr. Henty has a great power of infusing into the dead facts of history new life, and as no pains are spared by him to ensure accuracy in historic details, his books supply useful aids to study as well as amusement."—*School Guardian.*

The Dash for Khartoum: A Tale of the Nile Expedition. By G. A. HENTY. With 10 page Illustrations by J. SCHÖNBERG and J. NASH, and 4 Plans. Crown 8vo, cloth elegant, olivine edges, 6s.

" It is literally true that the narrative never flags a moment; for the incidents which fall to be recorded after the dash for Khartoum has been made and failed are quite as interesting as those which precede it." *Academy.*

BY G. A. HENTY.

"Surely Mr. Henty should understand boys' tastes better than any man living."
—*The Times.*

Reduced Illustration from "Tiger of Mysore".

Wulf the Saxon: A Story of the Norman Conquest. By G. A. HENTY. With 12 page Illustrations by RALPH PEACOCK. Crown 8vo, cloth elegant, olivine edges, 6s.

"The story shows Mr. Henty at his best." *Daily Chronicle.*

"*Wulf the Saxon* is second to none of Mr. Henty's historical tales, and we may safely say that a boy may learn from it more genuine history than he will from many a tedious tome. The points of the Saxon character are hit off very happily, and the life of the period is ably reconstructed."—*The Spectator.*

By Pike and Dyke: A Tale of the Rise of the Dutch Republic. By G. A. HENTY. With 10 page Illustrations by MAYNARD BROWN, and 4 Maps. Crown 8vo, cloth elegant, olivine edges, 6s.

"The mission of Ned to deliver letters from William the Silent to his adherents at Brussels, the fight of the *Good Venture* with the Spanish man-of-war, the battle on the ice at Amsterdam, the siege of Haarlem, are all told with a vividness and skill which are worthy of Mr. Henty at his best."—*Academy.*

BY G. A. HENTY.

"Among writers of stories of adventure for boys Mr. Henty stands in the very first rank."—*Academy*.

The Lion of St. Mark: A Tale of Venice in the Fourteenth
Century. By G. A. HENTY. With 10 page Illustrations by GORDON
BROWNE. Crown 8vo, cloth elegant, olivine edges, 6s.

"Every boy should read *The Lion of St. Mark*. Mr. Henty has never produced any story more delightful, more wholesome, or more vivacious. From first to last it will be read with keen enjoyment."—*The Saturday Review*.

By England's Aid: The Freeing of the Netherlands (1585–
1604). By G. A. HENTY. With 10 page Illustrations by ALFRED
PEARSE, and 4 Maps. Crown 8vo, cloth elegant, olivine edges, 6s.

"The story is told with great animation, and the historical material is most effectively combined with a most excellent plot."—*Saturday Review*.

Under Drake's Flag: A Tale of the Spanish Main. By
G. A. HENTY. Illustrated by 12 page Pictures by GORDON BROWNE.
Crown 8vo, cloth elegant, olivine edges, 6s.

"There is not a dull chapter, nor, indeed, a dull page in the book; but the author has so carefully worked up his subject that the exciting deeds of his heroes are never incongruous or absurd."—*Observer*.

Bonnie Prince Charlie: A Tale of Fontenoy and Culloden.
By G. A. HENTY. With 12 page Illustrations by GORDON BROWNE.
Crown 8vo, cloth elegant, olivine edges, 6s.

"Ronald, the hero, is very like the hero of *Quentin Durward*. The lad's journey across France with his faithful attendant Malcolm, and his hairbreadth escapes from the machinations of his father's enemies make up as good a narrative of the kind as we have ever read. For freshness of treatment and variety of incident, Mr. Henty has here surpassed himself."—*Spectator*.

"A historical romance of the best quality. Mr. Henty has written many more sensational stories, but never a more artistic one."—*Academy*.

For the Temple: A Tale of the Fall of Jerusalem. By
G. A. HENTY. With 10 page Illustrations by S. J. SOLOMON, and
a Coloured Map. Crown 8vo, cloth elegant, olivine edges, 6s.

"Mr. Henty's graphic prose pictures of the hopeless Jewish resistance to Roman sway adds another leaf to his record of the famous wars of the world. The book is one of Mr. Henty's cleverest efforts."—*Graphic*.

True to the Old Flag: A Tale of the American War of
Independence. By G. A. HENTY. With 12 page Illustrations by
GORDON BROWNE. Crown 8vo, cloth elegant, olivine edges, 6s.

"Does justice to the pluck and determination of the British soldiers. The son of an American loyalist, who remains true to our flag, falls among the hostile redskins in that very Huron country which has been endeared to us by the exploits of Hawkeye and Chingachgook."—*The Times*.

BY G. A. HENTY.

"Mr. Henty is the king of story-tellers for boys."—*Sword and Trowel.*

Reduced Illustration from "Knight of White Cross"

St. Bartholomew's Eve: A Tale of the Huguenot Wars.
By G. A. HENTY. With 12 page Illustrations by H. J. DRAPER, and a Map. Crown 8vo, cloth elegant, olivine edges, 6s.

"A really noble story, which adult readers will find to the full as satisfying as the boys. Lucky boys! to have such a caterer as Mr. G. A. Henty."—*Black and White.*

"What would boys do without Mr. Henty? Ever fresh and vigorous, his books have at once the solidity of history and the charm of romance. *St. Bartholomew's Eve* is in his best style, and the interest never flags. The book is all that could possibly be wished from a boy's point of view."—*Journal of Education.*

With Clive in India: Or, The Beginnings of an Empire.
By G. A. HENTY. With 12 page Illustrations by GORDON BROWNE. Crown 8vo, cloth elegant, olivine edges, 6s.

"Among writers of stories of adventure for boys Mr. Henty stands in the very first rank. Those who know something about India will be the most ready to thank Mr. Henty for giving them this instructive volume to place in the hands of their children."—*Academy.*

BY G. A. HENTY.

" Mr. Henty is one of our most successful writers of historical tales."—*Scotsman.*

The Lion of the North: A Tale of Gustavus Adolphus and the Wars of Religion. By G. A. HENTY. With 12 page Pictures by J. SCHÖNBERG. Crown 8vo, cloth elegant, olivine edges, 6s.

" A praiseworthy attempt to interest British youth in the great deeds of the Scotch Brigade in the wars of Gustavus Adolphus. Mackay, Hepburn, and Munro live again in Mr. Henty's pages, as those deserve to live whose disciplined bands formed really the germ of the modern British army."—*Athenæum.*

The Young Carthaginian: A Story of the Times of Hannibal. By G. A. HENTY. With 12 page Illustrations by C. J. STANILAND, R.I. Crown 8vo, cloth elegant, olivine edges, 6s.

" The effect of an interesting story, well constructed and vividly told, is enhanced by the picturesque quality of the scenic background. From first to last nothing stays the interest of the narrative. It bears us along as on a stream whose current varies in direction, but never loses its force."—*Saturday Review.*

Redskin and Cow-boy: A Tale of the Western Plains. By G. A. HENTY. With 12 page Illustrations by ALFRED PEARSE. Crown 8vo, cloth elegant, olivine edges, 6s.

" It has a good plot; it abounds in action; the scenes are equally spirited and realistic, and we can only say we have read it with much pleasure from first to last. The pictures of life on a cattle ranche are most graphically painted, as are the manners of the reckless but jovial cow-boys."—*Times.*

In Freedom's Cause: A Story of Wallace and Bruce. By G. A. HENTY. With 12 page Illustrations by GORDON BROWNE. Crown 8vo, cloth elegant, olivine edges, 6s.

" His tale of the days of Wallace and Bruce is full of stirring action, and will commend itself to boys."—*Athenæum.*

By Right of Conquest: Or, With Cortez in Mexico. By G. A. HENTY. With 10 page Illustrations by W. S. STACEY, and 2 Maps. Crown 8vo, cloth elegant, olivine edges, 6s.

" *By Right of Conquest* is the nearest approach to a perfectly successful historical tale that Mr. Henty has yet published."—*Academy.*

In Greek Waters: A Story of the Grecian War of Independence (1821-1827). By G. A. HENTY. With 12 page Illustrations by W. S. STACEY, and a Map. Crown 8vo, cloth elegant, olivine edges, 6s.

" There are adventures of all kinds for the hero and his friends, whose pluck and ingenuity in extricating themselves from awkward fixes are always equal to the occasion. It is an excellent story, and if the proportion of history is smaller than usual, the whole result leaves nothing to be desired."—*Journal of Education.*

BY G. A. HENTY.

"No more interesting boys' books are written than Mr. Henty's stories."—
Daily Chronicle.

Through the Fray: A Story of the Luddite Riots. By
G. A. HENTY. With 12 page Illustrations by H. M. PAGET. Crown
8vo, cloth elegant, olivine edges, 6s.

"Mr. Henty inspires a love and admiration for straightforwardness, truth, and
courage. This is one of the best of the many good books Mr. Henty has produced,
and deserves to be classed with his *Facing Death*."—*Standard.*

Captain Bayley's Heir: A Tale of the Gold Fields of Cali-
fornia. By G. A. HENTY. With 12 page Illustrations by H. M.
PAGET. Crown 8vo, cloth elegant, olivine edges, 6s.

"A Westminster boy who makes his way in the world by hard work, good
temper, and unfailing courage. The descriptions given of life are just what a
healthy intelligent lad should delight in."—*St. James's Gazette.*

Through Russian Snows: A Story of Napoleon's Retreat
from Moscow. By G. A. HENTY. With 8 Illustrations by W. H.
OVEREND, and a Map. Crown 8vo, cloth elegant, olivine edges, 5s.

The hero of this story, Julian Wyatt, is a careless, good-natured youth,
who becomes, quite innocently, mixed up with smugglers—when smuggling
was common in the south coast of England. The smugglers carry him to
France, and hand him over as a prisoner to the French; but he subsequently regains his freedom by joining Napoleon's army in the campaign
against Russia. The young Englishman takes part in the great battles of
Smolensk and Borodino, arriving at Moscow with the victorious Emperor.
Then, when the terrible retreat begins, Julian finds himself in the rear-
guard of the French army, fighting desperately, league by league, against
famine, snow-storms, wolves, and Russians. Ultimately he escapes, after
rescuing the daughter of a Russian Count; makes his way to St. Petersburg;
and then returns to England. A story this with an excellent plot, exciting
adventures, and splendid historical interest.

In the Heart of the Rockies: A Story of Adventure in
Colorado. By G. A. HENTY. With 8 page Illustrations by G. C.
HINDLEY. Crown 8vo, cloth elegant, olivine edges, 5s.

"Few Christmas books will be more to the taste of the ingenuous boy than *In
the Heart of the Rockies*."—*Athenæum.*
"Mr. Henty is seen here at his best as an artist in lightning fiction."—*Academy.*

One of the 28th: A Tale of Waterloo. By G. A. HENTY.
With 8 page Illustrations by W. H. OVEREND, and 2 Maps. Crown
8vo, cloth elegant, olivine edges, 5s.

"Written with Homeric vigour and heroic inspiration. It is graphic, picturesque, and dramatically effective . . . shows us Mr. Henty at his best and
brightest. The adventures will hold a boy of a winter's night enthralled as he
rushes through them with breathless interest 'from cover to cover'."—*Observer.*

BY G. A. HENTY.

"Ask for Henty, and see that you get him."—*Punch.*

The Cat of Bubastes: A Story of Ancient Egypt. By
G. A. HENTY. With 8 page Illustrations by J. R. WEGUELIN.
Crown 8vo, cloth elegant, olivine edges, 5s.

"The story, from the critical moment of the killing of the sacred cat to the
perilous exodus into Asia with which it closes, is very skilfully constructed and
full of exciting adventures. It is admirably illustrated."—*Saturday Review.*

Maori and Settler: A Story of the New Zealand War. By
G. A. HENTY. With 8 page Illustrations by ALFRED PEARSE, and
a Map. Crown 8vo, cloth elegant, olivine edges, 5s.

"It is a book which all young people, but especially boys, will read with
avidity."—*Athenæum.*

"A first-rate book for boys, brimful of adventure, of humorous and interesting
conversation, and of vivid pictures of colonial life."—*Schoolmaster.*

St. George for England: A Tale of Cressy and Poitiers.
By G. A. HENTY. With 8 full-page Illustrations by GORDON
BROWNE. Crown 8vo, cloth elegant, olivine edges, 5s.

"A story of very great interest for boys. In his own forcible style the author
has endeavoured to show that determination and enthusiasm can accomplish mar-
vellous results; and that courage is generally accompanied by magnanimity and
gentleness."—*Pall Mall Gazette.*

The Bravest of the Brave: With Peterborough in Spain.
By G. A. HENTY. With 8 full-page Pictures by H. M. PAGET.
Crown 8vo, cloth elegant, olivine edges, 5s.

"Mr. Henty never loses sight of the moral purpose of his work—to enforce the
doctrine of courage and truth, mercy and lovingkindness, as indispensable to the
making of an English gentleman. British lads will read *The Bravest of the
Brave* with pleasure and profit; of that we are quite sure."—*Daily Telegraph.*

For Name and Fame: Or, Through Afghan Passes. By
G. A. HENTY. With 8 full-page Illustrations by GORDON BROWNE.
Crown 8vo, cloth elegant, olivine edges, 5s.

"Not only a rousing story, replete with all the varied forms of excitement of a
campaign, but, what is still more useful, an account of a territory and its inhabitants which must for a long time possess a supreme interest for Englishmen, as
being the key to our Indian Empire." *Glasgow Herald.*

A Jacobite Exile: Being the Adventures of a Young English-
man in the Service of Charles XII. of Sweden. By G. A. HENTY.
With 8 page Illustrations by PAUL HARDY, and a Map. Crown
8vo, cloth elegant, olivine edges, 5s.

"Incident succeeds incident, and adventure is piled upon adventure, and at the
end the reader, be he boy or man, will have experienced breathless enjoyment
in a romantic story that must have taught him much at its close."—*Ar. .y and
Navy Gazette.*

BY G. A. HENTY.

"Mr. Henty's books are always alive with moving incident."— *Review of Reviews.*

Condemned as a Nihilist: A Story of Escape from Siberia. By G. A. HENTY. With 8 page Illustrations by WALTER PAGET. Crown 8vo, cloth elegant, olivine edges, 5s.

"The best of this year's Henty. His narrative is more interesting than many of the tales with which the public is familiar, of escape from Siberia. Despite their superior claim to authenticity these tales are without doubt no less fictitious than Mr. Henty's, and he beats them hollow in the matter of sensations."
—*National Observer.*

Orange and Green: A Tale of the Boyne and Limerick. By G. A. HENTY. With 8 full-page Illustrations by GORDON BROWNE. Crown 8vo, cloth elegant, olivine edges, 5s.

"The narrative is free from the vice of prejudice, and ripples with life as vivacious as if what is being described were really passing before the eye. . . . Should be in the hands of every young student of Irish history."— *Belfast News.*

Held Fast for England: A Tale of the Siege of Gibraltar. By G. A. HENTY. With 8 page Illustrations by GORDON BROWNE. Crown 8vo, cloth elegant, olivine edges, 5s.

"Among them we would place first in interest and wholesome educational value the story of the siege of Gibraltar. . . . There is no cessation of exciting incident throughout the story."—*Athenæum.*

In the Reign of Terror: The Adventures of a Westminster Boy. By G. A. HENTY. With 8 full-page Illustrations by J. SCHÖNBERG. Crown 8vo, cloth elegant, olivine edges, 5s.

"Harry Sandwith, the Westminster boy, may fairly be said to beat Mr. Henty's record. His adventures will delight boys by the audacity and peril they depict. The story is one of Mr. Henty's best."—*Saturday Review.*

By Sheer Pluck: A Tale of the Ashanti War. By G. A. HENTY. With 8 full-page Pictures by GORDON BROWNE. Crown 8vo, cloth elegant, olivine edges, 5s.

"Morally, the book is everything that could be desired, setting before the boys a bright and bracing ideal of the English gentleman."— *Christian Leader.*

The Dragon and the Raven: Or, The Days of King Alfred. By G. A. HENTY. With 8 page Illustrations by C. J. STANILAND, R.I. Crown 8vo, cloth elegant, olivine edges, 5s.

"A story that may justly be styled remarkable. Boys, in reading it, will be surprised to find how Alfred persevered, through years of bloodshed and times of peace, to rescue his people from the thraldom of the Danes. We hope the book will soon be widely known in all our schools."—*Schoolmaster.*

A Final Reckoning: A Tale of Bush Life in Australia. By G. A. HENTY. With 8 page Illustrations by W. B. WOLLEN. Crown 8vo, cloth elegant, olivine edges, 5s.

"All boys will read this story with eager and unflagging interest. The episodes are in Mr. Henty's very best vein—graphic, exciting, realistic; and, as in all Mr. Henty's books, the tendency is to the formation of an honourable, manly, and even heroic character."—*Birmingham Post.*

BY G. A. HENTY.

"As publishers of books of adventure for boys Messrs. Blackie & Son have no superiors."—*St. James's Gazette.*

Facing Death: Or, The Hero of the Vaughan Pit. A Tale of the Coal Mines. By G. A. HENTY. With 8 page Pictures by GORDON BROWNE. Crown 8vo, cloth elegant, olivine edges, 5s.

"If any father, godfather, clergyman, or schoolmaster is on the look-out for a good book to give as a present to a boy who is worth his salt, this is the book we would recommend."—*Standard.*

A Chapter of Adventures: Or, Through the Bombardment of Alexandria. By G. A. HENTY. With 6 page Illustrations by W. H. OVEREND. Crown 8vo, cloth elegant, 3s. 6d.

"Jack Robson and his two companions have their fill of excitement, and their chapter of adventures is so brisk and entertaining we could have wished it longer than it is."—*Saturday Review.*

Two Thousand Years Ago: Or, The Adventures of a Roman Boy. By Professor A. J. CHURCH. With 12 page Illustrations by ADRIEN MARIE. Crown 8vo, cloth elegant, olivine edges, 6s.

"Adventures well worth the telling. The book is extremely entertaining as well as useful, and there is a wonderful freshness in the Roman scenes and characters."—*The Times.*

The Clever Miss Follett. By J. K. H. DENNY. With 12 page Illustrations by GERTRUDE D. HAMMOND. Crown 8vo, cloth elegant, olivine edges, 6s.

"Just the book to give to girls, who will delight both in the letterpress and the illustrations. Miss Hammond has never done better work."—*Review of Reviews.*

BY ROSA MULHOLLAND.

Banshee Castle. By ROSA MULHOLLAND. With 12 page Illustrations by JOHN H. BACON. Crown 8vo, cloth elegant, olivine edges, 6s.

"One of the most fascinating of Miss Rosa Mulholland's many fascinating stories. . . . The charm of the tale lies in the telling of it. The three heroines are admirably drawn characters."—*Athenaeum.*
"Is told with grace, and brightened by a knowledge of Irish folk-lore, making it a perfect present for a girl in her teens."—*Truth.*

Giannetta: A Girl's Story of Herself. By ROSA MULHOLLAND. With 8 page Illustrations by LOCKHART BOGLE. Crown 8vo, cloth elegant, olivine edges, 5s.

"Giannetta is a true heroine—warm-hearted, self-sacrificing, and, as all good women nowadays are, largely touched with the enthusiasm of humanity. One of the most attractive gift-books of the season."—*The Academy.*

BY KIRK MUNROE.

At War with Pontiac: Or, The Totem of the Bear. By
KIRK MUNROE. With 8 page Illustrations by J. FINNEMORE.
Crown 8vo, cloth elegant, olivine edges, 5s.

This is a story of old colonial days in America, when Detroit was a
frontier fort, and the shores of Lake Erie were held by hostile Indians
under Pontiac, their famous chief. The hero is Donald Hester, a young
English officer, who goes in search of his sister Edith, she having been captured by the red-skins. Strange and terrible are his experiences; for he is
wounded, taken prisoner, condemned to be burned, contrives to escape,
and is again captured. In all his adventures he finds a magic talisman in
the Totem of the Bear, which was tattooed on his arm in his childhood by
a friendly Indian; while in the end there is peace between Pontiac and
the English, and Donald marries the great chief's daughter. One dares not
skip a single page in this most enthralling tale.

The White Conquerors of Mexico: A Tale of Toltec and
Aztec. By KIRK MUNROE. With 8 page Illustrations by W. S.
STACEY. Crown 8vo, cloth elegant, olivine edges, 5s.

"Mr. Munroe gives most vivid pictures of the religious and civil polity of the
Aztecs, and of everyday life, as he imagines it, in the streets and market-places
of the magnificent capital of Montezuma."—*The Times.*

Highways and High Seas: Cyril Harley's Adventures on
both. By F. FRANKFORT MOORE. With 8 page Illustrations by
ALFRED PEARSE. Crown 8vo, cloth elegant, olivine edges, 5s.

"This is one of the best stories Mr. Moore has written, perhaps the very best.
The exciting adventures are sure to attract boys."—*Spectator.*

"It is pleasant to come across such honest work as F. Frankfort Moore's *High-
ways and High Seas.* Captain Chink is a real achievement in characterization."
—*Scots Observer.*

A Fair Claimant: Being a Story for Girls. By FRANCES
ARMSTRONG. With 8 page Illustrations by GERTRUDE D. HAMMOND.
Crown 8vo, cloth elegant, olivine edges, 5s.

"As a gift-book for big girls it is among the best new books of the kind. The
story is interesting and natural, from first to last."—*Westminster Gazette.*

The Heiress of Courtleroy. By ANNE BEALE. With 8
page Illustrations by T. C. H. CASTLE. Crown 8vo, cloth elegant,
olivine edges, 5s.

"We can speak highly of the grace with which Miss Beale relates how the
young 'Heiress of Courtleroy' had such good influence over her uncle as to win
him from his intensely selfish ways."—*Guardian.*

BY GEORGE MACDONALD.

A Rough Shaking. By George Mac Donald. With 12 page Illustrations by W. Parkinson. Crown 8vo, cloth elegant, olivine edges, 6s.

'One of the very best books for boys that has been written. It is full of material peculiarly well adapted for the young, containing in a marked degree the elements of all that is necessary to make up a perfect boys' book."— *Teachers' Aid.*

At the Back of the North Wind. By Geo. Mac Donald. With 75 Illustrations by Arthur Hughes. Crown 8vo, cloth elegant, olivine edges, 5s.

"The story is thoroughly original, full of fancy and pathos. . . . We stand with one foot in fairyland and one on common earth."—*The Times.*

Ranald Bannerman's Boyhood. By Geo. Mac Donald. With 36 Illustrations by Arthur Hughes. Crown 8vo, cloth elegant, olivine edges, 5s.

"The sympathy with boy-nature in *Ranald Bannerman's Boyhood* is perfect. It is a beautiful picture of childhood, teaching by its impressions and suggestions all noble things."— *British Quarterly Review.*

The Princess and the Goblin. By George Mac Donald. With 32 Illustrations. Crown 8vo, cloth extra, 3s. 6d.

"Little of what is written for children has the lightness of touch and play of fancy which are characteristic of George MacDonald's fairy tales. Mr. Arthur Hughes's illustrations are all that illustrations should be."—*Manchester Guardian.*

The Princess and Curdie. By George Mac Donald. With 8 page Illustrations. Crown 8vo, cloth extra, 3s. 6d.

"There is the finest and rarest genius in this brilliant story. Upgrown people would do wisely occasionally to lay aside their newspapers and magazines to spend an hour with Curdie and the Princess."—*Sheffield Independent.*

BY HARRY COLLINGWOOD.

The Pirate Island: A Story of the South Pacific. By Harry Collingwood. With 8 page Pictures by C. J. Staniland and J. R. Wells. Crown 8vo, cloth elegant, olivine edges, 5s.

"A capital story of the sea; indeed in our opinion the author is superior in some respects as a marine novelist to the better known Mr. Clark Russell."—*The Times.*

The Log of the "Flying Fish": A Story of Aerial and Submarine Adventure. By Harry Collingwood. With 6 page Illustrations by Gordon Browne. Crown 8vo, cloth elegant, 3s. 6d.

"The *Flying Fish* actually surpasses all Jules Verne's creations: with incredible speed she flies through the air, skims over the surface of the water, and darts along the ocean bed. We strongly recommend our school-boy friends to possess themselves of her log."—*Athenæum.*

₊ For other Books by Harry Collingwood, see pages 21 and 23.

BY GEORGE MANVILLE FENN.

" Mr. Fenn stands in the foremost rank of writers in this department."—*Daily News.*

Quicksilver: Or, A Boy with no Skid to his Wheel. By GEORGE MANVILLE FENN. With 10 page Illustrations by FRANK DADD. Crown 8vo, cloth elegant, olivine edges, 6s.

" *Quicksilver* is little short of an inspiration. In it that prince of story-writers for boys—George Manville Fenn—has surpassed himself. It is an ideal book for a boy's library." *Practical Teacher.*

Dick o' the Fens: A Romance of the Great East Swamp. By G. MANVILLE FENN. With 12 page Illustrations by FRANK DADD. Crown 8vo, cloth elegant, olivine edges, 6s.

" We conscientiously believe that boys will find it capital reading. It is full of incident and mystery, and the mystery is kept up to the last moment. It is rich in effective local colouring; and it has a historical interest."—*Times.*

Devon Boys: A Tale of the North Shore. By G. MANVILLE FENN. With 12 page Illustrations by GORDON BROWNE. Crown 8vo, cloth elegant, olivine edges, 6s.

" An admirable story, as remarkable for the individuality of its young heroes as for the excellent descriptions of coast scenery and life in North Devon. It is one of the best books we have seen this season."—*Athenæum.*

The Golden Magnet: A Tale of the Land of the Incas. By G. MANVILLE FENN. Illustrated by 12 page Pictures by GORDON BROWNE. Crown 8vo, cloth elegant, olivine edges, 6s.

" There could be no more welcome present for a boy. There is not a dull page in the book, and many will be read with breathless interest. 'The Golden Magnet' is, of course, the same one that attracted Raleigh and the heroes of *Westward Ho!*"—*Journal of Education.*

In the King's Name: Or, The Cruise of the *Kestrel*. By G. MANVILLE FENN. Illustrated by 12 page Pictures by GORDON BROWNE. Crown 8vo, cloth elegant, olivine edges, 6s.

" The best of all Mr. Fenn's productions in this field. It has the great quality of always 'moving on', adventure following adventure in constant succession."—*Daily News.*

Nat the Naturalist: A Boy's Adventures in the Eastern Seas. By G. MANVILLE FENN. With 8 page Pictures. Crown 8vo, cloth elegant, olivine edges, 5s.

" This sort of book encourages independence of character, develops resource, and teaches a boy to keep his eyes open."—*Saturday Review.*

Bunyip Land: The Story of a Wild Journey in New Guinea. By G. MANVILLE FENN. With 6 page Illustrations by GORDON BROWNE. Crown 8vo, cloth elegant, 4s.

" Mr. Fenn deserves the thanks of everybody for *Bunyip Land*, and we may venture to promise that a quiet week may be reckoned on whilst the youngsters have such fascinating literature provided for their evenings' amusement."—*Spectator.*

BY GEORGE MANVILLE FENN.

"No one can find his way to the hearts of lads more readily than Mr. Fenn."—
Nottingham Guardian.

Brownsmith's Boy: A Romance in a Garden. By G.
MANVILLE FENN. With 6 page Illustrations. Crown 8vo, cloth
elegant, 3s. 6d.

"Mr. Fenn's books are among the best, if not altogether the best, of the stories
for boys. Mr. Fenn is at his best in *Brownsmith's Boy.*"—*Pictorial World.*

*** For other Books by G. MANVILLE FENN, see page 22.

BY ASCOTT R. HOPE.

Young Travellers' Tales. By ASCOTT R. HOPE. With
6 Illustrations by H. J. DRAPER. Crown 8vo, cloth elegant, 3s. 6d.

"Possess a high value for instruction as well as for entertainment. His quiet,
level humour bubbles up on every page."—*Daily Chronicle.*

"Excitement and cheerful enjoyment run through the book."—*Bookman.*

The Seven Wise Scholars. By ASCOTT R. HOPE. With
nearly 100 Illustrations by GORDON BROWNE. Cloth elegant, 5s.

"As full of fun as a volume of *Punch*; with illustrations, more laughter-
provoking than most we have seen since Leech died."—*Sheffield Independent.*

Stories of Old Renown: Tales of Knights and Heroes.
By ASCOTT R. HOPE. With 100 Illustrations by GORDON BROWNE.
Crown 8vo, cloth elegant, 3s. 6d.

"A really fascinating book worthy of its telling title. There is, we venture to
say, not a dull page in the book, not a story which will not bear a second reading."—*Guardian.*

Under False Colours: A Story from Two Girls' Lives.
By SARAH DOUDNEY. With 6 page Illustrations by G. G. KIL-
BURNE. Crown 8vo, cloth elegant, 4s.

"Sarah Doudney has no superior as a writer of high-toned stories—pure in
style and original in conception; but we have seen nothing from her pen equal
in dramatic energy to this book."—*Christian Leader.*

"This is a charming story, abounding in delicate touches of sentiment and
pathos. Its plot is skilfully contrived."—*Scotsman.*

The Universe: Or The Infinitely Great and the Infinitely Little.
A Sketch of Contrasts in Creation, and Marvels revealed and
explained by Natural Science. By F. A. POUCHET, M.D. With
272 Engravings on wood, of which 55 are full-page size, and 4
Coloured Illustrations. Twelfth Edition, medium 8vo, cloth elegant, gilt edges, 7s. 6d.; also morocco antique, 16s.

"We can honestly commend Professor Pouchet's book, which is admirably, as
it is copiously illustrated."—*The Times.*

"Scarcely any book in French or in English is so likely to stimulate in the
young an interest in the physical phenomena."—*Fortnightly Review.*

BY DR. GORDON STABLES.

For Life and Liberty: A Story of Battle by Land and Sea. By Dr. GORDON STABLES, R.N. With 8 Illustrations by SYDNEY PAGET, and a Map. Crown 8vo, cloth elegant, olivine edges, 5s.

When in 1861 war was declared in America between the North and South, the news greatly interested Osmond Lloyd, who was at school in England. Being of an adventurous spirit, and having relations in the States, the lad ran away from home with his chum Kenneth Reid, and the two made their way to America in the *Mosquito*. Their various adventures in that great conflict, both in the army and in the navy, are vigorously set forth in this narrative. Osmond was in the army of the Potomac, took part in all the campaigns, and won praise for his valour from the famous general, "Stonewall" Jackson.

Reduced Illustration from "To Greenland".

To Greenland and the Pole. By GORDON STABLES, M.D. With 8 page Illustrations by G. C. HINDLEY, and a Map. Crown 8vo, cloth elegant, olivine edges, 5s.

"His Arctic explorers have the verisimilitude of life. It is one of the books of the season, and one of the best Mr. Stables has ever written."—*Truth.*

Westward with Columbus. By GORDON STABLES, M.D. With 8 page Illustrations by A. PEARSE. Cloth elegant, 5s.

"We must place *Westward with Columbus* among those books that all boys ought to read."—*The Spectator.*

'Twixt School and College: A Tale of Self-reliance. By GORDON STABLES, C.M., M.D., R.N. With 8 page Illustrations by W. PARKINSON. Crown 8vo, cloth elegant, olivine edges, 5s.

"One of the best of a prolific writer's books for boys, being full of practical instructions as to keeping pets, and inculcates in a way which a little recalls Miss Edgeworth's 'Frank' the virtue of self reliance."—*Athenæum.*

BY ROBERT LEIGHTON.

Olaf the Glorious. By ROBERT LEIGHTON. With 8 page Illustrations by RALPH PEACOCK, and a Map. Crown 8vo, cloth elegant, olivine edges, 5s.

"Is as good as anything of the kind we have met with. Mr. Leighton more than holds his own with Rider Haggard and Baring Gould."—*The Times.*
"Among the books best liked by boys of the sturdy English type few will take a higher place than *Olaf the Glorious.* . . . ."—*National Observer.*

The Wreck of "The Golden Fleece": The Story of a North Sea Fisher-boy. By ROBERT LEIGHTON. With 8 page Illustrations by F. BRANGWYN. Crown 8vo, cloth elegant, 5s.

"This story should add considerably to Mr. Leighton's high reputation. Excellent in every respect, it contains every variety of incident. The plot is very cleverly devised, and the types of the North Sea sailors are capital."—*The Times.*

The Pilots of Pomona: A Story of the Orkney Islands. By ROBERT LEIGHTON. With 8 page Illustrations by JOHN LEIGHTON, and a Map. Crown 8vo, cloth elegant, olivine edges, 5s.

"A story which is quite as good in its way as *Treasure Island*, and is full of adventure of a stirring yet most natural kind. Although it is primarily a boys' book, it is a real godsend to the elderly reader."—*Glasgow Evening Times.*

The Thirsty Sword: A Story of the Norse Invasion of Scotland (1262-63). By ROBERT LEIGHTON. With 8 page Illustrations by A. PEARSE. Crown 8vo, cloth elegant, 5s.

"This is one of the most fascinating stories for boys that it has ever been our pleasure to read. From first to last the interest never flags. Boys will worship Kenric, who is a hero in every sense of the word."—*Schoolmaster.*

BY G. NORWAY.

A Prisoner of War: A Story of the Time of Napoleon Bonaparte. By G. NORWAY. With 6 page Illustrations by ROBT. BARNES, A.R.W.S. Crown 8vo, cloth elegant, 3s. 6d.

"More hairbreadth escapes from death by starvation, by ice, by fighting, &c., were never before surmounted. . . . It is a fine yarn."—*The Guardian.*

The Loss of John Humble: What Led to It, and What Came of It. By G. NORWAY. With 8 page Illustrations by JOHN SCHÖNBERG. Crown 8vo, cloth elegant, olivine edges, 5s.

"This story will place the author at once in the front rank. It is full of life and adventure. The interest of the story is sustained without a break from first to last."—*Standard.*

A True Cornish Maid. By G. NORWAY. With 6 page Illustrations by J. FINNEMORE. Crown 8vo, cloth elegant, 3s. 6d.

"There is some excellent reading. . . . Mrs. Norway brings before the eyes of her readers the good Cornish folk, their speech, their manners, and their ways. *A True Cornish Maid* deserves to be popular."—*Athenæum.*

With the Sea Kings: A Story of the Days of Lord Nelson.
By F. H. WINDER. With 6 page Illustrations by W. S. STACEY.
Crown 8vo, cloth elegant, 4s.

"Just the book to put into a boy's hands. Every chapter contains boardings, cuttings out, fighting pirates, escapes of thrilling audacity, and captures by corsairs, sufficient to turn the quietest boy's head. The story culminates in a vigorous account of the battle of Trafalgar. Happy boys!"—*The Academy.*

Grettir the Outlaw: A Story of Iceland. By S. BARING-GOULD. With 6 page Illustrations by M. ZENO DIEMER, and a Coloured Map. Crown 8vo, cloth elegant, 4s.

"Is the boys' book of its year. That is, of course, as much as to say that it will do for men grown as well as juniors. It is told in simple, straightforward English, as all stories should be, and it has a freshness, a freedom, a sense of sun and wind and the open air, which make it irresistible."—*National Observer.*

Gold, Gold, in Cariboo: A Story of Adventure in British Columbia. By CLIVE PHILLIPPS-WOLLEY. With 6 page Illustrations by G. C. HINDLEY. Crown 8vo, cloth extra, 3s. 6d.

"It would be difficult to say too much in favour of *Gold, Gold, in Cariboo*. We have seldom read a more exciting tale of wild mining adventure in a singularly inaccessible country. There is a capital plot, and the interest is sustained to the last page."—*The Times.*

A Champion of the Faith: A Tale of Prince Hal and the Lollards. By J. M. CALLWELL. With 6 page Illustrations by HERBERT J. DRAPER. Crown 8vo, cloth elegant, 4s.

"Will not be less enjoyed than Mr. Henty's books. Sir John Oldcastle's pathetic story, and the history of his brave young squire, will make every boy enjoy this lively story."—*London Quarterly.*

BY ALICE CORKRAN.

Meg's Friend. By ALICE CORKRAN. With 6 page Illustrations by ROBERT FOWLER. Crown 8vo, cloth extra, 3s. 6d.

"One of Miss Corkran's charming books for girls, narrated in that simple and picturesque style which marks the authoress as one of the first amongst writers for young people."—*The Spectator.*

Margery Merton's Girlhood. By ALICE CORKRAN. With 6 page Pictures by GORDON BROWNE. Cr. 8vo, cloth extra, 3s. 6d.

"Another book for girls we can warmly commend. There is a delightful piquancy in the experiences and trials of a young English girl who studies painting in Paris."—*Saturday Review.*

Down the Snow Stairs: Or, From Good-night to Good-morning. By ALICE CORKRAN. With 60 Illustrations by GORDON BROWNE. Crown 8vo, cloth elegant, olivine edges, 3s. 6d.

"A gem of the first water, bearing upon every page the mark of genius. It is indeed a Little Pilgrim's Progress."—*Christian Leader.*

BY HUGH ST. LEGER.

Hallowe'en Ahoy! Or, Lost on the Crozet Islands. By HUGH ST. LEGER. With 6 Illustrations by H. J. DRAPER. Crown 8vo, cloth elegant, 4s.

This is the strange history of the derelict *Hallowe'en*, in which is set forth: How she was found on the high-seas beyond the equator; how it befell that there was only a ghost on board; how the ghost was captured; how the vessel was cast ashore on a desert island in the Southern Ocean; how the crew, being Englishmen, took the disaster cheerily; and how at length, after many hardships and hairbreadth escapes, they floated their stout craft, bringing her back safe again to old England. And in this wonderful tale there is such wealth of fine enchantment that it will warp the hungry school-boy from remembrance of his dinner.

Sou'wester and Sword. By HUGH ST. LEGER. With 6 page Illustrations by HAL HURST. Crown 8vo, cloth elegant, 4s.

"As racy a tale of life at sea and war adventure as we have met with for some time. . . . Altogether the sort of book that boys will revel in."—*Athenæum.*

BY EDGAR PICKERING.

Two Gallant Rebels: A Story of the Great Struggle in La Vendée. By EDGAR PICKERING. With 6 Illustrations by W. H. OVEREND. Crown 8vo, cloth elegant, 3s. 6d.

These two rebels are two English youths who are shipwrecked and cast ashore in La Vendée, a province of France. Here they are rescued by the inhabitants, and in gratitude for this assistance they join the Vendéans in their revolt against the French Republic. The two young fellows maintain the English character for pluck in the various ambushes and battles in which they take part; and even when captured and condemned to the guillotine they contrive to escape by sheer reckless daring.

In Press-Gang Days. By EDGAR PICKERING. With 6 Illustrations by W. S. STACEY. Crown 8vo, cloth elegant, 3s. 6d.

"It is of Marryat we think as we read this delightful story; for it is not only a story of adventure with incidents well conceived and arranged, but the characters are interesting and well-distinguished."—*Academy.*

An Old-Time Yarn: Wherein is set forth divers desperate mischances which befell Anthony Ingram and his shipmates in the West Indies and Mexico with Hawkins and Drake. By EDGAR PICKERING. Illustrated with 6 page Pictures drawn by ALFRED PEARSE. Crown 8vo, cloth elegant, 3s. 6d.

"And a very good yarn it is, with not a dull page from first to last. There is a flavour of *Westward Ho!* in this attractive book."—*Educational Review.*

Silas Verney: A Tale of the Time of Charles II. By EDGAR PICKERING. With 6 page Illustrations by ALFRED PEARSE. Crown 8vo, cloth elegant, 3s. 6d.

"Altogether this is an excellent story for boys."—*Saturday Review.*

BY CHARLES W. WHISTLER.

A Thane of Wessex: Being a Story of the Great Viking Raids into Somerset. By CHARLES W. WHISTLER. With 6 Illustrations by W. H. MARGETSON. Crown 8vo, cloth elegant, 3s. 6d.

The story of young Heregar, a thane in the old kingdom of Wessex. Wherein is finely set forth,—how he was falsely accused, and unfairly outlawed as a traitor; how in his wanderings he discovered the war-galleys of the Vikings, and carried the War-arrow; how he withstood the raiding Danes at Bridgwater, and gathered the levies at Glastonbury; how he contrived an ambush, and completely defeated the Vikings at Parret mouth; and how, at length, he was inlawed again, and in reward of his valour made the King's Standard-Bearer. That is the noble story of Heregar.

His First Kangaroo: An Australian Story for Boys. By ARTHUR FERRES. With 6 Illustrations by PERCY F. S. SPENCE. Crown 8vo, cloth elegant, 3s. 6d.

This is a story of adventure on an Australian cattle-station. Dick Morrison accepts an invitation to spend a holiday in the bush, and has a good time. A band of bush-rangers also make things lively, for on one occasion the station is " stuck up", while a young Scotsman is kidnapped and rescued with difficulty. The story is full of healthy out-of-doors adventure, in fresh and attractive surroundings.

Three Bright Girls: A Story of Chance and Mischance. By ANNIE E. ARMSTRONG. With 6 page Illustrations by W. PARKINSON. Crown 8vo, cloth elegant, 3s. 6d.

"Among many good stories for girls this is undoubtedly one of the very best."—*Teachers' Aid.*

A Very Odd Girl: or, Life at the Gabled Farm. By ANNIE E. ARMSTRONG. Illustrated. Crown 8vo, cloth elegant, 3s. 6d.

"The book is one we can heartily recommend, for it is not only bright and interesting, but also pure and healthy in tone and teaching."—*The Lady.*

The Captured Cruiser: By C. J. HYNE. Illustrated by FRANK BRANGWYN. Crown 8vo, cloth elegant, 3s. 6d.

"The two lads and the two skippers are admirably drawn. Mr. Hyne has now secured a position in the first rank of writers of fiction for boys."—*Spectator.*

Afloat at Last: A Sailor Boy's Log of his Life at Sea. By JOHN C. HUTCHESON. Crown 8vo, cloth elegant, 3s. 6d.

"As healthy and breezy a book as one could wish to put into the hands of a boy."—*Academy.*

Picked up at Sea: Or, The Gold Miners of Minturne Creek. By J. C. HUTCHESON. With 6 page Pictures. Cloth extra, 3s. 6d.

Brother and Sister: Or, The Trials of the Moore Family. By ELIZABETH J. LYSAGHT. Crown 8vo, cloth elegant, 3s. 6d.

The Search for the Talisman: A Story of Labrador.
By HENRY FRITH. With 6 page Illustrations by J. SCHÖNBERG. Crown 8vo, cloth elegant, 3s. 6d.

"Mr. Frith's volume will be among those most read and highest valued. The adventures among seals, whales, and icebergs in Labrador will delight many a young reader."—*Pall Mall Gazette.*

Reefer and Rifleman: A Tale of the Two Services. By
Lieut.-Col. PERCY-GROVES. With 6 page Illustrations by JOHN SCHÖNBERG. Crown 8vo, cloth elegant, 3s. 6d.

"A good, old-fashioned, amphibious story of our fighting with the Frenchmen in the beginning of our century, with a fair sprinkling of fun and frolic."—*Times.*

Dora: Or, A Girl without a Home. By Mrs. R. H. READ. With
6 page Illustrations. Crown 8vo, cloth elegant, 3s. 6d.

"It is no slight thing, in an age of rubbish, to get a story so pure and healthy as this."—*The Academy.*

Storied Holidays: A Cycle of Red-letter Days. By E. S.
BROOKS. With 12 page Illustrations by HOWARD PYLE. Crown 8vo, cloth elegant, 3s. 6d.

"It is a downright good book for a senior boy, and is eminently readable from first to last."—*Schoolmaster.*

Chivalric Days: Stories of Courtesy and Courage in the
Olden Times. By E. S. BROOKS. With 20 Illustrations by GORDON BROWNE and other Artists. Crown 8vo, cloth extra, 3s. 6d.

"We have seldom come across a prettier collection of tales. These charming stories of boys and girls of olden days are no mere fictitious or imaginary sketches, but are real and actual records of their sayings and doings."—*Literary World.*

Historic Boys: Their Endeavours, their Achievements, and
their Times. By E. S. BROOKS. With 12 page Illustrations by R. B. BIRCH and JOHN SCHÖNBERG. Crown 8vo, cloth extra, 3s. 6d.

"A wholesome book, manly in tone, its character sketches enlivened by brisk dialogue and high-class illustrations; altogether one that should incite boys to further acquaintance with those rulers of men whose careers are narrated. We advise teachers to put it on their list of prizes."—*Knowledge.*

Dr. Jolliffe's Boys: A Tale of Weston School. By LEWIS
HOUGH. With 6 page Pictures. Crown 8vo, cloth extra, 3s. 6d.

"Young people who appreciate *Tom Brown's School-days* will find this story a worthy companion to that fascinating book. There is the same manliness of tone, truthfulness of outline, avoidance of exaggeration and caricature, and healthy morality as characterized the masterpiece of Mr. Hughes."—*Newcastle Journal.*

The Bubbling Teapot. A Wonder Story. By Mrs. L. W.
CHAMPNEY. With 12 page Pictures by WALTER SATTERLEE. Crown 8vo, cloth extra, 3s. 6d.

"Very literally a 'wonder story', and a wild and fanciful one. Nevertheless it is made realistic enough, and there is a good deal of information to be gained from it."—*The Times.*

Thorndyke Manor: A Tale of Jacobite Times. By MARY C. ROWSELL. With 6 page Illustrations by L. LESLIE BROOKE. Crown 8vo, cloth elegant, 3s. 6d.

"Miss Rowsell has never written a more attractive book than *Thorndyke Manor.*"—*Belfast News-Letter.*

Traitor or Patriot? A Tale of the Rye-House Plot. By MARY C. ROWSELL. Illustrated. Crown 8vo, cloth, 3s. 6d.

"Here the Rye-House Plot serves as the groundwork for a romantic love episode, whose true characters are lifelike beings."—*Graphic.*

BLACKIE'S NEW THREE-SHILLING SERIES.
Beautifully Illustrated and Handsomely Bound.

Hussein the Hostage: Or, A Boy's Adventures in Persia. By G. NORWAY. With 6 page Illustrations by JOHN SCHÖNBERG. *New Edition.* Crown 8vo, cloth elegant, 3s.

"*Hussein the Hostage* is full of originality and vigour. The characters are lifelike, there is plenty of stirring incident, the interest is sustained throughout, and every boy will enjoy following the fortunes of the hero."—*Journal of Education.*

Cousin Geoffrey and I. By CAROLINE AUSTIN. With 6 page Illustrations by W. PARKINSON. *New Edition.* Crown 8vo, cloth extra, 3s.

"Miss Austin's story is bright, clever, and well developed."—*Saturday Review.*

The Congo Rovers: A Story of the Slave Squadron. By HARRY COLLINGWOOD. With 6 page Illustrations by J. SCHÖNBERG. Crown 8vo, cloth elegant, 3s.

Reduced Illustration from "Cousin Geoffrey".

"No better sea story has lately been written than the *Congo Rovers*. It is as original as any boy could desire."—*Morning Post.*

THREE-SHILLING SERIES—Continued.

Under Hatches: or, Ned Woodthorpe's Adventures. By F.
FRANKFORT MOORE. With 6 page Illustrations by A. FORESTIER.
Crown 8vo, cloth elegant, 3s.

"The story as a story is one that will just suit boys all the world over. The
characters are well drawn and consistent; Patsy, the Irish steward, will be found
especially amusing."—Schoolmaster.

Menhardoc: A Story of Cornish Nets and Mines. By G.
MANVILLE FENN. With 6 page Illustrations by C. J. STANILAND,
R.I. Crown 8vo, cloth extra, 3s.

"They are real living boys, with their virtues and faults. The Cornish fishermen are drawn from life, and stand out from the pages in their jerseys and
sea-boots all sprinkled with silvery pilchard scales."—Spectator.

Yussuf the Guide: or, The Mountain Bandits. A Story of
Strange Adventure in Asia Minor. By G. MANVILLE FENN. With
6 page Illustrations by J. SCHÖNBERG. Crown 8vo, cloth extra, 3s.

"Told with such real freshness and vigour that the reader feels he is actually
one of the party, sharing in the fun and facing the dangers."—Pall Mall Gazette.

Robinson Crusoe. With 100 Illustrations by GORDON
BROWNE. Crown 8vo, cloth extra, 3s.

"One of the best issues, if not absolutely the best, of Defoe's work which has
ever appeared."—The Standard.

Gulliver's Travels. With 100 Illustrations by GORDON
BROWNE. Crown 8vo, cloth extra, 3s.

"Mr. Gordon Browne is, to my thinking, incomparably the most artistic,
spirited, and brilliant of our illustrators of books for boys, and one of the most
humorous also, as his illustrations of 'Gulliver' amply testify."—Truth.

Patience Wins: or, War in the Works. By GEORGE MAN-
VILLE FENN. With 6 page Illustrations. Cr. 8vo, cloth extra, 3s.

"Mr. Fenn has never hit upon a happier plan than in writing this story of
Yorkshire factory life. The whole book is all aglow with life."—Pall Mall Gazette.

Mother Carey's Chicken: Her Voyage to the Unknown
Isle. By G. MANVILLE FENN. With 6 page Illustrations by A.
FORESTIER. Crown 8vo, cloth extra, 3s.

"Undoubtedly one of the best Mr. Fenn has written. The incidents are of
thrilling interest, while the characters are drawn with a care and completeness
rarely found in a boy's book."—Literary World.

The Wigwam and the War-path: Stories of the Red
Indians. By ASCOTT R. HOPE. With 6 page Illustrations. Crown
8vo, cloth elegant, 3s.

"Is notably good. It gives a very vivid picture of life among the Indians,
which will delight the heart of many a schoolboy."—Spectator.

THREE-SHILLING SERIES—Continued.

The Missing Merchantman. By HARRY COLLINGWOOD.
With 6 page Illustrations by W. H. OVEREND. Cloth extra, 3s.

"One of the author's best sea stories. The hero is as heroic as any boy could desire, and the ending is extremely happy."—*British Weekly.*

The Rover's Secret: A Tale of the Pirate Cays and Lagoons
of Cuba. By HARRY COLLINGWOOD. With 6 page Illustrations by W. C. SYMONS. Crown 8vo, cloth elegant, 3s.

"*The Rover's Secret* is by far the best sea story we have read for years, and is certain to give unalloyed pleasure to boys."—*Saturday Review.*

Perseverance Island: or, The Robinson Crusoe of the 19th
Century. By DOUGLAS FRAZAR. With 6 page Illustrations. Crown 8vo, cloth extra, 3s.

"This is an interesting story, written with studied simplicity of style, much in Defoe's vein of apparent sincerity and scrupulous veracity; while for practical instruction it is even better than *Robinson Crusoe.*"—*Illustrated London News.*

Girl Neighbours: or, The Old Fashion and the New. By
SARAH TYTLER. With 6 page Illustrations by C. T. GARLAND. Crown 8vo, cloth elegant, 3s.

"One of the most effective and quietly humorous of Miss Sarah Tytler's stories. It is very healthy, very agreeable, and very well written."—*The Spectator.*

BLACKIE'S HALF-CROWN SERIES.
Illustrated by eminent Artists. In crown 8vo, cloth elegant.

A Musical Genius. By the Author of the "Two Dorothys".
Illustrated by JOHN H. BACON.

Hugo Ricardo has a genius for the violin, and is adopted by a wealthy musical amateur who has discovered his special gift. The lad studies hard, and fulfils the highest expectations of his new friend. But he never quite forgets his humble, unselfish brother the conjurer; and when he is called upon to make choice between affection for his brother and a wealthy home, he quickly chooses the former. The charm of this tale is in its naturalness, and in the engaging self-sacrifice of the two noble brothers.

For the Sake of a Friend: A Story of School Life. By
MARGARET PARKER. Illustrated by G. DEMAIN HAMMOND.

Stories of school life are common enough, but this tale of a girls' school in Melbourne is quite new. The vivacity of these Australian girls is not less attractive than the home-like brightness and freedom of the school. The heroine, Susie Snow, and her friend, Trixie Beresford, are the sweetest and cleverest of girls, and although there are jealousies, mistakes, and misunderstandings among the pupils at Stormont House, yet all comes right in the end.

HALF-CROWN SERIES—Continued.

Under the Black Eagle. By ANDREW HILLIARD. Illustrated by W. BOUCHER.

Ernest Wentworth is an English lad resident in Russia, and his great chum is a student called Gregorieff. As this student has secret dealings with Nihilists, the two friends become suspected of plots, and the final result is that both are apprehended, and exiled to Siberia. On the journey they contrive to leap from the convict-steamer, swim ashore in the darkness, escape from their pursuers, and make their way across "the Roof of the World" into Northern India.

The Secret of the Australian Desert. By ERNEST FAVENC. With 4 Illustrations by PERCY F. S. SPENCE.

Three white men, and a blackfellow called Billy Buttons, start on an expedition into the great Australian desert. Strange, uncanny, and terrible are their experiences in that vast wilderness. They meet with the cannibal Warlattas; find a mysterious burning mountain; discover traces of the lost explorer, Dr. Leichhardt; and only arrive back at their cattle-station after long and grievous wandering in the waterless desert. The vivid actuality of this enthralling narrative is due to the fact that the author has taken the material from his own thrilling experiences.

A Little Handful. By HARRIET J. SCRIPPS.

"He is a real type of a boy."—*The Schoolmaster.*

A Golden Age: A Story of Four Merry Children. By ISMAY THORN. Illustrated by GORDON BROWNE.

"Ought to have a place of honour on the nursery shelf."—*The Athenæum.*

A Rough Road: or, How the Boy Made a Man of Himself. By Mrs. G. LINNÆUS BANKS.

"Mrs. Banks has not written a better book than *A Rough Road.*"—*Spectator.*

The Two Dorothys. By Mrs. HERBERT MARTIN.

"A book that will interest and please all girls."—*The Lady.*

Penelope and the Others. By AMY WALTON.

"This is a charming book for children. Miss Walton proves herself a perfect adept in understanding of school-room joys and sorrows."—*Christian Leader.*

A Cruise in Cloudland. By HENRY FRITH.

"A thoroughly interesting story."—*St. James's Gazette.*

Marian and Dorothy. By ANNIE E. ARMSTRONG.

"This is distinctively a book for girls. A bright wholesome story."—*Academy.*

Stimson's Reef: A Tale of Adventure. By C. J. HYNE.

"It may almost vie with Mr. R. L. Stevenson's *Treasure Island.*"—*Guardian.*

Gladys Anstruther. By LOUISA THOMPSON.

"It is a clever book: novel and striking in the highest degree."—*Schoolmistress.*

HALF-CROWN SERIES—Continued.

BY BEATRICE HARRADEN.

Things Will Take a Turn. By BEATRICE HARRADEN.

With 44 Illustrations by JOHN H. BACON. Crown 8vo, cloth elegant, 2s. 6d.

"Perhaps the most brilliant is *Things Will Take a Turn* . . . A tale of humble child life in East London. It is a delightful blending of comedy and tragedy, with an excellent plot."—*The Times.*

The Whispering Winds, and the Tales that they Told. By MARY H. DEBENHAM. With 25 Illustrations by PAUL HARDY. Crown 8vo, cloth elegant, 2s. 6d.

"We wish the winds would tell *us* stories like these. It would be worth while to climb Primrose Hill, or even to the giddy heights of Hampstead Heath in a bitter east wind, if we could only be sure of hearing such a sweet, sad, tender, and stirring story as that of Hilda Brave Heart, or even one that was half so good."—*Academy.*

From "Things will Take a Turn". (Reduced.)

Hal Hungerford. By J. R. HUTCHINSON, B.A.

"Altogether, Hal Hungerford is a distinct literary success."—*Spectator.*

The Secret of the Old House. By E. EVERETT-GREEN.

"Tim, the little Jacobite, is a charming creation."—*Academy.*

The Golden Weathercock. By JULIA GODDARD.

"A cleverly conceived quaint story, ingeniously written."—*Saturday Review.*

White Lilac: or, The Queen of the May. By AMY WALTON.

"Every rural parish ought to add *White Lilac* to its library."—*Academy.*

Miriam's Ambition. By EVELYN EVERETT-GREEN.

"Miss Green's children are real British boys and girls."—*Liverpool Mercury.*

The Brig "Audacious". By ALAN COLE.

"Fresh and wholesome as a breath of sea air."—*Court Journal.*

HALF-CROWN SERIES—Continued.

The Saucy May. By HENRY FRITH.
"Mr. Frith gives a new picture of life on the ocean wave."—*Sheffield Independent.*

Jasper's Conquest. By ELIZABETH J. LYSAGHT.
"One of the best boys' books of the season."—*Schoolmaster.*

Little Lady Clare. By EVELYN EVERETT-GREEN.
"Reminds us in its quaintness of Mrs. Ewing's delightful tales."—*Liter. World.*

The Eversley Secrets. By EVELYN EVERETT-GREEN.
"Roy Eversley is a very touching picture of high principle."—*Guardian.*

The Hermit Hunter of the Wilds. By G. STABLES, R.N.
"Will gladden the heart of many a bright boy."—*Methodist Recorder.*

Sturdy and Strong. By G. A. HENTY.
"A hero who stands as a good instance of chivalry in domestic life."—*The Empire.*

Gutta Percha Willie. By GEORGE MACDONALD.
"Get it for your boys and girls to read for themselves."—*Practical Teacher.*

The War of the Axe: Or, Adventures in South Africa. By J. PERCY-GROVES.
"The story is well and brilliantly told."—*Literary World.*

The Lads of Little Clayton. By R. STEAD.
"A capital book for boys."—*Schoolmaster.*

Ten Boys who lived on the Road from Long Ago to Now. By JANE ANDREWS. With 20 Illustrations.
"The idea is a very happy one, and admirably carried out."—*Practical Teacher.*

A Waif of the Sea: Or, The Lost Found. By KATE WOOD.
"Written with tenderness and grace."—*Morning Advertiser.*

Winnie's Secret. By KATE WOOD.
"One of the best story-books we have read."—*Schoolmaster.*

Miss Willowburn's Offer. By SARAH DOUDNEY.
"Patience Willowburn is one of Miss Doudney's best creations."—*Spectator.*

A Garland for Girls. By LOUISA M. ALCOTT.
"These little tales are the beau ideal of girls' stories."—*Christian World.*

Hetty Gray: Or, Nobody's Bairn. By ROSA MULHOLLAND.
"Hetty is a delightful creature—piquant, tender, and true."—*World.*

Brothers in Arms: A Story of the Crusades. By F. BAYFORD HARRISON.
"Sure to prove interesting to young people of both sexes."—*Guardian.*

Miss Fenwick's Failures. By ESMÉ STUART.
"A girl true to real life, who will put no nonsense into young heads."—*Graphic.*

Gytha's Message. By EMMA LESLIE.
"This is the sort of book that all girls like."—*Journal of Education.*

HALF-CROWN SERIES—Continued.

Hammond's Hard Lines. By Skelton Kupford. Illustrated by Harold Copping.

"The story is very clever and provocative of laughter."—*Standard.*

"It is just what a boy would choose if the selection of a story-book is left in his own hand."—*School Guardian.*

Dulcie King: A Story for Girls. By M. Corbet - Seymour. Illustrated by Gertrude D. Hammond.

"An extremely graceful, well-told tale of domestic life ... The heroine, Dulcie, is a charming person, and worthy of the good fortune which she causes and shares."—*Guardian.*

Hugh Herbert's Inheritance. By Caroline Austin. With 4 page Illustrations by C. T. Garland.

"Will please by its simplicity, its tenderness, and its healthy interesting motive. It is admirably written."—*Scotsman.*

Reduced Illustration from "Hammond's Hard Lines".

Nicola: The Career of a Girl Musician. By M. Corbet-Seymour. Illustrated by Gertrude D. Hammond.

Jack o' Lanthorn: A Tale of Adventure. By Henry Frith.

My Mistress the Queen. By M. A. Paull.

The Stories of Wasa and Menzikoff.

Stories of the Sea in Former Days.

Tales of Captivity and Exile.

Famous Discoveries by Sea and Land.

Stirring Events of History.

Adventures in Field, Flood, and Forest.

"It would be difficult to place in the hands of young people books which combine interest and instruction in a higher degree."—*Manchester Courier.*

BLACKIE'S TWO-SHILLING SERIES.
Illustrated by eminent Artists.   In crown 8vo, cloth elegant.

NEW VOLUMES.

In the Days of Drake. Being the Adventures of Humphrey Salkeld. By J. S. FLETCHER. With Illustrations by W. S. STACEY.

Wilful Joyce. By W. L. ROOPER. Illustrated by HAROLD COPPING.

Proud Miss Sydney. By GERALDINE MOCKLER. Illustrated by G. DEMAIN HAMMOND.

The Girleen. By EDITH JOHNSTONE. Illustrated by PAUL HARDY.

The Organist's Baby. By KATHLEEN KNOX.

School-Days in France. By AN OLD GIRL.

The Ravensworth Scholarship: A High School Story for Girls. By Mrs. HENRY CLARKE.

Queen of the Daffodils: A Story of High School Life. By LESLIE LAING.

Raff's Ranche: A Story of Adventure among Cow-boys and Indians. By F. M. HOLMES.

An Unexpected Hero. By ELIZ. J. LYSAGHT.

The Bushranger's Secret. By Mrs. HENRY CLARKE, M.A.

The White Squall. By JOHN C. HUTCHESON.

The Wreck of the "Nancy Bell". By J. C. HUTCHESON.

The Lonely Pyramid. By J. H. YOXALL.

Bab: or, The Triumph of Unselfishness. By ISMAY THORN.

Brave and True, and other Stories. By GREGSON GOW.

The Light Princess. By GEORGE MAC DONALD.

Nutbrown Roger and I. By J. H. YOXALL.

Sam Silvan's Sacrifice. By JESSE COLMAN.

Insect Ways on Summer Days in Garden, Forest, Field, and Stream. By JENNETT HUMPHREYS. With 70 Illustrations.

Susan. By AMY WALTON.

A Pair of Clogs. By AMY WALTON.

The Hawthorns. By AMY WALTON.

Dorothy's Dilemma. By CAROLINE AUSTIN.

TWO-SHILLING SERIES—Continued.

Marie's Home. By CAROLINE AUSTIN.

A Warrior King. By J. EVELYN.

Aboard the "Atalanta". By HENRY FRITH.

The Penang Pirate. By JOHN C. HUTCHESON.

Teddy: The Story of a "Little Pickle". By JOHN C. HUTCHESON.

A Rash Promise. By CECILIA SELBY LOWNDES.

Linda and the Boys. By CECILIA SELBY LOWNDES.

Swiss Stories for Children. From the German of MADAM JOHANNA SPYRI. By LUCY WHEELOCK.

The Squire's Grandson. By J. M. CALLWELL.

Magna Charta Stories. Edited by ARTHUR GILMAN, A.M.

The Wings of Courage; AND THE CLOUD - SPINNER. Translated from the French of GEORGE SAND, by Mrs. CORKRAN.

Chirp and Chatter: Or, LESSONS FROM FIELD AND TREE. By ALICE BANKS. With 54 Illustrations by GORDON BROWNE.

Four Little Mischiefs. By ROSA MULHOLLAND.

New Light through Old Windows. By GREGSON GOW.

Little Tottie, and Two Other Stories. By THOMAS ARCHER.

Naughty Miss Bunny. By CLARA MULHOLLAND.

Adventures of Mrs. Wishing-to-be. By ALICE CORKRAN.

The Joyous Story of Toto. By LAURA E. RICHARDS.

Our Dolly: Her Words and Ways. By MRS. R. H. READ.

Fairy Fancy: What she Heard and Saw. By MRS. READ.

BLACKIE'S EIGHTEENPENNY SERIES.

With Illustrations. In crown 8vo, cloth elegant.

NEW VOLUMES.

The Little Girl from Next Door. By GERALDINE MOCKLER.

Uncle Jem's Stella. By Author of the "Two Dorothys".

The Ball of Fortune. By C. PEARSE. *New and Cheaper Edition.*

The Family Failing. By DARLEY DALE. *New and Cheaper Edition.*

Warner's Chase: Or, The Gentle Heart. By ANNIE S. SWAN. *New Edition.*

Climbing the Hill. By ANNIE S. SWAN. *New Edition.*

Into the Haven. By ANNIE S. SWAN.

THE EIGHTEENPENNY SERIES.—Continued.

Olive and Robin: or, A Journey to Nowhere. By the author of "The Two Dorothys".

Mona's Trust: A Story for Girls. By PENELOPE LESLIE.

[*Reduced Specimen of the Illustrations.*]

From "Pleasures and Pranks".

Little Jimmy: A Story of Adventure. By Rev. D. RICE-JONES, M.A.

Pleasures and Pranks. By ISABELLA PEARSON.

In a Stranger's Garden: A Story for Boys and Girls. By CONSTANCE CUMING.

A Soldier's Son: The Story of a Boy who Succeeded. By ANNETTE LYSTER.

Mischief and Merry-making. By ISABELLA PEARSON.

Littlebourne Lock. By F. BAYFORD HARRISON.

Wild Meg and Wee Dickie. By MARY E. ROPES.

Grannie. By ELIZABETH J. LYSAGHT.

The Seed She Sowed. By EMMA LESLIE.

Unlucky: A Fragment of a Girl's Life. By CAROLINE AUSTIN.

Everybody's Business: Or, A Friend in Need. By ISMAY THORN.

Tales of Daring and Danger. By G. A. HENTY.

The Seven Golden Keys. By JAMES F. ARNOLD.

The Story of a Queen. By MARY C. ROWSELL.

Edwy: Or, Was he a Coward? By ANNETTE LYSTER.

The Battlefield Treasure. By F. BAYFORD HARRISON.

Joan's Adventures at the North Pole. By ALICE CORKRAN.

Filled with Gold. By J. PERRETT.

Our General: A Story for Girls. By ELIZABETH J. LYSAGHT.

Aunt Hesba's Charge. By ELIZABETH J. LYSAGHT.

By Order of Queen Maude: A Story of Home Life. By LOUISA CROW.

The Late Miss Hollingford. By ROSA MULHOLLAND.

Our Frank. By AMY WALTON.

A Terrible Coward. By G. MANVILLE FENN.

Yarns on the Beach. By G. A. HENTY.

Tom Finch's Monkey. By J. C. HUTCHESON.

Miss Grantley's Girls, and the Stories she Told Them. By THOS. ARCHER.

The Pedlar and his Dog. By MARY C. ROWSELL.

Town Mice in the Country. By M. E. FRANCIS.

Phil and his Father. By ISMAY THORN.

Prim's Story. By L. E. TIDDEMAN.

EIGHTEENPENNY SERIES—Continued.

Down and Up Again. By GREGSON GOW.

Madge's Mistake. By ANNIE E. ARMSTRONG.

The Troubles and Triumphs of Little Tim. By GREGSON GOW.

The Happy Lad: A Story of Peasant Life in Norway. By B. BJÖRNSON.

A Box of Stories. Packed for Young Folk by HORACE HAPPYMAN.

The Patriot Martyr, and other Narratives of Female Heroism.

LIBRARY OF FAMOUS BOOKS FOR BOYS AND GIRLS.

In Crown 8vo. Illustrated. Cloth extra, 1s. 6d. each.

The Cruise of the Midge. M. SCOTT.

Lives and Voyages of Drake and Cavendish

Edgeworth's Moral Tales.

Marryat's The Settlers in Canada

Michael Scott's Tom Cringle's Log.

White's Natural History of Selborne.

Waterton's Wanderings in S. America.

Anson's Voyage Round the World.

Autobiography of Franklin.

Lamb's Tales from Shakspeare.

Southey's Life of Nelson.

Miss Mitford's Our Village.

Two Years Before the Mast.

Marryat's Children of the New Forest.

Scott's The Talisman.

The Basket of Flowers.

Marryat's Masterman Ready.

Alcott's Little Women.

Cooper's Deerslayer.

The Lamplighter. By Miss Cummins.

Cooper's Pathfinder.

The Vicar of Wakefield.

Plutarch's Lives of Greek Heroes.

Poe's Tales of Romance and Fantasy.

Also a large selection of Rewards at a Shilling, Ninepence, Sixpence, and Fourpence. A complete list will be sent post free on application to the Publishers.

The Best Book for Children.

Laugh and Learn: The Easiest Book of Nursery Lessons and Nursery Games. By JENNETT HUMPHREYS. Profusely Illustrated. Square 8vo, cloth extra, 3s. 6d.

"One of the best books of the kind imaginable, full of practical teaching in word and picture, and helping the little ones pleasantly along a right royal road to learning."—*Graphic.*

LONDON:

BLACKIE & SON, LIMITED, 50 OLD BAILEY, E.C.

BLACKIE'S
SCHOOL AND HOME LIBRARY.

Under the above title the publishers have arranged to issue, for School Libraries and the Home Circle, a selection of the best and most interesting books in the English language. The Library will include lives of heroes, ancient and modern, records of travel and adventure by sea and land, fiction of the highest class, historical romances, books of natural history, and tales of domestic life.

The greatest care will be devoted to the get-up of the Library. The volumes will be clearly printed on good paper, and the binding made specially durable, to withstand the wear and tear to which well-circulated books are necessarily subjected.

In crown 8vo volumes. Strongly bound in imperial cloth. Price 1s. 4d. each.

Dana's Two Years before the Mast.	Cooper's Pathfinder.
Southey's Life of Nelson.	The Vicar of Wakefield.
Waterton's Wanderings in S. America.	White's Natural History of Selborne.
Anson's Voyage Round the World.	Scott's Ivanhoe. 2 vols.
Lamb's Tales from Shakspeare.	Michael Scott's Tom Cringle's Log.
Autobiography of Benjamin Franklin.	Irving's Conquest of Granada. 2 vols.
Marryat's Children of the New Forest.	Lives of Drake and Cavendish.
Miss Mitford's Our Village.	Michael Scott's Cruise of the Midge.
Scott's Talisman.	Edgeworth's Moral Tales.
The Basket of Flowers.	Passages in the Life of a Galley-Slave.
Marryat's Masterman Ready.	The Snowstorm. By Mrs. Gore.
Alcott's Little Women.	Life of Dampier.
Cooper's Deerslayer.	Marryat's The Settlers in Canada.
Parry's Third Voyage.	Martineau's Feats on the Fiord.
Dickens' Old Curiosity Shop. 2 vols.	Marryat's Poor Jack.
Plutarch's Lives of Greek Heroes.	The Good Governess. By Maria Edgeworth.
The Lamplighter. By Miss Cummins.	Northanger Abbey. By Jane Austen.

To be followed by a new volume on the first of each month.

"We feel sure that they will form a collection which boys and girls alike, but especially the former, will highly prize; for whilst they contain interesting, and at times very exciting reading, the tone throughout is of that vigorous, stirring kind which is always appreciated by the young."— Sheffield Independent.

Detailed Prospectus and Press Opinions will be sent post free on Application.

LONDON:
BLACKIE & SON, Limited, 50 OLD BAILEY, E.C.

www.ingramcontent.com/pod-product-compliance
Lightning Source LLC
Chambersburg PA
CBHW030949110726
47900CB00004B/1191